FORGET
HER
NAME

ALSO BY JANE HOLLAND

FORGET
HER
NAME

Jane
HOLLAND

THOMAS & MERCER

Text copyright © 2018 by Jane Holland
All rights reserved.

Published by Thomas & Mercer, Seattle

www.apub.com

Amazon, the Amazon logo, and Thomas & Mercer are trademarks of Amazon.com, Inc., or its affiliates.

ISBN-13: 9781542046640
ISBN-10: 1542046645

Cover design by Ghost Design

Printed in the United States of America

For sisters everywhere

Prologue

Through the glass, everything is white, white, white. The winding road into the village resort, the Swiss chalets in the distance, the ski slopes, the high Alps beyond, all of them laced with thick, deep, white snow like a Christmas postcard.

Leaning both hands against the chill window frame, I press the tip of my nose to the glass. My breath mists up the glass in a wobbly circle round my face. The fog it makes on the window is stronger each time I exhale, the only warm thing in the room; then fainter as I breathe in. It's hard to make anything out through that fog. I don't really need to see outside though, since it's all the same lumpy, formless white. Even the sky is too pale to be grey.

It feels as though every drop of colour has been sucked out of the world, and this is what's left over. Total white. Pure as a pill.

Daddy comes back at last, snow still clinging to his boots and coat. He stamps his feet, looking at me.

'Cat,' he says heavily.

I run towards him for a hug, and we hold each other. He feels cold, too. Like a snowman.

I ask in a small voice, 'Where's Rachel?'

When he doesn't answer, I peer up at him, trying to read his face.

Daddy is pale, like the snow-laden sky. Even his lips are pale. He brushes my blonde fringe out of my eyes, gazing down at me. He hates the way it flops over my face, but I like the way I can look out at the world through it. Look out and know they can't see in.

'I thought your mother already spoke to you. I thought she told you—'

'I didn't believe her.' I raise my voice, trying to make him understand. 'Mum tells lies. She's always telling lies.'

'Sweetheart, don't say that. You know it's not true.'

I'm shaken by his calm acceptance of what is happening. He shouldn't be here in this horrid little room, talking to me. He should be out there, doing something to help my sister. She's the one who needs him today. Not me.

'Where's Rachel? Tell me.'

'I want you to listen very carefully, okay? No, you need to stop shouting and listen.' His hands drop to my shoulders, and he squeezes lightly as though to emphasise his words. 'I know this is hard. The hardest thing you've ever faced. But what your mother told you is true.'

'No, no . . .'

'Rachel is dead and we're never going to see her again. Never, ever again.' He pauses, searching my face. 'Do you understand me, Catherine?'

I feel numb. Like I'm out there in the cold with Rachel. Like nothing will ever be the same again.

'Yes, Daddy.'

'What did I just say? Repeat it back to me.'

'Rachel is . . .'

'Say it.'

'Rachel is dead.' I hear my voice wobble on those momentous words, and his face blurs through my tears.

I sniff loudly and look away. I hate crying. It makes me feel like a kid again. A little kid after a nightmare, helpless and frightened in the dark, even though I'm twelve now. Practically a grown-up, Mum always says.

His hoarse voice nags at me. 'And?'

He's crying too, I realise.

I push my own unhappiness away and focus on his. It's hard, but I can just about manage it without collapsing.

My sister is dead.

I struggle to understand what I'm feeling, but my thoughts slip out of reach even as I try to grasp them, bobbing away on a tide of grief, refusing to be pinned down. All I feel right now is this appalling numbness, and beneath it, a wicked, secret, niggling sense of relief.

'Rachel is dead,' I whisper, 'and she's never coming back.'

Chapter One

The woman cradling the baby starts crying again just as Sharon dumps a brown-paper parcel on my workstation.

'For you,' she says shortly, ignoring my startled glance, then turns to the crying woman, who is gazing in despair at the shelves of tins and packets she's not allowed to have. 'As my colleague told you, we need a letter of referral before we can release any food,' she tells the woman. 'I'm sorry, love. Those are the rules at the Tollgate Trust and we have to abide by them. Perhaps if you speak to someone at the benefits office? They have a fast-response scheme if it's an emergency. I can give you an information leaflet from the council if that's any help.'

The woman has a telltale split lip, and a fading bruise on her cheek. Teary-eyed, she glances at me as though hopeful that I'll intervene.

I look down at the paperwork on my desk instead, fiddling with my pen. I used to smile in a sympathetic manner when people came in without referral letters. But as Sharon explained to me, that often makes the situation worse.

'A smile can be taken the wrong way,' Sharon told me after a few uncomfortable incidents in my first week. 'They're already upset, yeah? So if you say no, but with a big smile, it looks like you're taking the piss.'

Most of the people who come in here are lovely people, really lovely. But a few of them are definitely on the edge. One man with mental health issues threatened to punch me in the face. Another spat at me, and the police had to be called. We're on the edge of Chalk Farm here, which is North London. Not a bad area, but there are pockets of trouble.

I came here initially to help out in a practical way. The constant sight of people sleeping rough on the streets of London finally got to me, and I wanted to be useful. But Sharon's training sessions were an eye-opener. 'Always be polite and friendly,' she told me and the other new volunteers. 'But if you can't help them because they don't have an official referral, don't give them any reason to get nasty with you. And that includes smiling too much. Got it?'

I got it.

The woman looks away, and I smile at the baby in the pink romper suit instead. She stares back at me with large, solemn blue eyes.

Sharon starts rummaging for an information leaflet for the woman. I put down my pen and examine the parcel, unsure what to make of it. At first glance I assumed it was another donation to the food bank. They come in quite frequently from anonymous donors. It's not particularly heavy though. And it's addressed to me personally, not the food bank, which is unusual in itself.

An early wedding present, perhaps?

I tear off the brown-paper wrapping. It's a plain cardboard box and inside is a snow globe.

I freeze, staring down at it.

I see the face of a familiar, smooth glass sphere, glittering water inside, half buried in a heap of protective white polystyrene chips.

It's Rachel's snow globe.

My fingertips touch the glass, hesitant. I could be mistaken. *Must* be mistaken, in fact. It can't be her snow globe. How could it be?

But when I brush away a few polystyrene chips, there on the black plastic plinth below the glass is my sister's name. Printed long ago in block capitals onto a stick-on label that's now smudged and peeling slightly at one corner.

RACHEL.

My hand starts to tremble.

'What on earth's that?' Sharon asks, peering over my shoulder.

The woman with the baby has gone, I realise.

Hurriedly, I cover the snow globe again and close up the cardboard box. 'Nothing,' I say. 'I mean, it's personal. Not for the food bank.'

'Okay, well, when you're ready . . . I've got a Mrs Fletcher here with a referral note from social services.' Sharon sounds impatient, as though I've been caught slacking. An East End accent that thickens when she's annoyed. Salt of the earth, as my father might say. Not that Dad is ever likely to come into the food bank and meet my boss. Thankfully. 'Could you possibly see to her if you've got a moment? Family of two adults, three teenagers, wheat allergy.'

'Of course, sorry.'

I shove the parcel out of sight under the desk, and turn to Mrs Fletcher with a broad smile. Smiles are allowed for people with the proper documentation. 'Hi, I'm Catherine,' I tell her cheerily. 'Have you brought a list of what you can't eat?'

Mrs Fletcher, a harassed-looking woman in her early forties, gives me a wary smile in return. 'Here.' She shoves a scrap of paper into my hand. Her hands are red and swollen, with a gold ring on nearly every finger, almost hidden by flesh. 'We've only the one kid with an allergy though. The rest of us need bread and pasta.'

'Don't worry, we'll get you sorted out.' I glance over the handwritten list, and then lead the way across to the food storage area. 'If you could just follow me, Mrs Fletcher?'

My heart is thumping and I feel a little light-headed. Who on earth would send me Rachel's old snow globe?

And why?

'This is the first time I've ever used a food bank,' Mrs Fletcher is telling me. 'I'm not out of work.'

'There's no need to explain, Mrs Fletcher.'

'We're not *poor*. Not homeless or anything. Been in the same flat three years now, never caused nobody any trouble. It's only because I'm on one of those zero-hour contracts. Only they've not called me in for two weeks, have they?' she adds bitterly. 'Like they think we can survive on thin bloody air.'

'Well, you've come to the right place. Let's cover the basics first.' I take a plastic bag and shake it out, then start filling it with standard items from the list on the wall above me. 'Sugar? Tea? Coffee?'

'Thanks,' she says to all of them, nodding.

Some of those who come here look embarrassed or start to excuse themselves, as if they've done something wrong by not being able to afford basic food for their families. They haven't, of course. Far from it. But a few still feel the need to explain.

I've noticed most are less defensive with Sharon and Petra though. My accent, probably. I don't sound like I fit in, my voice too cultured, even though I try to disguise it. 'Too posh', as Sharon often says. They instinctively see me as an enemy. Even aggressive. Someone who's had it easier than them. Someone who hasn't had to struggle for everyday needs. All true, of course. I can't deny my posh accent or my privileged background. But there are things they don't know about me, too. Things long-buried and forgotten about.

I say nothing though. What would be the point?

'Thanks, love,' Mrs Fletcher repeats, watching me select a family-sized packet of dried pasta. 'And some rice, maybe? That goes a long way, doesn't it?'

When the shopping part of the process is finished, I find a cup of tea for Mrs Fletcher so she can wait to speak to someone about additional help. Then I pop my head round the office door to ask Sharon if I can go for my lunch early.

She's surprised by the request. Turning from the filing cabinet, Sharon glances up at the clock on the wall. Her face registers slight irritation, but only the sort that comes with tiredness.

'You not feeling well?'

'I'm fine. I just have a few errands to run.' I manage a wry smile. 'It's been a bit manic recently, what with the wedding coming up.'

Sharon looks back at me indulgently. 'Of course. Three weeks on Saturday, isn't it?'

I nod.

'You must be so excited. Have you got the dress yet?'

'Yes.' I smile then, despite myself. 'I picked it up last week. It's so beautiful. I only hope I can do it justice.'

I'd gone for the 'mermaid' shape in the end, fitted closely from the sweetheart neckline down to the knee, then flaring out in a lavish display to the hem. Beautiful appliqué flowers cling to one side of the ivory satin bodice; the other side dazzles with tiny sequins. By not booking an expensive reception after the church, but inviting everyone to join us at a nearby pub afterwards for drinks and a finger buffet, we're saving a fortune. So I spent up on the wedding dress instead, maxing out my credit card on the beautiful outfit, which includes matching underwear and ivory satin pumps.

'Of course you'll be gorgeous, silly girl. All the men will be falling over each other to have a look at you.' Sharon winks at me, thick black mascara clumped at the ends of her eyelashes. 'And how's Dominic coping?'

'Not too bad. In fact, he texted me earlier to confirm all the tux rental details. My dad's the only one who's making a fuss.' I make a face. 'Sometimes I wonder if he actually *wants* me to get married.'

'Oh, it's just their way. Dads always hate losing their little girls.' Sharon returns to filing the paperwork she's been working through, happy with all this talk of dresses and weddings. 'Go on, you run along. Get your errands done. Me and Petra can cope.'

On my way out, I grab my jacket from my chair, and then tuck the parcel carefully under my arm with the woollen garment folded over the top.

I struggle outside into the grey, windy, North London street. It's too cold to walk far without a coat though. I stop a few doors down, put the parcel on the pavement as gingerly as if it contains a bomb, and shrug into my jacket. Then I tuck the box under my arm again, and hurry on to La Giravolta, the family-run Italian bistro on the corner where I usually eat a quick tuna sandwich or quiche for lunch.

As I hesitate in the doorway, peering inside, an acquaintance waves at me from across the room. Georgia from the book club. She's dining alone, the seat opposite conspicuously empty.

I wave back, then abruptly change my mind about going inside.

The last thing I need is to get sucked into yet another conversation about Dominic and the wedding.

Not today.

Head down, as though I've just remembered some urgent mission, I turn back into the wind. It tears at my unbuttoned jacket and I shiver, dragging the two sides together with one hand. *Bloody hell.* I've left my scarf and gloves behind in my hurry to get out. It's been a bitter start to November. My feet ache from standing since early this morning, and my hands are numb from the chilly, warehouse-like Tollgate Trust food bank, with its constantly open doors.

It's important work. Not paid, except for Sharon, who's employed full-time by the charity to run the place. Important and worthwhile nonetheless. I chose the position deliberately, aware that I was born with every advantage in life, while others just as deserving are less fortunate. And since my parents were happy to cover my rent while I found my feet in the world of work, that made a volunteering position possible. I have no real reason to feel guilty, of course. But it was time to give something back.

Good intentions aside, my feet still hurt.

I thread past two black-hijabbed women with buggies, then dart across the busy road in front of a lumbering double-decker bus, earning myself a glare from the woman driver. On the other side, I continue another few blocks until I reach the Costa coffee shop. It's blissfully warm inside, and nobody looks round when I enter. I check all the tables for anyone I know.

They are all strangers.

I get in the queue, the box still awkward under my arm. The man behind me glances at it curiously, but looks away when he encounters my gaze.

Finding a quiet seat at the back, I eat half my panini, sip on my latte, then push both aside and place the parcel squarely on the table in front of me.

The address label has been printed. It looks neat and professional. I check the underside but there's no return address, and no note inside to indicate a point of origin. The brown-paper wrapping is plain; the white polystyrene chips are generic. I can't imagine who could have sent it to me. And to the food bank, not my home.

I reach inside and pull the snow globe free of its rustling nest. My breath catches in my throat.

It wasn't a mistake. Or not on my part, anyway.

Even without my sister's name on the plinth, I would have known whose globe it was. I recognise the village scene inside, the miniature Swiss chalets, the white-capped mountain with its obligatory tiny goat. Rachel loved to shake and shake the globe, only laughing when our mother pleaded with her to be careful.

'Rachel, please don't,' Mum would say. 'You'll break it if you drop it.'

But of course *she* never dropped it.

The snow globe feels smooth and heavy in my hands, snug on its black plastic plinth. There's a thin crack across the plinth; I can see where it was mended. My father did that with superglue, then it had to be left to set for half a day.

I glance about the busy café, but nobody's looking my way. Nobody cares about this strange, unsettling reminder of my sister.

Only me.

It's like looking into the past. Like my childhood still exists inside a locked room in one of those snow-covered Swiss chalets, almost within reach, if only I could see through the white-out of the storm . . .

Then something else bobs round with the fake snow, bumping against the glass.

I cry out, almost dropping the globe.

An eyeball?

Not a joke-shop eyeball. A real, honest-to-goodness eyeball, white and fatty, with ragged bits of pinkish tissue still hanging off where it was cut out.

There's an eyeball in the whirling snow, staring back at me.

Chapter Two

Our flat is five minutes' walk from the Hanwell Cemetery end of Ealing Broadway, a large old Victorian house divided into one- and two-bedroom flats. We're on the top floor.

'Hello?' I ask warily, unlocking the front door.

There's no answer.

I kick the door shut and hurry straight into the bedroom of our one-bedroom flat, not pausing to strip off my thick scarf and gloves. The curtains are still drawn. The windows are narrow and the ceilings slope on the top floor, so the room constantly feels small and gloomy.

I flick on the light, breathing quickly after my fast walk from the bus stop, and look about the place. Books and open magazines lie everywhere, cups balance on book stacks, dirty plates gather dust on the floor, the wastepaper bin overflows silently in a forgotten corner. The double bed is still messy from this morning's scramble to get up in good time, the duvet thrown back in a tangled rush, one of Dominic's dark hairs on the pillow. A crumpled sock dangles over the lampshade.

It looks like the flat has been burgled.

Nothing unusual, then.

I bend and shove the anonymous parcel, still partially wrapped, under the bed. It slides into the narrow space with barely an inch to spare. Easy to remove though, and hidden from view when I step back to check.

'There.'

I'll deal with it later, I tell myself, and try to ignore the guilty thump of my heart. Dominic will be home any minute, and Rachel's snow globe isn't a conversation I want to have with my fiancé. Not today, anyway.

Dominic sheds like a bloody cat, I think, glaring down at the long strand of hair coiled on his white pillow.

I strip off my gloves and shove them into my coat pocket. With a grimace, I tweak the long hair off the pillow and drop it into the waste-paper bin, then plump up both head-dented pillows. Shaking out the duvet, I arrange it neatly across the bed. Straightening up, I eye the dirty sock on the lampshade, then decide to leave it there.

I don't want him to suspect anything is wrong.

'There,' I say again.

Before leaving the room, I pause in the doorway and glance dubiously back at the parcel's hiding place.

Will I even be able to sleep with *that thing* under the bed all night?

The front door bangs.

Closing the bedroom door, I turn with a quick smile. 'Dominic.'

'Hey, baby.'

Dominic looks exhausted, still in his blue hospital scrubs, his nurse's identity badge twisted up in a loop on its lanyard and stuffed into his top pocket. There's a dark shadow on his chin where he needs to shave. Twelve-hour shifts as a nurse practitioner in Accident and Emergency. Not easy to cope with.

He smiles wearily and kisses me on the lips. We nuzzle together for a moment in silence, his head on my shoulder.

I should tell him about the snow globe.

Only I can't.

'You're early,' I say instead. 'And I'm late.'

'Busy day?'

'Busy day,' I agree without elaborating. 'And the bus took forever to arrive. I was just going to make a pot of tea. Want some?'

'Gin would be more appropriate,' he says, 'and hold the tonic.'

'I expect that can be arranged,' I tell him lightly, but raise my head to study his face. I know that tone. 'What's happened?'

'Oh, you know . . . same old shit in A & E.'

'Dom, come on.'

'It's nothing. I'm knackered, that's all.' I raise my eyebrows, still waiting, and he adds reluctantly, 'An old lady died. Old ladies do that, don't they?'

He drags the identity badge up over his head and tosses it onto the hall table, then staggers past me into the tiny living room. I follow in silence, wishing there was something I could do to help. But he hates me fussing. Making an irritable noise under his breath, he reaches up and pulls off the hairband that holds his ponytail strictly in place during the working day.

'Except they're supposed to die at home, or on the ward,' he mutters, and throws himself onto the sofa, taking up all the space. 'Not in a bloody uncomfortable chair in a crowded corridor, after waiting nine hours to be seen by a doctor.'

I don't ask for details. He'll tell me more if he wants to. When he's had a crappy day like this, Dominic rarely wants a two-way discussion. He just wants to get the acid out of his system for a few minutes, which usually means bitching about Sally Weston, his manager in A & E, or the increasingly visible cracks in the NHS. Then he'll sink down in front of the television with a beer for a few hours and not mention it again.

I kneel on the rug beside him. 'Fuck.'

'Nobody even noticed.' He throws an arm across his eyes. 'She'd been dead maybe twenty minutes, half an hour, before anyone even thought to check she was still breathing.'

I lean my forehead on his shoulder. My heart aches for him. And for the old lady.

'This fucking government . . .' He kicks the far end of the sofa, and there's a distinct crack. 'Shit, sorry.'

'Don't worry about it.' I stroke his hair, trying to communicate how sorry I am without being mawkish. Dominic distrusts sentimentality; he says it clouds the important issues, that love is better without pity in the mix. 'What was her name?'

'Ida,' he tells me after a long pause. 'Her name was Mrs Ida Matthews, a widow. And she had a son, and three grandchildren.'

'Weren't they with her at the hospital?'

'On a winter holiday, she said. Two weeks' bloody skiing in the Alps.'

I tense, pushing away a sudden vision of Swiss chalets against a backdrop of snowy mountains . . .

'That's awful.'

'I left Sally trying to find a number for their hotel.' He gives a croak of humourless laughter. 'If I hadn't spent so long talking to her, we wouldn't even have known about them. She could have been lying unclaimed in the morgue for days.'

'You did your best.'

'Oh yes, I did my bloody best. No one can blame me. Or the doctor. Or the system. We were all doing our best under difficult circumstances, that's what the report will say.'

Dominic sits up suddenly, knocking me away. His eyes are damp and bloodshot. He stares at nothing, his face grim, then turns his head towards me and says, 'Sorry,' without actually meeting my gaze. 'You're only trying to help, and I'm being shitty. Come on.' Standing, he holds out a hand to me. 'Let's make supper together. I'll do us chicken pasta. You can tell me about your day.'

I think about my day, and my smile falters. 'You're too tired.'

'I insist.' He pulls me up effortlessly, six foot of pure brawn, and kisses me again, this time a lingering kiss that leaves me warm and ach= ing. 'Mmm, you're so good to come home to. I love this.' His fingers play with my short, ash-blonde hair. 'Soft hair, soft skin . . .' His hand slips down to my behind. 'Soft bumps.'

'I beg your pardon?'

To his credit, Dominic gives an embarrassed laugh. 'Curves, then. Though I like to think of them as bumps.'

'You mean like speed bumps?'

'Quite the opposite effect. Your bumps make me go faster, not slower.'

I grin at that, and kiss him back. My lips part and his tongue slips between them, probing delicately. I know what he's asking and don't pull away, slipping a hand down between our bodies. I take my time, my eyes shut tight, concentrating on him. It's the perfect distraction.

He starts to harden against my fingers, and his breathing quickens.

'Yes,' he mutters.

We don't make it to the bedroom. He makes love to me right there on the sofa, from behind, while I'm bent over, gasping. I don't know where he finds the energy, after his long shift at work. I close my eyes and try to close off from that other world. The one with eyeballs, and parcels from anonymous ill=wishers. Despite his fatigue, he makes love to me with a familiar, almost violent urgency that often accompanies days when he's witnessed a death at the hospital.

Afterwards, Dominic lies panting beside me.

'You didn't come,' he says.

It's not a question. All the same, I consider lying. Avoiding all the fuss by pretending he missed it in the rush of his own orgasm. But a greedy little voice in my head won't let me. Instead, I whisper, 'It doesn't matter', and wait.

'Of course it matters.' His hand pushes between my legs, bold and insistent, as I secretly hoped it would.

'What about the pasta?'

'Fuck the pasta.'

I stifle my cries against the cushions, my face hot and flushed, my legs shaking as though after some traumatic incident.

Dominic always seems to know what I need, physically. It's his gift, I tell him in a hoarse voice, but he's already moving away and doesn't hear me.

I consider showing him the snow globe.

But then I decide against it. He knows I had a sister who died young. But none of the details. And that's how I prefer it. I don't want him to know about my past.

About Rachel.

Chapter Three

After we've eaten the chicken pasta, we lie together on the sofa for an hour, limbs tangled in lazy torpor, and watch a late-night news programme where they're discussing the state of the NHS.

'Bloody fools,' Dominic growls, throwing an empty cigarette packet at the screen. 'What the hell do you know about it?'

He's a political animal.

I was vaguely apathetic before I met him, not even bothering to vote. But I take a keener interest in politics now, largely down to him and his highly vocal opinions. Dominic seems better informed than the guests we see on news shows, quickly grasps political nuances and complexities that other people miss. He snaps at the television when annoyed, as though the presenters can hear him.

I find his outbursts entertaining, but keep my amusement to myself.

As a nurse practitioner in a casualty department, he sees an even sharper side to social injustice than I do at the food bank, and I know it's real experiences that drive him, like the old lady's death today.

Protest marches, campaigning, political activism. Dominic has made no attempt to encourage me to take part in such activities. But I often join him anyway, making slogan banners long into the evening on Friday nights and sometimes carrying them, too, marching beside him and his activist friends at weekends.

The job at the food bank was his idea, initially. Though only after I'd expressed a need to do something worthwhile, rather than continue working in an exclusive Knightsbridge boutique, as I was doing when he met me.

Mum and Dad were astonished when I told them about the food bank. Dad even tried to stop me, saying he would find me 'something better' if I didn't like boutique work anymore. But Mum backed me up for once. 'Let the girl do what she feels is right, Robert,' she told him, and smiled at me.

A minor victory. Something to put on my mental shelf, along with other trophies, like my parents' acceptance of Dominic, and their grudging support when I chose to move out and rent a flat like most other people of my age that I knew. I still need their help with the rent, of course. But I won't be doing volunteer work forever, and my time at the food bank will help to build up my CV.

'I'm not a child,' I told my dad when he complained that our flat was too insecure, the area run-down and dangerous. 'I'm twenty-three, for God's sake.'

Dad said nothing. But his disapproval was palpable.

'You can't blame your parents, babe,' Dominic told me later, reassuring me that I was making the right choice. 'They live in a different world to us. People like that don't see why food banks are needed, just like they don't feel the need to protest. They think the answer is as simple as someone getting a job instead of a handout. Their lives are too comfortable for reality to ever intrude. They live in this soft, champagne-coloured bubble of money, and can't see anyone outside it.'

I couldn't argue with that.

Dad works at the Foreign Office, and is almost never at home. And Mum is a housewife, the Roedean-educated daughter of a diplomat herself. She doesn't work; in fact, I don't think she has ever had a job. Her obsessions include her looks, the large and immaculate London town house where I grew up, and hosting dinner parties for their circle of wealthy, influential friends. I can't imagine either of my parents having experienced hardship, let alone poverty and starvation. So how can they possibly understand my need to give something back to the society I can see falling apart around me? To do something altruistic with my life?

The news programme finishes just before midnight, and I glance at Dominic, lying curled up against me.

He's asleep, breathing deeply, his mouth slightly open.

'Poor tired baby,' I whisper.

He doesn't react.

As gently as possible, I extricate myself from his arms. I leave him sleeping on the sofa and creep into the bedroom without putting on the light. I don't want to wake him. Not yet, anyway. Listening for sounds of movement from the living room, I drag the parcel out from under the bed, then remove the snow globe in the semi-darkness.

It's cold, round and heavy in my hands. Like a marble head.

Ugh.

I carry it on tiptoe into the bathroom, then shut the door. As an afterthought, I turn the key in the lock.

I turn the globe upside down. The black plinth is easy to remove. Just a few twists and a click.

I hid a screwdriver in the cupboard under the sink earlier while Dominic was preoccupied with the pasta. I take it out now and slip it inside the rubber seal of the snow globe, wiggling it about. It's harder to dislodge than I thought it would be. After a few minutes of pointless fumbling and swearing, I'm tempted to give up. To throw the bloody thing away and forget it ever arrived.

But I need to be sure. So I persevere, and eventually the rubber cap shifts, water pouring down my arm in a sickly, glittery shower.

'Shit,' I say, inadvertently loudly.

Loud enough to wake Dominic? I listen at the door, suddenly tense, but there's no sound from outside the bathroom.

I don't want to involve Dominic in this. *Can't* involve him. How could I possibly explain a horror like this without sitting down to tell him the whole sorry tale of my sister Rachel? I can't bear to admit to any of that. After we're married, perhaps. But not before.

I know it's a form of dishonesty. But it's just too scary a thought. Rachel is the skeleton in our family closet. And what if it's hereditary?

Once I'm convinced Dominic is still asleep, I hold the globe over the sink and slowly let the rest of the water drain out, glitter and white snowflakes clogging up the plughole.

Then nothing is left inside.

Except the eyeball.

Gagging, I push a hand inside the narrow opening and grope about with my fingertips until I meet something soft.

I drop the eyeball twice while trying to retrieve it, my whole being repulsed by the cold, squidgy feel of it. Eventually I drag it out through the opening of the globe and hold it up to the flickering strip light above the sink; a fat iris with a whitish surround, staring dully back at me. Definitely organic, the flesh around the eyeball is a pale, yellowing pink, flecked with glitter. And it smells pretty awful, too.

Like it's already rotting.

Chapter Four

They're doing some kind of renovations at the back of St Hilda's Hospital in North London, where Dominic works. Scaffolding, hanging folds of plastic sheeting obscuring everything, planks and steel rods heaped to one side, a cement mixer churning away, and not a single workman in sight. I duck through an opening in the plastic and head towards the back stairs. There must be a bin lorry backing up somewhere through the chaos and debris, ready to empty the vast hospital bins at the base of the steps. I hear its high-pitched, warning *beep-beep-beep*, but where is it?

The sky is steel grey again, a mass of cloud hanging low over London's skyscrapers. Another grim day slipping rapidly into winter.

I hurry to get inside, out of the cold.

The large, skin-headed security guard, smoking a sneaky cigarette a short distance outside the back door, his peaked cap balanced on the low wall, barely glances at me as I pass. To be fair though, he must have seen me go through this entrance a dozen times with Dominic. Behind him, the sign says: *Strictly No Smoking Anywhere In This Area*.

I push through the double doors, trainers squeaking on the yellow flooring. They swing shut behind me, and the stifling heat of the hospital hits me like a wall.

I take the nearest flight of stairs, heading for the Garden Cafeteria where I sometimes grab a quick lunch with Dominic.

Today, I am not here to see him.

In fact, Dominic's not even here. He's on a half-day training course at St Mary's Hospital, a few miles west of the smaller St Hilda's. Something to do with managing hygiene and hospital superbug controls. I left him scrolling through an email circular with some dull and unwieldy subtitle like 'The perennial problem of hand-cleaning between patients in A & E'. Dominic looked intent on it, barely registering my kiss goodbye.

Louise is already there, head bent, reading something at a corner table. She's one of Dominic's colleagues at St Hilda's – an RNMH, Registered Nurse Mental Health. Smiling, she looks up as I approach, then closes her novel, marking the page with a strip torn from a napkin.

'Cat,' she says, unaware that I hate the way Dominic sometimes abbreviates my name when we're in company. 'How are you? You look great. Looking forward to the wedding?'

'God, don't mention that bloody wedding.'

Louise laughs and stands up to hug me. She isn't in uniform, as her shift doesn't start for a few hours. Instead she's casual, in high-heeled boots, deliberately ripped jeans, and a fluffy pink jumper that belies the discipline of her life. Her make-up is immaculate as always, her mascara crisp, lipstick unsmudged. She has straight black hair that falls sharply to just beyond her shoulders and hangs there, seemingly motionless. Never untidy, not a strand out of place. At work she wears her hair up in an old-fashioned bun, held in place with clips and pins.

I envy that impression of total control, even though I know it wouldn't suit me. It's also a little disconcerting. I prefer people who aren't quite perfect, perhaps because it makes me feel better about my own imperfections.

Louise tips her head to one side. 'So what's all this top-secret business about?'

'You didn't tell Dominic I wanted to meet you?'

'Of course not.'

I open my mouth, then shut it again. A sudden internal wobble. 'Let's get something to eat first, then we can talk. I'm starving.'

I'm not starving at all. But I feel uncomfortable under Louise's steady gaze.

'Whatever you like.'

Louise grabs her purse, and we move to the counter. The queue is short, thankfully, and the place offers pre-packaged sandwiches, which is easiest for both of us. Armed with coffee in paper cups and a sandwich apiece, we head back to the corner table.

'You're not having second thoughts, are you?' Louise asks, frowning as she sits down. 'About marrying Dom, I mean.'

Now it's my turn to say, 'Of course not.'

'But?'

I pretend to be preoccupied with my sandwich packaging. Though it's pointless trying to hide my nervousness, the way my hands are trembling. Louise is one of Dominic's closest work colleagues, and she's both intelligent and highly observant. Too bloody observant, frankly.

Perhaps I ought not to have asked someone so close to Dominic for advice about this. But ever since he introduced us in a nightclub, soon after I started dating him, I've felt a certain affinity with Louise, a natural connection between the two of us. Like I could tell her anything and she wouldn't judge me for it.

I just hope that proves to be true.

'But . . . I do have a problem.' I look up to find Louise watching me intently, and feel a sudden bloom of heat in my cheeks. 'Oh, not with Dominic. He's the love of my life. We're perfect together.'

'Agreed.'

I have to smile. There was the tiniest hint of warning in that one word, as if to say, 'Don't mess with my friend's heart.'

Louise is not jealous, of course. She's gay and happily in a relationship with Amita, a radiographer a few years older than her. But she looks after her friends.

'No, this is something totally different.'

I go to take a sip of coffee, but it's too hot to drink.

Louise unwraps her sandwich. 'Go on.'

I look about the half-empty café. Lunch is almost over now. I guess most staff have eaten and gone, because it's mainly visitors and the occasional dressing-gowned patient at the tables around us.

'The thing is,' I say quietly, 'someone sent me something odd in the post, and I'd like your opinion on it.'

'Sent you something? What, like a wedding gift?'

'No.' I pause, frowning. 'Actually, I don't know. Maybe it was meant as a wedding gift. I hadn't thought of it like that. Pretty sick gift though.'

'Sick?' Now she's looking bemused.

'I'm going to have to give you some background first,' I tell her. 'Otherwise it won't make any sense.'

'Shoot.'

'First, you need to promise you won't repeat any of this to Dominic.'

Louise, about to take a bite of her prawn mayonnaise sandwich, puts it down again. Her finely etched brows rise steeply. 'Seriously?'

'I'm sorry, I know that probably sounds ridiculous. But I don't want Dom to know.'

'Why not?'

'It's personal.'

'No way.' Louise shakes her head. 'I can't agree to lie to Dominic. I mean, he's my friend. I don't want to pull rank, but I've known him longer than you. Not much longer, agreed. But it counts.'

'Please, this is important.'

Louise looks at me closely. 'Jesus. Whatever this is about, it's really upset you, hasn't it?'

I nod, not trusting myself to reply.

25

'Okay.' Louise takes a deep breath, then lets it out slowly. 'I promise not to tell Dom. But only if I think, after hearing what you have to say, that he doesn't *need* to know.'

'That doesn't sound like much of a promise.'

'Take it or leave it.'

I consider for a moment, then nod. Though only because it's either confide in Louise or nobody. And right now I desperately need a second opinion. Otherwise I'm going to crack.

'I'll take it,' I say drily. 'You drive a hard bargain.'

Smiling, Louise raises her coffee in a mock toast. 'Never play me at cards. So, what is it I mustn't tell your husband-to-be?'

I reach into my coat pocket. The cold plastic of the bag in which I placed the eyeball rubs against my fingers. No backing out now; I have to tell someone.

'I had a sister,' I begin haltingly, and my chest tightens with just those words. 'Her name was Rachel.'

Chapter Five

'*Had* a sister?'

I nod and look away. Much to my embarrassment, my eyes fill with tears.

'Oh God,' Louise says at once, and puts her hand out across the table, brushing my arm. 'You poor thing, you're in pieces.'

'No, it's . . . it's okay.'

I breathe in deeply through my nose, then out again. Count to five in my head. The wave of panic begins to recede. But slowly, very slowly.

'I had a sister called Rachel,' I repeat. 'She died years ago, when we were kids. On a family holiday in the Swiss Alps.'

'I'm so sorry.'

'Dominic knows that much. But there's more.' It's hard, but I force myself to go on. 'Far more.'

'Go on.'

I take a tentative sip of coffee, my gaze on the blank, cream-coloured wall opposite. The coffee is still hot but no longer scalding. 'I wasn't with her that day, so I don't know exactly how she . . . Anyway, Rachel died on that holiday and life was never the same again.'

'I'm not surprised. It must have been traumatic.'

Blinking back tears, I shake my head. 'No,' I say with some difficulty. 'You still don't understand.'

Louise looks at me, frowning.

How on earth could she understand? Louise did not know Rachel, and has no idea what life has been like for our family; of the way that holiday in Switzerland split everything into 'before' and 'after' her death.

'Rachel had a snow globe,' I start again, not looking at her. 'There was this pretty Swiss village inside, a goat, you know the sort of thing. All that twee tourist stuff. My dad bought it for her on a diplomatic trip to Switzerland a few years before she died. She loved that snow globe. She used to shake it really hard, and then watch the snow slowly settle.' I swallow. My voice is hoarse and uneven, but I need to get this out. 'After Rachel died, I never saw the snow globe again. I thought Dad must have thrown it away. Because he couldn't bear to see it and remember, you know?'

Louise watches me with concern in her eyes. 'You okay, Cat?'

'Yeah, just about.' I nod, then take another sip before pushing away my coffee cup. It tastes bitter. 'Anyway, a few days ago, this parcel arrived for me at the food bank. Addressed to me by name. I thought it was just another donation. But when I opened the parcel, the snow globe was inside.' I pause. 'Rachel's snow globe.'

'Oh my God.' Louise looks shocked. 'You're sure it was hers?'

'Positive.'

'So who sent it to you?' She frowns. 'Your parents?'

'No, impossible. They would never have done something like that. There was no note with it either. But there was . . . there was something inside it.'

'What?'

Feeling sickened, I pull the plastic bag from my pocket and throw it across the table towards Louise.

'That was inside the snow globe.' I watch as Louise picks up the bag and stares at the contents. 'I had to drain the globe to . . . to get it out.'

'Is that . . . an eyeball?'

'Yes.'

'Jesus Christ.'

'That's why I wanted to see you today. Because I need you to check if that's a human eye or an animal's. If it's even a real eyeball at all.'

'Looks real enough to me.' She studies it closely, frowning. 'Though I'd say it's too large to be human.'

'But could you find out for sure?'

'I can do that, yes.'

'Thank you, I really appreciate it.' I pause, guessing from her expression that some further explanation is needed. 'I could have asked Dominic to check for me, of course. But I don't want him to know the truth about Rachel.'

'But why?' She looks puzzled. 'I mean, it's none of my business. But the two of you are getting married soon, for God's sake. I'm sure Dominic would understand.'

'I'm not sure he would. It's rather complicated, you see.'

'Families are always complicated.'

'Not like this.'

She studies me. 'It can't be that bad, surely?'

'Confidentially?'

'Of course.'

'Rachel was my older sister,' I say. 'Older by just over one year. But she was also an evil bitch and I wasn't sorry when she died.'

I can't believe I'm admitting the truth at last. I've never discussed Rachel's condition with anyone outside the family except a therapist when I was younger, and even he avoided using her name. As if it was unlucky. But now that I've started, I can't seem to stop. Not until Louise understands.

'I know that sounds awful,' I continue breathlessly, avoiding her shocked stare. 'But Rachel made my life a living hell from the moment I was born. She made my parents' lives hell too. She was . . . Rachel was like the devil.' My hands harden into fists, nails digging into my flesh. 'Total, stone-cold evil.'

Louise is staring at me in astonishment.

'You probably think I'm exaggerating. That it was just typical sibling rivalry between us. Tit for tat, some childish feud. But you'd be wrong. Completely, horribly wrong.' My voice starts to shake. 'The sort of things Rachel did would turn your stomach. I can barely bring myself to talk about it. I mean, she was sick. She must have been. No normal person would have done things like that.'

Louise takes my hand and squeezes it. 'Bloody hell, you poor thing. Please, you don't need to go on.'

'No, I do. There's . . . there's more.'

She waits.

'A few months before she died, Rachel trapped a stray cat in the shed. A young cat. More of a kitten, really. I wanted to run and tell our mum, but Rachel wouldn't let me. She made me stand there and watch. Watch while she tortured the poor little thing until it died.'

Louise is shaking her head in horror. As a mental health specialist, she must have heard some nasty stories in her time. But this is particularly gruesome.

'After it was dead, Rachel pulled its eyes out. It was so horrible. She slipped one into my water glass at bedtime. So when I went to take a drink . . .'

Louise puts a hand to her mouth, unable to speak.

I understand precisely how she is feeling, that creeping sense of horror, and decide not to finish the story. It speaks for itself anyway.

Instead, I gesture to the bag containing the eyeball. 'That,' I tell her, 'is pure Rachel. Only it can't be Rachel who sent it to me. Because my sister is long dead.'

I meet Louise's eyes deliberately. No more hiding. No more lying to myself.

'And nobody's happier about that than me.'

Chapter Six

After work on Tuesday I head for the bus stop opposite the food bank to begin the laborious trek across London to my parents' house in Kensington. It's been another difficult day and I'm dog-tired, my feet aching.

I'm also upset.

I know some of the people who come to the food bank are in terrible circumstances, but it still shakes me to learn exactly how they're living, often hand to mouth, in appalling housing conditions. There was a woman today who couldn't stop crying while I fetched her food. We had to stop while she took a breather. She was recently widowed and living out of a suitcase, with four young kids and only two damp rooms in a North London high-rise. One of her kids was a toddler, a girl who trailed round after her mum with a lost look in her eyes, constantly sucking her thumb.

Sharon had to take over in the end because I didn't know how to deal with my own distress. The worst stories have a tendency to reduce me to misty-eyed sympathy, and then I'm next to useless, forgetting even the basics of my training.

Sharon came to see me afterwards, saying, 'Don't worry, love. You'll get used to it.'

She's right, of course. I need to be more professional, not keep dissolving. The problem is, I'm not sure I want to 'get used to it'. To become so hardened to such tales of suffering that I no longer feel like crying.

A man sitting opposite me on the bus keeps staring and mouthing at me. I'm not sure what he's trying to say, but it looks like he's high on something.

I tug on the hem of my suede skirt, which is below the knee and hardly a come-on. I'm careful to look past him with no change of expression, but am secretly relieved when the man gets off five stops later, still glancing my way.

I've always been shy, and still have trouble with people who are noisy or aggressive, especially in cramped, crowded spaces like buses and tubes at rush hour. Brushing against people is one of my pet hates, and having to walk home alone in the late evening is another. But working at the food bank has made me more relaxed in certain situations. For instance, I no longer clutch my bag quite so rabidly on the bus, or stare rigidly ahead when walking down the street as though terrified someone will speak to me.

'But you said you were brought up in London,' Sharon exclaimed the first time I confessed one of my stupid little phobias to her and Petra.

'I was rarely here though, and when we were, we tended to take taxis everywhere.' I struggled to explain my unusual upbringing, aware that Sharon was brought up in a vast, sprawling family in the East End, with cousins and half-siblings on every corner. 'I was homeschooled, and we stayed in the house most days. Then later, after—' I caught myself. 'That is, when I was older, I got sent off into the country with a nanny.'

'You're so posh,' Petra said, smiling at me over the pallet of donated tins she was putting on the shelves. She's always smiling. A naturally sunny personality – surprising to me, given that Petra is an amputee

33

whose right arm was severed at the elbow in a cycling accident years ago. But she doesn't seem to let it bother her. 'I wish I'd had a nanny.'

'Oh, it's not as nice as it sounds,' I told her quickly. It wasn't entirely true – but the truth wouldn't be appropriate. That's what my mother would say. 'Anyway, I never really spent much time in the city until I finished my education. And then I found a job within walking distance of my parents' house, so I never had a chance to get used to . . . well, how big London is.'

Sharon grinned. 'Bloody enormous, isn't it? And it gets bigger whenever there's a tube strike on, you ever notice that?' She handed over a stack of forms. 'Here, my eyesight's crap. Can you sort through these for me?' Sharon hates reading and form-filling. 'Sorry to ask again. But you can sit in my office if you like. Out of the draught.'

I readily agreed, even though it was the third time this month that Sharon had asked me to fill out the forms. But I prefer the office with its two-bar heater to the chilly open floor of the food bank. Admin suits me better, too. Besides, Sharon is so good with people, it's a shame for her to be cooped up with paperwork when she could be talking to 'clients', as she calls the people who come wandering in every day, desperate not to look like they need a handout.

I have to change bus at the next stop. I sway to the exit as the driver corners at speed with brutal precision. Then I hop off in the cold, soon crossing the road at the lights and heading downhill towards a more familiar area.

I used to wait at this bus stop as a teenager, on my way home from shopping or a walk. In those days, I was less scared of the city. Less scared of living. Back then, I would sometimes have a sneaky smoke while waiting for the bus. Like the purple-haired girl in the skin-tight dress and thigh-high boots who's there today, oblivious to the icy winds, both hands cupped round the flame of her boyfriend's lighter as she sucks on a cigarette.

I don't smoke anymore, though Dominic occasionally has a ciga-rette after dinner or when he's feeling stressed after a long day.

Rachel used to smoke, I remember with a jolt. Whenever our par-ents weren't watching, she'd drag out a packet of fags – probably stolen from Dad, who sometimes indulged in those days – and light one up. Then crush it under her heel before Mum came in, blaming the smell on me.

'It wasn't me, Mum,' she would insist. 'You know I don't smoke. It was Cat.'

So Mum would turn to look at me accusingly. And I was only able to shake my head and mutter something incoherent, while Rachel smiled viciously at me behind Mum's back.

The bus arrives and I get on behind the young couple, touching my Oyster card to the pad while they giggle and head for the back row. It's impossible not to inhale the stale smell of smoke.

It's only a short ride to the stop nearest my parents' home, a large double-fronted house just off the Old Brompton Road. It's hidden by high iron railings long since taken over by an overgrown box hedge. There's a weeping willow in the garden, which gives the front rooms a melancholy tint in summer, and now, in winter, looks bleak and some-how lonely without its greenery. The dead willow leaves are still lying on the lawn, brown-edged and curling, even littering the gravelled front path, too.

There are lights on downstairs, though the curtains have been drawn to shut out the cold of the evening. I root automatically in my bag for my key, then stop and ring the bell instead. I no longer live here, as Dad has explained several times. It isn't appropriate for me to use my key unless they are both out.

My mum opens the door, a tall woman with ash-blonde hair like my own, only shoulder-length and more silvery.

'Darling, how are you?' Her eyes widen. 'Gosh, you've cut your hair rather short. I'm not sure what your dad will say about that. What on earth made you do it?'

Her smile falters slightly as she searches my face. But she continues without waiting for an answer. 'Still, it's lovely of you to visit us at last. We've both missed you. The house isn't the same. Of course, it's wonderful that you're so busy with your volunteering these days. But we'd love to see more of you.'

That's what Dominic would call a passive-aggressive greeting, I think drily. But I manage a polite smile in return. 'Hi, Mum. How are you?'

My mother is looking strained. Is that down to today's visit, or is something else bothering her? 'Oh, I'm fine,' she says vaguely as I kiss her on the cheek.

I slip past into the hallway, which smells heavily of flowers, and hang up my coat. I stop to admire the elegant white orchids on the hall table, then head for the living room.

'No, not in there. Your father's only just home from a meeting, I'm afraid. He went upstairs for a quick shower.' Mum gestures me further down the hallway. 'Let's sit in the kitchen instead, shall we? It's warmer in there anyway.' She pauses, then says with an unfamiliar teasing note in her voice, 'And I've got a little surprise for you.'

I follow her into the large, modern kitchen, with its beautiful chrome fittings kept at a high shine by Kasia, my parents' cleaner. She's Polish and very efficient. She taught me how to pronounce her surname once. Lecinska. Like 'let-chin-scar'. I always get the feeling Kasia doesn't like me, though I've done nothing to deserve that. But I often see her and my dad having a joke together, so maybe she's the kind of woman who prefers men to other women.

'No Dominic?' Mum asks, lifting a bottle of chilled white wine out of the fridge and holding it up. 'Chardonnay?'

'Just a small one, thanks.' I watch as Mum pours us each a large glassful, ignoring my request, then I take the wine with a perfunctory smile. *Going to be like that, is it?* 'Dominic's on evenings this week.'

'Must be hard, not having him there when you get in from work.'

'Not at all,' I lie, but know my mum won't be fooled. Our relationship is none of her business though, as I've told her before. 'I like having extra time to myself.'

To distract her, I turn on my heel, studying the room next door, just visible through an archway. Light-blue walls and a new, gilt-framed oval mirror facing me. I check my reflection in it, then hurriedly look away, not liking what I see. The cold wind has left my cheeks tinged red, and my blonde hair looks sharp as a hedgehog's bristles, sticking straight up over the crown. No wonder Mum stared at me on the doorstep. I look wild, like a changeling.

'Oh, you've redecorated the breakfast room,' I say, playing with the thin stem of my wine glass. 'Is that the surprise?'

'God, no, we had that done over the summer, while we were away in Barbados.' My mother draws out a chair and sits down, watching me.

I feel uneasy under her gaze and avoid looking at her, prowling the room instead.

'You must see the new decor in the guest bedroom, too,' she continues. 'I wanted pink wallpaper, had it all picked out. But your dad said no, it had to be something stylish and classic. In case one of his banker friends comes to stay. You know how conservative they all are, these business executives. So we went for grey and cream.'

'I'd have preferred pink.'

'Me too, absolutely.' Mum's voice has begun to tremble, as though she's uneasy. An impression she confirms a second later, adding brusquely, 'Do sit down, darling. You're making me nervous. You remind me of a caged animal when you pace about the room like that. A panther, maybe.'

'A blonde panther?'

My mother's mouth compresses, but she goes on smiling. 'Yes, a blonde one. I was so glad when you rang. So was your dad. It really has been too long since you came to see us, Cat.'

'Please don't call me that.'

There's a short silence.

'Sorry, I forgot. You prefer Catherine these days, don't you?' My mother takes a deep swallow of wine. 'So grown-up.'

I sit down and place the glass in front of me without having yet taken a sip. The chilled wine is already frosting up the outside of the glass.

'How's the job?' Mum asks brightly, then jumps up and fetches her handbag from beside the cooker, as though she's already forgotten asking. 'Here.' With her most generous smile, the one reserved for moments when she knows gratitude will shortly be in order, she hands me a small, gift-wrapped box. 'A little present for you, darling. I bought it for your Christmas present, but . . . well, you're here now. So go ahead, open it.'

Reluctantly, I jerk on the thin gold ribbon holding the wrapping paper in place, then peel back soft layers of crepe. Inside is a small blue jewellery box.

Harrods, it says on the lid in gold lettering.

I hesitate, suddenly wary. What on earth has Mum bought for me from Harrods, of all places?

'Shouldn't I wait,' I ask, 'if this is a Christmas present?'

'No, go on.' My mother is watching with childlike eagerness, almost as though the present is for her, not me. 'I can always buy you something else for Christmas. Besides, I want to see what you think.'

'I think you've spent too much money on me.'

'Oh, don't be silly. You're my daughter and it's not as though we're hard-up. Besides, my goodness, your bloody dad never lets me spend more than we can afford. Well, you know what he's like.' She laughs, but without any real humour. 'Ebenezer Scrooge, to a T.'

I don't laugh.

I'm remembering the young widow with sad, desperate eyes today. The one with four equally desperate kids, all crammed together in two dingy rooms, and barely any money to buy food.

Whatever's inside this jewellery box from Harrods, it would probably feed that whole family for six months.

'Yes, Catherine, open the damn box,' a deep voice says from behind us, startling me to the core. 'Let's see what Ellen has been hiding from me for weeks.'

Chapter Seven

I jump up, my heart suddenly racing. The box waits unopened on the table as I throw both arms about his neck.

'Daddy.'

He looks down at me with those dark, heavy-lidded eyes that always make me think of home and childhood. Not entirely happily, it has to be said. He glances at my mother. 'Sorry I'm late, Ellen. Traffic was insane, as usual.' He kisses my flushed cheek, then pinches it. 'Catherine, where have you been? You know I like to keep a very special eye on my daughter, to make sure she's not in any trouble. Yet weeks go by and you don't get in touch.'

'Sorry.'

'Too busy with Dominic to bother with your old mum and dad, is that it? Well, never mind, you're here now,' he says, in an echo of my mother earlier. His voice deepens with affection. 'Not sure about the drastic haircut. But if it makes you happy—'

'It does,' I say.

'Well then.' Despite the indulgent smile, there's an edge to his voice, making it clear he doesn't approve. 'Now, why don't you open that box? Put us all out of our misery.'

I turn back to the jewellery box, meaning to open the lid, but my hand shakes at his words and I suddenly can't bring myself to do it.

Why don't you open that box? Because I'm remembering my sister's snow globe, heavy and cold to the touch, an eyeball bobbing about inside, staring back at me.

'Go on, darling,' Mum prompts, her eyes shining.

I open the lid of the box.

Inside is a beautiful cat in profile, cast in silver and nestled against a bed of black velvet. The cat's back is arched as if it's spitting, tail raised, head forward. Its single eye winks at me under the kitchen spotlights. A tiny diamond, I realise. At the apex of its hunched back is a loop with a delicate silver chain threaded through it.

'What do you think?'

I look blankly round at Mum. 'It's a cat.'

'You always wanted a cat as a child. Do you remember? Because of your pet name. *Cat*. Only we were worried about all the traffic. Central London . . . A kitten might have got itself killed under a car's wheels, and we couldn't bear the thought of that.' She looks at my face, and concern creeps into her voice. 'Cat? What is it?' She glances at the silver necklace. 'You don't like it?'

It's all I can do not to scream in her face.

'No, it's . . .' I unthread the necklace from the box with unsteady fingers. 'It's lovely. Thank you.'

My parents say nothing, watching me.

'Daddy, could you possibly . . . ?' I smile, awkwardly miming putting on the necklace. 'These things are so fiddly.'

'Turn around,' he says in his deep voice.

I stand still while Dad positions the necklace around my neck. It fits perfectly. His warm fingers brush my skin, fumbling a little as he fastens the clasp.

'It is a little fiddly,' he agrees after a few seconds, breathing heavily next to my ear. 'There,' he says at last, and steps back. 'All done.'

I close the lid of the jewellery box and straighten the silver cat on my chest. It hangs to just above my cleavage. I'm pretty sure Dominic will love it.

'Thank you.' I smile politely at Dad, and then at Mum. 'It's super. Thank you so much.'

'You're welcome, darling,' Mum says, beaming. 'Oh, it does suit you.'

Dad says nothing.

'If you don't need me, I think I'll go up to my old room for a bit,' I tell them, wishing my voice did not sound so high and breathless. 'I've got one of my headaches coming on. Probably the wine.'

My mother glances at my face. 'Do you need painkillers?'

'It's fine, I have something in my bag.'

'Of course.'

I glance vaguely about the kitchen. 'Unless you need help?'

'God, no. We're only having steak and salad. Your dad's agreed to cook the steaks, and Kasia made us a big salad before she left tonight. It's in the fridge, chilling.'

'Like the wine,' Dad says, and winks at me.

'Then I'll see you both later.'

'Should be ready about seven thirty.' Mum smiles broadly, gripping the back of one of the kitchen chairs. Her knuckles look almost white under the spotlights. 'You have a nice lie-down, Cat. I'll send Daddy to let you know when dinner's ready.'

'I told you, please don't call me that.'

I turn and leave the room, feeling their gazes on my back all the way out. The hall is brightly lit, but the first floor is in darkness. I don't put the lights on though, finding my way upstairs without any help, my hand sliding along the smooth wooden banister.

One. Two. Three. Four. Five . . .

In my head, I count all the stairs up to the second floor, reaching twelve and stopping. It's pitch-black at the top of the house. My bedroom to the right. Rachel's to the left. Her room locks, mine doesn't. I can still see marks on the wooden frame of her door where there used to be a bolt, too. On the outside, to keep her safely locked in when she was having one of her violent tantrums. Our shared bathroom lies straight ahead.

The house is silent up here.

Oppressively so.

I tuck the necklace under my knitted top, but I can still feel it there. The silver cat is cold against my skin. Cold and heavy.

Pushing the door to my room open, I grope along the wall for the light switch.

The light comes on.

I look up, straight into Rachel's eyes.

Chapter Eight

Of course, it isn't Rachel. It's just my own reflection in the full-length mirror opposite. But it frightens me enough that I gasp, take a sudden step back.

Someone – Kasia, perhaps? – has hooked one of my old black evening dresses on a hanger over the framed edge of the mirror.

For a second, looking into the mirror is like looking through a second doorway. A doorway into the past, and not a very flattering one.

Rachel was thinner than me, and slightly taller too, being older. Otherwise we were quite similar, so that people often mistook us for each other. In this instant though, I glimpse Rachel as she might have looked if she'd survived into adulthood. The narrow face filled out, her long hair chopped unflatteringly, hips somewhat broader, the suggestion of a rounded belly where Rachel was flat as a board. A slight coarsening of the features, too, which shocks me, examining myself in contrast to my dead sister.

There was always an air of elfish malevolence about Rachel that has kept her ever young in my memory. But if she'd lived, she might have looked very different by now. Perhaps even unrecognisable, if encountered on the street.

I lied about the headache.

My primary impulse downstairs had been to escape. To flee the claustrophobic atmosphere of the kitchen, where I'd felt – and acted – like a child again. That's how it always seems to go when reunited with my parents. Pure regression, everything driven by kneejerk reactions that date back to childhood. One excellent reason for avoiding them all this time, though I can hardly admit that to my mother.

Daddy, I called him.

As though I were a little girl in short socks, and he was my hero. The best man in all the world.

'Ugh.'

I drop backwards onto the bed, which is made up with fresh linen as if they told Kasia I'm staying the night. I won't stay, of course.

But dinner won't do any harm.

The mattress creaks beneath me in its wooden frame as I shift, getting comfortable. A sleigh bed, both ends curved like a Russian troika. My initials are carved into the wooden scroll at the head end.

There's a photograph on the wall: me and Dad, soon after we returned home from Switzerland, taken by Mum in the back garden.

I look young and vulnerable. No make-up, my clothes ill-fitting. I would go on to lose a lot of weight in my mid-teens, my body a kind of stranger during adolescence. By contrast, Dad looks easy and self-assured in jeans and shirtsleeves, his top button undone. No tie, I notice. He took several months off work after Rachel's death, which pleased me as I got to spend so much time with him alone.

Dad's arm is round my shoulder, hugging me close. His smile is warm and open. Yet there's a sadness about him, too. A distance in his eyes.

We had just lost Rachel.

His hair was only faintly threaded with silver in those days. Tall and broad-shouldered, but with a leanness that made his jeans sit low on his hips, he dominates the shot. Behind us stands the gigantic magnolia tree that is still the focal point of the garden, especially in spring when its petal buds open into vast, waxy-leaved, bowl-like flowers. Even now I can almost smell that rich, citrus scent that is always so overwhelming when sitting beneath it in the shade . . .

Did Dad love Rachel more than me when we were kids? Was I some kind of consolation prize for him after her death?

I often wonder, yet never dare ask him directly. And with my adult mind, it's a possibility that makes little sense. Rachel was an unpleasant child, always in serious trouble, always doing something not merely mischievous but downright appalling.

Yet my parents usually like to pretend that she was normal.

'You shouldn't speak ill of the dead,' they told me once, after an inadvertent mention of Rachel and some dreadful crime she'd committed. Their disapproval was tangible.

Rachel, the saint.

Canonised after death, and quite undeservedly.

I bring out the cat necklace from under my top, straightening it on my chest. I both love it and hate it at the same time. A conflict which hurts and causes me confusion. The very fact that my mother can buy me a gift like this, and not know how painful it must be, makes me question my own memories.

Yes, I wanted a cat as a child. A soft, fluffy kitten who would run after dangled wool and cuddle up to me at night.

But there was a very good reason they decided against getting a cat. Because of Rachel's hatred for animals. Not least the day she tortured and killed that unfortunate stray in front of me. And further traumatised me by plucking out its eye, and . . .

The snow globe.

I close my eyes and push that memory away. It's easier to do than I feared. But then, it was always quiet here at the top of the house. The windows are specially double-glazed to be soundproof, and the noise of traffic below is barely audible. That's one reason I spent so long up here after Rachel's death. I felt cocooned, a rook in a high nest, cut off from the rush and confusion of the city below. Like I was all alone in the world, and nothing could bother me. Not even the most troubling memories of my sister.

I let myself drift into sleep. I'll mention Rachel's snow globe at dinner. That's why I've come to see them, after all.

We eat in the dining room, not the breakfast room, which surprises me. The dining room is long and very grand, and normally reserved for when my parents have company. And I hardly count as 'company'. But the table was laid by Kasia before she left, Mum tells me. It has been covered with a cream damask tablecloth, and laid with wine and water glasses, and slender silver cutlery. There's a floral centrepiece too, white roses with delicate green candles, and for each person a damask napkin enclosed in a silver-plated napkin ring.

There's an empty seat opposite me. No place setting, but the seat is there.

I glance at it briefly, and then away.

'How's Dominic getting on at the hospital?' my mother asks, and I smile, turning to her, only too happy to talk about someone other than myself.

While I describe Dominic's recent issues at St Hilda's, I'm aware of my dad watching me, his eyes intent. Such close scrutiny makes me uneasy, but I keep talking. I know what he's thinking. That Dominic isn't good enough for me. Such crap. None of the boys I've dated have ever been good enough for him. At first I was disheartened by his patent disapproval of Dominic – 'A male nurse?' Dad had repeated when I first mentioned his job, clearly horrified – but Dominic himself persuaded me to let it go.

'Parents never like the guys their daughters date,' he assured me, grinning. 'Don't worry about it.'

I did worry though, but secretly, and certainly didn't allow Dad to influence my choice of boyfriend.

Dinner over, Mum disappears into the kitchen to make a pot of coffee, again rejecting my offer of help.

I stay at the table, talking politics with Dad.

'Are you happy with this man?' he asks suddenly, reaching for my hand.

'Of course I am.'

'You'd tell me if you weren't? You wouldn't hide it from me?'

'Don't be silly, you know I would.' Embarrassed, I pull my hand away, and feel his gaze narrow on my face. 'Look, everything's fine. You don't need to worry.'

'Your mum said you sounded unhappy on the phone. She thought there might be a problem.'

'Not with Dominic.'

He nods slowly, his expression giving nothing away. 'Okay.'

'I love Dominic.' I have to struggle not to raise my voice. Would he be this overprotective if I were his son? 'How can you even think that? For God's sake, I'm marrying him in a few weeks.'

'People change their minds sometimes.'

'I haven't changed my mind.'

'Okay,' he repeats, but continues to watch me closely.

'I wish you wouldn't treat me like this.'

'Like what?'

'Like some stupid kid who doesn't know her own mind.' My mother comes back in, carrying a tray of coffee. 'I told you before, everything's going fine with our wedding plans. We know what we're doing. So you don't need to worry. Either of you.'

Mum looks worriedly from me to my father. 'I only left you two alone for five minutes. Don't tell me you've argued again?'

'Not at all,' my father says smoothly.

He reaches out again and pats my hand before I can stop him. A deeply patronising gesture, though I know Dad's probably unaware of his own latent sexism. I suppress my little burst of temper and say nothing.

'Typical dad–daughter stuff, that's all,' he says easily. 'And it seems we've had a false alarm. No probs with the delectable Dom, after all.' He sniffs the air appreciatively. 'That smells amazing, Ellen. It's been a long day. Endless bloody problems at work. I could murder a cup of coffee.'

Mum pours us all a cup of coffee, her movements precise and studied. Then she sits back in her place and smiles at me. It looks like she's brushed her silvery-blonde hair while out of the room. There's not a strand out of place.

The perfect society hostess.

'So, darling,' she says, 'if the wedding's still on, and you and Dominic are still madly in love, what on earth's bothering you? I don't want to come across as one of these irritating mother-hen types, but you did sound a little upset on the phone. And you hardly ever pop over to see us these days.' She searches my face, then her smile fades. 'Oh God, you're not . . . you're not expecting, are you?'

I almost laugh out loud, but then see a similar look of alarm etched on my dad's face. 'Of course not. It's nothing like that.'

'Let's hear it then.' Dad sips his black coffee and settles back in his seat, crossing his long legs. Like a crane fly, we used to say as girls, giggling at him in shorts. Daddy-Long-Legs. 'What's this visit about?'

I take a deep breath. 'Rachel.'

Chapter Nine

A thick silence follows my sister's name, as I guessed it might.

My parents never like to discuss Rachel with me, not even in passing conversation. Mum is sitting so still, she seems to be holding her breath. My parents look at each other down the length of the dining table as though I've said something explosive. *Talk about the black sheep of the family*, I think, gulping down a mouthful of hot coffee to hide my nerves and only succeeding in scalding my mouth.

I can hardly blame them for that reaction, of course. My own memories of my older sister are not exactly fond. In fact, I still have nightmares . . .

Dad puts his cup down carefully.

'Rachel?'

Looking directly at him, I say, 'A parcel arrived for me at the food bank. I don't know who sent it. But when I opened it . . . Rachel's snow globe was inside.'

He stares at me. 'Her snow globe?'

'With an eyeball inside it.'

My mother makes a noise of protest, a hand at her mouth. 'Oh God.'

'It was a horrible shock. Which I imagine was the whole point.' Noting my mum's sudden pallor and wide eyes, I say, 'Though it turned out not to be as gruesome as it appeared. I took it to Louise – she's a nurse at the hospital, a friend of Dominic's – and she confirmed my suspicions. It isn't human.'

My mother lets out a shaky breath. 'You mean it was a fake? One of those joke-shop eyeballs?'

'No, it was a real eyeball.' I think back over the phone call from Louise. 'Just not human. Probably a cow's eye, Louise told me.'

'Oh my God,' Mum says faintly.

'They're quite easy to get hold of, apparently. Butcher shops have them. And abattoirs. Places like that.'

Dad stirs at last, sitting forward with obvious interest. 'So who on earth sent you this . . . cow's eyeball?'

'I told you,' I say, 'I don't know. There was no sender's address on the parcel. And nothing inside either.'

'How convenient.'

'What's that supposed to mean?'

But he sidesteps the question, asking instead, 'What did Dominic say?'

Now it's my turn to feel uncomfortable. 'He doesn't know.'

For a moment, nobody says anything.

My father frowns, studying my face. 'You're telling us you received something that ghoulish in the post . . . and didn't tell your fiancé?'

I shrug.

'Why, may I ask?'

'I didn't want to alarm him,' I say, not entirely untruthfully.

'You didn't want to *alarm* him?' my dad repeats. 'Darling, don't be ridiculous. The man works in a hospital. He can hardly be squeamish.'

That wasn't what I meant, of course. I hesitate. 'It's complicated.'

'I see,' he says drily.

Mum glares at him. 'Robert.'

'Oh, very well.' He shrugs, a vague hunching of his shoulders. But I can tell he doesn't believe a word I've said tonight. He's just humouring me for Mum's benefit. And perhaps mine, too. 'So let's see if I've got this right. The cow's eyeball was inside Rachel's snow globe?'

'Yes.'

'And you're certain it was her snow globe? Not simply a similar-looking one?'

'Yes,' I say again.

'But how can you be so sure?'

'Well, for a start, "Rachel" was written on the plinth. It was a typed label, just like the one I remember.' I'm struggling to sound credible, hearing myself and thinking wildly: *I wouldn't believe this either*. 'Obviously, I should have brought it with me. But to be honest, I didn't think you wouldn't believe me. And I couldn't stand to look at the horrible thing again. I've hidden it.'

'Hidden it?'

'In our flat,' I tell them.

He glances at my mother again.

I look from one to the other, reading their shuttered expressions with dismay. They think I'm losing it.

I want to leave. That's my first unhappy impulse. Leave now before they humiliate me any further. Snow globes and eyeballs. What must they be thinking? I made a mistake coming here tonight. I could have been snug at home in front of the telly, or falling asleep in a deep bubble bath, waiting for Dominic's key in the door. He's my rock, my safe haven.

I should have told Dominic instead. He would have believed me without question. He would have understood how much this incident is shaking my confidence. He wouldn't speak to me as if I were deranged. But I didn't want to drag him into the nightmare of my past.

I'm angry now. Angry and confused.

'I thought maybe . . .'

Dad raises his brows, his searching glance on my face again. 'Yes?'

'That maybe it was you.'

'Me?'

'Who sent me the snow globe.'

Mum says something in quick denial, clearly distressed. But I miss it in the sudden grate of my dad's chair on the marbled floor of the dining room.

'Get up.'

I stand in confusion, staring at him. Is Dad throwing me out? He grabs for my wrist. His fingers curl round the narrow bones like a manacle, and he squeezes, jerking me forward.

'Come with me, Catherine.'

I'm scared for a second, but he isn't threatening me. Not with violence, anyway. His voice is one I recognise from childhood. That 'you're in trouble now' tone. It makes me instantly defensive.

'Why?'

'There's something I need to show you.'

Flushed and breathless, I try to shake him loose. 'No.'

Dad isn't expecting resistance. I see the flash in his eyes. He refuses to let go, tightening his grip. 'Now you listen to me—'

'Ow, that bloody hurts.'

'Robert!' Mum exclaims.

He looks round at her, releasing my wrist. But his face is dark with anger. Anger or shame, I'm not sure which. Maybe a touch of guilt, too. And he should be bloody guilty, the way he just treated me.

'Follow me,' he says abruptly, and leaves the room.

When I stride angrily after him into the hall, Dad is already heading upstairs.

'Up here, Catherine.'

I hesitate, then follow him.

There's an old, dark-wood chest on the landing outside the guest room, ornately carved, gleaming with polish. My father is waiting beside it with folded arms.

I approach him warily, mistrusting the look in his eyes. I can smell beeswax from the polished chest, and a faint scent of flowers mixed with chemicals emanating from the pale-blue-and-white carpet.

Kasia has been hard at work up here too, I think.

I look down at the chest. I recognise it as having stood at the foot of my parents' bed once. It held linen then, I recall. Neat stacks of freshly laundered sheets and duvet covers, all beautifully ironed and folded, a sachet of lavender slipped between the sheets at intervals to keep the linen scented. Mum sometimes sent me tiptoeing into their bedroom at night to fetch fresh sheets for my bed – there were embarrassingly frequent bed-wetting occasions in my childhood – and I remember lifting the lid quietly, so quietly, to avoid waking Dad, and then dragging out armfuls of clean, lavender-scented sheets.

Now the chest has been moved onto the landing for some reason. Somehow I doubt it still holds linen.

'Open it,' he tells me.

'Why?'

'Just open it.'

It's obvious that he won't be happy until I've performed this stupid little charade for him. So I kneel, feeling ridiculous, and open the heavy, creaking lid of the chest.

Inside the chest are things I recognise from childhood. Not my things though. It's a jumble of old dolls and teddy bears, stuffed animals, toys, Christmas annuals and a few much-thumbed paperbacks. Some collections of poems, some paranormal romances and an illustrated paperback of Lewis Carroll's *Through the Looking-Glass*. I hesitate over that, pick it up, then put it back.

'These are Rachel's,' I say, and glance up at him, frowning. 'So what?'

I try to close the lid, but his voice stops me.

'Take another look.' Dad's watching me, his face unreadable in shadow, the landing light behind his head. 'A proper look, please.'

Reluctantly, I pluck a teen novel out of the chest and flick through it. It's one of the paranormal romances. Witches in a coven, fixing love potions or making up curses. There's occasional red pen in the margins, too. Some kind of commentary on the text? I try to skim through quickly, not reading my sister's angry scribble. But a few words leap out at me.

SLAG, one angry note reads, heavily circled and underlined, with five exclamation marks. Another states simply, *LIAR*. There are numerous scribbled doodles, too. Animals with sad expressions. Heart shapes with dark-red crosses scored through them. Then, on one page, a completed hangman picture, the dashes filled out beside it in childish capital letters.

<u>C</u> <u>A</u> <u>T</u>

Shuddering, I drop the book back into the chest as if it's burning my fingers.

'Okay, so you've cleared out her old bedroom at last. It was about time. What's your point?'

Dad studies me for a moment, until I grow uneasy under his stare. 'Catherine, please, don't play games. It's not funny. We both know it's in there. You can't pretend it's not.'

I stare up at him, confused.

'What are you talking about?'

'The snow globe.' He sounds angry again. 'You're right, I finally got around to clearing out Rachel's room a few weeks back. Kasia helped me sort this lot out. We threw some stuff away too. Took her old clothes to a charity shop.' He pauses. 'It's something we should have done years ago. Ridiculous to hold on to it all. Like keeping a shrine.'

I look away, uncomfortable.

'If it had been up to me alone,' Dad continues, 'I'd have thrown the whole lot out. I mean, what's the point? But your mother got upset. She wanted to keep a few things at least. Personal items.'

'So?'

'So the snow globe is in there. I put it there myself. Bloody thing was leaking, but your mother wouldn't hear of me throwing it out. So I wrapped it in a plastic bag.'

I glance into the chest again. It isn't completely full. The soft toys and the stack of tatty annuals take up most of the room. But there are plenty of smaller items at the bottom. I bend over the chest and carefully move my sister's possessions aside, one by one, searching right down to the wooden base.

There's no plastic bag. No snow globe.

'Well, it's not there now.'

'Impossible.'

I stand aside while my father bends too, searching the chest with mounting urgency. 'Where the hell?' He flings Rachel's toys aside, practically emptying the contents onto the landing. 'I don't understand.'

I fold my arms across my chest. I want to stay calm. To be adult about this, as he had asked me to be. But my heart is beating fast, like I've been running, and there's a familiar flush spreading over my cheeks.

He straightens at last, his face pale. 'You're right,' he says heavily. 'It's not there anymore.'

'So you were wrong,' I say, unable to keep the hurt and anger out of my voice. 'I wasn't playing games.'

'It would appear not.'

'You could at least apologise for accusing me of lying.'

I wait for an apology.

My father says nothing, of course. He's rigid, his brows drawn together.

'For God's sake,' I mutter.

I slam the chest shut and glare round at him. I'm his only surviving child. Yet I might as well be a stranger, the amount of suspicion and uncertainty I can see in his face.

'When are you going to start believing *me* for a change, Dad?'

Chapter Ten

There's a fire engine skewed to a halt outside Gloucester Road tube station, and several police cars parked alongside it. There are no sirens, but flashing blue lights bounce eerily off glass all around the station. As I approach, I see that the entrance to the station has been cordoned off, the concourse empty except for one bearded police officer on the phone. A noticeboard has been dragged out into the street, where it's flexing back and forth, in danger of being blown down by the wind. On it someone has written in black marker pen *Station Closed Due To A Serious Incident*, followed by two alternative stations within easy walking distance.

Wrapping my scarf tighter against the chill wind, I smile at the policeman, then start to trudge on towards the next station.

Inside, I'm still in turmoil. Dad denied having anything to do with that parcel. But should I believe him?

After all, by his own admission, he's the one who cleared out Rachel's room. He saw the snow globe, even noticed it was leaking. Perhaps he took the opportunity to play a nasty trick on me. But I know what Dominic would say if asked. What possible motivation could my father have for doing that?

Because he holds you responsible for Rachel's death, an inner voice taunts me.

I cross the road, raising my chin.

No, I'm not going back there again. Back to my demons, to that dark place where taking my own life seemed like the only way out. That's the person I was years ago. A 'troubled teen', the doctors called me, though in fact the black dog pursued me into my early twenties, too. But with therapy and medication, I managed to push beyond those horrors, and into the light again.

There's no way I'm falling back into that negative way of seeing the world. Believing everyone is against me. That everyone in my life is lying to me.

There's a man huddled in a shop doorway a few hundred feet from the tube station. Cardboard wedged beneath him, dog crouched at his side in the damp folds of a blanket. There's a rough sign partly tucked under his feet as he tries to sleep, turned away from the bitter wind, his body hunched.

HELP, the sign says simply.

I stop beside the sign, and fumble in my bag for change. *Shit*, I think, and check my pockets, too. I don't have anything besides coppers and a few banknotes.

The dog doesn't move, but the man half turns under the blanket, gazing up at me expectantly. His eyes are heavy-lidded, dark and liquid, and he's wearing a woollen hat to keep out the cold.

'Here,' I say in the end, and hand him a five-pound note.

'Bless you,' he says hoarsely.

The flat is in total darkness when I push through the front door, armed with two bags of shopping from the late-opening supermarket on the next block.

It's all quiet inside. Surprisingly cold, too.

'Dom?'

I kick the door shut behind me and listen. Nothing. Maybe he's going to be home later than expected. Sometimes the hospital asks him to work an extra hour or two if things get really hectic in Accident and Emergency.

'Dom?'

But he's not there.

I wander into the kitchen and stab at the light switch with my elbow. The place is a mess as usual. We need to spend some time tidying up if it's going to look nice for this weekend, when we've invited friends over for drinks.

Dumping the shopping on the kitchen counter, I frown.

Why the hell is it so cold?

I strip off my gloves and coat, and check the prepayment meter, situated on the wall above the television. The catch is fiddly and I have to stand on a chair to reach the box. But there's still a tenner to go before it runs out. Dominic is pretty good at remembering to keep it topped up.

I unpack the shopping hurriedly, then put the oven on a medium heat, partly to warm the room but also because I've bought a packet of frozen vegetable rissoles for Dominic's supper. He likes that kind of thing. Putting the kettle on to boil, I set out two mugs for when he finally comes home, then stand warming my hands in the rising steam.

Bloody hell, it's absolutely freezing in here. I stamp and hug myself. Perhaps I should put my coat back on.

Have we left a window open by accident?

I wander out again into the dark hallway. Sure enough, there's a severe draught coming from the bathroom door, which is slightly ajar. I stare at it, then give the door an experimental push with my foot. As it creaks wider, I feel an icy blast of air.

The building is an old Victorian villa, renovated into flats that overlook the mainline railway tracks, most of the windows at the back old-fashioned sash jobs. Useful for the fire escape below, but heavy and unwieldy. The bathroom window is open, the lower half sucking out all the warmth in the flat.

I slam the sash window down and fasten it, shaking my head. 'Dom . . .' He usually takes a shower before work. He must have opened the window for ventilation, as there's no other way to air out the bathroom when it gets steamy, but then forgotten to shut it before leaving for the hospital.

It's now almost as cold inside the flat as outside.

Whacking up the two storage heaters to their maximum output setting, I duck into the bedroom to fetch my warm, blue-flannel dressing gown. Comfort clothing for when I'm feeling at my most miserable.

I hit the light switch, and stop, suddenly unable to breathe.

My chest contracts painfully.

'What the hell?'

There on the bed is my wedding dress, removed from its protective cover and laid out as though ready to be worn. Last week I picked it up after a few minor alterations needed to be made, and hung it on the back of the bedroom door in an opaque bag supplied by the bridal shop. 'It's unlucky to see the dress before the wedding,' I told Dominic, who laughed at my superstitious nature. My dream dress, as I'd described it to my mother tonight over dinner, telling her how impatient I was for Dominic to see me wearing it on the big day itself.

Only it's no longer beautiful.

Someone's taken a pair of scissors to my wedding dress, cutting it into ribbons. There are large, fierce rips in the sweetheart bodice, and all the way down the clinging, mermaid-style skirt. Shreds of satin lie on the floor and the bed. Sequins sparkle from odd corners of the bedroom as though they were deliberately torn off and scattered about like mock confetti.

But the most shocking thing is the thick, gooey red substance splashed across the shimmering white.

Paint?

'Oh my God.'

I take a few impulsive steps forward, as if to snatch up my ruined dress, even though it's far too late to rescue it.

That's when the smell hits me.

Blood.

Chapter Eleven

The blood's sickening, iron-rich stench is unmistakeable now that I'm close enough to touch it. Not that I do, frozen by the bed, staring down at the dress, not quite able to believe what my eyes and nose are telling me. It's too horrific to be true. Yet the evidence is right there in front of me. Somebody has not only maliciously ripped my wedding dress to shreds, they've also covered it in what smells like blood.

'No, please . . .'

Gagging at the vile stench, I run to the front door of the flat, fumble with the catch and throw it open.

Our flat is on the top floor. That seemed like a good idea when we chose it, so far from the noise of the street below and reminiscent of my childhood bedroom in my parents' house, the rook's nest. My refuge against the world. Now though, it's too far from the safety of other people.

Up here, anything could happen and nobody would know . . .

Below, I hear the street door bang shut. The old wire letterbox on the back rattles. A gust of frozen air swirls up the stairs, and I shiver without my coat. Suddenly there's the sound of echoing voices in the hallway on the ground floor.

Somebody has just come in from the cold evening.

Two somebodies.

'Well, there's still time to run away. You're not married yet.'

It's a woman's voice, followed by mutual laughter, and the swift reply: 'I don't want to run away. I want to marry her.'

The woman's voice is only vaguely familiar. But I know the other voice as well as I know my own.

Deep and lightly amused, with a South London accent, the man is saying, 'Besides, she'd soon find me if I ran away. I sometimes think Cat's psychic, she always seems to know what I'm thinking.'

'Dominic?' I interrupt them, hanging almost too far over the banister in my panic, staring down. It's increasingly hard to breathe, especially with my chest pressed against the rail. 'Dominic . . . oh, thank God.'

From below, I catch the flash of his face looking up three floors. A pale oval of surprise and concern. 'Catherine?'

'I need you. Come up, quick.'

'What's the matter?'

'Hurry, please.' I'm gasping. 'Please, Dom.' Snatching at the chilly air, my lungs aching, I can't seem to stop myself from sliding to my knees.

'Okay,' he says, beginning to run. 'Hang on, I'm on my way.'

'Quick, quick.' I'm repeating myself stupidly. Like a trained bird in a cage. My hands grip the banisters like claws as I twist my head and stare down, trying to see through the bars. It's ridiculous to feel jealousy at a moment like this. But I do, all the same. 'Who was that woman with you? I can't see her. Who is it?'

He takes the stairs two at a time, his face flushed. 'It's nobody,' he says, rounding the stairs below, almost as breathless as me after the speed of his ascent. 'Only Laura, from downstairs.'

'Laura?'

Dominic is nearly at the top of the house, carrying a small white plastic bag that swings violently back and forth as he rounds the stairs. 'From Flat Two. You know Laura. The woman with glasses. And the racer bike.' He reaches me and stops, staring down into my face. 'Christ, you look awful. What on earth's the matter?'

'Why were you with Laura? You came in with her from the street. I heard you.'

'She was at the Chinese takeaway.'

'What?'

'I grabbed a chow mein on my way from the tube, and she was there. So we walked back together.' He sounds bewildered. 'Baby, you're crying. What's all this about?'

Now that he's here, I can't seem to tell him what's happened. What I've seen. Instead, I wave him towards the flat. The door is still open. And inside . . .

'I found . . .'

But the words die on my lips.

'What? You found what?' He bends and kisses my mouth. His lips are cold, though, like the inside of the flat, and I don't respond. He searches my face. 'Sweetheart, you're worrying me. And you must be freezing to death out here without a coat. Come on, let's get you inside.'

He bustles me through the door, suddenly the healthcare professional, his touch carefully solicitous rather than intimate.

'Right,' he says, and locks the door behind us, even putting the metal chain on. 'Now, what's upset you, baby?'

'In . . . there,' I manage to say, pointing to the bedroom door. That too is still open, the light on inside. Just as I left it.

'In the bedroom?'

I nod frantically.

He frowns and hands me the plastic bag containing his Chinese takeaway. I hold it close, the smell of chow mein wafting up as I watch him approach the bedroom, his stance cautious and wide-legged, like a dog expecting trouble.

He stops on the threshold and leans round the bedroom door, peering inside.

In my mind, I replay what I saw. My wedding dress lying across our bed like a dead bride. Cut into pieces, smeared with blood. Its beauty ruined forever. The vile smell is still in my nostrils. It feels like I'll never get rid of it.

'Dom?'

But Dominic doesn't reply. He's unmoving, standing like a statue in the doorway to the bedroom.

I hold my breath. A sudden fear floods me. Was the appalling desecration of my wedding dress real?

Or did I imagine it?

Chapter Twelve

There were instances in my childhood where strange things happened, and then turned out afterwards not to have been real. Though I'm still convinced Rachel was behind most of them. All those cruel tricks my sister loved to play on her victims. She was particularly skilled at emotional sleight of hand. Turning the screw in our minds until we cracked. Most of Rachel's little games were barely significant, taken on their own. Minor acts of deception or theft. Yet they always caused upset, nonetheless. Things disappeared with frightening regularity, never to be seen again. Here one minute, gone the next. Like the snow globe that vanished from the wooden chest at my parents' house.

Though that's since turned up, I remind myself. And not in a pleasant way.

Yes, my sister would have been delighted with all this chaos.

If the wedding dress was her work, Rachel would have turned and laughed at me, shaking her head. 'Oh dear, poor Catty gone a bit mental, has she?'

Will Dominic do the same?

'Jesus.' He moves abruptly, disappearing inside the room. I wait, my heart thundering with sickly nerves. Then I hear a faint rustling noise, and his breathing speeds up. 'Jesus Christ.'

I follow him to the door.

No, the violated dress is real.

He's picked up one of the severed, bloodied strips of satin, and is examining it with all the care and specialist attention he might give a wounded patient at the hospital.

'Did you do this?' he asks blankly, not looking round at me.

'God, how can you ask me that?'

'Then who?'

'I have no idea.' I shrug helplessly, though he still isn't looking in my direction. 'I just walked in and found it like this.'

'How long ago?' He glances back at me, his eyes speculative. 'You were planning to see your parents tonight, weren't you? I thought you might stay over.'

'I couldn't.'

'Why?'

'I just . . . I couldn't, okay?'

'Did you have an argument with them?'

'Sort of.'

'Right.' He sounds calm, but I know he isn't. 'So you came home, and . . . what then? Can you talk me through what happened?'

'I was late back.' I'm hesitant, unsure what he wants to hear. 'Like you. The place was dark. Bloody freezing too.' A thought occurs to me, and I shudder. 'Oh shit, the bathroom window. That's how he got in.'

'He?'

'Well, whoever did this. I don't know, do I? Some fucking pervert. Some freak.' I'm angry at his attitude, but am still careful not to mention Rachel. I hate the idea that he won't want to marry me if he finds out just how crazy my sister was. Some of these things can be hereditary, after all, and he mentioned once that he'd like to have kids one day. 'I guess you must have left the window open after your shower this morning.'

'No, I always shut the window afterwards. I make a point of checking it before I leave the flat.'

'But—'

'It wasn't me, Catherine. If the bathroom window was open when you came home, then presumably someone climbed up the fire escape and pushed it open from the outside.' He makes a face. 'It's an old window. The catch is frail, and the frame's rotten in places. If someone wobbled it about enough, maybe it came loose. I'll take a look in a minute.'

Someone climbed up the fire escape . . .

The snow globe, the gross eyeball. Now this break-in. An emerging, hostile pattern. Then there's the nature of the incident itself. My wedding dress targeted. Not any other kind of clothing. It's exactly the sort of horrible prank Rachel would have loved to inflict on me. Something intrusive, disturbing, impossible to pin down. And deeply personal.

Except that my sister is dead.

I sneak a look at him. There's no point sharing my fears with Dominic. He may be my fiancé but he never met Rachel. He's heard stories about her, of course. The stories I could bear to share with someone outside our family. But he can't possibly understand the full extent of her evil. You had to be there, I think bitterly. To grow up under Rachel's shadow, to breathe her poisonous presence into your lungs, day in, day out. To feel that toxicity in every pore of your body and know you'd never entirely wash it out.

'What is this stuff, anyway?' He bends to the sequinned bodice, sniffing one of the thick, red smears. 'God, it's grim. Smells like—'

'Blood,' I say.

'Yes, almost certainly.' He glances round at me, his eyes wide, an arrested look on his face. 'It'll need to be tested.'

'Tested?'

I have visions of him handing the remains of my wedding dress to someone at the hospital, maybe a lab technician. It's not an idea I'm comfortable with. Not something this personal.

'By the police.'

At first, I can't comprehend what he just said. Then his words begin to filter through the waves of horror I'm feeling after seeing the dress again. Its stark, bloodied reality.

'The police,' I repeat slowly. 'You want to call the police?'

'Catherine, someone broke into our flat. Went through our things. Totally trashed your wedding dress.'

'I know, it's just . . . I feel violated.'

'That's perfectly understandable. And the last thing I want right now is to have the police here, traipsing round the place, asking questions. I've had a full day at work, I'm dog-tired, my chow mein is getting cold . . .' He turns back to study the shocking display on the bed. 'But we can't let whoever did this get away with it.'

It's deliberate, the way the dress has been placed on the bed. The bed where we sleep together. And I can see him thinking the same thing.

'Have you checked everywhere else?' he continues.

'What do you mean?'

'Whoever did this probably looked over the whole flat. Maybe stole something.' He peers past me into the hallway. 'They might still be here.'

I can't speak, but shake my head. There's something so vile, so abhorrent about the idea of a stranger coming into our home, invading our private space, touching our things . . .

He drops the shred of satin he'd been examining. 'Hey,' he says softly, and takes me in his arms. 'I'm not going to let anything happen to you. You hear me?'

'But who could have done this? To us? To my lovely wedding dress?'

'I don't know. But I'm going to bloody well find out.' He looks into my face, his eyes serious, watchful. 'You sure you're okay?'

I manage a slight nod. Though in truth I'm far from okay.

'That's the spirit.'

He kisses me firmly, then reaches into his pocket for his mobile phone. Seconds later he's talking to a police officer as calmly as if he's discussing work. I stand listening to his level tone, unable to take my eyes off the ruined dress while Dominic gives the police our address and a few other details. Then he rings off.

'Could be an hour before they get here,' he tells me. 'Maybe two.'

'That long?'

'It's not a priority.' He sounds terse, yet seems to accept the long wait as painful but necessary. No doubt it's something he's used to at work. The endless frustration of lengthy waiting times. 'Look, I'm going to check out the rest of the flat. You stay here.'

'I'm coming with you.'

'Catherine, for God's sake . . .'

'I'm not staying in here alone. Not with that.' I shudder, nodding towards the dress. 'It stinks, for one thing. And for another, it's horrible. Like something out of a nightmare.'

'I know. Come here.' Dominic puts a comforting arm about my waist, lets me lean my head against his warm shoulder for a moment. But I can sense his impatience. 'All right, I won't leave you in here. But keep behind me, okay?'

'You genuinely think there's still someone in the flat, don't you?'

'I'm not taking any chances.'

'Right, I'm definitely coming with you,' I say. 'It's always the girl left behind on her own who gets horribly murdered.'

'You watch too many horror films.'

But he keeps a tight hold on my hand as we creep out into the hallway.

Together we check the rest of the flat, quiet, careful, listening hard. But there's nobody here. Only us, and the unpleasant knowledge that someone else has been in our space, prowling about, touching our private things.

I feel sick just thinking about it.

Trying to regain a sense of normality, I turn off the unwanted oven, then find a bowl and decant his Chinese meal from its foil box, a tangle of lukewarm noodles and fleshy king prawns. I give it a quick spin in the microwave to heat it up again.

Dominic, who's on the sofa, googling 'what to do after a break-in' on his iPhone, refuses to eat at first. 'Not right now,' he tells me, waving the food away.

But I insist.

He shovels chow mein absentmindedly into his mouth between Google searches, and I keep him company, peeling and eating a satsuma, perched on the edge of the armchair opposite. I try to think of something else but can't manage it. My mind keeps flashing back to that ruined dress on the bed, the stink of blood.

Animal or human though?

The police will be able to tell with their forensic tests, I expect.

It's well over an hour before there's a knock at the front door to the flat.

'At last,' Dominic says, not bothering to hide his impatience. He jumps up to open the door. 'In there,' he says, directing the police officers – a male constable and a female sergeant – towards the bedroom.

The officers look shocked at the state of the place.

'Christ! They really did you over.' The constable sounds horrified, shaking his head as he steps over debris in the hallway.

'Oh, no, sorry,' Dominic says, moving a few bags to one side and picking up an old jacket that's been on the floor for weeks. 'This is our mess. This is normal.'

The male officer grins, moving on. But his female colleague is unamused, giving me a hard, assessing stare.

'I'm Pauline,' she says, and shakes my hand. 'This is Ahmed.'

Dominic introduces himself, and then I give my name, too. Ahmed writes it all down in his notebook. Throughout their visit we all use each other's first names, like we're best mates already. Dominic seems easy with this informality. I find it a little creepy.

They examine the bed with its vile contents, and Pauline looks horrified. 'Good God,' she mutters, and nods to Ahmed. 'Take some pictures of that, would you?'

'Yes, Sarge.'

She looks round at me. 'The dress yours, is it? Big day coming up soon?'

I nod.

With his phone camera, Ahmed takes a few photographs of the dress, and then of the bathroom window where our intruder presumably got in. But they both seem less interested once they discover my wedding dress is the only casualty.

'Just to be clear, the dress was torn up, but nothing was taken?' Pauline sounds puzzled. 'TV, laptop, electrical devices, jewellery, all still here?'

'Yes,' Dominic says firmly.

'And nobody was hurt?'

'No.'

'We weren't even at home,' I point out.

We follow the two police officers into the living room.

'So you're sure nothing was taken?' The sergeant takes off her cap and smooths back short red hair, glancing round at the mess. 'Must be hard to tell. You've checked all your documents? Passports, birth certificates, that kind of thing?'

I look at Dominic, uncertain.

'Sometimes people take the oddest things,' she continues. 'Not just TVs and iPads, but bank statements and credit card receipts. Even diaries and old birthday cards. Anything that will help them find your personal details. Your mother's maiden name, your favourite colour. For hacking personal accounts and identity theft.' She pauses, looking from Dominic to me. 'You're positive no one's mucked about in your papers?'

'Let me take another quick look,' I say.

Rather wearily, I traipse back into the bedroom to check. My diary is still in the bedside drawer, my bank and credit card statements look untouched in our tabletop file holder, and I rarely keep old correspondence anyway. I had my phone with me, of course. And my iPad is still safe in my top drawer.

'Nothing taken. So this looks increasingly like a malicious attack,' says the constable, who's followed me into the bedroom. He stops to write something in his notebook, then bites the end of his black pen. He's stout, with a thin goatee. 'A grudge, maybe? A personal vendetta against one of you. Something like that.'

'Yes,' the sergeant agrees, drifting into the room with Dominic behind her. Her cap is tucked under her arm now and she's holding a clipboard, the top sheet folded over. 'Can either of you think of someone who might bear a grudge against you? Maybe a friend who isn't happy about the two of you getting married?'

Dominic laughs. 'Not at all.'

'What about ex-girlfriends?'

He looks embarrassed. 'I'm not in touch with any of them. And besides, none of them were that serious.'

'How about you?' The constable glances at me.

I shake my head.

'What about old school friends?' Pauline asks. 'Or enemies?'

'I was mostly home-educated,' I say reluctantly. Dominic knows about my unconventional schooling, of course, but it's still uncomfortable to be the centre of attention. 'We had a nanny who taught us.'

The two police officers glance at each other. I know what they're thinking. *Posh bitch with a nanny.* The old silver-spoon prejudice.

Then Pauline frowns, looking about at our meagre furnishings. It's obvious she's wondering what went wrong in my life. Where all the money went.

She asks an unexpected question.

'*Us?*'

Too late, I realise my slip.

Chapter Thirteen

I never talk to people about Rachel. Or as little as humanly possible. It might seem cold, but I've found silence the best protection against bad memories that might otherwise swamp me.

When Dominic looks at me too, his gaze searching, I scrabble for the right thing to say. 'Me and my older sister.'

'How's your relationship with your sister? Could she have done this?' The sergeant considers me, fiddling with her clipboard.

I shake my head.

'How does she feel about your marriage?'

My throat seems to be silted up with sand. Somehow I manage to say, 'She's dead.'

Pauline shifts from one foot to the other. 'I'm sorry.'

'It was a long time ago.'

'Right.' She glances at her colleague, then asks more confidently, 'So how about college friends? Or someone at work?'

'I didn't go to college. Or university.'

Another silence.

'I was never very academically . . .' I shrug, not looking at Dominic. 'I volunteer at a food bank. But I doubt anyone there would have done something this nasty. They're all thrilled about the wedding.'

Dominic nods. 'Same here.' With a wry smile, he indicates his scrubs and ID badge, not having had a chance to change yet. 'Nurse in A & E, as you can see. Triage, mostly. I've got no enemies there.'

'That you know of,' I say.

He raises his brows. 'That I know of,' he repeats slowly, looking at me. 'Yes, true enough.'

'Though this attack looks like it was aimed more at you, Catherine,' the sergeant says. 'It was your wedding dress that got cut up, after all. Not something belonging to Dominic. Pretty vicious attack, too.' She studies the dress on the bed. 'Looks almost . . . frenzied. Like whoever did this really hates you and wants you to know it.'

My skin crawls and I say nothing, horrified.

Ahmed clears his throat.

'Do you mind if we take the dress away?' Pauline nods to her colleague without waiting for permission. 'Bag it up, would you? We'll get forensics to check out the bloodstains. But my guess is, it's animal, not human.'

'Hold on, aren't you going to dust for prints?' I ask, staring at her. 'The bathroom window must be where they got in. There may be fingerprints.'

'It's not really a big enough priority,' she says apologetically. 'Nothing was taken, after all. Feels like a prank to me. A nasty prank, agreed. But with so many more serious crimes on our caseload, I'm afraid there isn't enough here to justify calling a crime scene investigator.'

'Seriously?'

Pauline sighs at my tone, and puts a hand to her radio. 'I can let forensics know, if you insist. But I can't promise when it will happen. There was a shooting earlier. You may have seen it on the news. Some kid, only fourteen years old, shot dead on his way home from school. His mum's in the hospital, too. Our duty forensics officer is on scene. It could be several hours before she can get here. In fact, you may not even get a visit until tomorrow.'

'Tomorrow?' Dominic glances at the bed, aghast. 'But . . . we don't have anywhere else to sleep.'

The sergeant shrugs, waiting. 'You still want me to make the call?'

I study Dominic, who is clearly exhausted, his shoulders slumped, then shake my head. 'No, it's okay,' I tell her reluctantly. 'You do what you have to do.'

I'm not happy though. I can't believe that someone can invade our home and it isn't considered a high enough priority for the police to check for fingerprints.

'Whoever did this must be sick in the head,' Dominic mutters, watching as the constable puts on thin latex gloves and starts to bag up the sticky shreds of wedding dress.

Ahmed is sympathetic. 'Not the first time we've seen something like this, mate. There are some sick people out there, trust me. Usually turns out to be a disgruntled ex, though.'

Dominic makes a helpless gesture. 'I told you, I don't have any ex-girlfriends who'd be that bothered about me marrying Catherine.' He holds out a hand to me, his smile wry. 'Not exactly God's gift, am I, darling?'

I say nothing, but lace my fingers with his.

Pauline takes us briefly through a witness statement. First she suggests what we should say and then scribbles our responses on her clipboard. When she's written down all the details, she reads out the finished statement and asks us to confirm it's correct. I sign first, then Dominic.

'That's about all we need at this stage,' she tells us briskly. 'We'll check if there are any CCTV cameras covering the back of the building, and let you know if we find anything.'

Ahmed strips off his gloves and pushes them into his pocket. He smiles reassuringly as he shakes both our hands. 'Good to meet you. And good luck with the wedding.'

'Thanks,' Dominic says, grinning.

The sergeant's radio crackles with another call-out. Pauline turns away to speak into it briefly, then comes back into the room.

'Okay, we have to leave urgently, I'm afraid. But someone will be back in touch soon.' She nods to Ahmed, then smiles at me. 'It's a real shame about your wedding dress. But it could have been worse. A dress isn't a person; you can always replace it. All the same, I'd seriously suggest fixing the lock on that bathroom window as soon as possible. Crime prevention, yeah?'

On his way out, Ahmed hands me a police incident reference number in case I need it for insurance purposes.

Dominic cuddles me in silence for a few minutes after they've gone. His strong arms feel comforting and familiar. But it's going to take more than a hug to wipe out the memory of what happened to my wedding dress.

'It's finished now, okay?' Dominic peers into my face. 'I don't want you to fret about this. That policewoman was right. It was horrible to come home to, but I'm sure it'll turn out to be a one-off.'

'How can you be sure?'

'I see all sorts of wacky shit at the hospital. This isn't so crazy. People can behave very strangely when they get an idea in their heads.'

'But what idea has someone got about me?'

'Christ knows.' He squeezes me tight. 'There's probably no logical explanation. Don't get hung up on it.'

'And why wouldn't they dust for prints?'

'You heard what she said. Nothing was taken. Nobody was hurt. It wasn't a high enough priority. And they got a call to go elsewhere.' Dominic makes a face. 'Policing is like nursing. It's a high-pressure job, you're constantly reacting to circumstances, and some things will automatically take precedence over others.'

'But there was someone here, for God's sake. *In our flat.*'

'I know, and I'm angry about it too.' He shrugs. 'It's not a reflection on how upset it made you, babe. That's just the way things go sometimes. The police made a judgement call based on the evidence to hand. Enough said.'

Staring into the bedroom, I shudder. I'll have to lie down on that bed tonight, knowing that our flat has been invaded, my privacy violated by some crazy person or persons. How can I even think of sleeping here? It's too horrific.

'I could have been attacked if I'd been in the flat at the time. Do you realise that?'

'But you weren't.'

'I need to change the bedding,' I mutter, and pull away from him. 'We can't sleep under that duvet cover tonight.'

'Good idea. I'll find a fresh cover.'

'There should be one in the airing cupboard. Bring a clean sheet too. And matching pillowcases, if you can find them.'

I strip off the duvet cover with loathing, then the sheet and pillowcases, and carry them in a bundle to the washing machine. It's late, but I put the machine on anyway, then wash my hands thoroughly with soap and hot water.

By the time I return from the kitchen, Dominic is already making up the bed again with clean linen, his movements deft and professional, as though he's at work.

'What if the police are wrong,' I ask, leaning against the door frame to watch him, 'and whoever did it comes back for another go? Only next time they take a pair of scissors to me, instead of my clothes?'

'Not going to happen, baby.'

'Easy for you to say. You're rarely here on your own. And you're a man. I'm no weakling, but I'm not exactly built to defend myself against crazies, either. It didn't seem like the police cared about that.'

'There is another possibility, of course.'

I take a deep breath. 'Go on.'

'Maybe,' Dominic says carefully, bending to smooth out creases in the bottom sheet, 'the police didn't bother taking it seriously because they think one of us did it.'

'One of us?' I repeat blankly.

'I just got that feeling at the end there, didn't you? Like they felt this could be a domestic. Rather than a break-in by a third party.'

'That's ridiculous. Why on earth would I cut up my own wedding dress? I only just bought it. And you weren't even here. They can't have thought that, surely?' I groan, a sudden realisation hitting me. 'It's going to cost a fortune to replace the dress. And at such short notice too. The wedding's less than three weeks away.'

'Then we'll make a claim on the contents insurance,' he says, and shakes out the duvet to fill the cover properly.

'The new dress will have to be completely off the peg. No time for alterations. And it has to match the bridesmaids' dresses.' I'm thinking out loud. We only have two bridesmaids, one of them Louise, the other a second cousin of mine called Jasmine. She lives in Birmingham and I barely know her, but Mum insisted I should have a family member as a bridesmaid. Their dresses have sequinned bodices just like the dress that was bagged up and taken away. 'Though I suppose it won't be the end of the world if they don't match exactly.'

'It'll work out fine, stop worrying so much.' Dominic finishes plumping up the pillows, then turns to take me in his arms. I close my eyes, leaning thankfully into his warmth. His voice deepens. 'I love you, Catherine. That's all that matters.'

'I love you too.'

And I really do love him. With all my heart.

'Don't tell my parents about this, okay?' I add. 'Not until we know for sure what's going on, anyway. They'd only freak out. I couldn't bear that. Not on top of everything else.'

'Whatever you say.'

I try to relax, enjoy being cuddled, feeling safe again. But behind tightly closed eyes, I'm still fretting. And not only about my wedding dress. I should have told Dominic about the snow globe. The truth about Rachel, too. We're going to be married soon, he deserves to know the worst. But I love him too much to cause him worry, especially after tonight's horror show.

Is love all that matters though? I wonder. Is love enough? No matter who you are and what you've done?

Once Dominic is finally asleep, I climb softly out of bed and tiptoe through to the bathroom, barefoot and in my pyjamas. I'm exhausted but unable to sleep, so I might as well get up and try to do something. Besides, ever since the policewoman asked if anything else had been taken, the question has been weighing heavily on my mind. But I couldn't check before now. Dominic has barely let me have a moment to myself since the police left, even talking to me through the bathroom door while I brushed my teeth and got ready for bed. So I didn't get a chance to make sure the snow globe is still under the bathroom sink. Not without risking his suspicion.

Why would whoever cut up my wedding dress also want my sister's snow globe? It's a ridiculous thought. Yet I have to check. If only to set my churning mind at rest.

Locking the bathroom door behind me, I gently open the cupboard under the sink and crouch to look inside.

The box is open, empty.

Rachel's snow globe is no longer there.

Chapter Fourteen

The empty box frightens me more than the sight of my ruined wedding dress.

Where has her snow globe gone?

Who would take such a thing? Or even know it was here, hidden under my bathroom sink among the half-empty shampoo bottles and shower gel?

My skin crawls as I imagine the unknown intruder searching quietly through every room in the flat for this one specific object — opening drawers, looking in cupboards, until finally they came to the bathroom . . .

What does it mean? What does any of it mean?

My heart is racing and I'm trembling like I've been in an accident. Adrenaline, I realise, and try to control myself. But the terror won't be controlled. I gulp and swallow, unable to comprehend what's happening.

Perhaps my memory's at fault. I was so tired when I finished cleaning the snow globe the other night, it's not impossible I made a mistake. It was still wet. Perhaps I left it out of the box, hiding it further back in the cupboard while leaving the empty box at the front.

I search through the mess under the sink, moving things aside and removing others. It's a dark, cramped space, dominated by pipes, spare toilet rolls, and boxes of tampons. Once I've checked behind those, there's nothing left that's big enough to hide a snow globe.

It's definitely not here.

There's a sudden noise beyond the bathroom door. The unmistakeable creak of a floorboard under someone's foot.

I freeze. Has the intruder come back again? Though my logical mind knows the front door is locked, the safety chain on, and the bathroom window behind me is shut and fastened.

'Catherine?'

I sag with relief, then hurriedly close the cupboard under the sink and stand up. 'Just a minute,' I say, flushing the toilet. I run the tap for a moment, washing my hands. Only then do I unlock the door. 'Sorry, did I wake you?'

Dominic looks past me into the bathroom, his face unreadable. 'You okay? You've been in there a while.'

'No, I'm fine. I just couldn't sleep.' I make a face, trying to step past him so I can close the door behind me. 'Can't get the wedding dress out of my mind.'

'So you thought you'd clear out the cupboards instead?'

I stare at him, taken aback by the sardonic tone, then glance over my shoulder to see what he's looking at.

Shit.

Two shampoo bottles and an old bar of soap are still on the floor by the sink. I must have shifted them out of the cupboard while searching, then forgotten to replace them in my hurry.

'Oh,' I say, struggling to sound casual as I gesture towards the bottles. 'No, I was, erm, looking for . . .'

'This?'

I look back at him, and gasp in shock.

Dominic is holding something in his cupped hands, like an offering.

It's my sister's snow globe.

My gaze lifts to his face. There's nothing to be frightened of. I know that. This is Dominic and I love him. We're going to be husband and wife soon. I trust him with my life. Yet I'm afraid.

'I don't understand,' I say, and hear the fright in my voice. I take a quick step back, stumbling, and come up against the cold seat of the toilet. 'Dominic?'

'This belonged to your sister,' he says, still holding it out to me, 'didn't it? It was Rachel's snow globe.'

'Yes,' I whisper.

'Only you wanted it for yourself. You were jealous that she'd got this beautiful present from your dad. So you stole it from her.'

'That's not what happened.'

'That's not how you remember it, you mean.'

'What?'

'It's okay.' His voice softens, becomes reassuring, his gaze locked with mine. 'I know all about the snow globe. I spoke to your dad on the phone earlier. He told me everything.'

I can't believe what I'm hearing. 'Everything?'

Dominic nods. 'He told me how, when you were kids, you stole the snow globe from Rachel's rucksack. Only you dropped it. There was a crack in the base, he said, and all the water drained out. So you put it back in her rucksack, and you didn't admit that you'd taken it. You blamed her for breaking it instead.'

'No.'

'You lied to your parents about dropping it.'

'No,' I say again.

'You lied because you saw a chance to get your sister into trouble. She'd been teasing you about your stutter, and you were angry. Blindingly angry. You wanted to get back at her.'

'I didn't need to do anything to get my sister into trouble. Rachel was perfectly capable of getting into trouble all on her own.'

He raises his eyebrows, looking at me in silence.

'And I didn't have a stutter,' I add bitterly. 'Rachel used to upset me so much, it made me n-nervous, that's all.'

'Of course.' Again, Dominic nods, seeming to understand what I'm saying. Even to sympathise with me. Then he looks down at the snow globe. 'But this did belong to her, didn't it? You took it from your parents' house tonight and then came up with a story about someone having sent it to you.'

'It wasn't a story.'

'Okay. Though I didn't notice it arriving, Catherine.'

'It was sent to me at the food bank, not here. It came with the other parcel deliveries. Only it was addressed to me personally. You can ask Petra,' I add. 'Ask Sharon. They were there. They saw it arrive.'

'Fair enough. So why not show me the snow globe at once?' His gaze searches my face. The skin prickles on the back of my neck. 'Why hide it under the sink like you're ashamed of it?'

'I didn't know how you'd react,' I say. 'And from the way you're being now, it's obvious I was right to be worried.'

'And how am I being?'

'You don't believe me, do you?' I swallow hard, fighting an urge to cry. 'We're getting married in a few weeks. To have and to hold. Forever and ever.'

'I know.'

'Yet I tell you this, and you don't believe me.'

'In my defence, it's not an easy story to believe. It's . . . well, pretty far-fetched. Some anonymous person steals this from your dad's house and sends it to you?' He holds up the snow globe. 'At the food bank where you're volunteering?' He hesitates. 'I want to believe you. But you're making it very hard for me.'

'Look!' I bend to the cupboard under the sink, tearing the door open so fiercely it almost wrenches the hinge off. The empty parcel is there at the front. Grabbing it, I shove the box towards him. 'See? It's addressed to me.'

He does not move, still looking straight at me. 'Sender's address?'

'There isn't one. And the label's printed. Do you think I didn't check those things? It was sent to me anonymously. But I know why.' I let the box drop, since he refuses to take it. It falls on its side on the bathroom lino, white polystyrene chips spilling out. 'He sent it to taunt me.'

His eyes narrow on my face. '*He?*'

'My dad.'

'Your dad?' He looks bemused now. 'Why on earth would your dad do something like that?'

'Because he hates me.'

'For God's sake—'

'He blames me for Rachel's death,' I burst out.

There's a grim silence.

Dominic studies my face. Then his frown finally relaxes, as though he's come to some unspoken conclusion. He offers me the snow globe again. This time I take it with unsteady hands.

The glass sphere is still warm from his touch. I look down at the Swiss chalets and snowy mountains, the tiny goat. Everything inside is damp and glittering, even though there's no longer any water in it.

I remember the eyeball, and shudder.

'Look, there's something wrong here,' Dominic says slowly, as if he's trying to work things out on his own. 'You told me Rachel died in an accident when you were kids.'

'Yes,' I whisper.

'A skiing accident, you said. In . . . Switzerland, wasn't it?'

'The Swiss Alps.'

'So how can your dad possibly blame you for that?'

Chapter Fifteen

Without answering, I drop into a crouch and place the snow globe back in its box. As soon as I have closed the lid, I feel better.

When I straighten, Dominic is still watching me, his arms folded. There's a war in his face between wanting to trust me and the suspicion my dad has seeded in his mind.

'Well?'

'First, answer me this,' I say, my tone brittle. 'Who rang who?' He looks mystified. 'Did you call my dad or did he call you?'

'He called me,' Dominic says quietly, 'on my way home from work. He told me what happened when you turned up. How upset you were.'

'I'm surprised he noticed.'

'Actually, he sounded very worried about you. He asked me to check how you were.' When I shake my head in disbelief, he sighs. 'Look, I know what you're thinking.'

'I doubt it.'

'Your dad only has your best interests at heart. As do I.'

'So which lie did he use this time? He thinks I'm having another nervous breakdown, is that it?'

'*Another?*'

My laugh is humourless. 'My parents were always "worried" about me after Rachel died. Forever taking me to the doctor, to specialists. They said I was depressed.'

'Maybe you were.'

'I wasn't depressed. I was just trying to get back to being me. Rachel was always the centre of attention. The centre of the whole world, it sometimes felt. After she died, I thought maybe, just maybe, my parents might be interested in me for a change.'

He looks taken aback. 'That's not very . . .'

'Nice?'

He shrugs.

'You didn't know Rachel, or you wouldn't judge me for craving a little attention. She wasn't just your average spoilt brat who thinks she's a princess. Rachel was . . .' I screw up my face, struggling to make my point without sounding like a bitch. 'She made our lives miserable.'

'You already told me that,' he interrupts impatiently. 'When we first started dating, remember? You said she was a nightmare to live with.'

'I didn't tell you the whole truth. There's more. And some of it . . . some I can't tell you. It's too horrible.'

'Oh, come on. You were just a couple of kids.'

'Even kids can be dangerous.'

Again, he shrugs. He thinks I'm exaggerating.

'I didn't matter to them, and that's the truth. I was the out-of-focus sister.' My voice stumbles, but I press on, determined to make him understand. 'Do you have any idea how that feels? To grow up like that? Always the quiet one, the sensible one, the one who had to pick up the pieces, the one who never got what she wanted because Rachel always had first choice.'

'Okay.' He leans against the door frame, watching me. 'So why does your dad blame you for Rachel's death? How were you involved?'

'Me?'

'Catherine, there must be a reason.' He frowns. 'How exactly did Rachel die? You said she was skiing that day.'

I pick up the box containing the snow globe and cradle it in my arms.

'I don't know what happened,' I say simply. 'I think she'd gone out on the piste with Dad, while I stayed behind with Mum. Mum had a cold, so she didn't want to go out in the snow. Or maybe it was me who had the cold.'

'You can't be sure?'

'My memory of that day is kind of hazy, except for when Dad came to tell me about Rachel. I remember that part perfectly. But the rest is fuzzy round the edges.' I make a face. 'Not surprising, really. It was years ago. And I was only a kid.'

'What did he tell you?'

'There was this place . . . I suppose it was a hospital of some sort. I remember waiting there with Mum, though she'd gone off somewhere. To the toilet, I expect, or to grab coffee. And Dad came in. He looked awful.' I feel my breathing quicken at the memory. 'He said Rachel had died. And that was it. I flew home with Mum the next day, and Dad flew home a little later. I guess he had to wait for them to . . . release the body.'

'She was buried in England?'

'Cremated.' I look at him. 'Her ashes are in Dad's study. They think I don't know, but I spotted it when I was looking for an insurance document for my mum once, when he was away from home.'

'It?'

'The urn containing her ashes. He keeps it in the bottom drawer of his filing cabinet. Mum showed it to me after the funeral, so I recognised it at once.' I grimace. 'Promise me you won't stick me in a filing cabinet when I die.'

He smiles then. 'I promise.'

With careful hands, he takes the parcel away from me. 'Come here,' he says, putting it back on the floor. He pulls me towards him, ignoring how stiff and reluctant I am to be hugged.

'He can't have it both ways,' he whispers in my ear. 'He can't blame you for Rachel's death if you weren't even with her that day.'

'Dad loved her so much though.'

'He loved you both. *Loves* you, I should say,' he corrects himself. 'He was in a complete state when he rang. He told me about the eyeball in the snow globe.'

I close my eyes briefly. 'Shit.'

'When were you going to tell me about *that*?'

'Never.'

'Yet you went to Louise behind my back,' he says, his tone accusing.

'Louise had no right to—'

'She hasn't said a word. Your dad told me you'd spoken to her, that's all.' He shakes his head as though he's disappointed. 'You and Louise. I thought she was my friend. The two of you kept me out of the loop on this.'

'Don't blame Louise. She wasn't happy about it either. I just didn't want you to find out about . . . my family history. About how bad Rachel was. The things she did.' I finish fiercely: 'I wanted you to think I'm normal.'

'Baby, I do think you're normal. A perfectly normal woman with a perfectly normal reaction to disgusting things like eyeballs being sent to you through the post.' His arms tighten round me. 'Where is it now?' he asks.

I have to think for a moment. 'Louise still has it.'

'Good. She can keep it.'

'I'm sure my dad sent it. He's the only one who had the opportunity. Except for Mum. And I can't see her even looking at an eyeball, let alone stuffing one inside a snow globe as a nasty trick.'

'Sweetheart, your dad asked me to keep a close eye on you while you get through this. Begged me, even.' Dominic pulls back, studying me with sympathy. 'That doesn't sound like someone intent on upsetting you, does it?'

'I guess not.'

'Your dad was very explicit on the phone.' His voice deepens with significance. 'He told me to watch out for you, to make sure you don't do anything stupid. That's why I was checking under the sink earlier. In case you had some . . . I don't know . . . pills or something hidden in there. That's when I found the snow globe.'

'For God's sake, I'm not *suicidal*.'

'I'm glad to hear that. Because I don't think I could live without you.' Dominic puts a finger under my chin and tips my face up towards his, then kisses me on the lips. Slowly, and with a loving tenderness that melts my resistance.

I close my eyes and lean into his kiss. My skin tingles with anticipation, and it's hard not to touch him back when he strokes a hand down my spine. I can't push him away when he's like this with me. And he bloody well knows it.

'I agree with Robert. You need to be looked after properly. Whoever sent that snow globe is out to hurt you. To upset you.' Dominic looks at me intently. 'And they've already succeeded, haven't they? First the snow globe, then the wedding dress . . .'

'I still think it was Dad,' I say. 'I told you, he's always been off with me. Like he thinks the wrong daughter died.'

'That's not true. Your dad is on your side. But whoever is doing this, it ends here. Enough is enough.'

I smile through my tears when he pulls my hand to his lips and kisses it. A typically gallant gesture, and precisely why I fell for him in the first place. Dominic may not have a white charger, but he knows how to make me feel swept off my feet.

'If I'm going to be any kind of husband to you,' he adds firmly, 'I need to stop stressing about my work constantly and start thinking about you instead. I want us to start married life on the right foot, not looking behind us all the time, wondering who the hell's out there.' He leads me back to the bedroom, his arm about my waist. 'Which is why I texted your dad after the police left, and agreed to his suggestion.'

My throat tightens. 'What suggestion?'

He closes the bedroom door after us and pulls me closer, kissing my mouth. 'That we should move into their place after the wedding,' he says in my ear. 'Where you'll be safe from whoever got hold of the snow globe and sent it to you.'

I stop, pulling away from him in shock. 'What?'

'The top floor of their house is all ready to be turned into a mini-flat for us, your dad said. A bedroom, bathroom and sitting room. He's been clearing it out.' Dominic peers at me in surprise. 'He said he told you about it.'

'Dad told me he was tidying out Rachel's old room. But not why.'

'It's a fantastic offer. Not only safer for you, but cheaper too. He says there'll be no rent to pay. And the commute will be far shorter. We can make our own meals. We can be as self-sufficient as we want.'

'You've got to be kidding.'

'I know it goes against the grain. I know it's not the way we imagined married life would be . . . You and me together in our cosy little flat. Nobody else around.' He kisses me on the lips, as though trying to cajole me out of my disapproval. 'But it's the answer to everything. You must see that, baby. This way we can start saving for a deposit on our own place.'

'I don't like it.'

'Hey, it's not ideal, moving back in with your parents. Far from it.' He gives a half-laugh. 'But it wouldn't be forever. And I know how much you get on with your mum. I thought you'd be pleased at the idea of spending more time with her. Aren't you?'

'Not if it means we lose . . . this.' I look around at the untidy bed=
room, my eyes misty. 'This is our place, Dom. We've been happy here.
So happy.'

'And we'll get our own place again in the future, and be happy
there too. Even happier, because we'll be owners, not tenants. Don't
you want that?'

He's so persuasive, it's hard to argue with him. And deep down, I
know Dominic's probably right. With everything that's been happening
lately, maybe the best option is for us to move into my parents' home.

Like he says, it wouldn't be forever.

I rub a hand across my face, suddenly exhausted. It's been such a
long day. 'Yes, I suppose so. When you put it like that.'

'That's settled then.'

He turns off the light without any further discussion. We climb
back into bed and lie together in the darkness, listening to the wind
blowing and the muted sounds of traffic below.

Eventually his breathing slows, and I realise he's asleep.

I lie there, turning events over in my mind, unable to sleep, and
can see how Dad sending me the snow globe doesn't make sense. Not
after finding my wedding dress cut up tonight. I can't imagine my father
doing something that vile and creepy. And I'm not sure he's capable of
scaling our rusty old fire escape and climbing in through a bathroom
window, and then rushing home to meet me for dinner. Not at his age.
The same goes for Mum. And I can't imagine that Kasia had anything
to do with it.

Which means there's only one person who could have destroyed
my wedding dress.

And she's dead.

Chapter Sixteen

'You look beautiful,' Dad says, patting my hand.

We are sitting in the back of the sleek white limousine as it pulls up in front of the Parish Church of Christ the Saviour in Ealing. I can see people waiting by the main entrance, the high steeple soaring above them into a grey, wintry sky. My two bridesmaids, sheltering in the arched stone porch, peek out and wave cheerily at the car. Their limo has parked further up the lane that runs beside the church. I can see the chauffeur leaning against the bonnet, having a cigarette.

My head still hurts from too many drinks last night. I hadn't meant to go out at all. But Louise turned up at my parents' house, where I've been staying alone for the past few days, with a bottle of wine and some chocolates. And then my cousin Jasmine arrived and all my careful plans for an early night were blown out of the water. An hour later, we were in the pub at the end of the road, playing a drinking game.

I glance up at the sky through the back window of the limousine. It looks cloudy, but no sign of rain yet. It's forecast for later today though, and everyone outside looks cold. The women are holding on to their hats in the stiff breeze. In top hats and with tails flapping, Dominic's ushers peer down the path to check I've arrived safely, then one nips back inside the church. To tell the organist I've arrived, presumably, and give Dominic's best man the nod.

We went through it all at the wedding rehearsal. Twice. It should go like clockwork, the vicar said, assuming no last-minute problems.

So far, so good.

I'm nervous, all the same. Not sick-nervous, thankfully. But my knees are a little shaky, and the distance between the limousine and the church door suddenly looks like a long way.

Dad studies my face. 'You okay, darling?'

'I'm fine.'

'Sure?'

'It's my wedding day, Dad. Of course I'm fine.' I manage a tremulous smile. 'Better than fine, in fact.'

My lips are numb though, and it feels as if all the colour has drained from my face. Probably last night's excesses still having an effect, even after several large glasses of water and some pick-me-up Alka-Seltzer. Or the chilly weather. This new wedding dress, while not as elegant or clinging as the mermaid style, is almost as flimsy. And mid-December is not exactly the right weather for short puff sleeves and a low-cut bodice.

'I can ask the driver to take us back home, if you've changed your mind,' he tells me, his voice low and earnest. 'It's not too late. We wouldn't be cross.'

I stare at him. 'Changed my mind?'

'You look so pale . . .'

'I told you, there's nothing wrong.' The chauffeur has come round and opened the door next to me. I gather my flouncy white skirt in one hand, my bridal bouquet in the other. The delicate white roses smell amazing. Wind tears at my hair arrangement and I fear for my silk rosebud tiara, carefully pinned in place by the hairdresser less than an hour ago. 'Come on, let's get inside before we get blown away.'

I climb out and the smartly liveried chauffeur gives me a helping hand, his smile admiring.

'Lovely dress,' he says.

'Thank you.'

My father appears from the other side of the car, still looking uncertain, and takes my arm, guiding me towards the entrance porch. The wind drags on my skirt, but I just laugh. My nerves are still there, my legs trembling, but I'm excited now, too. 'You look gorgeous, love!' somebody shouts from the street, and I turn but can't see who it is.

One of the ushers is talking to my father, but in such a low voice I can't hear what's being said.

'Problem?' I ask nervously.

My dad squeezes my hand. 'They're ready,' he says in my ear, 'if you are.'

'I'm ready.'

My bridesmaids come running up, giggling. Louise looks skinny and smashing as always, her face rosy with cold. She hugs me briefly, then whirls aside, and there's my cousin Jasmine, grinning too.

'You make a fantastic bride,' Jasmine tells me. She sniffs my bridal bouquet enthusiastically. 'Oh, those roses and freesias smell amazing. Super combination.' She does a quick twirl. 'See, not a spot of dirt.'

I was worrying before she and Louise left the house earlier, after the visiting hairdresser had finished with us, that Jasmine would get her bridesmaid dress dirty. She's got the most spectacular looks, dark-skinned and stunning, with a fabulous afro crown teased to perfection; her father is originally from Jamaica, her mother one of my mum's cousins. But, by her own admission, she's a bit of a tomboy. She nearly tore the hem of her dress running downstairs too quickly this morning, and I was fretting by the time she left in case she shut the dress in the door of the limousine, or caught it on one of the vast holly bushes near the church door.

'I'm impressed,' I tell her.

'So what's up? You look a bit peaky.'

'Just nervous.'

Jasmine mock-punches my arm. 'You'll do brilliant, babe.'

I smooth out the skirt of my new wedding dress, wishing I still had my other one. It shimmered, and clung in all the right places, and made me look thinner than this one does with its big white lace flounces. But I push that thought aside. I'm not going to let the memory of what happened to that dress darken my wedding day.

'Is he here?' I ask in a whisper.

Louise, adjusting her bridesmaid's tiara, looks round at me, perplexed. 'Who?'

'Dominic, of course.'

'You bet. In fact, he insisted on getting here a full hour early, Richard said.' Jasmine laughs, throwing her head back. 'They couldn't believe it when I said we were out on the razz last night. They had pizza and watched an action film on the telly, then got an early night. Apparently Dominic was terrified of oversleeping.'

I smile.

Dominic's best man, Richard, is one of his work mates from the hospital. He's a big guy with a bushy brown beard and hardly any hair, despite only being in his late twenties. I can just imagine him and Dominic sprawled on the sofa at our flat in front of a film, discarded pizza boxes everywhere, reminiscing about good times as single blokes.

'Time to go,' Jasmine says.

The wind whips Louise's hair into my face and I blink, suddenly nervous again. *Of course I'm fine.* That's what I told my father in the car. But is it true? Am I ready to marry Dominic? Marriage is such a huge step.

I peer inside while everyone is fussing around me. The parish church interior is vast and surprisingly ornate. It's a Church of England service, but quite High Church. There are painted ceilings, and fluted pillars on both sides of the carved wooden pews, and the glow of candle-light is everywhere, augmenting the dull December daylight that comes streaming through the stained-glass windows. The pews to the back are empty, but further forward several rows are full. Mostly Dominic's friends and work colleagues, by the look of it, though I recognise his aunt and uncle from photos. Since both his parents are dead, and he's an only child, he was only able to invite a few members of his family to the wedding, which breaks my heart. Though my own family is hardly well-represented either, and he more than makes up for it with his friends, who are numerous and noisy.

Georgia and some of the others from my book club have come along too, even though I haven't been recently. And I spot Petra and Sharon seated together near the front, heads bent, presumably reading the order of service pamphlets that are on all the pews. Unless they're on their phones. Online shopping while they wait for the bride . . .

The organist has been playing an upbeat tune to keep everyone happy while they wait. We heard it from outside while the bridesmaids were getting into position behind me. But as I step through the porch door on Dad's arm, there's a short, pregnant pause, then the organ strikes up with the familiar opening bars of Wagner's Bridal Chorus . . .

I see my mother, in the front pew, turning to look at us. Her face lights up under the cream brim of her hat.

Tears come to my eyes, and I stumble over the worn stone step.

'Careful, darling.' Dad clutches my arm. Then he asks again, hanging back slightly, watching me, 'Are you sure you're okay, Catherine? Do you need a minute?'

'I'm fine,' I repeat fiercely.

He gives a nod and we start the long walk to the altar. I only hope it's true and I'm not kidding myself. Because if I trip up out of sheer nerves, and fall on my face going down the aisle . . .

Then I see Dominic, waiting for me in front of the altar. Everything comes rushing back into focus, like a zoom lens suddenly tightening on one vital spot. To my relief, the numbness vanishes and I can feel again. All my love for him, all our adventures together since we met, all the excitement and passion of our lovemaking, even the tender way he kissed me goodbye before I left for my parents' house a few days ago.

I find myself breathing fast, my heart thumping wildly as if I've been running.

'I love him,' I gasp.

Dad jerks his head towards me. 'What's that?'

I shake my head silently.

'I'm here for you, Catherine,' he says. 'Just lean on me.'

But I don't lean on him. I stand straight and walk firmly, arm in arm with my father, towards the man in the grey-striped morning suit who has turned now to look at me.

I smile.

Dominic smiles back, his mouth broadening with pleasure as he looks me up and down. By the time he takes my hand, I'm no longer trembling. His own hand is cold, almost clammy. But his touch is reassuring.

Our eyes lock.

'I love you,' he mouths.

I want to say it back, but I'm too nervous in front of all these people. I feel a sense of purpose though, listening to the vicar as the marriage ceremony begins. A sense of destiny, even. This wedding is the start of our new life together.

I glance sideways at Dominic, and he turns his head, meeting my gaze. He looks so solemn, suddenly pale against the white of his formal shirt.

Is he nervous, too?

'I love you,' I mouth back at him, his anxiety making me braver.

His hand squeezes mine and he shoots me a grin. Back to the old, mischievous, loving Dominic.

All the same, I think, I won't take his surname.

And I won't promise to obey.

Chapter Seventeen

The reception afterwards is a simple 'do' above a pub off Ealing Broadway, because I refused to let my parents contribute to that too. They're already paying for the honeymoon – a week in the Lake District, at Dominic's suggestion, far from the demands of our work – and I hate the thought of being any more beholden to them. It's bad enough that we've agreed to move into the top floor of their house. Though Dominic's right to say it gives us a chance to save up towards a deposit for our first home.

Mum and Dad are standing near the bar, looking uncomfortable. They're more used to expensive hotels in Kensington than something this informal.

But it's not that bad. The staff have made a real effort, with a gorgeous finger buffet, and champagne already being handed out on our arrival from the nearby church. Plus, there are sprays of green and white flowers everywhere, courtesy of Louise, who has been kindly helping out with arrangements.

After the inevitably rambling speeches and toasts, someone puts some soft rock music on and Dominic grabs my hand and whirls me up into an impromptu dance.

'My beautiful bride,' my new husband whispers in my ear, spinning me round and round until I'm dizzy. 'I can't wait to get you into bed, Mrs Whitely.'

'Miss Bates,' I correct him, breathless.

'Oh God,' he groans. 'I forgot. You want to keep your maiden name and stay your own woman, not take on the heavy chains of patriarchy.' His hand tightens around my waist and he pretends to leer down at me. 'Though maybe it's not such a bad idea. Now I can be a married man and still see Miss Bates on the side.'

I laugh. 'Bad man.'

'Your bad man.'

'I'm just glad you went through with it and didn't run away.'

Dominic tips his head to one side, perplexed. 'Sorry?'

'You should have seen your face. I thought you were about to faint.'

'When?'

'In the church.'

'That's another lifetime ago,' he says. 'Bloody place was freezing, anyway. And you were late arriving.' He pauses. 'I did get cold feet, though.'

My heart almost stops. 'What?'

'Yes. I thought my toes were going to develop frostbite, I was sitting in that damn pew so long.'

I laugh and breathe again. 'Sorry about that. The hairdresser took ages.'

'I was beginning to wonder if I should prepare a little speech. Just in case you didn't show and I had to tell the congregation to go home without their finger buffet and champagne.'

'I hope you would have kept the pressies, though.'

'Absolutely.' He grins at me. 'We're not giving anything back. Not even if we split up tomorrow. Have you seen that big parcel with the gold bow?'

My heart stutters, glancing towards the large pile of presents arranged at the back of the room. 'The one with . . . with polka dot wrapping paper?'

'That's it. From Jasmine, apparently. I hope it's a coffee machine.' He leers again. 'Hey, you never told me your cousin was so sexy. Bloody hell. I nearly had to beat the groomsmen off when she turned up at the church with Louise; she was getting mobbed. And once I'd had a peek, I could see why.'

'Hey.' I shove at his chest, mock-annoyed. 'Married, remember?'

'Oh yeah.' He makes a face. 'Damn.'

We both laugh and keep dancing. But I suddenly have two left feet, it seems, and Dominic has to stop me from colliding with the buffet table.

'Careful,' he whispers, and steers me back across the room.

His best man, Richard, is dancing with Louise. They make way as we sweep past, no doubt afraid I'm going to knock into them.

I'm not usually this clumsy.

Dominic was only joking, I tell myself, and try to calm down.

He's mine now, I have to remember that.

All mine.

———

The reception is starting to wind down for the evening; the room is a little less crowded and my parents have already gone home, taking our wedding gifts with them for safe-keeping. Louise has called a taxi to take us to the hotel where we're staying tonight. A little romantic interlude before we take a train up to the Lake District tomorrow, for a week at a rented cottage near the shores of Lake Windermere. I've been looking forward to it for ages.

I look across the room and see Dominic talking to Jasmine. It's silly but I can't help feeling ludicrously jealous, especially when he touches her arm, and she touches him back at once, smiling with genuine amusement. As if she is the bride, not me.

You never told me your cousin was so sexy.

Good grief.

I chug back the last of my wine and hand the empty glass to a passing waiter. I have to stop letting my imagination run away with me. Or we're going to need marriage counselling at this rate. We haven't even had our wedding night, and already I'm watching my husband for signs of infidelity.

Seconds later, Dominic bends to Jasmine's ear, speaking above the loud, pumping beat of the music. I see Jasmine turn her head, staring up at him, wide-eyed.

As if he's just told her something shocking.

'Okay, it's here,' Louise says, bounding up to me, flushed and out of breath. She hands me a closed umbrella. 'Quick, you'll need this. It's raining cats and dogs.'

'What are you talking about?'

'Your taxi, of course. To take you to your hotel? It's waiting outside.' She shakes her head, smiling. 'Bloody hell, girl. Come on, shake a leg. How much wine have you had?'

'Not enough,' I mutter.

But Louise has already gone and doesn't hear. She calls Dominic over with a frantic wave. 'Taxi's here. And the meter's running.'

Dominic comes towards me and kisses my forehead. 'Ready?'

I nod silently.

Jasmine has followed him, a look of consternation on her face. She glances at me, still frowning, then away. I get the impression she doesn't want to talk to me. Which is odd, as she was madly talkative earlier in the evening, discussing her wild life in Birmingham and her passion for stock car racing.

What the hell did Dominic say to her?

'I'll grab my coat,' Dominic says, then disappears towards the cloakrooms.

Louise runs after him. 'Get mine too, would you?' she calls. 'Or I'm going to get soaked.' Her hair is already wet, and she's long since lost the tiara she was wearing at the ceremony. She must have been standing outside waiting for the taxi. Or popped out to talk to the driver when the cab finally arrived.

I'm left alone with Jasmine.

My cousin hesitates, then looks around at me, a question in her wide, dark eyes. But whatever she wants to know, it's obvious she's not going to broach the subject right now.

'I've had a lovely time, Catherine,' she says. 'The wedding was such brilliant fun. Especially the speeches. Don't know when I've laughed so much. Your dad's sense of humour is a bit on the dry side, isn't it?' She pauses awkwardly. 'Well, I hope you two have a great honeymoon up at the Lakes. I've never been there, but I've heard the countryside is beautiful. Even at this time of year.'

I can't stay quiet any longer. 'Jasmine, what is it?'

'Sorry?'

'I saw you two together.'

She looks alarmed. '*What?*'

'Don't bother to deny it.' I'm breathless with panic, worrying about what's wrong, what she's hiding from me. I grab her hands and squeeze them. 'Please, what's the matter? What did Dom say to you?'

'N-nothing,' she stammers.

'Tell me, for God's sake. I have to know.'

'It's nothing, honestly. I got a . . . a postcard, that's all.'

'A postcard?'

'I thought it was a sick joke, so I just put it in the bin. That's what I was telling Dominic.'

A sick joke.

'What kind of postcard?'

She shrugs. 'It was a picture of the Alps. Ski slopes, snow, those cute wooden houses, you know.'

I do know, and I stare at her in horror.

'It was a prank, probably. That's what Dom said when I told him. He didn't want me to mention it to you.' She squirms, looking uncomfortable under my intent gaze. 'He said you've had some trouble recently too. People sending you weird shit.'

She tries to pull away, but I hold her hands tight. 'Forget all that,' I say. 'I need to know what was written on the postcard.'

'Dominic said not to—'

'For Christ's sake, tell me!'

She is surprised by my tone. 'It was only a few words. But look, the postmark was Westminster. So it wasn't actually from Switzerland, you know? Like I say, most likely some sick prankster . . .'

I can't seem to catch my breath. 'What did it say, Jasmine?'

'It said, "I see you, Catherine",' she whispers.

I see you, Catherine.

'And the signature?'

I already know what Jasmine's going to say. But I refuse to believe it. 'Rachel.'

Chapter Eighteen

The Lake District is breathtakingly beautiful, just as I had always imagined it would be. Off the tourist tracks, long majestic vistas of dark lakes nestle between slopes scattered with rocky outcrops and thick with trees. We spend a gloriously happy week in a cottage overlooking the gloomy water. Windermere is the perfect winter honeymoon location. Stunning scenery, quiet and isolated, yet with plenty of pretty restaurants and cafés open for when we can't be bothered to cook for ourselves. It isn't too cold either, despite being so close to Christmas. Chilly and often icy, yes. But nothing too extreme, thank goodness.

It snows on the third and fourth day, but not heavily. Just enough to dust the hilltops with white, and ice the village pavements, leaving them slippery underfoot.

We sleep late most days, our limbs tangled together under warm sheets. Then we put on thick layers of clothing and hiking boots, and walk out, hand in hand, to explore the lake and picturesque village. When the weather's too bad for walking, we stay in beside the cosy flicker of an open fire, such a lovely contrast to the storage heaters in our flat.

We watch films in the long evenings, and feed each other marshmallows dipped in chocolate fondue, sometimes making leisurely love on the rug or in the bedroom with its huge bed and decadent black satin sheets.

We have been locked in our own little heaven for six days and nights now. Locked in and ecstatic about it, deaf to the demands of our lives back in the city.

'How did your mum find this place?' Dominic asks, staring out over dark waters on our last day there. 'I mean, it's fantastic, but . . . Jesus, these hills, these lakes. It's like something out of a film.'

As we watch, a few errant snowflakes spin out of the looming grey sky, threatening more bad weather on the way. Luckily, we'll be on the train back to London first thing in the morning, so there's little danger of getting snowed in now. But the increasing chill in the air is unmistakeable.

I shiver. 'Someone recommended it to her, I think.'

'By someone, you mean . . .'

'Probably a diplomat.' I smile at his wry shake of the head. 'What?'

'What kind of family have I married into?'

I lean against him, wearing only his T-shirt and a pair of fluffy slippers. It's a little cold for such a skimpy outfit, but we only recently got out of bed after another lovemaking session, and the open fire he's kindled should soon warm the small cottage.

'I could ask the same of you,' I say.

Dominic keeps staring out at the chilly weather, but I can feel his stillness. 'Now what's *that* supposed to mean?' he says.

'Well, you said some of your relatives would be at the wedding. But I only met your aunt and uncle for about five minutes, and I barely caught a glimpse of your cousins . . .'

'They left early,' he says, an odd note in his voice. 'I told you they couldn't stay long.'

Have I hurt his feelings?

Dominic lost his mum and dad in a house fire, some terrible accident while he was in his first year at university, and I feel awkward sometimes that mine are both still alive. Which is crazy, of course. But it's hard not to wonder how he feels about his family, especially when he has so few relatives and I have . . . well, not that many. But more than him.

'Hey, sorry.' I snake my arms about his waist, and stand on tiptoe to kiss his throat. He looks down at me, and again there's that hurt look on his face. 'I was only teasing. And your aunt was lovely.'

His smile is grudging. 'Yeah, Aunty Grace . . . she's a laugh. Always my favourite aunt when I was a kid.'

'So you do have *other* aunts.'

'I'm not in touch with that side of the family anymore. Not since my parents died.' There's a wistful note in his voice. 'You're lucky, you know. Being so close to your mum and dad.'

'Too close sometimes,' I mutter.

He turns away, putting a couple of fresh logs on the hearth and poking the embers with a fire iron. We've had a relaxed last day together so far, drifting from the bed to the lunch table and back to bed without much conversation, neither of us willing to upset the easy dynamic between us. But there's something we still need to discuss, regardless.

I sit on the large white sofa and pull my slippered feet up beneath me, trying to get warm. 'We haven't talked about Jasmine yet.'

I don't recognise my voice, it sounds so thin and breathless.

He straightens, but does not look at me. There's a slight flush in his cheeks, as though bending too close to the fire has overheated him.

'Jasmine?'

'I know you spoke to her at the wedding.'

He nods, giving nothing away. 'Yeah, she texted me the next morning, said she'd been indiscreet. Too much beer.'

'Indiscreet?'

'I asked her not to get into it with you.'

I wait for him to explain. But Dominic says nothing more, carefully replacing the fire iron on its stand.

'So?'

His gaze meets mine at last, curiously hard. 'So?' he echoes me.

'She told me about the postcard.'

'A fake,' he says dismissively. 'I knew it would upset you. Perhaps even ruin the honeymoon. That's why I didn't say anything. Jasmine knew it too, otherwise she would have contacted your family as soon as it arrived. The fact that she didn't is pretty much self-explanatory.'

'But why would someone do that? Send her a fake postcard from . . . from my sister?'

I can't bring myself to say her name out loud. Even thinking it is hard. As if naming my dead sister might give her the power to be alive again.

Which is ridiculous.

Rachel.

Her name has been a secret darkness at the heart of our honeymoon. I don't want that darkness to persist into our marriage, too. I'd rather spend a peaceful last evening here with my husband. Maybe play some Scrabble or a game of chess. Or watch another film. Or perhaps make love again.

I have to exorcise her though, whatever the cost.

'Some people are like that,' he says. 'They thrive on hurting other people. On sowing the seeds of unhappiness in relationships. Especially marriages.'

'You think someone is trying to break up our marriage?'

He shrugs.

'Someone who doesn't want the two of us to be together,' I say slowly, trying to work it out. 'And who knows exactly which buttons to press. So it has to be someone who knows me well. And who knows about Rachel. Maybe someone who knows more than I do about her death.' I stare at the flickering fire, half mesmerised by the flames. 'After all, I was a kid when it happened, and my parents wanted to protect me. That's why they never discussed it afterwards, I guess.'

I frown, thinking about the eyeball in the snow globe, and my ruined wedding dress, and now Jasmine's postcard. There's a pattern here. A vile, twisted pattern of hostility and attack. But I can't see what it means.

'Well, it's a nice theory,' I continue, a little unnerved by Dominic's silence. 'But who the hell ticks all those boxes? I don't know anyone who's so bothered about us getting married that they'd go to all this bloody trouble.' I pause in my little rant, looking up at him. 'Do you?'

Dominic's expression is grim, yet he says nothing. He stands and opens a wooden chest, taking out a soft tartan blanket, which he shakes and drapes around my shoulders. Physical comfort instead of words. Perhaps I prefer it. Right now, the fact that he's here for me should matter more than what he says. Or doesn't say.

'Thanks.' My voice is husky. I pat the sofa, which suddenly feels very big. 'Join me?'

Dominic hesitates, then sits next to me. The sofa gives slightly under his weight and I slump towards him, not very gracefully. The T-shirt rides up, revealing my bare thighs. I see his gaze flicker across them, slowly moving higher. His hand finds my shoulder, then caresses my collarbone, the curve of my throat, his fingers trailing across my cheek.

'You think too much,' he tells me softly.

'Better than too little.'

'Not when you're on your honeymoon.'

'Shit, sorry.' I bite my lip at the quiet accusation in his voice. I'm not sure how I got there, but I'm on the verge of tears. 'I'm ruining our honeymoon, aren't I? We were having such a peaceful time up here, hiding away from everything, and now . . .' I suck in a deep breath. 'Rachel always finds a way to spoil things.'

'Forget Rachel,' he says, almost angry.

Shaken, I meet his gaze.

'I don't want you to think about her again, you hear me?' he continues. 'Rachel is dead and gone. She can't hurt you anymore.'

God, I want to believe him. To forget about my sister. To dismiss all the things that have been happening lately. It would make everything so much easier if I could just shut her out of my head.

I close my eyes as he kisses me.

Rachel is dead and gone. She can't hurt you anymore.

So who sent that postcard?

Chapter Nineteen

Sharon calls me into her office just after nine o'clock on my first day back at work after the honeymoon. She has changed her hair, I realise, as I follow her into the warm room. She used to wear it loose over her shoulders, all bouncy, honey-blonde, dyed curls. Now it looks stricter, coiled up in a bun at the back of her head. She has toned down her lipstick, too. Usually scarlet, it's a darker red today, and less glossy. As if she means business.

'How was the Lake District?' she asks, indicating that I should close the door.

'Fantastic, thank you. The scenery was breathtaking.'

'Sounds lovely. Did you do much walking?'

I smile, though I'm still puzzled by this unexpected summons. If Sharon has something to say, normally she would do so in front of everyone else. Is this just about the honeymoon?

'We went out a couple of times. It was a bit cold for anything major.'

'Snowed, did it?'

I nod, and Sharon makes a wry face.

'That's the Lake District in December, love,' she says. 'I did say you should have gone to Benidorm.'

'And you were right. I hate flying though, so . . .' I shrug. 'By the way, we both absolutely love the cruet set. Thank you so much.'

'No problem.' Sharon looks uncomfortable again, but manages a thin smile. 'You'd better sit down.'

I sit in one of the plastic chairs in front of her desk.

'Is there a problem?' I ask.

'A problem?' Sharon sits behind her desk, smiling at me in a perfunctory manner. 'I'm not sure I would put it like that, no.'

'So why am I here?'

She looks annoyed by the question, as if I'm straying from the script in her head. Picking up some papers, she shuffles them, glancing at one or two, then hands them to me.

'You recognise these?'

I study the first few sheets. It's paperwork I sorted out for her in the weeks before my wedding. Simple accounting for the food bank. Part of her job as manager here – but knowing I have an affinity with numbers, Sharon often gives me the forms to fill out while she mans my workstation.

A quid pro quo arrangement that suits us both.

There has never been a problem before.

I nod, still mystified, and offer her the papers back again.

'No, keep them for now.' Sharon sits back. Her face is troubled. 'I didn't notice the issue until last week, when I had to provide our monthly figures to the charity.'

'Issue? What issue?'

Her mouth tightens. My tone obviously irritates her.

'You have no idea what this is about, Catherine?'

I don't like the way she emphasises my name.

Now I'm irritated, too.

'None whatsoever, sorry. Should I?'

I flick through the loose sheets again, checking the details on each. Some people I recall perfectly. The ones with the worst stories. Others are harder to place. A few were dealt with by different volunteers, or they came to the food bank outside my shift times.

There's nothing here that strikes me as wrong.

Sharon taps the desktop with one painted fingernail, studying me through narrowed eyes. 'Okay, let's do this properly. You know how you have to input the details on the computer, then print out two copies for the files?'

'Of course.'

'And each printout has to be signed at the bottom, in the box that says "Handling Officer"?'

'Yes.'

'And you're supposed to leave that part blank so that I can add my signature later?'

A cold feeling creeps over me. Did I sign the printed forms by mistake? Guiltily, my hand clenches the sheets, staring back at her.

I did rush through some of those forms in the weeks before the wedding, my head full of flower arrangements and invitations and packing up our stuff for the post-wedding move to my parents' house. Plus, of course, the horror of the snow globe's arrival.

'Look at the signature on each sheet.'

I look down at the first sheet, expecting to see my own name in the box left blank for the Handling Officer's signature.

My heart stutters.

There's a name written in the signature box. Signed in bold, black ink. The scrawl is not quite legible, almost underdeveloped. As though the writer hasn't fully decided yet how to sign their name.

A familiar, sloping signature, all the same.

Just one word.

The sheets in my hand begin to tremble.

This is fear. Sudden, primal, brain-numbing fear.

When I don't say anything, Sharon clears her throat. Her look is cold, brittle. She doesn't understand, and who can blame her?

'Well?' she says. 'Do you have an explanation for me? Any explanation at all?'

I shake my head, my heart thumping. I don't know what to say. Or if I can even speak. My tongue feels as if it's stuck to the roof of my mouth. I'm in hell, I think. A nightmare, only it's for real.

Sharon glares at me. 'Who the hell is Rachel?'

Chapter Twenty

I meet Louise for lunch at La Giravolta, the Italian bistro on the corner. It's her day off on the new shift rota, but she looks tired, like she ought to be in bed. She's pale, her black hair limp on her shoulders, and there are shadows under her eyes which a few dabs of concealer have not managed to erase. It must be all the night shifts she's been doing, I decide. Dominic is exactly the same after a long stint on nights. He keeps me up too, as I find it so hard to sleep when he's not in the bed with me. It's even harder now that we've moved in with my parents.

'How are you?' Louise asks, standing up to kiss me on the cheek. She sits down again, her hand going automatically to her wine glass, and I realise she has started drinking without me. 'Dominic said you had a wonderful time on honeymoon. Slept late nearly every day. God, what I wouldn't do for a whole week of lie-ins.'

'So book some holiday leave,' I say lightly as I take my seat. I nod to her glass. 'Is that a dry white?'

'House Chardonnay.'

I turn to call the cheerful waitress, Bianca, who knows me well. 'Two lunch menus, please. And a bottle of Chardonnay.'

'*Pronto.*'

Bianca disappears into the kitchen, singing softly under her breath in Italian.

'Oh, you know me.' Louise shrugs. 'I get so bored on holiday.'

'Same here,' I say, though it's not entirely true.

'Not on your honeymoon though.' She winks at me and drains her wine. 'Sounds like you two spent most of your time in bed.'

I blush, and glance about the restaurant. 'Shush.'

'Prude.'

'Lush.' I nod at her empty wine glass. 'I didn't think I was that late. How long have you been here?'

'I only had a glass while I was waiting. And not long. Fifteen minutes?' She looks at me with suddenly intent eyes. 'So come on, spill. What was so urgent you had to speak to me today?'

First, I check over my shoulder, as though I half expect Sharon to be standing in the bistro doorway, which is ridiculous. Then I flick through the photos on my phone for the snap I took of one of the forms. I had to do it sneakily while Sharon was out of the office for a few minutes, dealing with an unfortunate young woman who'd started screaming at Petra. It made me nervous, knowing I was breaking all the rules. But it was my only chance to get a photocopy of my dead sister's apparent 'signature'.

I hand the phone across the table, and she studies the photograph while Bianca arrives with the menus and wine. She drags the cork out of the bottle with ease, then pours two large glasses. I pretend to study the menu until Bianca's gone, then close it and look at Louise impatiently.

'Well?'

'Sorry.' She is as mystified as I was on first being handed the forms. 'What am I looking at?'

I point out the signature. 'I'm certain I left that box blank for Sharon to sign. So how the hell did that signature get there?' I lean forward, hoping she can advise me. Louise is always so level-headed. 'And why would someone pull a trick like that?'

'To get you into trouble, presumably,' she says, studying the photo again. 'So did you?'

'I told you,' I say hotly. 'I didn't write that.'

'No, crosspatch. I meant, did you get into trouble?'

'Oh. Sorry, I didn't mean to jump down your throat.' I make a face. 'A slapped wrist, that's all. Though it wasn't very pleasant. Sharon didn't believe a word I said. She thinks I signed the wrong name deliberately.'

'Why?'

'She's been giving me her paperwork to complete. That's against the rules, and I think she assumed I wanted someone at the charity headquarters to notice.'

'Like signing "Mickey Mouse" on a cheque?'

'Exactly.'

'So did you tell her who Rachel is?'

'God, no. I denied the whole thing.' I drink some wine, which is dry and nicely chilled, but rather sharp. 'Sharon would think I was mad if I told her the truth.' When Louise looks perplexed, I add, 'How does "My dead sister signed it" sound to you?'

She grins. 'Fair enough.'

Bianca comes back to take our order. 'What can I get for you ladies?' she asks briskly.

Without bothering to open the menu again, I order my usual lunch, a tuna salad baguette, and add a bowl of green and black olives to start.

Louise orders the Special of the Day, Fusilli Giravolta, served with salad and garlic bread. 'I bet it's delicious,' she says, flirting a little with the waitress.

Bianca smiles, her whole face lighting up. 'Our new chef's speciality. He stole the recipe from his Sicilian grandmother, or so he claims.'

'Sicilian?' Louise raises her brows. 'He should be careful. She sounds positively dangerous.'

Bianca laughs. 'That's what my brother says.'

'Is he a chef too?'

'Giacomo? No, he's a locksmith.' She points to a stack of business cards in a holder next to the salt cellar, then plucks one out and hands it to Louise, smiling self-consciously. 'Please, take one. In case you ever get locked out . . .'

Someone calls her from the kitchen and she hurries away, threading her way through the tables with one quick look back at Louise.

'You're such a wicked flirt,' I tell Louise, shaking my head. 'What would your girlfriend say?'

'Amita knows what I'm like. She's okay with it, so long as I don't go too far.' She studies the business card, then passes it to me with a shrug and leans back against the alcove seat, her smile mischievous. 'Besides, it doesn't hurt to browse occasionally. Just in case something better turns up.'

There's a crash behind me and I jump, my heart pounding as I look round. But it was only a wine glass, knocked off a table. People are laughing. A few clap mockingly.

I slip the card into my bag, then glance at the clock on the wall opposite to check the time. Still forty minutes before I have to be back at work. Plenty of time for both of us to eat, and even have a coffee afterwards.

'Have you told Dominic about this business with Rachel's signature?' Louise asks suddenly.

'He's at work.'

'But will you?' She studies me curiously. 'You didn't tell him about that eyeball in the snow globe. He cornered me about it a few days before the wedding. Gave me quite a talking-to.'

'I'm sorry.'

'That's okay. I can handle irate men.' Louise hands back my phone in a conspiratorial manner. 'But this is probably something you need to discuss with your husband, rather than me. And besides, I don't know anything much about Rachel, except what you told me at the hospital.'

'I haven't told Dom much either.'

'However bad it is, you have to tell him,' she says bluntly.

I know Louise is right, but I hate the thought of having that conversation.

'I've told him most of it,' I say.

'Most?'

'There's more.' I lower my voice and lean forward. I don't want anyone else to hear what we're talking about. But it's time I was straight with Louise about the extent of my sister's mental health issues. 'There's always more with Rachel.'

Louise leans forward too, intrigued. 'Go on.'

'Oh God, where do I start?' I shake my head. 'Rachel used to hear voices. Voices in her head. Devils on her shoulder, telling her what to do. Bad stuff, usually.'

'Sounds like schizophrenia.'

'I thought it was just a neat way of getting out of trouble. Though Mum did say that when she was little, Rachel was always looking for angels in the ceiling.'

'I beg your pardon?'

Bianca stops next to our table and puts down a bowl of olives. 'There you go,' she says, smiling at Louise before disappearing again.

Louise watches her go, then makes an appreciative noise, gazing at my side order.

'Have one,' I say.

'Thanks, they look delicious.' She selects a fat green olive. 'Sorry, you were saying Rachel saw angels?'

'Not literally. Looking for angels in the ceiling means she never looked directly at Mum's face, like normal babies do when they're nursing. That she found it hard to make an emotional connection with other people.' I shrug. 'That's what Mum told me anyway.'

'Interesting.' Louise plays with the stem of her wine glass, frowning. 'Did Rachel have a Statement of Special Educational Needs?'

'Neither of us went to school. Mum taught us at home, mostly. Though we had a nanny who looked after us for a time, while Mum was busy doing other stuff. She often sent us away.' I shrug. 'I suppose we got underfoot in London, you know.'

The weather outside looks grim. I watch a crowded bus lumber past outside the bistro, people behind the steamed-up windows staring vacantly ahead or looking down, presumably at their phones. It's still early afternoon, yet already the sky is darkening.

It's not long until Christmas, I realise with a start. I've been so busy with work this year, and the wedding, I've barely noticed the festive season creeping up.

Louise steals another olive with an apologetic smile. 'These are gorgeous. I could eat them all day.'

'Help yourself,' I say. 'I'm not sure if being homeschooled helped or hindered Rachel's development, to be honest. Rachel was always in trouble. Perhaps she would have done better at school.'

'Sounds like she needed proper help, not condemnation,' Louise says, a little tartly.

I look at her, and realise that she doesn't understand. But how could she?

'Rachel was troubled, yes. But more than that. She was evil.'

'Evil?'

I choose my words carefully. 'Rachel didn't care about other people. She was only interested in getting her own way. So she would say anything to get what she wanted. Do anything, however appalling.' I draw a deep breath. 'Then, afterwards, she'd walk away as if nothing had happened, leaving someone else to pick up the pieces.' I make a face. 'Sometimes literally.'

'Sounds like a right bundle of laughs, your sister.'

I smile, though it's not funny really. Not deep down, not with what I'm going through. But Louise will think I'm strange if I don't smile.

'Yeah, absolutely,' I say. 'Rachel was a real party person.'

'And you killed her.'

Chapter Twenty-One

I stare at her, the smile frozen on my lips. 'Wh-what?'

Louise starts to reply, but Bianca reappears at that moment with our lunches and we both fall silent. She hands us our plates, checks we have cutlery and, finally, clears away the now-empty olive bowl.

'Have a good meal, ladies,' she says with a smile, and then breezes back towards the kitchen.

'Sorry, I shouldn't have said that,' Louise says quietly once Bianca has disappeared. 'What I meant to say was, you *think* you killed her.'

I don't know how to respond to that.

'Look, I know this is none of my business.' Louise gives her knife and fork a quick, fastidious rub with her napkin. 'But Dom told me how your sister died. That it was a skiing accident, and you can't remember much about the circumstances. Only that your parents refused to talk about it afterwards, and now they get edgy whenever her name comes up.'

I look away, uncomfortable.

A woman about my own age at a nearby table is staring at us. Spiky red hair, an aggressive expression. I meet her eyes, then glare. *Nosy, much?*

She glances hurriedly away.

My pulse is racing. I'm beginning to regret asking Louise to meet me for lunch. This is too much, on top of the shock of seeing Rachel's name all over that paperwork. My nerves are still too raw, too painfully scraped, to deal with what Louise is saying.

'That's about right,' I say huskily.

I pour us both some more wine from the bottle, deliberately generous. Though I notice she's been easing off since I arrived. Only a third of her glass was gone. Unlike mine. This has not been the comfortable, easy conversation I had envisaged. Quite the opposite, in fact. But the wine is helping.

'So in some part of your brain,' Louise says, 'deep in your subconscious, you may think you were involved in her death, based simply on the way your parents behaved at the time.'

'Pure psychobabble,' I say, irritated by her tone.

'Maybe, maybe not.' She looks at me steadily. 'How old were you when she died?'

'Twelve. I'd only just had my birthday.'

'And Rachel?'

'Thirteen and three-quarters,' I say promptly.

Rachel used to say that a lot, as a silly joke. Then she died and got stuck at that age forever. *Thirteen and three-quarters.*

The joke was on her in the end.

'There you are, you see.' Louise shrugs, as though this explains everything. 'You were an adolescent.'

'So?'

'Adolescence is one of the most sensitive ages for trauma, barring infancy. All those shifting hormone levels, all that identity crisis shit that gets thrown at you during puberty, it makes mental trauma of the kind you suffered all the more dangerous.'

'Dangerous?'

Louise smiles drily. 'Don't look so worried. All I mean is, trauma at that age can have a long-lasting effect. It can turn inwards and eat away at you for the rest of your life.'

'So,' I say, putting down my baguette, 'you think losing my sister at that age may be affecting me now.'

Her gaze flickers across my face, but Louise merely says, 'Perhaps', and continues to eat, mopping up some of her thick sauce with a slice of garlic bread.

A suspicion strikes me.

'You think I did it myself, don't you? You think I was the one who signed Rachel's name on those sheets.'

Louise stops eating, and meets my eyes. 'Did you?'

'Of course I bloody didn't.'

'Have you considered it to be a possibility?'

'No.'

'You might have done it without realising what you were doing.'

I stare. 'Without . . . what?'

'In a kind of fugue state,' she says. 'It's like a trance where you forget who you are and what you're doing.' When my eyes widen, she makes a face. 'Please don't bite my head off. It can happen, especially when someone's under a lot of unusual stress.'

'How am I under stress?'

'Getting married is one of the most stressful events in a person's life. Don't you know that? It's only beaten by getting divorced and moving house.'

'I was not stressed out by marrying Dominic,' I say, though part of me acknowledges that to be a lie. 'I love him.'

'No one says you don't. And I know you're upset, but this is hard for me too. Believe me, we all have your best interests at heart.' She pauses, biting her lip delicately. 'Have you considered, for instance, that you might have cut up your wedding dress yourself and simply have no memory of doing it?'

I blink in horror. 'No, absolutely not.'

'Or maybe taken your sister's snow globe and posted it to yourself with . . . with the eyeball inside?'

'Why would I do something like that? Now you're being ridiculous.' My heart is thudding. I stand up, pushing my chair back. 'I've had enough of this. I'm going back to work.'

'Wait, please. Sit down.'

My chest is heaving and I feel like screaming. But something in her tone makes me stop and sink slowly back into my chair.

'There is a particular phenomenon, Catherine,' she says slowly. 'A condition. And it's not your fault. I've seen people with this condition brought into casualty, often after an episode of self-harming, and it's much more common than people realise.'

'What are you talking about?'

'Survivor's guilt.'

I shake my head, looking away. I don't want to hear this.

'People who've survived a traumatic event where others died,' she continues gently, 'even when they don't remember it properly, can experience an overwhelming sense of guilt. It's so strong sometimes, it can change the way they behave. In extreme cases, it can even make them take on certain facets or behavioural traits of loved ones who didn't survive, like a kind of penance to the dead person.' She hesitates, then adds, 'Openly, or on a subconscious level.'

'Bullshit.'

'It's a well-recognised condition.'

'Has D-Dominic been talking to you about this?' Hearing the slight stutter in my voice only annoys me further. My heart races when she says nothing, merely watching me. But there's a flicker in her eyes again, a touch of guilt. 'Oh God.'

'Catherine . . .'

I feel the telltale blush of anger fill my cheeks and can't control it. 'This is Dominic's theory, isn't it? Not yours at all. He's the one who thinks I'm going mental.'

'That's such an unhelpful word.'

'Oh, I'm so sorry.' My voice is a hiss, and she stares at me, clearly startled. 'How would you describe my condition, then? In your expert opinion?'

'I'm not a doctor, it's true,' she says slowly, 'but I am an experienced mental health specialist, and I don't think we should—'

'Has "survivor's guilt" made me hysterical, would you say? Hysterical and hormonal? Or does Dominic think it's worse? What did he tell you?' My voice starts to rise, even though I know people are looking our way. The woman with spiky red hair is staring again, but I ignore her. 'Am I a bit on the flaky side, perhaps? Unhinged? Disturbed?'

I pause, barely able to hear myself through the thunder of blood. Yet the final word forces itself out anyway.

'Mad?'

Chapter Twenty-Two

Back at work, I try not to catch Sharon's eye. Lunch with Louise has not helped me work through my confusion about the signatures on the paperwork. In fact, I feel worse, and keep checking over my shoulder, as though afraid my colleagues are looking at me sideways. Though I'm sure Sharon won't have told anyone else about the forms. After all, she could get into trouble for having handed over that paperwork to a subordinate instead of doing it herself.

People who've survived a traumatic event where others died, even when they don't remember it properly, can experience an overwhelming sense of guilt.

Is Louise right? Am I simply going through some kind of post-traumatic experience, triggered by the stress of getting married?

Thankfully the rest of the afternoon goes quickly. Sharon does not speak to me again, working in her office most of the time, head bent over her desk.

I wonder what she thinks about me.

That I'm crazy, perhaps.

I cringe at that possibility, and feel inexplicably cold, too. The tips of my fingers tingle as though I've been touching glass. *I'm not crazy*, I tell myself. But it's getting harder to believe that, despite Louise's insistence that I am not mad.

Merely *stressed*.

I'm not alone in feeling stressed, of course. As I have daily proof of in this job. The world is getting darker and colder for everyone, not just me. I'm getting ready to leave for the day when a young woman barges in through the entrance doors, pushing a buggy and looking flustered. She stares around the place, then fixes on me. Her eyes widen, and she heads in my direction, biting down hard on her lip as though repressing the urge to scream.

I know that expression. It's very common in the food bank. It's the look of a woman at the far edge of what she can deal with, in need of only one push before total collapse.

'Hello?' She stops walking. 'I need food. My kid's starving.'

'Of course.'

She's surprised by that response. I see it in her face. She expected a struggle. To be knocked back by the system.

The woman parks the buggy in front of me. Her child is about two years old, a sallow-faced girl with huge eyes. She's clutching a fluffy soft toy to her chest. Some kind of cat, perhaps?

'Do you have a referral?' I ask, smiling down at the child.

'A what?'

'You need a referral to use the food bank. It's usually a letter from social services, or a reference from a GP.' She just looks mystified. 'I'm afraid we can't help you without one,' I add.

'Are you kidding me?'

Sharon comes out of her office and stands listening.

'I'm really sorry,' I tell the woman awkwardly. 'But I could make a phone call.'

'Catherine?'

I ignore Sharon, not even looking in her direction. 'It might be possible to arrange some emergency cover,' I say to the woman, 'if you're really desperate. I'd just need some details from you.'

'What kind of details?' the woman asks in a suspicious tone, though I can see she's thawing.

'Your name and address, for starters.' I get out a notebook and pen. 'Don't worry, it's all confidential.'

'Thanks, Catherine, I'll deal with this,' Sharon tells me, and there's a warning note in her voice. She turns to the woman, her manner brisk and unemotional. 'We only deal with direct referrals.'

'But I've come a long way,' the woman says. 'I had no money to top up my Oyster card. I had to walk.'

'And I'm sorry you've had a wasted trip.' Sharon's smile is utterly fake. I can tell she has decided this woman is going to make trouble. 'Let me fetch you an info sheet on how to go about getting a referral.'

'I don't want one of them.'

'It's the best I can do, I'm afraid.'

'Says you.' The woman looks Sharon up and down. Her finger stabs towards me. 'I want her. Not you. Got it?'

'I'm in charge here.'

The woman starts to say something, but Sharon interrupts. 'I'm sorry.' Her voice has risen slightly, but she's still in control. 'If you don't want the information I've offered, then I think you'd better leave.'

Heads have turned towards us. Petra comes out of Sharon's office too, a clipboard under her arm stump. She looks across at me and raises her eyebrows. I shake my head.

'What if I don't want to leave?' the woman asks, her voice also rising.

Nobody says anything.

'I need help.' The woman jiggles the buggy from side to side and the child cries out in fear. 'She needs food. Are you going to stand there and say no?'

'I'm sorry,' Sharon says again.

'You're not fucking sorry. You've got everything. What have we got, eh? Nothing.' Abruptly, the woman wheels the buggy about and strides furiously towards the exit. 'And none of you give a fuck.'

She bangs through the double doors, and I listen to the unhappy wail of her child with a sinking heart. This isn't why I came to help out here – to turn people away who are in absolute need.

Sharon sees my expression. 'I offered to help her get a referral. You heard me. She didn't want my help. This may be a charity, but we have rules about referrals. We have to do things by the book.'

I grab my bag and run after the woman.

'Catherine, don't!'

But I ignore Sharon's warning.

———

Dusk is falling outside. The street lights have come on. I walk down the road and soon spot the woman, who has not gone far. She has stopped at the corner by La Giravolta, head down, while her daughter continues to cry.

'Hello?'

She looks up at my voice. She is shaken and upset. 'What do you want?'

'I don't want to offend you, but I thought maybe . . .' I'm not sure how she will react as I start to rummage in my handbag for my purse. I take out a twenty and hand it to her. 'Just to tide you over. If you want it.'

She stares at the note in disbelief, then takes it. 'Thank you.'

'You're welcome.'

'I'll let you have it back.'

'No, it's fine.'

'Honestly,' she says, pushing the note deep into the front pocket of her jeans. 'Cross my heart. Soon as I get my social through.'

I smile and say nothing, but we both know that's unlikely to happen. Not in her circumstances.

'What's your name?' she asks abruptly.

'Catherine.'

Her smile surprises me. 'That's a nice name.'

She does not tell me her name in return and I don't ask.

The child is leaning forward in the dusk, peering round the side of the buggy at me, curious and damp-eyed. She's still clutching the soft toy to her chest.

I grin at her, and the little girl shrinks away, instinctively wary.

'Right, better get this one home for her tea. It's nearly dark.' The woman is no longer looking at me or the kid. She's staring ahead at the oncoming car lights with a distracted expression, her mind already elsewhere. 'See you later, yeah?'

And with that, she's gone.

As I watch her push the buggy down the road, a car drives past in the opposite direction with excruciating slowness, perhaps waiting for the lights ahead to change.

The car is a silver Jaguar.

The driver's window is partly open, an old familiar Christmas carol blasting out into the evening. 'Good King Wenceslas'. One of my mum's favourites, it always reminds me of home and the sweetly nostalgic Christmases of childhood. I listen with a smile, singing along to the refrain under my breath.

The driver looks at me.

I glance at him casually, still smiling, and our gazes lock. Just for a fraction longer than is entirely comfortable. Long enough for me to pause, wondering if I know him. He certainly looks as though he knows me.

My dad used to drive a Jag when I was a kid. This one isn't quite the same as his; Dad's was an older model with one of those silver leaping jaguars on the bonnet.

The driver is in his sixties, I'd guess. Grey hat, iron grey moustache, his coat collar turned up. He's unsmiling, head turned, staring straight at me. Not ahead at the road.

My smile fades.

The lights ahead change to green.

For a few seconds he doesn't react, still looking at me, then one of the drivers behind sounds a horn, and he drives on, suddenly accelerating.

A moment later, the Jaguar is lost in traffic ahead, rear lights red in the darkness, soon indistinguishable from all the rest.

Chapter Twenty-Three

Mum and Dad have been arguing again. I can tell as soon as I walk into the kitchen.

Mum's face is bright with fury, her cheeks flushed, eyes wide and damp. Dad is standing by the kitchen window, staring out at the dark garden. From the way his silvery hair is ruffled, I guess he's been running a hand through it in agitation.

When he turns towards me, I recognise the sullen, shuttered look on his face. It's clear she's been nagging him about something, as only Mum can, in that shrill, persistent way she has. But what about?

'Catherine, darling, there you are at last.' Mum gives me what is meant to be a brave, appealing smile. 'You're so late this evening. I was just saying to your father that he should go out in the car to pick you up from . . . that place where you work.'

'The food bank. I'm a volunteer.'

'That's right.' She sounds apologetic, but I know she isn't. 'I hate it when you don't get back on time. I worry.'

There's a heaped plate of scones on the kitchen table. Fresh-baked, by the gorgeous smell of them.

'It's nearly Christmas, Mum. I had to stay late at work, then I did a spot of present-shopping on the way home.' I drop my bag on the table and help myself to a scone. It's cheese, I realise. 'These smell amazing. Kasia's?'

'Well, I certainly didn't bake them myself,' Mum says sharply.

Kasia wanders in from the cold pantry at that moment, carrying a whole cooked ham. It looks delicious, breaded on one side and dotted with black cloves.

'Hello.' I look at her, surprised. 'I didn't know you were still here.'

Kasia shrugs, saying nothing. But her English is not brilliant, so she rarely says much to anyone.

She places the ham carefully on a steel platter in the middle of the table, as though ready for carving. Then turns to wash her hands at the sink, her back very straight, long blonde hair twisted up in a neat chignon for work. Willowy-thin, with angular hips and a perpetually sulky face, Kasia Lecinska is not the friendliest of people. But she's an excellent cleaner, and not too bad at baking either.

Certainly my mother says she couldn't cope without her.

I frown though, perplexed to see her still here. Kasia usually keeps such regular hours, having a young family of her own, and it's nearly seven o'clock.

I glance at my mother. 'Are you having a dinner party tonight?'

'Don't be ridiculous.' Dad glares at me. 'I asked Kasia to stay on until you got home, that's all. Just in case she was needed.'

'Needed for what?'

He hesitates. 'You were late. We weren't sure what had happened.'

'I'm only half an hour late.'

'Forty-five minutes,' my mother corrects me, her face strained.

'Even so, it's not exactly . . .' I stop and look from her to my father. They both seem so tense. As though something has happened. A sense of dread creeps over me. My mouth is horribly dry. 'I don't understand. What's the matter?'

'Nothing,' my mother says quickly, but I don't believe her.

'I didn't realise I was on a timetable.' It did take me a while to calm down after Sharon blew up at me. But even so . . . 'I'm sorry, I suppose I've got used to doing my own thing.'

'We expect you to keep regular hours under this roof.' Dad's voice grates at my nerves. 'Our house, our rules. Remember?'

I stare at him, speechless.

'Of course, you're free to come and go as you please—' Mum begins in a placating tone, but Dad interrupts her.

'No, she bloody isn't,' he insists. I haven't seen him this angry since the night he took me upstairs to look at Rachel's toy chest and we found the snow globe was missing. 'Not when we don't know how stable she is.'

I turn, hearing the door open, and see that Dominic has come into the kitchen.

'What . . . what do you mean?' I feel suddenly rigid, as though something inside me – my heart, perhaps – has turned to stone. 'How *stable* I am?' I look at my husband pleadingly. 'Dom, what are they talking about?'

Dominic says quietly, 'Louise gave me a call at work this afternoon. She's worried about you.' He pauses. 'We all are.'

'Louise?' I echo, shocked.

'It's okay. She told us what happened at the food bank today. About the paperwork you signed as Rachel.'

'That *I* signed . . . ?' I shake my head in instant, furious denial. It's important to stay calm, I know that. Yet how can I? My chest is tight and I can hardly breathe. 'She had no right to say anything. I told her in confidence. And why the hell is everyone assuming it was me?'

Dominic looks at me in silence, his eyebrows raised.

My parents say nothing, either.

Kasia, typically expressionless, hangs up her apron beside the range, then slips out of the kitchen without meeting my eyes. God only knows what she makes of all this, our crazy English family.

Meaning to go upstairs to my room, I make for the hall door but blunder into Dominic. He grabs me by the shoulders, his face sympathetic. 'Darling, please.'

'Please what? Please don't have a nervous breakdown? Please don't crack up?'

'She's hysterical.' My father, of course, ready with his expert male opinion. 'We should call her doctor.'

'Oh, why bother with a doctor? Why not just give me a good slap?' I turn on him, tasting salt in the corner of my mouth. The familiar brine of sorrow. Though this time it's more like rage. Long-suppressed rage escaping as tears. 'I'm sure you're dying to give me a good slapping, aren't you, Dad?'

My mother says something in quick protest, but I don't catch it over my father's roar of anger. 'How dare you?' He comes towards me, fists by his side but clenched tight nonetheless. 'After everything we've done for you . . .'

'So why say it was me who signed that paperwork?' I almost scream at them, and duck away from Dominic, who's trying to restrain me. This isn't his battle, it's mine. It's been mine for a long time, and I know all the manoeuvres. 'Why not admit the truth?'

An awful silence falls again.

Mum looks frightened now, a hand at her mouth.

Dad stops where he is, staring at me. There's some expression in his eyes that I don't quite understand.

'And what truth is that, Catherine?' he asks.

'That Rachel isn't dead. That she didn't die like you told me. That my sister is still alive somewhere.' I'm gasping, and barely recognise my own voice. Or the words coming out of my mouth. They feel sharp and pointed, like knives I'm throwing at my enemies, my parents. 'And she's coming back to finish what she started, and destroy my life.'

Chapter Twenty-Four

Upstairs in our self-contained flat, I sink down on the white leather sofa and bury my face in my hands.

I want to cry but dare not.

They denied it, of course. What did I expect? They looked at me as if I'm going crazy. Even Dominic. He thinks I've lost my mind or am about to lose it.

Perhaps I am crazy.

But the last thing I want is for Dominic to find me crying up here on my own like a kid. He would only assume I can't cope. That I need help. Not simply his, but of the professional variety. Someone Louise knows at the hospital, perhaps. Or Doctor Holbern, the doctor who used to see me occasionally in my teens, when I would get 'hormonal', as my dad used to put it, and do stupid stuff.

Doctor Holbern. A strangely angular man with a ginger beard. He had long legs that he would cross and recross as he sat listening to me. As if he could never get comfortable. I haven't seen him in ages.

Dad's probably on the phone to him right now.

The thought frightens me.

I'm not going crazy. I didn't send myself Rachel's snow globe with a bull's eye inside it. And I didn't sign any documents at the food bank in my dead sister's name.

Unless I did, and have simply blanked it out of my memory.

'No way.' I rock back and forth, making a moaning noise under my breath. 'I didn't do any of that. I'm not mad.'

Except I'm acting mad. Rocking back and forth. Talking to myself.

I sit up, then close my eyes and try to centre myself. To focus my energy on feeling calm again. I practise the deep-breathing technique Doctor Holbern taught me years ago. In and out. In and out. Drawing the air right to the base of my stomach, then letting it go again, slow and deliberate, out through my nose.

My chest heaves and I catch my breath, struggling against the rhythm. The technique doesn't seem to be working this time.

I raise my head, listening for Dominic's tread on the stairs.

But he doesn't come.

What are they talking about down there?

'I think you should go and lie down,' Dominic said after my out-burst. I didn't argue with him. By that point I was only too happy to escape the claustrophobic atmosphere of the kitchen.

I thought he would be right behind me. But there's no sign of him. The room is silent, my rapidly beating heart somehow obscenely loud here.

I look around at the clean, black-and-white-striped wallpaper, the pristine glass and chrome furniture. The freshly painted door stands slightly ajar.

This used to be Rachel's bedroom when we were kids, but Mum and Dad have cleared it out and turned it into a bright, modern sitting room for us. Rachel's dusty old curtains have finally gone, replaced by Roman-style blinds in stern black. I haven't opened them yet, but I know that view intimately. This side of the house overlooks the street, the quiet evenings often disturbed by sirens or car horns. There's a flat-screen television and a DVD player where Rachel's bed used to be. Before the new wallpaper went up, her old pop posters and the various pictures she had painted as a kid were taken down.

Rachel's 'art'.

The walls are blank now, except for a rectangular mirror that hangs just above the single bookshelf. That's new, too. Perhaps that's why it feels strange to be in here. Sitting in Rachel's private space, making it my own. My sister would hardly approve. But then she never approved of much.

A sob wells up from deep inside, and I fight against it, my throat tight.

'Shit.'

I hate feeling like this. Like a child, helpless, unable to make my voice heard above Mum and Dad. It's stupid to still feel like this at my age. I'm an adult. I shouldn't feel intimidated by my own parents. I should be able to explain myself and say how I feel. But now that I'm back living under their roof, in the same rooms where I grew up, it's not easy to change my habit of deferring to Dad. Even when I know he's wrong.

Someone is coming heavily up the stairs.

I recognise that tread.

'Dom?' I stand up awkwardly, wiping damp eyes. I don't want my husband to see me broken. I need him to think I'm okay, that I'm functioning. 'I'm in here.'

He comes in and our eyes meet.

'Darling,' he says, shaking his head. He disapproves of my accusations. Of course he does. He's just like them, deep down. He doesn't understand.

I feel angry and scared at the same time. But I dare not show it. My fingers buzz with some kind of nervous vibration, like pins and needles, and I hide them from him, shoving my hands behind my back.

'They drive me up the wall.'

'Christ, I can see that.' His eyes are warm and sympathetic. He holds out his arms, as though everything is forgiven. 'Come here, baby.'

I cross the room and let him hold me. It feels good. But I'm still guilty about the way I behaved downstairs. Uncomfortably so.

I lean my head on his chest and close my eyes. 'Sorry.'

'Don't apologise.'

'I totally lost my cool.'

'I know.' He laughs softly. 'It was impressive. Like standing too close to Mount Etna when it's erupting.'

'I wasn't doing it for effect.'

'Of course you weren't.' He strokes my hair, and laughs again. 'It was still impressive though. My little volcano.'

'Oh God. What must they be thinking?'

'That their little girl isn't quite so little anymore, I expect. But you have nothing to be ashamed of. It's about time they stopped treating you like a child.'

His arms tighten about me, strong and comforting. I take several deep breaths and instantly feel better. Calmer, able to face the world again.

Dominic knows when I'm hiding something from him, though. He always knows. Putting a gentle finger under my chin, he tips my head back. 'Hey, you okay in there?'

I gaze up at him silently.

He makes a noise under his breath, then kisses me. I kiss him back, hungry for affection. We sway together, and after a few minutes his hands slide down my spine, pressing me hard against him.

He's aroused, I can feel it.

Then he cups my breast, running his thumb firmly over my nipple. 'Dom . . .'

He doesn't answer as he guides me backwards in a few shuffling steps to the sofa. I sit down, startled, his weight on top of me, and we keep on kissing.

His breathing has quickened, his tongue in my mouth. My heart hammering painfully, I cling onto his shoulders, my eyes shut tight, and hope he's only playing. He likes to do stuff like this sometimes, to make love spontaneously, and push things too far. It's not something I'm hugely comfortable with. But I think Dominic enjoys that element, too. Knowing that he's forcing me beyond my limits, taking me places that I would never otherwise go.

Tonight though, I'm not in the mood to be pushed.

'Not here,' I say, our mouths close together. I panic, my skin in a cold sweat. 'Let's go in . . . in the bedroom. Please.'

He ignores me. Perhaps he thinks I'm play-fighting.

'Dominic, no.'

I fight him in earnest, and he growls in my ear like an animal. A second later, he grabs my wrists and forces me back against the sofa cushions so I can't get away. Then he crushes my mouth under his, effectively silencing me.

This isn't a sex game anymore. It's for real.

Chapter Twenty-Five

Dominic's kisses are an assault. Or that's how they feel. I wrench my head sideways and struggle for air. I'm suffocating under him. I can't bear it any longer.

'I said no, Dominic.' I twist away, breathless and shaking. 'I wasn't joking, okay? I'm not in the mood.'

For a moment he stays where he is, kneeling on the sofa, his chest heaving. Then he pushes away from me and stands up, adjusting his clothing.

'Sorry,' he says thickly. 'I forget sometimes that you . . . that we have different tastes.'

'What's that supposed to mean?'

He makes a helpless gesture. 'Nothing.'

'Dom?'

He runs a hand through his hair. 'I'm not trying to get at you. It's just sometimes you can be a bit too passive in bed.'

'Too passive,' I repeat blankly.

'For me.'

'What, so now we're sexually incompatible? That's news to me, Dominic. Perhaps you could have discussed that with me before we got married.'

'I thought . . . I assumed . . .'

But he doesn't finish. He makes an angry noise under his breath and buries his head in his hands.

I stare at the wall and say nothing. The minutes pass, both of us silent and unmoving. I recall Rachel lying on her bed in here once, reading a vampire novel. It looked interesting, a glossy, exciting cover with a snappy title, but she wouldn't let me see it. 'It's mine,' she kept saying, her voice mean and taunting. 'It's a teen romance. With sex and everything. Not suitable for *little girls*.' Though she could barely have been thirteen herself. But she thought of herself as mature, of course. Almost an adult. And I suppose she was frighteningly precocious.

Sometimes you can be a bit too passive in bed.

If Rachel had still been alive, would she have caught Dominic's eye when we first started dating? Might he have preferred my more exciting sister to me?

I push the awful thought away. But it's unsettled me, my hands clenched into fists. I shouldn't have moved back into my parents' house with Dominic. It was a mistake. There are too many bad memories here.

Dominic stands up eventually and turns, studying me. He holds out a hand. 'I'm sorry,' he says, and I can tell that he means it. That he's worried by my silence. 'That was a bad call. I misjudged your mood. I shouldn't have treated you so roughly. Or said . . . that.'

I stand up too, taking his hand. I feel numb inside after our row. But perhaps he's right, at least in part. Perhaps I'm not as demonstrative towards him as I should be. He's my husband, after all.

'It was a misunderstanding,' I say.

'All the same . . .'

'I love you,' I whisper.

He smiles then, the deep frown lines disappearing. His whole face lights up, as if the sun has suddenly appeared from behind dark clouds. 'I love you too, Catherine.'

'I meant what I said though.'

'About?'

'About Rachel still being alive.'

He shakes his head, then gently strokes a finger down my cheek. 'You know that's actually impossible, right?'

'Is it?'

'Your sister died years ago, sweetheart. There was no misunderstanding about that. It was a skiing accident. Your parents were there, you told me that yourself.'

'Yes, but I didn't attend her funeral,' I say urgently. 'Mum flew home with me after the accident, and Dad stayed on to collect the body. They said the funeral would upset me too much.'

He frowns. 'But you told me she'd been cremated. That you've seen her ashes. In your dad's study.'

'But how can I be sure they're Rachel's ashes?'

He raises his eyebrows. 'Darling . . .'

'Look, my parents never talked about Rachel afterwards. Not once. They wouldn't even hear her name mentioned. Like it was taboo. I tried a few times, but they always changed the subject.'

His brows contract. 'Okay, I agree that's odd.'

'Then, about a year after she died, I asked Mum if we could scatter Rachel's ashes in the back garden. She said no, but I kept on at her. I'd been having nightmares about her, and I thought it would help me . . . you know, lay her to rest. Eventually Mum yelled at me to shut up, then burst into tears.' My hands tighten into fists at the memory of that appalling row. 'I'd never seen my mother like that before. She's usually so calm, so easy-going.'

Dominic nods, watching me.

'I was so shocked by her reaction,' I continue, lowering my voice, even though I know my parents can't possibly hear me, 'I never brought the subject up again. I didn't dare.'

'Poor baby.'

I pull away from him. 'I'm serious, Dom. *This* is serious.'

'Sorry, I wasn't trying to diminish what you're feeling.' He takes a step back, respecting my need for space. 'I just thought you might need comforting.'

'What I need are answers.'

'So go and ask your parents again. Keep asking until you get the truth.'

'Oh, come on.' I shake my head in frustration. 'Now you're being naïve. You saw what Mum and Dad were like down there. They might not have said anything, but they looked at me like I'm crazy.'

'Because you touched a sore point.'

'I know, right?' I shake my head, remembering Mum's white face, the unspoken fear behind her fury. 'This probably sounds weird, but it's almost as though they're . . . afraid.'

'Afraid of what?'

'I don't know exactly. It's obvious they want me to forget about Rachel. To forget everything about her.' I meet his eyes. 'Even her name.'

He reaches for my hand and I let him take it. His thumb caresses the soft skin of my palm. 'Listen,' he says quietly, 'maybe they just want to protect you from what happened to Rachel.'

'But I don't know what happened. I don't know how my sister died. Only that she did.'

'Right,' he says, squeezing my hand more firmly, 'then we'll get changed out of our work clothes, and go downstairs and ask them. Okay?'

I stare at him. 'Are you serious?'

'Of course I'm serious.' He heads for the bedroom, pulling me gently behind him as if he's taking me to bed. 'We'll ask them together.' He pauses, then adds, 'Straight after supper.'

'Why not right now?'

'Because supper's almost on the table and we don't want Robert to get another bout of indigestion.' Dominic pulls a face as if he's in pain.

'Christ, you know what he's like . . . all those gurgling noises. Belching discreetly behind his napkin when he thinks no one's listening. Better wait until dinner's gone down before mentioning the dead daughter, don't you agree?'

'Dom, please.' I'm laughing, but reluctantly. I'm worried my parents may hear us downstairs. 'Hush, not so loud.'

Dominic ignores me and gives several deliberate, pretend burps, kicking the bedroom door open. He flicks on the light. And stops mid-belch, dropping my hand as he stares at the wall opposite.

'Christ,' he says, his voice hoarse.

I look past him, still grinning at his irreverent impersonation of my father, and freeze in shock, too.

Someone has drawn on the wall above our bed in bright red lettering. Lipstick, I think at once, recognising the shade with a curious absence of shock. One of my own red lipsticks, in fact, is still lying on the white duvet, twisted up and with its lid off.

It's a rough hangman's gibbet and noose, exactly like the one in Rachel's book from the toy chest, with the same three-letter word filled out beneath it in scarlet scrawl.

C A T

Chapter Twenty-Six

I can't bear to look at the bedroom wall, so I wait in our sitting room opposite with the door closed while Dominic fetches my parents from downstairs. They come upstairs quickly but protesting, saying food is on the table, waiting for us.

I slip out and stand on the landing, arms folded, leaning unsteadily against the wall while Dominic takes them into our bedroom. I'm trembling and I hate it. But how else am I supposed to feel, under the circumstances?

I'm under attack.

But who's doing this? And why?

The obvious answer isn't one I want to contemplate. It makes me feel physically sick. And, to be honest, a little frightened, too.

Mum gasps at the sight of my name on the wall, which makes me feel better. At least I'm not being oversensitive. But Dad merely comes out of the bedroom and looks at me.

I know immediately what he's thinking.

'It wasn't me,' I say angrily.

'I didn't say it was.'

'You didn't need to say anything. I can see it in your face.'

'What nonsense.'

I feel the sting but it barely registers. That's how accustomed I am to my father putting me down.

'But *did* you do it?' he adds.

'Of course not.'

Dad grunts, looking at me steadily. I get the strong impression he doesn't believe me. Then he turns and enters our bedroom again.

After a momentary hesitation, I follow him, arms folded defensively across my chest.

Inside, Mum looks at me, then away, as though she does not know what to say. To my relief though, Dominic smiles reassuringly at me and puts an arm about my waist. I can't quite bring myself to smile back at him. *I'm not alone*, I tell myself. *Not this time.*

My father studies the writing on the wall with great deliberation. 'Right.' He clears his throat. 'Well, let's not overdramatise this. What are we going to do about it?'

Let's not overdramatise this.

'For God's sake,' I begin, but Mum interrupts me, her voice brisk and businesslike.

'I'll fetch something to clean it off. That's the first thing to do. Now, let's see, lipstick . . . what will shift lipstick off wallpaper?'

'It's oil-based,' Dominic says.

'Yes.' Mum touches his shoulder briefly, flashing a smile at him. 'Hot water and some Jeyes, perhaps. Kasia will have just the thing under the sink, I'm sure.'

My father says, 'Kasia's gone home, remember?'

'I'm perfectly capable of opening a kitchen cupboard, Robert,' Mum says, and I'm not imagining the coldness in her voice. Maybe she's on my side after all, even if she doesn't show it. Though I don't like the way this conversation is going. It's all about damage control, not investigation. 'I can put on a pair of Marigolds when an emergency occurs.'

'Hold on a minute.'

My voice cuts through their deliberations. My father looks at me warily. Mum bites her lip, a touch of impatience in her face.

I don't look at Dominic.

'Before you start scrubbing lipstick off our bedroom wall, wouldn't it be a good idea to take a photo of it first?'

Mum stares. 'A photo? Whatever for?'

'To preserve the scene.' I look round at them, shocked at their apparent slowness. 'For the police.'

'Catherine,' Dominic begins, holding me close.

'For God's sake, it's evidence,' I burst out. 'What's wrong with you all? Someone's broken in here and written that . . . that horrible thing on our bedroom wall. And none of you seem to think it's worth calling the police.'

Dad looks at me wearily. 'Catherine, it's not like that.'

'Then what is it like?'

'Perhaps Dominic should take you downstairs while we clean up this mess.' He turns to my husband with a significant nod. 'We won't be long. You could have a glass of wine.'

I swear, and my mother winces.

'Why will no one say out loud what's staring us in the face?' I point at the obscene scrawl of the hangman's noose with my name beneath it. 'Rachel did this.'

Nobody says anything.

'Are you going to deny she's behind it?' I turn and glare at Dad, who is shaking his head. 'Seriously?'

'Darling,' he says heavily, 'your sister's dead, and you know it.'

'Do I?'

It's not entirely a rhetorical question, yet none of them answers me. It's as if I've made myself ridiculous just by asking it. Except it's not ridiculous. Someone wrote my name on the wall to intimidate and scare me. And it's working.

In the ensuing silence, I feel my face grow hot. 'Okay, then. How did she die?'

'Please . . .'

'How did Rachel die, Dad?'

He looks at Dominic, and there's a kind of pleading in his face now. 'I really think you should take your wife downstairs. Let us deal with this.'

Your wife.

How very Victorian of him. It makes me sound like a parcel that's been handed from one responsible male to another. And a problematic parcel, at that.

'Why can't you just answer the question, Dad?' I turn to my mother, who has been standing pale and silent all this time. 'Mum?'

'It was a . . . a skiing accident, you know that,' she begins, hesitantly, then stops at a glance from Dad. 'Sweetheart, why don't you do as your father says? You're overwrought. You're not yourself. Look, we don't have to do this now. We can talk about . . . about Rachel later. When the wall's been cleaned.'

'Fuck the wall,' I say, and my parents look shocked.

Dominic's arm tightens about my waist. 'Catherine,' he says, his tone gentle but warning. 'I'm sure your parents only want what's best for you.'

'And what the hell would you know about it?' I ask him wildly. I'm sick of their lies and subterfuge. Sick of the sense of impending horror that's been hanging over me for weeks now. Ever since the mysterious arrival of the snow globe with its vile contents, and the destruction of my wedding dress. Someone did those things to me. And my money is on Rachel. 'I've had enough of this.'

I pull away from Dominic's grasp, and stumble out of the bedroom.

'Catherine?'

Ignoring my mother, I run downstairs, past the empty space on the landing where Rachel's chest had been, and down the next flight of stairs, all the way to the kitchen.

I grab my handbag from the kitchen table and let myself out the side door. I'm not really sure where I'm going, but I need to get out of the house, to get as far away from them as possible.

I realise mistily that I'm including Dominic in that 'them' now. It feels as though he's subtly crossed over to their side. Without me realising it, he has become one of my doubters and attackers. Which is insane and appalling. We only recently got married. Nonetheless, how else am I supposed to interpret the looks he and my father were exchanging up there, and the tacit way he agreed with their diagnosis?

You're overwrought.

The humiliation of that dismissal is almost too much to bear. Outside the side door, I stop and take several deep breaths, trying to calm down. They used to say that when I was a child. *Go to your room, Catherine. You're overwrought.* Like I'm a piece of iron that's been twisted out of shape.

I feel a sob in my chest and suppress it, too furious even to cry.

It's quiet and dark in the back garden, though the city sky glows as always, an eerie orange-black. I feel my way along the wall, glancing back once. The magnolia is a vast shape in the centre of the small garden, far too large for its space, spiralling out with stark, winter limbs to the red-brick walls on either side. On summer nights I've often lain beneath the magnolia and peered up at the luminous sky through its branches.

Not tonight though. There's a crisp, chill feel to the air this close to Christmas, and my breath is steaming. The ground is hard as ice.

Passing the lit window of my father's downstairs study, I glance in and for a second think I see someone looking back at me. A wild-eyed creature, hair in a mess; gaunt-cheeked, eyebrows arched in a perpetual question.

I'm shocked and jump, but then realise the truth.

That wild thing is me.

It's hardly surprising I look so mad. I've been driven half-crazy by the way they're all treating me. Their absurd refusal to even discuss Rachel's death. If she died at all, which I'm beginning to doubt.

Now *that* sounds crazy, I think. Even to me.

Someone touches my arm, and I cry out, backing against the wall instinctively, hands out, ready to defend myself.

'Hey, calm down. It's me.'

'Oh God, Dominic.' I clasp my chest and glare at him. He looms large in the darkness, almost menacing. 'You startled me.'

'Sorry.'

'Why did you come after me?'

He's out of breath, his cheeks slightly flushed. His gaze meets mine. 'Because I love you. Or had you forgotten that?'

'If you love me so much, why let my dad talk about me like that? As if I wasn't there?' I mimic my dad's voice. '*Take your wife downstairs.*'

'I know, he's a dinosaur.'

'Then why not say so? Why not stick up for me?'

'I'm sorry if you felt unsupported. It wasn't deliberate.' He grimaces. 'The way you were biting everyone's head off . . . I was just trying to keep the peace.' When my chin wobbles, he groans. 'Hey, come here. Let me give you a hug.'

I didn't realise until this moment how much Dominic's apparent side-taking had distressed me. To have him come after me, apologising, offering me a hug, fills my heart with love for him.

It also pushes me over the edge into tears.

'Darling,' I say brokenly, and he holds out his arms.

'Come on.' He hugs me, his face nuzzling against my throat. 'It's bloody freezing out here. Let's go and grab something to eat.'

'I'm not going back inside.'

'Of course not. I wouldn't dream of asking you to. You've had a shock and the last thing you need is to be patronised by those two.' Both our coats are draped over his arm. He must have grabbed them on his way out. He helps me into mine, then pulls on his own jacket and pats his pockets. 'Good, I've got my wallet. How about some pizza? Sit-in, not takeaway. That Italian place down the road.'

'With the striped awning?'

He nods, and then glances at my face. 'Shit.' He takes my hand and kisses it, an old-fashioned gesture that nearly makes me cry again. 'Hey, please, no more tears. I can't bear to see you cry. Did you think I'd let you go off on your own and not come after you?'

'It crossed my mind.'

'Poor love.' He rubs the back of my hand against his cheek, which is scratchy with stubble. 'You scarpered like a hare. I didn't know you could move that quickly.'

I laugh shakily. 'Good to know I can still surprise you.'

'I would have come after you sooner,' he says, and tucks my arm under his as he leads me down the path to the front of the house, 'only I stopped to give Robert a piece of my mind.'

I stare at him sideways. 'You had words with Dad?'

'Bloody right. Speaking to my wife like that.' He grins, and glances at me wryly. 'Did you really think I wouldn't stand up to him? I told him not to be such a fool. Someone is obviously trying to scare you. He can't just dismiss it as . . . I don't know, some kind of acting-out on your part.'

'So he definitely thinks I wrote it?'

'Of course.'

'Bastard.' I hesitate, almost not daring to ask the obvious question. 'What about you? Do you think I did it? To get everybody's attention?'

'Now you're being silly.'

I close my eyes. 'I had to check. If Dad's so convinced I drew that hangman on the wall myself, I thought maybe you would be, too.'

'Well, he's either suffering from a lack of imagination . . .'

'Or?'

'Or there's something else at work here.'

'Meaning?'

We reach the street corner, which is fairly quiet now, and cross the road. The Italian restaurant at the end of the next block is lit up, a waiter standing outside having a sneaky cigarette in the cold.

Dominic stops and frowns. 'Look,' he says, 'it's not really any of my business. I've come in late to this situation. But I can see how upset you are and, all joking aside, you're my wife and I love you.'

Somehow I manage a smile. 'I love you too.'

'If you ask me though,' he continues slowly, almost thinking aloud, 'your parents are hiding something. I saw how they were when you asked them about Rachel's death, and you're right, it's clear they don't want to talk about her. Or not to you anyway.'

'But why?'

'Perhaps they're afraid of saying the wrong thing. Of not being able to control the message.'

'I don't care about any of that.'

'No.' His gaze holds mine. 'It was a long time ago and you were only a child. But Rachel was your sister, and you have a right to know how she died.'

My heart is beating erratically. 'Agreed.'

'So my advice is, write them a letter.'

'A letter?'

'Yes, why not? Take an hour to sit down and ask them in a letter what happened to Rachel. But be sure to ask them to write you a letter back, rather than talk to you about it.'

'Good God, what makes you think they'd agree to that?'

'Because a letter is less confrontational. Therapists use the technique all the time in conflict resolution, especially between close family members where emotions can run high.' He kisses me lightly on the lips. 'The idea is, your parents are more likely to agree because, in a letter, they get to control the message. Whatever the message is.'

I shiver, but nod, saying nothing.

Whatever the message is.

Chapter Twenty-Seven

The next day is my day off work. While Dominic is at the hospital in the afternoon, I go out to a café where I can be private, and write the letter.

Dear Mum and Dad,

Dominic suggested I should write you a letter to explain how I feel about what's happened recently, and things we've never discussed – like Rachel. He thinks it's easier to say in a letter something that would be hard face-to-face, and I agree. So if you want to reply to me in a letter too, that would be fine.

First though, I want you to know that I love you both, and won't ever blame you, whatever you tell me. All I want is the truth.

Here's what I already know.

Rachel died in a skiing accident when we were on holiday in Switzerland. I was twelve, she was nearly fourteen. It would have been her birthday the following week. Rachel was really excited, looking forward to it. I remember the place we stayed at, that big white hotel just outside the village, and the ski resort. And I remember waiting on my own for news after the accident, and then Dad coming to tell me Rachel had passed away.

That moment is really clear in my memory.

But my other memories of the holiday are confused and fuzzy. I'm not sure if that's because I was in shock over what happened, but it means I can't actually recall what happened to Rachel that day, or how she died, or whose fault it was – if anyone's.

I can't remember much about what happened when we got home, either. Mum, you told me that she was cremated, only I wasn't allowed to be at the funeral because I would have been too upset. Then Dad got that posting in Dubai, and it was years before anyone mentioned her name again.

But now I'm not sure if everything you told me is true. Because odd things have been happening. Things that remind me of Rachel's nasty tricks. And I don't want to be horrible about my sister when she can't defend herself, but we all know she could be really unpleasant at times. And it's somehow connected to me marrying Dominic.

First I got Rachel's old snow globe through the post, with a cow's eye in it. Then someone broke into our flat and cut my wedding dress to bits, and covered it in what looked like blood. I know I should have told you about that, and I'm sorry, but I didn't want you to get upset. The police still haven't come back to us about that. At the wedding, Jasmine told me she'd received a postcard from Rachel, with some sick message saying I was being watched. And somebody signed Rachel's name on some paperwork at the food bank, and I don't know how they managed that, but it wasn't me, I swear it. Then last night, there was the lipstick hangman on the wall. With my name on it. So it's clear this is all aimed at me.

I know it makes no sense to believe Rachel could be behind this, because she passed away over ten years ago. But not knowing for sure is driving me mad. So can you please tell me – very clearly and in as much detail as possible – what happened that day in Switzerland? That would put my mind at rest.

I'm sorry, I know this must be really distressing. Rachel was your daughter. But she was my big sister too and, despite everything, I loved her. So I want to know what happened to her, even if it turns out it was somehow my fault that Rachel died. Because that's the only reason I can think why you would try to stop me talking about it.

Anyway, Dominic says I don't open up enough, that I bottle stuff up and it makes me ill. So this is me, opening up.

With all my love
Catherine

After that I leave the café. It's so cold outside, I pull up the collar of my coat, wishing I'd brought a scarf. The sky is grey and leaden again. But the shopfronts look gorgeous, all lit up for Christmas with flashing baubles and tinsel garlands, window edges white with spray-on snow, carols playing as I pass the open doorways.

I go back to Mum and Dad's house, feeling as if a weight has been lifted. Dominic was right to tell me to write the letter. It was absolutely the right thing to do.

To my surprise, the front door is ajar.

I go in and stop a moment, listening. The house is quiet, except for some rustling further down the hallway.

'Hello?' I say.

There's a sudden silence.

The passage is dimly lit, but there could be somebody there. Is that a shadow moving, or is it my imagination?

'Hello?' I repeat more loudly, my back to the front door.

Kasia appears in the kitchen doorway, a dripping mop in her hand. A strong smell of bleach wafts down the hall. She stares at me, clearly impatient. 'Yes?'

'Where is everyone?'

The cleaner shrugs, a slight flush of exertion in her sallow cheeks. 'Your father . . . he goes to the office. I think your mother goes Christmas shopping.' She glances down at the trail of drips left by her mop, her expression distracted. 'I clean the floor.'

She's wearing make-up again, I notice. Black kohl eyeliner, mascara, dark-green eyeshadow. As I recall, she never used to wear make-up to work. Now I rarely see her without it.

I remember the tension I've sensed between her and Mum since moving back in. I thought it was over me, that the presence of two more people in the house had laid unwanted extra duties on Kasia. But perhaps there's another reason. A more sinister reason.

'When did my dad go out?' I ask.

Kasia shrugs, still studying the wet floor. 'Five minutes? Ten? You just miss him.'

Her lipstick is smudged and her hair tousled. The top three buttons of her white blouse are undone. Her short skirt looks remarkably unsuited to housework.

I've seen my dad looking at her covertly.

No . . . impossible.

Dad wouldn't be unfaithful to Mum. Not in a million years.

Or would he?

Kasia's married, too. Or has small kids, at any rate. She could be divorced, I suppose. I realise with a shock that I don't actually know much about Kasia Lecinska. Except that her Polish surname is pronounced 'let-chin-scar' and she didn't like me moving back in here with Dominic. That last is just instinct on my part, of course. A chilly atmosphere whenever I walk into a room where she's working.

But perhaps Kasia wishes we weren't here at all. Perhaps there used to be less chance of being disturbed while my mother was out of the house . . .

That bright-red lipstick.

Everything inside me comes to a boil.

'Did you do it, Kasia? Last night. The writing on the wall.' I study her suddenly startled face. 'Was it you?'

Chapter Twenty-Eight

Kasia is instantly on the defensive. 'I don't know what . . . what it means,' she says warily, her accent thickening.

'I think you know perfectly well what I'm talking about. Someone wrote my name on my bedroom wall last night. Along with a hangman's noose. You understand what a noose is?'

I demonstrate with a quick-jerk gesture of being hanged, and she gazes back at me in horror.

'Oh, for God's sake.' I fumble in my coat pocket and drag out the offending lipstick, a smooth black tube. When we got home last night, I found my mother had closed it and left it on my dressing table. Pulling off the lid, I screw it up to show her the mashed stump of scarlet lipstick. Or what's left of it. 'With this. See?'

Kasia looks at it, her brows contracting. 'Lipstick?' She sounds perplexed. 'On the wall?'

'A sick joke.'

'Yes.'

'You did it.'

Her eyes widen, then she understands. 'No.'

'Who else could have done it?'

'I don't know.' She backs towards the kitchen door again, staring at me, the wet mop banging against her leg. 'I clean the floor. Your mother asks me.'

And with that, she's gone.

I'm half tempted to follow her into the kitchen, but don't. What good would it do?

I twist the lipstick down and replace the lid. The click is loud in the silence.

I don't care what my parents believe. I didn't do it.

So who did? Could it really have been Kasia?

By the time Dominic and I got back to the house last night, my parents were in bed and all the lights were off. We crept up to our bedroom, hand in hand, trying not to make too much noise. The wall above the bed was still damp, but clean of any lipstick. There was a faint reddish smear where the hangman's noose had been.

I know somebody went up to our bedroom yesterday and left that drawing on the wall for me to find. And maybe it *wasn't* Kasia. But that doesn't mean she doesn't know who did it. She could have let someone else into the house. Or failed to shut the front door, as she apparently did today, so that anyone could just walk in off the street.

As Dominic said, whoever did it wanted to frighten me.

But who? And why?

Unable to answer that, I head for my father's study instead. The door is often locked because his work at the Foreign Office sometimes involves keeping sensitive documents on the premises.

To my relief though, like the front door, his study isn't locked today.

I don't want to hand the letter over in person, that would be too embarrassing. But I'd dreaded having to leave the letter somewhere more public like the kitchen, for instance. Even if I know Kasia would never dare to open and read it, the very fact that I'm writing to my parents when we live under the same roof must seem strange. Especially after my accusation just now.

I hate people knowing my business. My dad calls it being 'secretive'. But if so, I got it from him. As a diplomat, he often has to be secretive.

I've never understood why being secretive is a strength for him, but a weakness for me.

Double standards.

In my dad's study, the full-length curtains are still closed, the lights off. I guess he didn't come in here before leaving for the office today, or not for long. I love this room, always have. It feels so snug. The walls are insulated with floor-to-ceiling bookshelves, several shelves of rare calf-bound volumes from the seventeenth and eighteenth centuries housed in a glass-fronted cabinet. A few early editions of Milton's *Paradise Lost* are among his collection.

I don't bother putting on the lights. There's enough daylight creeping in around the curtain edges to navigate my way across the room to his large, leather-topped desk.

I pull the letter out of my handbag, and smooth it out. I've sealed it inside a plain white envelope, and written *Mum and Dad* on the front.

It seems ridiculously formal.

But Dominic's right; this is the least painful way to get answers. Assuming they reply and don't just ignore my letter.

There's a photo frame on his desk. It's a photograph I don't remember seeing before. A holiday snap of Mum on some windswept beach when she was much younger. A baby in a swimsuit is squirming on her hip. Is it me or Rachel? It's hard to tell, the baby's face is hidden under a pink sun hat and those chubby legs could belong to either of us.

I lean the envelope upright against the photo frame where Dad can't fail to see it. There's a creaking noise in the hallway and I turn my head.

The study door is ajar.

'Hello?' I say.

There's someone outside the door, I'm sure of it. No sound, but I can feel a change in atmosphere. A sense of someone standing there and listening. Breathing quietly.

I frown, straightening. 'Kasia? Is that you?'

No answer. But the light levels in the room flicker, then steady again, as if someone has just slipped soundlessly past the door, blocking out the light for a second.

I stiffen and stare at the partly open door, holding my breath.

Is someone else in the house?

Chapter Twenty-Nine

I go to the door and open it, jerking it back. 'Who's there?'

The passageway is empty.

I stare up and down it, then lean forward to peer up the staircase. Nothing.

'Bloody hell.' I start to turn away, then realise I've missed something. The cellar door.

It's usually shut, but today it's open. Not fully open, but a crack . . . Like someone went down there to retrieve something – a bottle of wine, some china or linen – and forgot to shut it afterwards.

Hesitantly, I go to shut it, and hear something from below. Just the faintest echo of a cry from the dark pit of the cellar. Like a hungry baby, starting to whine.

I listen and it comes again. No, not a baby's cry. A mewing sound.

A cat?

I stand there motionless, stunned.

We don't have a cat.

Reluctantly, I open the cellar door and look down the steps to the cellar. 'Kasia?'

There's no reply. It's pitch-black down there.

I leave the door ajar and head for the kitchen. I want to find Kasia. But the kitchen is empty, and she isn't in the breakfast room either. I check the two dim and chilly pantries. No sign of her anywhere.

The side door to the back garden is locked and bolted from the inside. So Kasia does know how to use a key, I think wryly, rattling the door as I try it. But at least that means she's unlikely to be outside.

So where is she?

I didn't hear her go upstairs while I was in the study. But there was that fleeting shadow across the door . . . going in the wrong direction, I thought at the time, back towards the kitchen. But perhaps I made a mistake and it was Kasia heading upstairs with the vacuum or a basket of clean laundry. She usually checks the bedrooms are tidy, of course. Makes the beds, does a quick vacuum round, and brings down any cups or glasses left upstairs. But normally that gets done first thing, shortly after she arrives.

I leave the kitchen and go back along the hallway to the partly open cellar door.

I can hear mewing again, louder now, more desperate.

'Hello?' I say loudly. 'Is anyone down there?'

I put a foot on the creaky old stairs down into the cellar, then stop, holding my breath as the mewing continues. If it is a cat, it's sounding more and more distressed.

I grope in darkness for the light switch, but fail to find it.

Shit.

I click my fingers and purse my lips, making a beckoning noise instead. 'Pussy cat? Here, pussy . . .'

There's a brief silence, then the mewing starts again. Only this time it's more high-pitched. I can hear what sounds like thin, scratching noises, too. As though the poor defenceless thing is trapped somewhere down there, and is terrified.

My hands are trembling. 'No,' I say, shaking my head.

I can't bear this torment much longer. The air of the cellar is so cold, it's almost like being outside. My palms are clammy, my heart thudding. I clap my hands over my ears, but the mewing is somehow still there, echoing inside my head.

I fight off dark memories, but they won't stop coming. I'm remembering the last time I heard a cat make a sound like that. The day Rachel caught a kitten in our shed and tortured it to death in front of me, taking pleasure in its helplessness.

I did nothing to stop her that day. I felt just as helpless in the face of my sister's viciousness and mania. She was older than me and stronger.

But I'm not a child anymore.

And Rachel is dead.

Is Kasia behind this cruelty? Why is she doing it?

'Leave that cat alone!' I shout down into the darkness, and slam my hand against the wall inside, so hard it dislodges some of the crumbling plaster. 'Stop it, you bitch! Can't you see you're hurting her?'

Abruptly, the mewing stops.

I lean forward with a kind of angry roar, groping for the light switch and snapping it on. The bulb is unshaded and right beside the stairs, blinding me . . .

I overbalance, miss my footing and fall.

My arm flails out, clutching for the wooden banister, but it's too old and smooth. I slither down several steps before cracking my head on the rough cellar wall and landing in an awkward heap at the bottom, my right ankle twisted painfully beneath me.

'Shit, fuck.'

Swearing under my breath, I scramble back to my feet and hop forward a few steps, wincing in agony the whole way, unable to put much weight on my hurt ankle. I shouldn't be trying to move at all. But I'm not hanging around like an idiot at the bottom of the stairs. I've got no idea who else is down here. Or what else they've got planned for me.

My head hurts badly, my eyesight is muzzy. I can see dusty boxes, and a storage chest and shelves, and rack upon rack of wine bottles all the way to the back wall. There's only one light bulb though, up at the top of the stairs. It's still swaying where I knocked into it as I tumbled. I stand in that dark, cramped space as the bare bulb swings back and forth, the long shadows rising and falling.

I try the double switches at the bottom of the stairs, but the light at the top snaps off, plunging the cellar into darkness, and I hurriedly switch it back on. There should be another bulb down here. Is it missing? I peer up at the empty fitting hanging above my head. Somebody has taken out the bulb.

Shakily, I look into the darkness and purse my lips again, making a soft beckoning noise. 'Pussy? Puss-puss?'

But the panicked mewing has stopped.

It's so cold in the cellar, my breath is making little clouds. The air is damp, too. I can see mould and dark stains near the base of the wall in front of me. Rising damp. The cellar is a great place for storing wine, but not so wonderful for human beings.

I hop on a little way further, and look about for the cat, moving boxes and checking behind an ancient Welsh dresser full of unwanted china.

Just in case.

There's no cat, of course. There probably never was a cat. But there is a grimy old filing cabinet. With one drawer open, files and papers spilling out onto the dirty floor.

I lean on the dresser and stare at the mess of files on the concrete. The floor is dusty, but the files look pristine. As if they were dropped here recently. Perhaps even in the last few minutes . . .

There's a sound behind me. I turn clumsily and too late.

The light switch clicks off, and the cellar is enveloped in velvety blackness, only a faint glimmer at the top of the stairs.

My breath goes out of my lungs in one blind moment of panic. I back away, my instinct to hide behind the dresser, and nearly fall again in the darkness, coming up against the cold, damp wall. I gasp, tearing at the air, then can't seem to stop gasping. It feels like I'm being suffocated, as if there's a weight on my chest, stopping me from breathing. My hands are shaking too, stretched out in front of me to ward off some unseen attacker.

Then I hear it.

Someone is running lightly up the stairs.

The cellar door slams shut at the top, and I hear the key turn in the lock.

Shit.

I've just been locked in the cellar.

My first instinct is to run up the stairs and thump on the door, demand to be let out. I don't move though. My ankle is not up to running anywhere, and it feels safer to stay where I am for now, listening hard, trying not to lose control.

Someone *was* down here.

Someone who managed to entice me into the cellar by making those scared mewing noises, pretending to be a trapped cat. But whoever it was has gone now, and I'm alone in the pitch-black, my heartbeat loud in the silence.

I swallow down sickness at my own stupidity.

Groping along the wall, I make my way slowly, limping and hopping, back to the bottom of the stairs. My ankle is so bloody painful, I have to bite my lip to avoid crying out. Finally, my searching fingers touch something cold and flat and plastic.

The light switch.

I click it down and the bulb at the top of the stairs comes back on, light flooding the cellar again.

'Kasia?' I raise my voice. 'Kasia, this isn't funny.'

I wait, but the door at the top of the stairs remains firmly shut. Fury makes me almost hysterical.

'You come back here right now!'

I'm crying, I realise, and wipe my face with the back of my hand. Blood.

Chapter Thirty

I stare down at the blood in shock. A bright streak of red along my knuckles. I check gingerly, using only fingertips, and discover more blood. Thicker, darker red, trickling down my forehead from my hairline.

I must have cut my head when I fell down the stairs.

How bad is it?

I feel gently around the edge of the wound. It's not a deep gash, thank goodness, but deep enough to be bleeding quite heavily. And I did give my head one hell of a whack against the wall, I remember now.

'Kasia?' I glare up at the shut door. 'I'm not joking. Unlock the door.'

There's no answer.

Perhaps she can't hear me, I tell myself, and lean against the wall for a moment to take the weight off my ankle.

It has to be Kasia who tricked me, then turned off the light and ran away. I have no idea why she would do it, but she's the only other person in the house.

A shiver runs through me, and not simply because the cellar is so cold. I feel sick and light-headed. My hands are shaking. It's all too much. I thought it was fear at first, but this is a natural physical response to falling down stairs and hitting my head on the wall.

I'm not just bleeding, I could be concussed. And somebody has locked me in the cellar.

I don't have a phone – it's still in my bag, which is on Dad's desk – so I can't ring for help. I don't know the exact time. But it must be early afternoon. If Kasia doesn't come, I'll have to wait for someone else. How long will Mum spend Christmas shopping? Is Dominic finishing at two or eight today? Sometimes he works extra hours when they're short-handed. Dad could return at any moment, but it's rare for him to come back early once he's made the effort to head into the office rather than working from home.

So this is a waiting game.

I'm shivering more violently now. A combination of shock and this cold atmosphere. Huddling on the bottom step while I wait for help is an appealing thought. But it's also dangerously seductive. I can't let myself sink into torpor, I decide, and limp back towards the filing cabinet instead. If Dominic was here, he would say I need to keep moving, keep awake, occupy my mind with something . . .

My father's files, I think, picking one of the documents up to study it.

What was Kasia doing, messing about with them?

The top sheets are typewritten, full of impenetrable legalese and dense small print. Some look quite old. One dates back over ten years.

I begin stuffing them back into the manila folder, not really paying much attention to their content. Foreign Office documents, probably. Not top secret, I'm sure, but privileged information.

There's a slim black notebook with the papers. Dusty now, from the floor. I pick it up, wipe it off and flick idly through its densely handwritten pages. Then stop, my chest suddenly ice-cold with dread.

A familiar name has caught my eye.

Rachel.

I scan the page. Some kind of report about a hospital stay, with personal observations. I don't understand all of it. But no doubt Dominic will. There's a drugs section, with names and abbreviations that mean nothing to me. And a list of symptoms at admission. Mania, aggressive behaviour, spitting, hearing voices . . .

Psychosis.

I hold the book up to the light and look through it properly, checking for more references to Rachel.

Most are meaningless to me, written in some kind of shorthand. Others are simple reports, of visits from doctors or further hospital admissions. A few contain detailed information about Rachel's condition. Much of what is in the reports goes over my head, but it's clear Rachel had some serious mental health issues.

No surprise there.

But what makes me suck in a breath is that two of the handwritten reports near the back of the book are dated after our skiing holiday in Switzerland. Not long after, but the following spring.

After Rachel's death.

How is that possible?

There's a noise from upstairs. Someone in the hallway, a deep male voice calling, 'Hello? Anyone in?'

'Down here,' I shout. 'In the cellar. I need help.'

Reluctantly shutting the black notebook, I push it into my waistband at the back of my jeans and cover it with my top. Then I hop as quickly as possible to the bottom of the stairs, grimacing at the spikes of pain shooting through my ankle. Though the throbbing in my head is beginning to match it as I stare up at the naked bulb. There's a misty halo around the light that I can't seem to shake by blinking.

Double vision? And a cracking headache? I may have a concussion. I feel a trickle down my forehead, too. My wound appears to be bleeding again.

'Hello?' I call up again, even louder, though raising my voice makes the jagged ache in my head even worse.

Someone rattles the cellar door. Several times, unsuccessfully.

'I've been locked in. You need to—'

Then I hear the key being turned, and the door opens. I stare up, shielding my eyes against the light.

'Oh, thank God.'

'You all right down there?' A woman in a black uniform peers down at me. She seems vaguely familiar. 'Hello, is that Catherine?'

I clutch onto the wooden banister, staring up at her, unable to answer. I feel sick.

'What's happened here? God, that looks nasty. Banged your head, did you?' When I nod, putting a hand to my bloodied forehead, she turns to the man beside her. 'I think you'd better call an ambulance, Constable.'

It's the police.

Chapter Thirty-One

They came to see me about the wedding dress, Pauline explains as we wait in the living room for the ambulance.

'We've only just had the lab report back,' she says, trying to make me comfortable in a straight-backed leather armchair. 'I know, I'm sorry about the delay.' She makes a face. 'Cuts, what can I tell you? And it wasn't high priority, I'm afraid. Your husband gave us your new address when he contacted us last week. He was very keen to bring the investigation to a close. Again, I'm sorry it's taken so long.'

'That's okay,' I say.

I recall Pauline and Ahmed visiting the flat after the break-in, though it upset me so much to remember what happened to my lovely wedding dress, I'd tried not to think about it.

'So what did the forensics report say?'

Pauline is at the window, looking out for the ambulance, so Ahmed replies. 'Pig's blood. No other DNA. Whoever did it used gloves, I expect.' He shrugs. 'Without other evidence, there'll be no further action. We're putting it down as a prank.'

I feel deflated, although I'm glad it's not human blood. Still grisly, of course, but not actually murder.

But for something so horrible to be dismissed by the police as a mere prank . . .

Pauline comes back from the window and checks my head wound with careful, professional fingers. She notices my expression. 'I'm sorry. I know that must be a disappointment. But it's a good thing really. Someone messing you about, that's all. Nothing more sinister. Destruction of property, of course. Breaking and entering too. But without further evidence . . .' She smiles at me encouragingly. 'Feeling better?'

'Much, thank you.'

'How did you get locked in the cellar, anyway?'

I hesitate.

I don't know whether to tell them about Kasia or wait to speak to my parents first. Another prank, perhaps. And it's possible Kasia didn't realise I was hurt.

It's also possible it wasn't her.

I don't want to start accusing people of things they didn't do. Everyone is already so overprotective of me, I don't want to give them any reason to think I'm not coping. Besides, the idea that anyone would have done this deliberately is absurd.

'I thought I heard a cat . . . then I lost my footing.' I manage a smile, though it's hardly convincing. Not that they'll be surprised by that. The double vision has abated since they helped me hop up the cellar stairs laboriously, but I'm still in pain and the dizziness has returned. 'The cleaner must have seen the door open and locked it. A stupid accident. That's all.'

'Right.' Pauline studies me thoughtfully. 'And where is this cleaner now?'

'Kasia?' Uneasy under her searching gaze, I look away. 'I'm not sure. I shouted for her, but she didn't seem to hear me.'

'And your parents?'

'Out.'

Ahmed has been glancing through his notebook, but stirs at this, instantly helpful and smiling. 'You want me to give them a ring? Let them know you're hurt?'

'No, I'll be fine.'

The constable nods, though I can see he's curious. He glances about the room, taking in the elegance of his surroundings. 'Perhaps your husband then.' He checks his notebook. 'Dominic.'

I say nothing, feeling dizzy.

'Have a sip of this, you don't look so good.' Pauline hands me the glass of water she sent Ahmed to fetch and which I haven't touched yet. 'I think we should call him, don't you?'

'I didn't even know Dominic had been in touch with you.'

'Well, there you go. Keeping secrets already.' She smiles, as though to show that she's only joking. But I don't find it very amusing. 'How's your head?'

'Still throbbing.'

Ahmed glances past her out of the window. 'Here's the ambulance now.' He heads for the door. 'I'll let them know where we are.'

At that moment, there's a commotion at the door.

It's my mother, home from her shopping expedition. I hear her voice, high-pitched and worried, thrown by the unexpected discovery of a policeman in her house. 'What on earth . . . ? What's happened? Has there been a burglary?'

I struggle to stand up. 'My mum—'

'No, don't try to move,' Pauline tells me, before hurrying out into the hall to explain to my mother what's happened.

I'm alone at last.

Swiftly, I take the notebook out from the waistband of my jeans. There aren't many good hiding places I can easily reach with a swollen ankle, but I've had twenty minutes to consider what to do.

Leaning as far over from the armchair as I can without overbalancing, I slide the notebook under the glass-fronted cabinet behind me.

I catch the base of the glass door by accident, and the display of cut-glass crystal and china inside rattles. But the notebook disappears underneath the cabinet, and a few seconds later I'm sitting upright in the armchair again, as if nothing has happened.

At that instant, the door is pushed wide open and my mother stumbles in, breathless and unhappy, carrying four heavy bags of Christmas shopping in both hands, her smart Gucci leather handbag in the crook of her arm.

She's been to Harrods and Harvey Nicks, I realise, noting the logos on the gift bags. That kind of shopping expedition would normally leave her smiling and sated. But her eyes are wild, looking down at me in horror.

'Oh my God, darling. What on earth have you done to yourself?' She dumps her bags and bends over me, clucking with her tongue. She was always very capable with minor injuries when I was a kid. But she seems bewildered and a little lost for what to do. This is something a sticking plaster and some antiseptic cream won't fix, I guess.

'We did offer to call you,' Pauline says.

Traitor, I think, flashing the policewoman a sharp look.

'You should have done. You should have called me. Oh, your poor head.' My mother touches the gash on my forehead. 'The police officer says you fell down the cellar stairs. How in God's name . . . ?'

I decide not to go through it again. Not with Pauline listening. 'It's nothing serious, probably just a sprained ankle,' I start to say, trying to sound calm about it all, but Pauline interrupts.

'Concussion may be a possibility,' she says, correcting me. 'Catherine gave her head quite a nasty bash, as you can see. But the bleeding's stopped now, which is a good sign.'

My mother stares at her. 'So she called you? The police?'

'We were here about another matter. It was lucky we found her. She could have been stuck down there for hours.' Pauline smiles, and holds out her hand. 'I'm Pauline and this is Ahmed. May I ask your name?'

'Ellen,' Mum says warily, and they shake hands. 'Ellen Bates. What other matter?'

'It's not important,' I tell her.

She'll find out soon enough about the wedding dress, when Dad reads the letter I've left in his study.

To my relief, Pauline ignores the question. 'Don't you worry, we're whisking your daughter off to hospital to be checked over. Soon be right as rain.'

Just as she says this, two paramedics in green uniforms appear in the doorway – a middle-aged man and a young, freckle-faced woman.

'Where's Kasia?' my mother asks, standing back to let them pass. 'Why isn't she here? She should be here.'

'I don't know,' I say.

'Hello, Catherine,' the young paramedic says with a friendly smile. 'I'm Frieda and this is Medhi.' She puts her green emergency kit down beside the armchair and snaps on a pair of latex gloves. 'Hurt your ankle too, did you?'

'Yes.'

The police had already taken my trainer and sock off my right foot, so she sets to work examining the swollen ankle, her fingers cold through the latex, pressing gently.

'Yes, it's sprained, I'd say. Not too badly though, to judge by the amount of swelling. A cool-pack and a few hours' elevation should see that right. Your head's another matter. We'll need to take you into A & E for that, okay? Get you checked over by a doctor.'

I am just agreeing reluctantly when there are footsteps on the stairs, quick and light. Suddenly Kasia is there in the doorway. Her hair is messy and her cheeks look a little flushed, like she's been sleeping.

'There you are,' my mother exclaims, sounding almost angry, which surprises me.

Kasia stares in at us, her expression shocked.

'Wh-what's going on?' She looks at the police uniforms in horror, then spots me in the armchair, my swollen ankle resting on a footstool, the paramedic strapping on some kind of cold compress. 'Catherine?'

Her gaze lifts to my mother's face, and I see guilt there at last. 'Was there accident?'

My mother's face is cold. 'Where have you been?'

'Upstairs.'

'And you didn't hear anything?'

Kasia glances at the police, then shakes her head. 'I'm so sorry, Mrs Bates. I was . . . I was . . .'

'Were you asleep?'

The cleaner bites her lip deeply, looking ashamed. 'Just a little sleep. Half-hour in the guest bedroom. I was up all night with my little one.' She taps her mouth. 'Teething.'

'Well, you're here now.' My mother's face is stiff with outrage. 'You'd better make yourself useful. Call my husband. Let him know what's happened and tell him to ring me later. I'm going to the hospital with Catherine.'

Kasia blinks. 'Call . . . ?'

'His mobile.' My mother adds impatiently. 'The number is on the wall by the kitchen phone. Really, Kasia. Wake up.'

'Yes, Mrs Bates.'

She disappears.

Frieda, the paramedic, smiles up at me as she finishes strapping my ankle. 'Right, that should reduce the swelling. Ready for a ride in an ambulance?'

Chapter Thirty-Two

Shortly after my arrival at St Hilda's, being pushed into A & E in a wheelchair as though I'm an invalid, Dominic appears at my bedside, out of breath, as though he's run all the way from the staffroom.

'Catherine, are you okay? Sally told me you'd been brought in with a head wound. What the hell happened?' While my mother explains, he snaps on a fresh pair of latex gloves and tilts my head sideways with professional care. If he's horrified by her story, Dominic doesn't show it, soon calming down and even winking at me when he hears the part about the cat. 'Well, the good news is, this cut isn't as serious as it looks. No stitches required. The bad news is, I think my wife may be crazy.'

'That's not funny,' I say crossly. 'I wasn't imagining it. I definitely heard mewing.'

He dabs the wound gently. 'Maybe a neighbour's cat got in.'

'That doesn't explain the light turning off, and me getting locked in,' I say hotly. 'Dom, someone else was down there.'

'Who?'

I hesitate. 'I didn't see exactly. But I heard footsteps.'

'It sounds like a mistake of some kind.' He frowns, concentrating on what he's doing. 'An accident, I'm sure.'

'Seriously?' I lower my voice. 'After everything that's happened lately, you don't find this a little bit suspicious?'

His eyes flick to mine, then he reaches for some bandaging. 'You're worrying your mum,' he says softly.

I glance over his shoulder at my mother's pale face, and relent.

'Okay, maybe it was a . . . an accident.' I'm suddenly glad he's the one taking care of me. I'm not very keen on hospitals. Not when I'm the patient, anyway. 'I was convinced I heard a cat though. I feel like such an idiot.'

He grins.

As soon as my mother excuses herself to ring my dad, I ask Dominic to close the cubicle curtains, and tell him what the police said about the wedding dress.

'Pig's blood?' he repeats blankly, then shrugs. 'No wonder they're not interested in pursuing it. But I'd love to know who was responsible for ruining your dress. Some sick bastard who deserves a punch in the face.'

I shudder. 'Please, let's just forget about it.'

'Sure, if you want.' Dominic bends and kisses me on the lips. 'I was frantic when Sally told me you were in A & E,' he murmurs. 'You've got to take better care of yourself, Mrs Whitely. You hear me?'

'Miss Bates,' I remind him. 'And don't you forget it.'

'You stubborn feminist,' he says, and laughs when I poke my tongue out at him.

The curtain rattles, and he straightens.

Mum comes back in, looking flustered, her hair blown about by the wind. 'I couldn't get hold of Robert. He's not answering his phone. I left a message instead.' She sighs. 'I'll stay with you though. I just hope it doesn't take forever.'

Dominic stays with me and Mum while I'm examined by one of the duty doctors. I am checked for signs of concussion, and an X-ray is taken of my swollen ankle, which reveals no broken bones. As he thought, the gash on my forehead is not deemed serious enough to need stitches, but it is thoroughly cleaned and covered with a large plaster, padded with cotton wool. After a few hours I am given the all-clear and Dominic is granted permission to take me home himself.

'Early clock-off today,' Dominic says cheerfully, helping me out of the wheelchair. During our long wait, he's managed to wrangle a pair of crutches for me. 'Ever used these, darling?'

I shake my head.

'Come on, one under each arm.'

Once I'm steady on the crutches, Dominic helps me out to the taxi rank. His manager, Sally Weston, who's been hanging around the cubicle too, insists on coming to see us off. I get the feeling she's curious about me.

It's already dark outside. There's a Christmas tree outside the hospital's main entrance, strung with lights and baubles that wink and sway. The night air is cold, with a bitter, gusting wind that leaves me shivering.

'Don't forget concussion can still develop several days after a bang on the head. Watch out for any headache, dizziness, nausea . . .' Sally begins to recite the list of symptoms, then grins at Dominic's expression. 'Sorry, Dom. You know what to look for, of course.' She opens the back door of the waiting taxi for us. 'Good to see you again, Catherine. Take care, both of you. We should go for drinks sometime.'

'Sure,' Dominic tells her smoothly.

Mum has come after us, hunched in her coat and fussing about me. But she's not really needed with Dominic there, and she knows it.

'I'm sorry,' I tell him.

Dominic helps me hop into the back of the black cab, while Mum sits on one of the pull-down seats. 'What on earth are you apologising for? You fell down a flight of stairs, you great softie.' He puts the crutches on the floor. 'This is hardly self-inflicted.'

I can tell from Mum's briefly raised eyebrows that she does not agree. But she sees me looking and smiles. 'Are you okay, darling?'

'I'm fine.'

'You know what? I'm going to invite Jasmine to stay over Christmas.' Mum shifts her feet to one side as Dominic climbs in beside me. There's a firm note in her voice, as if everything is already decided and there's no point even arguing about it. 'I discussed it with your dad on the phone while you were in Radiography, and he agrees it's a good idea.'

I stare at her. 'Jasmine?'

'Why not?' she demands. 'The two of you are second cousins and you don't see enough of each other. And the poor girl's on her own this Christmas because everyone else is flying off to . . . I don't know, the Caribbean or somewhere. Only she can't go because she stupidly let her passport lapse and it was too late to renew in time. Anyway, it will be lovely to have her for Christmas, and I've already been on the phone to her mother too. Barbara is ecstatic about the idea.'

Barbara is Jasmine's mum, and one of Mum's first cousins. I glance at Dominic, who shrugs and looks away, a wry smile on his face.

'But where will she stay?' I ask.

'The guest bedroom, of course. I'll get Kasia to give it a quick tidy-out. Oh, darling, it will be lovely for you. You're off over Christmas, aren't you?'

There's a slight strain behind the question. I know she hates me volunteering at the food bank.

'Yes, I was meant to finish the day after tomorrow. Back again the day after Boxing Day.' I make a face, touching the padded plaster on my forehead. 'Assuming I'm fit. I must look a mess. And I doubt they'll want me hopping about on crutches.'

'You won't need crutches for more than a day or two,' Dominic reassures me.

'The doctor said it was a bad sprain.'

'It looks worse than it is. The swelling will go down quite rapidly, you'll see.'

I'm not sure I believe him, given how painful my ankle is right now. But I say nothing. Besides, I've got other things to worry about. Like Jasmine coming to visit.

I like Jasmine, but I'm uncomfortable now, and not simply because of the pain in my ankle. Just the mention of my cousin is a reminder of what she told me at the wedding. Of the unsettling postcard she received, supposedly from Rachel.

'I'll have to ring Sharon tonight,' I say, trying to distract myself. 'Let her know what's happened. That I can't work until after the holidays.'

'It's okay, let me do it,' Dominic says at once, and turns on his phone. The screen lights up the indulgent look on his face. 'I think I've got her number in my contacts list.'

'Thank you,' I say softly.

He gives me a sideways smile, then focuses on the phone screen.

I sit back and close my eyes, trying not to worry too much. I love how protective he's being with me. It's like he senses I'm nervous about Jasmine's visit, and wants to reassure me. I only hope his love will be enough to keep me sane, when everything else in my life seems to be falling apart with alarming speed.

When we get home, Dad is waiting for us in the brightly lit porch while Dominic supports me over the threshold. Seeing him reminds me of the letter waiting in his study. Has he found it already? Has he read it?

There's no sign of Kasia, I realise, looking past him into the empty hallway. But it's getting late. She must have left to be with her kids. I'm glad. And not just because I'm still a little suspicious she deliberately locked me in the cellar. I don't like the thought of her and Dad being home alone together for so long. The horrible idea that they're having an affair has got hold of me now, and I can't seem to shake it, even though I'm sure it can't be true. All the same, I avoid his gaze.

It ought to be a relief to be home.

But it isn't.

Quite the opposite, in fact. I find myself shivering again, even though the hall feels suffocatingly warm after the cold night air.

'Good grief, girl, what on earth have you done?' is my father's opening question, staring at my crutches in disbelief. 'I got your mother's message. What were you doing poking around in the cellar?'

'She took a tumble, that's all,' Dominic tells him coolly, and then gives him an even more truncated account of my misadventure than the one Mum told my father in the hospital.

To my surprise, Dad doesn't lay into me for my clumsiness but merely watches in silence as Dominic helps me hobble up the stairs. I half expect Mum to follow, but she disappears into the kitchen instead. To mix herself a stiff gin and tonic, probably. She hates hospitals even more than I do.

Dad follows her, vanishing before we're even at the top of the stairs. Perhaps he wants a drink, too. A drink and a proper explanation.

'Bloody hell,' I whisper in Dominic's ear, 'I think Dad's scared of you.'

'It's the scrubs,' he whispers back.

Briefly, I consider asking Dominic his opinion of Kasia, and whether she may have set her sights on my dad. But I dread his answer. What if he agrees with my suspicions? Worse, what if he admits to finding Kasia attractive himself?

I don't think I could bear to hear that. I'm not feeling strong enough.

Not tonight.

'Home sweet home,' he mutters when we reach our suite of rooms at the top of the house. I throw myself down on the bed, and he lands beside me, careful not to hurt my bandaged ankle.

Nasty little memories keep slipping back into my mind – the eyeball in the snow globe, Jasmine's cryptic postcard, the forms at the food bank signed *Rachel*, the unseen figure who locked me in the cellar – but I push them away with as much force as I can muster.

'What are you thinking?' he asks softly.

'Nothing.'

We look at each other. Our lips meet, and his tongue slips into my mouth, exploring gently. Then his hand strokes over the curve of my hip, pulling me into him. I can feel he's interested in taking it further. Here and now. Whether or not I'm in pain.

'The doctor said I should get some rest,' I point out after a few minutes, by which time he is already breathless.

'No problem,' he murmurs, and pulls down the strap on my top, bending to kiss my exposed breast. 'You lie there, take it easy. I'll do the hard work of undressing you.'

'But my parents . . .'

'Forget about them. Focus on this instead. On feeling good.' He kisses my mouth, demanding now. 'It was quite a turn-on to see you on that trolley in A & E. In your loose hospital gown, with some doctor bending over you.'

'Seriously?'

'No doubt about it.'

'Sicko.'

'Maybe.' He laughs, then cups my breast in its black bra. 'You're sexy when you're helpless though, did you know that?'

After we've made love, Dominic and I lie together in panting silence until our hearts have slowed and the sweat on our bodies is beginning to cool. It's dark outside the window, that pale, glowing, never-quite-black darkness of the city. I stare straight up at the ceiling, and avoid looking at the wall where my name was written.

Dominic is the first to break the silence.

'What were you really doing in the cellar?' he asks suddenly.

I don't answer, pretending to be asleep.

Chapter Thirty-Three

I decide it will be good to have Jasmine here for Christmas. It should take the spotlight off me. She's so vibrant and cheerful; it's hard not to smile whenever she's in the room. Even if everything inside is dark and silent.

But I still need to broach the subject of Rachel.

'Dad, did you get my letter?' I ask tentatively, finding him alone in the kitchen just before Jasmine is due to arrive from Birmingham.

He's got his back to me, chopping herbs for our dinner: fresh parsley and dill for a sauce to accompany the salmon. I see him stop momentarily, then he carries on chopping the parsley.

'Yes, I did.' To my relief, he sounds calm.

'And did you show Mum?'

'Yes, I did,' he repeats in the same way. 'And thank you for being so candid with us. It can't have been easy, putting that down on paper.'

'No, it wasn't easy.'

Dad turns his head and studies me, his expression unreadable. Then he says carefully, 'I take it you've confided all this to Dominic?'

'Of course.'

'I see.' He pauses. 'Jasmine will be here soon. We can't sit down and discuss Rachel with you and Dominic while she's in the house.'

'Why not?'

'What happened with Rachel is private. Our family business. It's not something we want to share with a guest.'

'But Jasmine is family.'

'Not close family,' Dad says deliberately, as though this makes a difference. 'And Christmas should be a time of peace and joy, Catherine. I'm afraid there's not much joy to be had out of discussing your sister's demise.'

And that's an end to our discussion, apparently.

When Jasmine arrives from Birmingham, carrying a suitcase and gifts, I greet her with the others, then take advantage of the commotion to slip away from the kitchen and retrieve the notebook. It's almost the first time I've been on my own since I got back from the hospital. Everyone insists on treating me like an invalid, although all I have is a cut on my temple and a sprained ankle.

Gently, I close the living room door to shut out the noise of Jasmine's welcome, and turn on the lights. The room is quiet and empty.

I lean my stick against the armchair and lower myself gingerly to look under the glass-fronted cabinet. But there's nothing there.

Someone has taken the notebook.

I stare at the space where I hid it. I can't believe it's gone.

'What the hell . . . ?'

Someone comes along the hall from the kitchen, where Jasmine is being treated to wine and cake, and I clamber to my feet, wincing at the sudden strain on my ankle.

But whoever it is keeps on going and heads slowly up the stairs. Now they are calling, 'Catherine? Where are you, darling?' It's my mother, undisguised concern in her voice. 'Jasmine has brought Christmas presents. Why don't you come and help her put them under the tree?'

I don't answer.

Hurriedly, before limping out of the room, I check all the surfaces and shelves, in case Kasia has been cleaning in here and, after finding it, put the notebook to one side to be claimed later.

But there's no sign of it.

Who took the notebook from its hiding place? And where the hell is it now?

On Christmas Eve, Dominic takes me and Jasmine out to the pub for drinks with some of his colleagues. We grab a meal first at Sushi Hiroba in Holborn, the sort of Japanese restaurant where the food goes around on a conveyor belt and you help yourself. It's busy and fun, and a good way to avoid the chaotic atmosphere at home. We left Mum and Kasia struggling to manoeuvre a gigantic turkey into the fridge, while Dad alternately stirred a vast vat of mulled wine and brought bottles up from the cellar for a drinks party they're giving tonight for their friends and a few of Dad's colleagues from the Foreign Office. We were also invited, of course, but excused ourselves.

'I doubt there'll be anyone there who's under forty,' I tell Jasmine as we lean forward to select colour-coded dishes from the revolving belt. 'But we can head back early after the pub, if you want.'

'I love your mum and dad to bits, God bless them,' Jasmine says, turning heads with her hoarse Brummie accent, 'but to be honest, this is more my scene.' She gestures to the sharply dressed young professionals around us, and raises her voice above the din of their chatter. 'I'd rather stay in the pub than go back to the house, if that's all right. Posh parties like that terrify me. What if I end up stuck next to some toffee-nosed ambassador? I wouldn't have a clue what to say.'

Dominic grins, pouring soy sauce over yellowtail sushi. 'You could always tell him about your love of stock car racing,' he suggests lightly, and she giggles.

After dinner, we take a taxi to meet his colleagues at a pub called The Ship and Shovell, near Victoria Embankment. Louise's choice, apparently, because it does good ales. We have to stand outside at a barrel table, as the pub is packed with festive drinkers.

I wish I could sit because my ankle aches. First day without the walking stick I've been using to replace the crutches that have gone back to the hospital. But I don't want to spoil the evening by mentioning it.

'You okay?' Dominic says in my ear.

'Never better,' I lie.

He examines my face. 'Back in a minute,' he says suddenly, and disappears into the pub.

His colleagues emerge a moment later. Louise is carrying a tray of drinks, and Sally has bought several bags of peanuts. I wave my hand until they spot us and head in our direction. Louise is walking awkwardly in heels that look new.

'Merry Christmas,' she says, putting the tray down. 'I hope I got everyone's order right.'

Sally dumps the bags of peanuts on the table too, and then tucks a loose strand of blonde hair behind her ear. 'Nuts, anyone?'

'Me,' Jasmine says, and helps Louise tear open the bags of peanuts for sharing.

Sally's phone rings and she turns away to answer it.

Louise watches Sally anxiously as though worried they are going to be called back to St Hilda's for some major emergency. I hope not, watching Sally, too. This is Dominic's first night off in ages. I don't know how he wrangled it but maybe he had to promise extra overtime later this week.

But Sally is laughing, her head back, chatting with whoever it is in a relaxed way. Not a work call, thank God.

'So, we didn't have much of a chance to talk before. How have you been since the wedding?' I ask Jasmine, raising my voice to be heard above the revellers and the sound of constant traffic.

'Not too bad, thanks.' She hesitates, glancing back over her shoulder at the pub. No sign of Dominic returning yet. 'By the way, about that postcard . . .'

I feel suddenly cold, and not just because of the chill December air. 'The postcard supposedly from Rachel?'

'Yeah.' She looks unhappy. 'I'm so sorry about that. I felt really bad afterwards.'

'What do you mean?'

'Mentioning something like that to you on your wedding day.' Jasmine makes a face. 'Your mum rang me later, tore a strip off me.'

I'm confused. I don't remember mentioning the postcard to Mum at the time. So how did she know about it? Dominic probably told her, I realise. He's so overprotective, always looking out for me – even when I don't need him to. They all are, in fact. It's like being suffocated in cotton wool.

'If I'd known . . . ' Jasmine says.

'Known what?'

She opens her mouth, then closes it again and shakes her head.

'Jasmine?'

'Nothing,' she says abruptly. 'Forget it.'

'No, I want to know. If you'd known what?' When she still doesn't say anything, I lean in closer, meeting her worried gaze. 'Please, Jasmine. This is important. What exactly did Mum tell you?'

'Look, I'm sorry. She asked me not to say.'

'Not to say *what?*'

I don't mean to, but I've raised my voice.

Dominic comes up behind us unnoticed and puts a bar stool down next to the barrel. 'There you go,' he says to me. 'Now you can sit down.'

'Darling, that's so thoughtful of you,' I say, and perch on the bar stool with relief. My ankle feels less painful immediately. 'That's much better, thank you.'

'You okay?'

'Fine, thanks.'

'So,' Dominic says lightly, standing opposite and glancing at us both in turn, 'I feel like I just interrupted something. Who asked you not to say what, Jasmine?' His smile is steady but it still worries me. I know what he's like when he thinks I'm hiding something from him. 'Family secrets?' he adds. 'I'm one of the family now, you know. I get to hear about all those skeletons in the closet.'

Jasmine looks at me, her eyes wide and apprehensive.

'Girl talk,' I tell him quickly.

'Hey, Dom, what do you think of this?' Sally waves him over to see something on her smartphone that she and Louise have been laughing over.

Reluctantly, he turns to his boss. 'What do I think of what?'

Jasmine mouths, 'Sorry,' to me behind his back.

I smile and take another sip of my white wine. I don't want to drink too much. I'm already a little woozy and it could be a long night. As I put the glass down again, my gaze moves to Sally. She's put the smartphone away, but is still looking at Dominic, a secret little smile on her face.

Taken aback, I flick a quick glance at Dominic, and he's looking at Sally, too.

Also smiling.

A splinter of pain enters my heart.

It's only a look, I tell myself. And indeed, a split second later Sally turns away to talk to Louise. Dominic returns to me and Jasmine, who is telling an anecdote about her mum and a pot of soft cheese, though I haven't really been listening. Dominic grins at my cousin, adding something to the story. A flippant remark that makes Jasmine burst out laughing.

I laugh too, mechanically. But I'm still only half listening, agonisingly aware of the beating of my heart, deafening to my ears.

His boss.

God, he wouldn't, surely?

We only just got bloody married. It makes no sense that he'd be playing around behind my back. Yet that look between them . . . what else could it mean?

Perhaps it's a silly thing from the past. A one-night stand with his manager that he omitted to mention, long before I came along. I can't hold something like that against him.

All the same, Dominic's my husband now. He shouldn't be looking at another woman like that – with that peculiarly intimate smile on his lips. It hurts just to remember it.

My hands curl into fists. Dominic's been so demanding in bed lately. Almost brutal at times. I've been pretending I haven't noticed the change. But I can't keep hiding from the likeliest reason for this change in behaviour: I'm not exciting enough for him.

But Sally is?

I feel sick, and have to look away, struggling to breathe normally.

'You okay?' Jasmine asks.

Now Dominic turns to look at me. Louise and Sally, too.

Louise is concerned. 'Cat, what is it?'

I fix them with my brightest smile, even though my heart feels like it's breaking. 'Nothing. It's just my ankle. You know, the odd twinge.'

'Ouch.' Louise pulls a sympathetic face. 'Poor you. And at Christmas too.' She drains her glass of ale. 'I should have given you a call when Dom told me. I feel bad about that. But it's been so hectic at work. You sure you're okay?'

'Honestly, I'm fine,' I say.

'Let me get this straight,' Jasmine says. 'You fell down the cellar steps?'

'That's right.'

Sally is watching me now. Her smile is knowing. As if she thinks I'm one of those stupid, clumsy people who spend their lives getting into one scrape after another. 'Head better now too?'

I manage a nod, remembering how friendly she was at the hospital that night, waving goodbye as the taxi pulled away. 'All sorted.'

'Kasia was telling me all about it this morning.' Jasmine looks perplexed. 'She said you thought you heard an intruder.'

'A cat.'

Her eyebrows shoot up. 'A cat? A cat in the cellar?' She frowns. 'Hold on, you don't have a cat.'

I look at Dominic.

He puts his arm round my waist, his smile warm and understanding. 'If Catherine says she heard a cat, then she heard a cat.'

Which is a very unsubtle way of saying he thinks I didn't hear any such thing, but however crazy I am he is willing to support me one hundred per cent.

A group of hatted and scarved carol singers come into view, heading towards us from the pub round the corner, where we've heard them singing for the past half an hour. They stop a few yards away and start to sing 'In the Bleak Midwinter', two of their members walking among the drinkers, rattling buckets for a charity collection. Dominic puts a few quid in the bucket for us while I listen to the beautiful lyrics in a kind of trance. I think unwillingly of Rachel and the day she died: 'Snow lay frozen, snow on snow, snow on snow . . .' Why can't I think of that day without feeling guilty? Is it because part of me was glad that my sister died, part of me wanted her dead? But how can I ever admit that to anyone?

Who would understand such a reaction? They would think I was a monster.

Chapter Thirty-Four

Dominic wanted to get a cab, but I told him I could manage the Tube. Though I hadn't realised how packed it would be this late on Christmas Eve. With most lines closing soon for the holidays, the station is so busy we have to fight our way down the platform. Dominic helps me, and I put my arm around his shoulders. Though I don't really need it. My ankle is far less painful now. But I like the way he's holding me close. Or am I holding *him* close? Making sure he doesn't stray?

Louise and Sally are just behind us, laughing and chatting with Jasmine.

'We're only going one stop, then we have to change,' Louise says to Dominic. She and Sally live near each other, so they can go back together. 'I just hope we haven't left it too late. It's nearly eleven.'

'Sorry?' Dominic can't hear her over the noisy rush of a train barrelling into the station. 'What did you say?'

There's a loud disturbance behind us and I glance back. Some kind of deep-voiced, drunken chanting. A crowd of young men are pushing their way down the platform, maybe heading home after a Christmas party, singing some festive song with alternative lyrics.

Sally looks at them contemptuously. She probably has to deal with guys like that all the time in A & E. She moves between me and the track, a little unsteady on her feet. She kept a cocktail umbrella from one of her drinks and is twirling it in her mouth like a purple flower.

'Merry Christmas,' Jasmine says, nudging me.

'Merry Christmas,' I reply automatically, aware that Dominic's arm is no longer around my waist. He is pulling Sally by the sleeve, tugging her back from the danger zone beyond the yellow line.

'Careful,' he tells her.

Sally says something, and he bends his ear close to her lips to hear it. They're both dangerously near to the edge of the platform now, their heads together, deep in conversation. A conversation I can't hear.

'I'm really sorry,' Jasmine says loudly.

I glance at my cousin. She's pretty drunk too, I realise. Her words are beginning to slur and her eyes are shining.

'What about?'

'Before,' she says, and then leans against me while she fiddles with her heel strap. I suck in my breath, the ache in my ankle gnawing as she puts too much weight on my shoulder. 'God, these heels are killing me. I should have listened to your mum and worn trainers.'

I feel the change of atmosphere as our train approaches, pushing air out of the dark tunnel, little crackles and flashes of light surrounding its approach.

The crowd is pressing so close, it feels dangerous, out of control. There's no room. No more room to move. So many people all desperate to get on the same train. It isn't easy to catch my breath, I'm being so crushed.

Someone shoves me from behind. A nasty push, right in the small of my back.

I try to look round, but can only turn so far. There's a mass of young men behind me, dressed for a night out on the town, swaying together mindlessly like plankton in an ocean current. They're all chatting and singing, looking past me without seeing me, waiting to board the train . . .

All except one man, who's clearly not with them. He's right behind me. Middle-aged, with a moustache, a grey hat, collar turned up.

He's not looking at the train like everyone else, but straight at me, with hard grey eyes that seem to pierce right through me.

Creepy.

The air is shuddering. Old newspaper is whipped up and about the platform walls as the incoming train begins to brake. The crowd shifts heavily as yet more people pour onto the already crowded platform, eager to get on board. We are all being forced towards the edge of the platform, including me and Jasmine.

'Shit,' I say, and grab at the person in front of me for balance.

It's Sally.

'Sorry.' I release her. 'People shoving me from behind . . .'

The crowd heaves forward convulsively, like a muscular spasm. It's as if I'm being swallowed. I grab at arms and shoulders, and cling on, trying to save myself from being knocked to the ground. I've lost Dominic in the chaos and I can't see Jasmine or Louise. I stumble into the person in front.

Suddenly there's a terrible cracking thud ahead of us, like a ball hitting a cricket bat, only more muffled.

I try to see over the crowd but all I can see are heads and the silver-and-red flash of the side of the train going past. Then it brakes more violently and I see passengers in the lit-up carriages being thrown forward.

A woman is screaming.

'Dom?' I shout, my voice rising in panic. 'Dominic? Where are you? Dominic?'

Jasmine pushes through the crowd towards me, saying, 'Excuse me, excuse me,' to everyone. Her expression is strained as she reaches my side. 'It's okay, I've got you,' she says, putting an arm round my waist. 'You can lean on me.'

'Jasmine, what the hell's happening? Where's Dominic?'

'No, trust me, you don't want to look.' I see the horror in her eyes as she tries to stop me pushing past. 'I think someone's gone under the train.'

Chapter Thirty-Five

My first appalled thought is that Dominic has fallen under the tube train.

But he appears behind Jasmine a few seconds later, looking as tense as she does, and I feel my heart jolt back into life.

'Dom,' I say, holding out my hand to him, and he draws me close. 'Oh God, Dom.'

'I'm here, baby.' He kisses me on the lips. 'Don't freak out, okay?'

'Jasmine says someone was hit by the train.'

'Yeah, some old guy. Poor bastard . . . he must have tripped and fallen onto the tracks, I guess.' Dominic catches me by the shoulders and holds me still, shaking his head. 'Hey, stay back. There's nothing anyone can do for him, and it's not a pleasant sight.'

There's an announcement over the loudspeaker system, but I can't seem to focus on it. The crowd is slowly beginning to disperse. I don't want to look, and turn my head the other way, shuddering. There's a hat lying on the ground a few feet from us. I stare at it in shock, then let Dominic lead me away.

The police keep us at Embankment station for ages, taking names and witness statements from those nearest the edge of the platform. I don't say much, as I didn't see anything. The platform is closed while they deal with the incident, and we all have to file out of the station to be questioned. It takes nearly an hour and it's freezing and dark outside. Once it's over, we're told the Underground is closed now until Boxing Day, so give up on that idea and cram into a taxi instead. Sally and Louise drop us off outside a Chinese takeaway near my parents' house, then head home together with contributions towards the final fare from all our pockets.

We shouldn't still be hungry after the meal we had earlier, but we are. All the booze and stress, I suppose. We grab some food at the takeaway, mercifully still open, and arrive back at the house at one in the morning. To my relief, my parents' guests have all gone and the house is in darkness, though remnants of the party are still in evidence, the dishwasher on its rinse cycle and half-empty wine glasses everywhere. In the kitchen, over a hot drink and our Chinese food, Dominic tells me and Jasmine that he saw the dead man 'fly' past him, as he puts it.

'I think maybe it was a suicide,' he decides in the end, 'not accidental. But obviously I can't be sure. There were so many people near the edge of the platform. It looked like he jumped. But maybe he was pushed and lost his footing.'

'There'll be CCTV on the platform,' I say, trying not to sound as shaken as I feel. 'The police should be able to work it out.'

Jasmine looks unconvinced. 'In that crush of people? It was so crowded, I nearly fell under the train myself. And the quality on those CCTV films isn't brilliant. I doubt they'll be able to see much.'

I help myself to some noodles, staring down at them.

'I wonder who he was,' Dominic says.

I say nothing. But my mind keeps flashing back to the only thing I saw as people dissipated in panic from that end of the platform.

The grey hat, trampled on the ground . . . no sign of its owner.

My hand shakes and I put down my fork.

It must have happened directly in front of where I was standing.

My heart feels like it's beating incredibly slowly. As if the blood in my veins has turned thick and treacly. Was it me who pushed that man onto the tracks? I remember grabbing at someone's arm in the chaos, and feeling them shift under my weight. Then I pushed hard.

Looking back, I realise I can't be sure where anyone was. Or exactly what happened. But there's this dark tide of guilt inside me. Guilt and fear.

'Catherine?' Dominic leans over to kiss my cheek, and I grab his shoulder, holding on desperately. He laughs. 'I'm not going anywhere, stop panicking.'

'I thought for an awful minute it was you.'

'Me?'

'Under the train.'

His laughter stills. 'Why would you think that?'

'I don't know.' I manage a smile, wanting to reassure him. But inside I feel like jelly. 'Just being silly, I guess.'

'Time for bed,' he says firmly, and puts down his fork.

Jasmine takes the hint and starts clearing up the takeaway. She has barely touched her food, I notice. Not surprising, perhaps, after what happened in the tube station.

'You two go upstairs,' Jasmine says in a low voice, scraping her plate into the bin. 'I can sort this out.'

'You're sure?'

'Of course.' Her voice drops to a whisper. 'You don't look too good, Cat. Best go to bed.'

I head off down the dark passageway to the stairs. I hate being treated like a kid. Yet people seem to treat me like one on a regular basis. Maybe I'm behaving like a kid, too.

Someone is coming downstairs. It's Dad. He looks old and weary in his dressing gown, his hair dishevelled.

'Oh, Catherine, thank God you're not hurt,' he says as I flick the light on. He hurries to embrace me. 'Jasmine's text only just came through.'

'Text?'

'About what happened in the tube station. So terrible.' He studies my face sympathetically. 'Her text said you were very upset.'

'I thought I knew him,' I blurt out.

'The man who went under the train?' He sounds stunned.

'Maybe not *knew*, exactly. I thought I'd seen him before, that's what I meant. Quite recently.' I trail off under his searching gaze. 'I could have been mistaken.'

I look down at my feet. My ankle isn't hurting as much anymore, which is one good thing, at least.

'Of course you were mistaken, darling,' says Dominic, appearing at my side. He strokes my cheek with the back of his hand. 'You were traumatised by what happened, you weren't thinking straight.'

I say nothing.

Dominic gives my father a reassuring smile. 'Robert. Did we wake you?'

'No, I wasn't asleep, I was . . . reading. Ellen is asleep though, so we'd better keep our voices down.' Dad is frowning, his gaze still on me. It's unnerving. 'Catherine, may I ask where you thought you might have seen him before, this man?'

I think back to that day at the food bank. The woman with the buggy and the attitude. The woman I followed out into the street to give her some money.

'I saw him outside the food bank once. He was driving a Jag.'

'And that was the only time?'

I nod. 'He was the same man who was on the platform tonight. I'm sure of it.'

My father is silent.

Dominic shakes his head, making a tiny noise under his breath. 'Sweetheart,' he says, 'I don't want to hurt your feelings. But how can you possibly know it was the same man?'

'The hat,' I say simply. 'That grey hat he was wearing. And the moustache.'

'Hardly conclusive.'

Jasmine comes out of the kitchen, whistling softly. She stops at the sight of us all huddled in the hallway.

'Merry Christmas,' she says.

'Of course,' Dad says blankly. 'It's Christmas morning, isn't it? Merry Christmas to you all.' He glances at the hall clock. 'Well, if everyone's safe and in one piece, I'd better get back to bed. Your mother will expect me to be on turkey duty first thing in the morning. Goodnight.'

'Goodnight.'

Dad turns and heads back upstairs. Jasmine follows him, yawning.

'Oh hell,' she says halfway up, looking back down at Dominic. 'I forgot. The window in my room won't shut properly. It's probably freezing up there now. Any chance of a hand, Dom? Maybe some WD-40 too?'

'More likely some elbow grease,' he says with a grimace. Then he gives me a quick smile and heads up the stairs after her. 'I'll only be a few minutes. You okay to go up on your own?' he asks.

'I'm fine,' I say, though in truth my ankle is aching again. I have a horror of people fussing over me. 'I'll see you in bed.'

I turn off the hall light.

The ground floor is dark and silent now everyone has vanished, but the landing light is on above. I walk up carefully, clinging to the banister in case my ankle decides to give way again.

I pause at the top of the stairs, hearing a muffled thud from the guest room. Dominic, presumably, trying to shut Jasmine's window so she doesn't have to sleep in an icebox. Further along the landing, my father's bedroom door is ajar. My parents have separate rooms, just like the Queen and Prince Philip. They always have had, for as long as I can remember.

Perhaps if I talk to Dad on his own about what happened tonight, he'll be more likely to believe me. I just can't get it out of my head that I'd seen that man before . . .

I knock lightly on Dad's bedroom door and put my head round when there's no reply. The room is empty. The only light comes from a Tiffany-style glass lamp on the table next to his armchair, giving the room a discreet yellowish glow. Dad's en-suite door is also open, the bathroom in darkness.

Where's he gone?

I listen. There's a rumble of low voices through the wall. Coming from my mother's bedroom on the other side. I suck in my breath. Dad must have nipped in there to speak to Mum before heading back to bed, even though he said she was asleep. Perhaps he wanted to tell her what happened at the tube station. About what I *thought* I saw. Before I've even had a chance to give my side of the story. Once again, I can't even go out for a drink with friends without everyone getting involved.

I am just about to retreat when I see it.

The black edge of a notebook, half hidden under some papers on the bedside table.

I wasn't asleep, he had said. *I was reading.*

Chapter Thirty-Six

I can't be sure, but it looks like the black notebook I found in the cellar. The one I hid under the cabinet in the living room. The notebook that mentions Rachel and her various psychoses and treatments. It disappeared and now here it is again on my dad's bedside table.

I slip off my shoes and creep across the floor towards it.

'Catherine?'

I jerk round so fast, I twist my ankle again and cry out in pain.

It's Dominic.

'Bloody hell, woman,' he says, almost angrily. He hurries across the room to grab me in his arms, taking the weight off my leg. He looks down at my bare foot. 'Are you hurt? You said your ankle was better.'

'It *is* better. I was just—'

'Trying to do too much before it's properly healed.'

'Obviously.'

'You're going to end up back in hospital if you're not careful.' He glances round at the empty room. 'What are you doing here anyway? I thought you were going straight up to bed?'

Before I can think of a credible excuse, my parents appear in the doorway, looking at us in complete bemusement.

'Yes, Catherine,' my father says, an edge to his voice. 'I'd like an answer to that question too.' He thrusts his hands in the wide pockets of his dressing gown and does not move from the doorway, effectively blocking my escape. 'You know my room is out of bounds. I bring official papers up here sometimes. Maybe not top secret, but sensitive documents all the same. What were you doing in here?'

I hesitate, my face flushing with embarrassment as they all stare at me.

'I wanted . . .'

'Yes?'

'To find Rachel's ashes.' It's the only reasonable excuse that comes into my head, so I blurt it out. 'You said once that you kept her ashes in one of your cabinets. Or maybe I saw her urn in here when I was a kid.' Except that was in his downstairs study, I realise too late, but press on regardless. 'I can't remember now. But the door was open, so I thought . . .'

'You thought you'd do some bloody sleuthing,' Dad says sharply.

I nod, trying not to look back at the notebook.

Mum is pale and staring. In a plain white nightie with a high buttoned collar, she looks oddly prim and Victorian.

'Your father showed me your letter, darling,' she says, glancing from my father to me. 'What . . . what on earth do you want with your sister's ashes? Is this because of what you said in the letter?'

I say nothing, but look pleadingly at Dominic.

'I get the feeling Catherine wants to see Rachel's ashes,' Dominic tells them, 'because she needs to be sure that her sister really is dead.' He nods at me, his voice carefully neutral. 'Am I right?'

'Spot on,' I say huskily.

'You can't have missed how much stress Catherine's been under lately,' Dominic continues, looking at Mum and Dad, 'with all the odd things that have been happening. Plus the feeling that perhaps you haven't been as open with her about how Rachel died as you might have been.'

I see Dad's eyes narrow.

'I know it sounds strange,' Dominic says, 'but it's actually very simple. If Catherine could see Rachel's ashes for herself, maybe even scatter them somewhere, I think she would be able to finally accept that her sister is at peace. And her life could go back to normal.'

Dad looks unconvinced, but Mum leans against the door frame, giving me a broken smile. 'Oh, darling, you should have said something before. If that's all it is, of course you can see your sister's ashes. Can't she, Robert?'

My father hesitates, then gives an abrupt nod.

'Now?' I ask, deeply surprised.

'In the morning,' Dad says firmly. He points at his digital alarm clock. It's after two o'clock. 'Her ashes aren't up here. They're in my study downstairs. But it's rather late to go rummaging about looking for funerary urns,' he says. 'Especially on Christmas morning. We all have a busy day ahead. And in fact, I believe your husband is working a shift at some point tomorrow.'

'I am indeed,' Dominic says ruefully.

'Well then.' Dad kisses Mum on the cheek. 'You'd better go to bed, Ellen. I'm sorry I woke you. I'll see you at seven, all right?'

When she has gone, my father steps aside to let us leave his room. He smiles at me in passing, but I can tell he's not happy. It's just an act. There's a strain in his face that wasn't there before. Like he's been holding a string taut, using all his strength, but is about ready to give up and let go.

'You two have a good night. We'll talk more in the morning.' He pauses. 'Please try not to upset yourself, Cat.'

Cat.

He hasn't called me that in years.

Upstairs on the top floor, pale moonlight streaming through our bedroom window, Dominic kisses me on the lips in a languorous fashion, and then sits me down on the bed and starts to help me undress. His hands are cool on my body, first checking my ankle, which is less swollen, and then working his way slowly upwards.

'There you go,' he whispers in my ear. 'You'll see Rachel's ashes tomorrow. Maybe even get to scatter them. How's that for a Christmas present?'

'It's pretty ghoulish, as Christmas presents go.'

He pulls back to look at me, frowning. His eyes glitter in the moonlight. 'What's the matter? I thought this was what you wanted. To know for sure that Rachel's dead.'

'Yes.'

'But you're still not happy. I don't understand.'

'It's not that.'

'Okay.' He kisses my throat hungrily. 'What then?'

I consider how to answer that. I'm still thinking about the notebook, wondering how I'm going to get access to it again without Dad finding out. Whatever's in it, he doesn't want me to know. Which means I must read it.

I haven't mentioned the notebook to Dominic. I should do. It feels so deeply personal that even talking about it out loud could be dangerous, but he's my husband. He deserves to know.

Yet even as I open my mouth, caution makes me change what I was going to say. 'That man tonight,' I whisper. 'The one who died.'

Dominic stops trying to unbutton the front of my dress. 'For God's sake . . .'

'I can still see his face. His hat.'

'Don't think about it,' Dominic says soothingly. 'It wasn't your fault, baby.'

'I know it wasn't my fault.'

He gives up on undressing me. 'So what's up?'

'He knew me too. I saw it in his face. He looked at me tonight, on the platform before the train came in, and he *recognised* me.'

Dominic sucks in a harsh breath. 'Darling,' he says, 'it hurts me to hear you talking like this. You didn't know that guy, and he didn't know you. And no amount of soul-searching is going to bring the poor bastard back to life. It's only going to torment the hell out of you.'

I search his face in the darkness. 'You think I'm imagining it? That this is all just . . . I don't know . . . guilt, because he went under the train right in front of us?'

'Don't you?'

I close my eyes, suddenly uncertain. Could I have made a mistake? Was he the same man I saw outside the food bank, or not? I picture his face behind the wheel of the silver Jag, then try to match it to the man in the tube station.

My uneasiness grows.

'I'm not sure of anything anymore.'

'Darling, it was a perfectly natural mistake to make. He looked at you, yes?'

'Yes.'

'So you made eye contact with this guy. You made a connection. Then a few seconds later . . .'

I put my hands to my face. 'Don't, please.'

'You're not to blame. So you can stop thinking it's your fault.'

'My fault?' I stare at him.

'Of course,' he says gently. 'Look, I feel guilty too. Guilty that I didn't spot what was in his mind. That I didn't pull him back from the edge . . . It was a traumatic event for everyone there, not just you.' He strokes my cheek lovingly. 'You're a sensitive soul though, and you've had one hell of a tough week. Plus, you were drinking tonight.'

When he puts it like that, I can see my mistake. The only thing I'm guilty of here is bringing everything back to myself. Of being self-obsessed.

It's an unpleasant realisation.

'I feel like such an idiot.'

'Maybe.' He leans forward to kiss me. 'But you're my beautiful idiot,' he murmurs against my mouth. 'My very sexy idiot.'

'I'm sorry.' I sigh. 'I'm so sorry.'

'Forget it,' he whispers, pushing me back on the bed. 'I love you.'

'I love you too, Dominic. I love you forever.'

Chapter Thirty-Seven

We wake late the next morning, our naked bodies still entwined, to a gorgeous smell drifting through the house: turkey and roast potatoes. Dominic is awake before me, and it's his hand playing with my hair that brings me back to full consciousness.

Rachel, I think. It's my first thought. Her ashes.

My body goes cold. When I open my eyes Dominic is gazing at me, a smile on his lips.

'Hey, sleepyhead.'

'Hey.'

I snuggle against him, pushing away all thoughts of my sister with surprising ease. Perhaps she has finally lost her ability to frighten me.

'Did we do it twice last night or did I imagine it?' I say.

His grin disarms me.

'Twice, definitely,' he says. 'Though it was morning, both times. We went to bed very late.'

I smile at him. 'And I thought we'd have less sex once we were married.'

'Who told you that?'

'I guess I just assumed. My parents have separate rooms. That must be for a reason. Married people fall out of lust, don't they?' I stroke down his body, and smile at his intake of breath. 'Three times, just to make sure we've still got it?'

'I thought you'd never ask.'

He rolls me over onto my back, kissing me hotly, then cups my breast.

'Catherine! Dominic!' my mother shouts up the stairs. 'Lunch will be ready soon.'

I giggle. Dominic turns and calls back, 'We'll be down in a minute.'

He regards me hungrily as I slip out of bed and hunt through the drawers for clean clothes suitable for Christmas lunch with the family.

'Nice view,' he says, smiling.

I throw a pair of lacy knickers at him, and he growls, climbing out of bed after me.

'Hey, put me down,' I insist as he grabs me, 'you big bear.' He lets me go and I turn back to my lingerie drawer. 'They're too polite to say so, but I was probably supposed to help with lunch.'

'I doubt you'll be missed in the kitchen.'

'What does that mean?'

'That your skills lie in a different direction to cooking,' he says with a grin, and ducks when I try to hit him.

'Very funny. All the same, I should go down and lay the table or something. I hate feeling like a parasite.' I push him away as his arms come round me again, groping and squeezing. 'Seriously, don't.'

Reluctantly, Dominic opens his arms to let me escape.

'Fine,' he says languidly. He picks up his dressing gown. 'I'm going to take a quick shower. But you're far from being a parasite. You need to be here right now. And your parents know it.'

I watch him go, unsure if he's offended or not. I'm also not entirely certain what his parting comment was about. *You need to be here right now. And your parents know it.* What does that even mean?

I find a matching black bra and thong. Then I pull a dress out of the wardrobe and throw it on the bed. It's a black-and-silver dress, skin tight, clinging in all the right places. Or the wrong places, depending on your point of view. I have no idea why I chose that one, my brain somewhere else, or maybe switched off entirely. Dominic bought it for me last Christmas but I've never worn it on the grounds that it's too damn revealing.

And this is a family Christmas. Not a night out on the town.

'Cat, darling?' my mother calls up from the bottom of the attic stairs. 'Are you on your way down?'

'Coming!' I shout back. Hurriedly, I pull on the bra and thong. 'Just getting dressed. Dom's in the shower. Sorry, we'll be right there.'

Mum says something I don't catch, and then wanders away again.

Lunch is probably imminent.

'Oh, what the hell.'

I drag on the little black-and-silver dress and find some heels that won't turn my ankle over on the way downstairs. Then I drag a brush through my hair and give myself a light dusting of make-up, even though I don't normally wear much at home. But the dress will look odd without any make-up at all.

I hesitate, and search in my jewellery box for the silver cat necklace my mother bought me from Harrods. It seems like a good occasion to wear it.

It suits the dress perfectly.

Downstairs, the smell of food is delicious and mouth-watering. I glance at the hall clock. It's nearly half past one already. I suddenly realise how hungry I am. I had no idea how late it was. I lose all sense of time in bed with Dominic, like a captive princess in a fairy-tale castle, sleeping away my life. Well, not always sleeping.

I grin, remembering his urgent lovemaking.

'Ah, Catherine, there you are at last.' My father stands in the doorway of the dining room, holding out a glass of pink champagne. He looks me up and down, then adds, 'What a lovely dress.'

'Thank you.'

I search his face, but he appears cheerful and unconcerned. There's no sign that he even remembers our conversation from last night.

'Aperitif?' he asks.

I take the champagne and drink some without hesitation, though the bubbles always go up my nose and make me tipsy quicker than ordinary wine.

'Do you need me to do anything?' I ask.

'Of course not, darling. Jasmine's been helping your mother for the past hour, and she says everything's nearly done.'

Good old Jasmine, I catch myself thinking, rather spikily, and am surprised by my sudden feelings of dislike for her.

What's wrong with me today?

Dad ushers me into the dining room, where the roast turkey is on the table, ready for carving and covered lightly with foil to keep it warm. I check briefly under the foil. It looks and smells delicious.

'You know your mother,' Dad is saying, a little awkwardly, as though he's sensed my mood and is trying to keep the peace. 'She hates too many people in the kitchen when she's cooking. Distracting her, getting underfoot. I'm sure she'll shout once she's ready for me to carry in the serving dishes.'

I say nothing, but knock back some more champagne.

Dad glances at my clinging black dress again, then at the cat necklace I'm wearing. He bends to turn on the Christmas tree lights, nestled among baubles in the branches of the real pine tree. They start flashing merrily away to the background sound of Christmas carols.

'There,' he says, straightening, his voice slightly muffled, 'that's more Christmassy.'

'I really should offer to help her.'

'Don't be silly.' Dad pulls out a chair for me. 'Come and sit down.'

'But—'

'Sit,' he insists.

Uncomfortable under his gaze, I sit down and let him pour more champagne into my glass. I don't argue, oddly thirsty today. Dominic appears, looking clean and fresh from the shower, his hair still wet. His eyes widen at the sight of my dress, then he smiles, his expression almost wolfish.

'Love the outfit, darling,' he says, taking the seat opposite without waiting to be asked. 'Thanks, just half a glass,' he says as my father offers him some champagne. 'I'm working tonight. Sorry, did we miss all the hard graft?'

'Not to worry, you're our guests today. And guests don't cook in this house.'

My mother calls from the kitchen, a strained note in her voice, and Dad hurries out of the room, suddenly looking distracted.

Dominic grins at me across the table, then lifts his glass in a mock-salute. 'Well, Merry Christmas. This is the high life.'

'Don't. I feel awful.'

'Why?'

'We slept in and now they're doing all the work. On Christmas bloody Day.' I take another deep gulp of champagne, the bubbles tingling and fizzing on my tongue. 'It's not right.'

'Nonsense,' he says crisply. 'They're your parents and they want you to feel at home.'

'People who are genuinely at home help out with the housework.'

'You've got an excuse, though. You're not well.'

I stare at him, perplexed. 'My ankle, you mean? That's hardly an illness. And don't try to say I had a concussion too. Because the doctor said I was fine.'

Dominic looks at me, silent for once, and then fiddles unnecessarily with his knife and fork. I get the impression he's annoyed with himself. As though he's said something he didn't intend to. Or wasn't supposed to.

'Wait,' I say slowly. 'You think I'm . . . ill?'

'Forget it.'

'I don't want to forget it.'

'Catherine, please don't make a scene,' he says gently, but with an odd tension in his face. 'Remember that it's Christmas, yeah? Peace and goodwill to all men. I just meant you've been a little down lately. Anyway,' he adds, 'you shouldn't worry so much what your parents think. You need to be your own person.'

I want to say more, but Jasmine and my parents parade into the room at that moment, their arms full of steaming food bowls. Dominic jumps up to help, but I just sit and stare at the turkey until my father twitches off the foil and starts to carve it up, his long knife flashing in and out of the white breast.

We eat lunch without saying much, though Dad insists on regaling us with a story about the Christmas Eve when he and Mum first met. They got stuck in an elevator together in New York for over twelve hours. I know the story well and don't listen properly, smiling dutifully in all the right places instead.

Dominic, to whom the story is new, listens with rapt attention, and laughs out loud at the punchline: 'So after that we had to get married, of course.'

Even Jasmine grins, though I'm sure she will have heard it before. But then, my bubbly cousin is far better company than me. More sociable, more animated. Constantly smiling. Smiling at my husband.

'How did you two meet?' she asks Dominic, glancing at me.

'Well, it wasn't quite as dramatic as that.' He laughs, brushing my fingertips across the table. 'Was it, baby?'

'Not dramatic at all,' I mutter.

I see the flash in his eyes. 'I was leafleting round here on a Saturday morning, on my bicycle, and managed to drop the bloody thing on one of Ellen's pots—'

'It was a very expensive terracotta herb pot,' Mum says, interrupting, 'housing a delicate young fennel. You squashed the poor thing flat.'

'I offered to pay,' Dominic says mildly.

My mum makes a face at him.

'Leafleting?' Jasmine repeats, looking puzzled.

'Save our NHS,' I say, not looking at him. 'He was knocking on doors and stuffing leaflets through letter boxes. Wearing a bloody T-shirt with "Save Our NHS" across it, and a matching baseball cap. After he'd rung the bell and apologised for the damage he'd done, he had the nerve to ask me to the pub with the other activists; bored me half to death with his endless slogans.'

'But as you can see, slogans or not, Catherine was smitten at first glance,' Dominic tells Jasmine, his tone rich with satisfaction.

My dad gets up and refills my glass with champagne. 'Dominic?' he asks politely, holding out the bottle.

'Not for me, thanks, Robert,' he says, covering his glass. 'Night shift, remember?'

After the meal, we move to the sofas in the living room to open our presents. My parents have bought us a large, silver-framed, oval mirror for our bedroom. It looks like an antique – and is, Mum is keen to tell me. Early Victorian, apparently. I show it to Dominic, who is deeply impressed, and we both thank her.

Dominic has bought me a gorgeous new dressing gown: grey silk, with pink and yellow butterflies on the back.

I kiss him lingeringly as a thank you, and see the heat in his eyes, hurriedly disguised when my father glances our way.

Jasmine exclaims in delight, unwrapping her gift. 'I love charm bracelets,' she says, thanking my mother, who is watching her fondly. 'Thank you so much. This is perfect.'

I've bought my parents tickets to a West End musical of their choice. I can see Dad isn't too excited but I know Mum will love a night out in town. And she adores musical theatre.

I unwrap my last present, which is from Dad. It's a fine, leather-bound, illustrated edition of *Alice's Adventures in Wonderland*.

My heartbeat seems to snag on something.

It was Rachel who enjoyed those old Lewis Carroll novels.

Not me.

'Thank you,' I say huskily, and try not to meet his eye.

Dad smiles. 'You're welcome.'

A genuine mistake, I decide. Not an attempt to wound me. I put the book with my other presents to be taken upstairs later. Maybe I should try reading it. Find out why Rachel enjoyed it so much. And it is a beautiful object.

I insist on making a pot of coffee for everyone after the wrapping paper debris has been cleared away, and this time nobody rejects my offer. Too full to move, I suspect. Dominic slips out to join me in the kitchen, but hinders more than helps, his arm constantly round my waist, bumping my hip and kissing me whenever I stand still for long enough.

'Stop it,' I tell him, mock-sternly.

'I can't help it, I find you edible today,' he whispers in my ear, glancing back to make sure we're still alone. 'It's your high heels, and this dress. It makes you look amazing.'

'I am amazing,' I say tartly.

'Like a sex bomb.'

'You have a one-track mind.'

'I told you, it's this dress.'

'And last night, in bed? I wasn't wearing anything then.'

'God, you tease.' He groans in mock torment. 'Better give me that tray before I bend you over the kitchen table. Can you imagine your dad's face if he walked in?'

I grin and allow Dominic to carry through the tray of cups and a silver coffee pot, while I follow.

'I like your arse in those jeans,' I say, *sotto voce*, and am rewarded by him wiggling his behind suggestively as he turns through the living room doorway.

Dad looks at us suspiciously, but I merely smile and sit down again. Dominic's right. This may be Dad's home, but he invited us to live here, we didn't invite ourselves. And I need to stand up to Dad's disapproval. Not let him constantly intimidate us into a meek acceptance of his old-fashioned rules.

Besides, if I can't flirt with my husband at Christmas, when can I?

Jasmine is standing by the window, looking out at the lengthening shadows. Dusk falls so quickly at this time of year.

'That was a delicious lunch, thank you,' I say to my parents, watching as Dominic pours us each a cup of steaming coffee. 'And the presents are fantastic. But I haven't forgotten what we talked about last night.'

They look at each other warily.

'You said I could see Rachel's ashes.'

There's a sudden silence in the room.

Dominic stops pouring and looks up at me. Then he continues what he was doing, but his smile has gone.

'I'd like to see her ashes today, please,' I say as firmly as I can. 'And maybe I could scatter them in the garden under the magnolia tree, if you don't object.' I pause. 'Before the light goes.'

Chapter Thirty-Eight

'I don't think that would be a good idea—' Mum begins hesitantly, but Dad cuts across her with a gesture that looks almost angry.

'No, if that's what Catherine wants. Maybe it is a good idea.'

'Robert?' Mum sounds almost scared.

He ignores her and gets up without accepting the cup of coffee Dominic is holding out to him.

'Come on,' he says calmly, 'let's do it right now. Like you say, Cat, the light goes quickly this time of year.'

My mother stares at him, a blind panic on her face now. 'Robert, no . . .'

'Be quiet, Ellen.'

Mum raises a fluttering hand to her mouth.

Dad looks at me, an uncompromising line to his mouth, then nods at my high heels. 'Better put some wellies on. It's muddy outside. You can borrow a pair, if necessary.' He leaves the room. 'I'll fetch the urn.'

I glance at Dominic, who touches my arm.

'Well done, darling,' he whispers.

We all troop back into the kitchen, heading for the side door where the outdoor shoes are kept on a long wooden rack. I select a muddy old pair of my mum's wellies and slip them on, checking inside first for spiders. Dominic and Jasmine both insist they'll be fine in trainers. My mother is still looking frightened, but she also exchanges her expensive indoor shoes for a pair of boots. I probably look very odd in this clinging, too-tight dress and wellington boots. It's not really an appropriate outfit for scattering a loved one's ashes. But there's no time to change.

Besides, Rachel is surely beyond caring what I wear to her second 'funeral'. She is beyond everything now.

By the time we have each grabbed a warm coat, Dad has returned with something in his hands: it's a small, black-and-white marble funerary urn.

I stare at it, my insides suddenly tightening.

'Hey, relax.' Dominic gives my hand a good squeeze. 'I'm here with you, remember? Everything's going to be okay.'

The lawn in the back garden crunches underfoot, crisp with frost from where today's thin December sunshine failed to reach it. The fences and trees of surrounding properties have a tendency to block out the afternoon sun, making the summers feel shorter and the winters longer. But it's still the garden where I grew up, and I love its dark, muddy little corners.

The vast old magnolia tree is stunning even in winter, its stark branches tipped with soft, velvety-looking buds ready for an early London spring. The earth beneath is iron-hard, the grass patchy round the roots.

I walk beneath the spreading magnolia branches and look up at the darkening sky. It won't be long until dusk falls.

'Here,' I say, and turn to my father, who is still cradling the marble urn. 'Rachel loved this tree. If she could speak, she'd say this is where she'd want her ashes scattered.'

'Are you sure about this, Catherine?' Dad searches my face. 'We can always do it another day.'

'No, now is perfect.' I glance back at Dominic for reassurance, and he nods, smiling. 'I want to do this.'

I could wish for a glorious summer day instead, blue skies above and all the birds singing. But this is the only day we have.

Dad hands me the urn with great reverence. I remove the lid and place it gently on the frosty ground. Then I start to tip the contents of the urn out.

The ashes puff out in a series of little gasps, surprisingly soft and insubstantial, like grey-black clouds. I turn slowly, letting them drop and scatter naturally in the air. There's hardly any wind today, but they drift away all the same, like tiny black seeds pollinating the trunk of the magnolia and the rough soil beneath.

Some of the ash attaches itself to my wellies, and I stare down at the grey-pitted green rubber, my breathing suddenly shallow.

I'm shocked, I realise, and more than a little uneasy. It's as though Rachel insists on remaining with me, even if only for a few more minutes, until I brush her off my boots like a stain. It's as if she knows even from beyond death what I'm doing today, how I'm struggling to shed her influence over my life, to lay her ghost to rest at last.

'Oh God.' I stagger backwards.

'Catherine?'

Dad sounds alarmed.

I see concern on Jasmine's face too, her eyes wide with surprise, and fight to get a grip of myself. Bloody hell. What is going on inside my head today? I was on the point of bolting, of running back towards the house in panic. Which is absurd.

Very deliberately, I slow my breathing, then tip the urn up again.

It's not empty yet.

'I think that's enough,' Dad says urgently, and steps forward as though to take the urn away from me.

Suddenly Dominic is next to me, steadying my trembling hands with his own, his hip brushing mine. Like we're two halves of the same person.

'No,' Dominic says, looking straight at my father, 'let her finish. It was never going to be easy. But this is important. It's a laying-to-rest. She can't stop now.'

I don't think I've ever loved him as much as at this moment.

With Dominic beside me, I turn and scatter the last soft ashes across the trunk and base of the magnolia tree. I try not to think too much about what I'm doing, about the terrible significance of the act. But of course there's no escaping the truth. Deep down, this is an exorcism. It's an emotional and spiritual banishment of the big sister I feared so much, the sister whose death I've always secretly doubted. The ash proves to me that her life ended, and everyone here knows it.

I've been waiting for this for so long, now that I'm here at last it feels as if a silent earthquake is taking place inside me. An upheaval so total and overwhelming, the shock waves have only just begun . . .

'Goodbye,' I say under my breath. 'Goodbye, Rachel.'

Chapter Thirty-Nine

Dominic has left for his night shift at the hospital. My parents and Jasmine have disappeared next door to old Mr and Mrs Bishop's house for Christmas drinks. I leave it a good ten minutes to make sure nobody's coming back, then head straight upstairs to Dad's bedroom.

The door is locked.

I rattle the handle, annoyed and more than a little taken aback. Dad almost never locks his door. Did he guess what I was planning? Why is he trying to stop me?

A locked door won't stop me for long. I know there's a spare key in Mum's room. It's in a small box on the mantelpiece in case of emergencies, and her room is never locked.

It takes me all of two minutes to find the spare key, unlock Dad's bedroom door and slip inside.

The spacious bedroom is dark and gloomy. The curtains are drawn to keep in the heat, but there's a small gap in the middle. I don't want to put on the light in case he happens to look out from our neighbour's house and see it. It's unlikely. But if the locked door is an indication that he knows I'm after the notebook, it's better to be safe and do this in darkness.

Slowly, I creep across the carpet until I reach his bedside table, which is covered in books and papers.

I check under the papers first. Then among the pile of books.

The notebook isn't there.

'Shit.'

My hands curl into fists at my side, my heart thumping loudly. Where the hell has my father put it? I'm even more convinced now that he guessed my intention and has hidden it somewhere.

But why is it such a big bloody secret?

From what I saw of the notebook in the cellar, it's a record of Rachel's 'problems' – whatever they were – and was written by my dad. Some kind of informal diary of her treatment. Which makes it all the more interesting to me, since I know so little about what was actually wrong with my sister.

As I stand there, staring in frustration at the empty space where I last saw the notebook, I catch a soft click somewhere in the quiet house. Like a door being closed, or a floorboard easing under the pressure of a foot.

I turn my head, holding my breath in apprehension. The door to Dad's room is partially open, the landing outside brightly lit . . .

I can't be caught in here.

Have my parents come back early from the neighbours' drinks party? Maybe they've forgotten something. Or have come back to pressurise me into going along too, not wanting to leave me alone in the house. Jasmine tried to persuade me to go with them, promising it would be more fun than it sounded, especially with her there. My mother was insistent, too. I was forced to lie. I told them I had a headache and was going to sit quietly and watch television.

I didn't like lying to Mum, especially after she was so loving towards me earlier, sitting with me on the sofa for an hour when I finished scattering Rachel's ashes. But I needed a chance to look for the notebook undisturbed.

There's that click again.

I wait, listening hard. But I hear nothing more. It could have been the boiler coming on or turning off. That's the likeliest explanation. Yet I remain unmoving.

It's ridiculous, but despite the silence that's settled over the big house now, I can't shake the sensation that I'm not alone. That someone else is here with me.

I tiptoe back towards the doorway, grimacing at every creak of the floor.

That's when I see the notebook.

Dad's tweed jacket is hanging on the back of the door, and there's a black notebook sticking out of the pocket. It looks exactly like the one I've been looking for.

There's no time to feel triumphant, but it's hard not to be excited. My heart thuds as I pull the notebook out of the pocket, and flick through it quickly, just to check it's what I came for.

It's the same book, I'm sure of it. That's my dad's handwriting. The same endless lists of symptoms and treatment schedules. The name 'Rachel' leaps out at me again. And my own name too, here and there, scattered through the pages.

Catherine.

Underlined in red every time.

Chapter Forty

I hear a noise downstairs again, and freeze instantly. It's not the heating this time. Too loud for that. A door being closed, perhaps.

Has Dad come back to check on me?

I try not to panic. There's still time to get out of his room without being noticed. But I need to hide the notebook, too. I can't risk anyone else seeing me with it.

Not even Dominic.

I fumble with the rucked-up flap on Dad's pocket, trying to conceal my theft, and something falls to the carpet. Something small, white and rectangular.

I bend and pick it up.

It's a blank white card.

I turn it over.

A business card. I move closer to the light coming from the landing through the gap in the bedroom door and read the embossed black writing.

Jason Wainwright. Private Investigator.

Why on earth has Dad got a business card for a private investigator in his jacket pocket? Is it something to do with his work at the Foreign Office? There's a mobile number, an email address and a website. No postal address, but it does state *London offices* under the name.

Another odd noise from downstairs. Not a click or a thud this time, but a thin, pathetic cry.

Like a cat mewing.

I shove the business card back into Dad's jacket pocket. What the hell? Am I imagining the sound of a cat in the house again?

But no, there it is, clear and unmistakeable, breaking the silence.

A cat, mewing.

This is way beyond funny, I think angrily. If somebody's playing a trick on me it's downright cruel. Especially if it's a real cat in distress.

I hurry out of his bedroom, lock the door behind me and return the key to the box on my mother's mantelpiece. Then I head upstairs to our flat and push the notebook as far under the bed as I can reach. It's not the world's most original hiding place but it will have to do. I can always move it later. Right now, I need to check out the cat sound. Nobody is making a fool out of me twice.

I head downstairs more slowly, favouring my weak ankle. I can still hear mewing. The living room and the dining room are both dark and empty. I make my way cautiously past the closed cellar door.

The kitchen is dimly lit. One spotlight is on over the range, its bulb angled away to shine on artfully exposed brickwork.

I spot a brief flicker of movement under the pine table, and gasp. My hand goes instinctively to my heart.

'What's that? Who's there?' I ask.

The movement comes towards me, gradually getting closer to the head of the table. Like I'm being tracked.

'Jesus.'

Then it emerges out of the shadows. Two green eyes raised in curiosity, followed by a narrow body with glossy dark fur, and a tail held high, curved in a question mark.

A cat. A young black cat, looking lost and in need of some love.

'Oh my God,' I whisper.

So it *was* a cat I could hear. This time at least, I wasn't imagining things.

But how did a cat get into my parents' kitchen?

I crouch to stroke its head, and the graceful creature purrs weakly, tilting its neck back for more.

'Hello, gorgeous. What on earth are you doing here?'

It doesn't have a collar, though I suppose it could have been micro-chipped by its owner. It looks very young, almost too young to be away from its mother. Not that I know much about cats. We were never allowed to have pets as a child, due to Rachel's tendency to mistreat animals. I guess we just never got around to getting a cat once she was gone.

The cat necklace swinging round my neck is attracting the cat's vivid green stare.

At the sound of soft laughter, I look up to find a figure watching me from the darkened archway that leads into the utility room.

'Dominic? You startled me,' I say, straightening up and staring at him. 'What are you doing home?'

'Happy Christmas,' Dominic says. He looks down at the black cat, who is weaving between my ankles, purring more loudly now.

I don't understand at first. Then I get it.

'It was you,' I say slowly. 'You brought the cat in here.'

He smiles.

'For me?' I ask.

'You said you'd always wanted a cat.'

'But Mum and Dad . . .'

'It's okay, I got their permission first. It won't be a problem.'

He bends down and strokes the cat.

'No name yet,' he says lightly. 'I thought you might like to choose one.'

'He's *my* cat, then?'

'Cat's cat.'

I don't know what to say. Tears are pricking my eyes.

'Thank you,' I say, and kiss him on the cheek. I scoop the cat up off the kitchen floor and cuddle it. 'Is it a girl or a boy?'

'Boy,' says Dominic.

I can't believe I actually have a cat of my own. A real live cat to name and to love. And to love me back, I hope. The warm, lithe body wriggles against my chest though, hating captivity even for those few seconds. When I resist, there's a cross mew and a sharp scratch at my wrist.

I open my arms and watch, disappointed, as the cat springs to the ground and stalks away, its tail high and twitching. That taunting question mark, whisking back and forth.

'Ouch.'

'Yeah, better watch out,' Dominic says wryly. 'Even kittens have sharp claws. He's not used to you yet. Or this house.'

'Well, he's only a kitten.'

'Nine weeks old.'

'But where did you—'

'Sally's cat had a litter back in the autumn. I put first dibs on this one, soon as I saw him. Totally black.'

'Like a witch's cat.'

'Exactly.'

I pretend to punch him, and he grins.

'He can be your familiar,' Dominic says, and laughs when I make a face. 'Look, I know looking after a pet is a big responsibility.'

'Too right. I haven't the faintest idea where to begin.'

'I don't want you to worry about anything. Sally's given me a diet sheet for the first month, and instructions on how to look after him. He's not quite house-trained yet, she says.' He grimaces. 'Which didn't exactly please Ellen. But I promised her we'd clean up any accidents.'

'Of course we will.'

He searches my face. 'So you like?'

'Hugely.'

'Because I wasn't sure . . .'

'It's the best Christmas present I've ever had.'

Dominic holds my gaze like a thread between us. 'Seriously?'

'Totally.'

He covers his face with his hands.

I frown, watching him. 'Hey, what's the matter? You okay?'

His hands drop from his face and he looks back at me with a curious intensity. His eyes are shiny with unshed tears. 'I don't know what to say. Except . . . you make me happy.'

'You're so sweet, Dom.'

I put my arms around him, and lean my head against his shoulder.

For a moment I'm tempted to tell him about the notebook. But some inner voice of caution warns me against it. Not until I've had a chance to examine it. I mean, what if there's something in the notebook about me? Something embarrassing? Something that might make him think differently about me? I don't think I could bear that.

So instead I whisper softly, 'Thank you for getting me the perfect present.'

'The *purr*-fect present?'

I chuckle, my head still nestled against him. 'I love you so much, darling. Even if you do crack some truly appalling jokes sometimes.'

He laughs too, and cuddles me in his arms, strong as an oak.

'Hey.' I draw back to stare at him. 'How are you at home, anyway? Aren't you supposed to be working at St Hilda's tonight?'

'Surprise.' Dominic tips his head to one side, his smile charming and apologetic at the same time. 'I told you a little porky, sorry. I'm down to work tomorrow, not tonight. I had to pretend I was going out to work or you would have wanted to know where I was going when I went to collect His Nibbs there.' His eyes crinkle up at the edges as he smiles. 'And that would have spoilt the surprise.'

I glance back at the cat, who is busy playing with the tassels on one of Mum's pine-chair cushion covers.

'Dom, did you ever bring him here before?'

'No, why?'

'Because I heard a cat just before I fell down the cellar steps, remember?' I feel his sudden stillness and bite my lip, wishing I hadn't said anything. I try to cover the awkwardness with a casual shrug. 'Anyway, it's not important. I could have sworn I heard a cat that day, that's all.'

He's still got that charming smile on his face, though it looks forced now.

Does he think I'm crazy?

'I probably imagined hearing a cat,' I add.

'Right,' Dominic says, but doesn't pursue it. He leans forward and kisses me hungrily on the lips instead. 'You know the best bit about me not being at work tonight?'

I raise my eyebrows, smiling.

'I get to take my wife to bed early,' he whispers in my ear, 'and make as much damn noise as I like, because everyone else is at that party next door.'

Chapter Forty-One

On Boxing Day morning, still smiling about Dominic's unexpected gift, I have a lazy breakfast of fruit and yoghurt, then politely decline to go out shopping with my mum and dad.

'But, darling, the sales will be on,' my mother says.

'All the more reason to stay home,' I say firmly. 'I can't afford to spend money on anything. Even reduced stuff. Honestly, you know Dom and I are saving for a deposit on a place of our own.'

'Your father will help you out with a deposit. Won't you, Robert?' Mum smiles at him.

Dad has been reading *The Times* over breakfast, but lowers it now to nod at me. 'Of course.'

'And that's very generous of you, Dad. But you know how Dominic feels about that. He's proud, he doesn't want charity.'

'It's not charity when it's your own parents,' Mum says.

'Well, he doesn't like the idea.' I flash her a brittle smile. She means well but she doesn't understand. 'Maybe I'll shop online instead. There are always great bargains this time of year.'

'It's so much more fun in the shops though. And we could have lunch somewhere nice afterwards. You always used to enjoy that.'

I hate having to keep saying no like this. I can see the disappointment in her face. But it's important that I stay home today. And it's not something I can share with her.

I avoid Dad's searching gaze.

'Someone has to look after the kitty,' I remind them. 'I'm going to call him Panther. Where is he, by the way?'

There's a silence.

'We made a little bed for him in the utility room,' Mum says hesitantly. 'But I'm sure he won't need much attention. Probably best if you avoid disturbing him for now. Let him get used to a new house.'

'Good idea.'

A horn sounds outside. Their cab has arrived. Dad lays aside his newspaper, and Mum fetches her handbag. I follow them into the hall to wave them off at the door. Dad hates shopping, which probably explains why he looks so grim.

'Look, you two have a great time,' I say as they climb into the taxi together. 'I'll be fine here with Jasmine and Panther. Don't spend all your money, okay?'

'Now you're being silly, darling,' Mum says, but I can see she's relieved by my cheerful mood this morning.

Once their cab has pulled away, I hurry inside and head straight upstairs to check on Jasmine. To my delight, she's still asleep, the room dark when I knock gently and stick my head round the door.

I climb the stairs to my own little flat, and shut the bedroom door. Then I sit down on the edge of the bed and open my laptop.

Jason Wainwright, I type into the Google search box. *Private Investigator, London*.

The main website is not very exciting. A few pages of testimony from former clients, Jason Wainwright's CV, and some discussion of prices for various different services, including investigatory work like 'tailing' and 'staking out' individuals and addresses.

Nothing surprising there.

But when I widen my search beyond the website, glancing down the list of other results, I find a news report that leaves me stunned. Then several more, all on the same topic. The same name.

Jason Wainwright.

I gasp, my eyes widening as I read.

Man Dies After Being Hit By Tube Train

I scan the sparse details, feeling sick. A recent widower, after thirty years of marriage, Jason Wainwright ran a private investigation service, and was described as 'reclusive' and even 'depressed' by neighbours. Nobody seems to have expressed surprise at his death. Not even the police, though they were reported as 'investigating' the circumstances of his sudden death at Embankment tube station on the Circle and District lines.

The word 'suicide' is not mentioned in any of the reports I find.

But what else could it have been?

His late wife's name was Joyce. I wonder how she died. The report doesn't say.

What on earth was Dad doing with this guy's business card in his pocket, and how is the dead man connected to me? Because he has to be connected in some way, surely? It seems too much of a coincidence for Jason Wainwright to have died only a few feet away from me at the same time as Dad was in contact with his firm. Especially after the way he looked at me, his gaze so intense.

But why contact an investigator in the first place? Is something wrong? Something Dad can't handle through his usual Foreign and Commonwealth Office contacts?

Perhaps he hasn't even heard about Wainwright's death yet. We told him about the suicide at the tube station, of course. But it never occurred to me that Dad might know the man who died. How can I ask though, without revealing that I've been going through his pockets?

I get down on my knees and retrieve the black notebook from under the bed. Dad hasn't mentioned it's missing. Either he hasn't noticed or has decided not to say anything.

The cover is a little dusty. I wipe it with my sleeve, then climb into bed, still in my pyjamas, and put pillows against the headboard so I can read comfortably. As an afterthought, I lean over and grab a magazine from the floor, then open it to a random page and set it in front of me. That way, if Jasmine comes in and surprises me, I can hide the notebook behind the magazine.

I open the notebook to the first page. It seems to be written in code. But when I look more closely, trying to decipher the tiny squiggles, I realise it's shorthand. I didn't notice that in the cellar.

Luckily, ten pages into the notebook, shorthand gradually turns to longhand. Whole words emerge first. Then full sentences, with the rare incomprehensible squiggle. So the first ten pages are completely indecipherable.

Frustrated, I turn back to the first page that isn't all in shorthand, and start to read. Slowly, frowning, struggling to work out the sporadic shorthand squiggles from the context. Not entirely without success.

'Rachel' is only occasionally written in full. Sometimes it's 'Rach'. Most times it's merely a capital 'R'. Written with a flourish, and sometimes circled for emphasis. Just as I find instances of 'Catherine' and 'Cat', but also 'C'.

My name is always underlined in red.

> Rachel getting worse. Several episodes of mania last weekend. She had to be . . . restrained . . . harming herself. I wish we could find a cure for this. If there is a cure, which the specialists seem to doubt.

I run my finger along the handwritten text.

Tuesday evening, we gave up and had to call Dr H out again. I begged, but he refused to increase meds. Too dangerous, he said. She's already on the maximum recommended dosage. After the doctor left, R. had what looked like an epileptic fit. I ran for the phone, but while I was gone, she climbed out of the window.

I can't make out the next words, but press on,

. . . back at midnight, in a police car. She was spitting and scratching by then. More like a wild animal than a girl.

I glance up at the door but it's still closed. I can hardly believe what I'm reading. I mean, I knew Rachel was a total headcase. But involving the police?

It sounds like she was lucky not to be arrested.

We took her to hospital but they could find nothing seriously wrong. Transferred to the psychiatric ward though, just in case. We were there most of the day, waiting to see if she would be committed this time. Doctor H came in later to examine her. He said the fit was most probably faked. That she did it to distract us, perhaps so she could . . .

Some determined crossing out at the bottom of that page. Heavy and black. I turn it over, but can't make out anything on the other side of the paper. Whatever was written at the end of that paragraph, Dad must have decided it wasn't fit to be recorded.

So she could . . . what?

Pack a bag? Phone a friend? Run away?

Dr H.

Doctor Holbern. He used to see me in my teens occasionally. Depression, etc. But it was nothing like this shit, thank God.

I continue reading.

> Eventually discharged with a follow-up appointment next week. But a committal can't be far off if she keeps this up. I told Dr H we couldn't bear the thought of her in a secure unit. Not long-term.

A secure unit?

A few pages later, this:

> She's gone too far this time. Nearly killed herself. A total nightmare. It was all I could do to keep our name out of the papers.

Some more heavy crossing out. As though he was worried who might read this, which doesn't surprise me. It sounds like a really serious incident. Though I don't remember anything about it. I would have been quite young at the time, and I doubt my parents would have shared such dramatic news with me. Not where Rachel was concerned, at any rate.

> Dr H gave me the website of a specialist clinic in Switzerland. Unorthodox procedures but has helped a few stubborn cases. Am going to contact the director tomorrow. For all our sakes. This can't go on.

Switzerland.

I suck in my breath, reading that page over again. Presumably that's why we went on that family holiday to Switzerland. So Rachel could be assessed by a specialist in childhood psychosis. Perhaps she was given some dangerous and unorthodox new treatment, and died because of it. And my parents have been living with the guilt ever since, maybe hiding the true cause of her death behind this elaborate fiction of a family skiing accident.

Is this the secret they've been keeping from me all these years?

It would certainly explain why I can't remember actually skiing on that holiday, or seeing Rachel die in an accident, or anything to do with that terrible day except Dad coming in to tell me she was dead. The rest is a kind of white, senseless blur.

Because we weren't there to ski, we were there to cure Rachel.

And we failed.

'Poor Rachel.'

I close my eyes. I didn't like my sister much, she was a Class A bitch at times. But she didn't deserve to die, and then for the truth of what happened to be hushed up forever.

'What the hell did they do to you, Rachel?'

Flicking on five pages, I find a list of medications Rachel was pre-scribed and study it. It goes on for over half a page, incredibly. The medical names mean nothing to me.

Dominic would know precisely what these meds are for, of course. He would know how and why they're prescribed, and their various side effects.

But I can't show him the list. He mustn't know I've stolen the note-book. He wouldn't understand my compulsion to know about Rachel. I'm not even sure I understand it myself. But I do know he would call it an unhealthy obsession, and tell me to give the notebook back to Dad. They all think I'm incapable of making my own decisions.

I'll have to look up these drugs on the Internet. Though I can haz-ard a guess right now that they're mostly antipsychotics.

Doctor Holbern prescribed antidepressants for me once. Some hor-monal surge in my early teens, triggered by a boy I'd met who wasn't interested in me. Typical teenage angst. The phase only lasted a few months, I'm sure. Perhaps I was trying to compete in some sad way with my dead sister, to be as much trouble to my parents as Rachel had been. But who could ever be as much trouble as Rachel?

There's a new fear bubbling up inside me now.

I'm trying hard to ignore it.

Now that I'm married, I haven't been as careful taking the pill as I used to be. In time, I could end up with my own child, my own daughter. What if she turns out to be anything like Rachel? I don't know how I'd cope with a kid like that.

I can only hope her madness – I hate that word, it feels so judgemental, but Rachel's behaviour had to stem from some serious mental health issue – isn't hereditary. But what if it is, and I have a child who starts behaving like Rachel as she grows up?

I need to know this stuff. They shouldn't be hiding it from me.

I start reading Dad's notes again, skipping frantically back and forth between medication lists and routine hospital trips, looking for more information about that specialist clinic in Switzerland.

Then I come to something that almost stops my heart.

Switzerland is definitely the way to go, even if it changes all our lives forever. But it's so unfair. What did we do to deserve Rachel? It's as if we're being punished for something, only we have no idea what. I just wish we could have our lovely Cat back.

Chapter Forty-Two

The bedroom is dark when I hear someone creeping in. For a moment, I feel confused and disoriented.

I remember having lunch with Jasmine in the kitchen, then we watched a Boxing Day film with her until my parents came home from the shops. Then I told them I had another headache and came up to bed. Mum tried to offer me some medication, but all I would take upstairs with me was a cup of soothing camomile tea.

Obviously it worked, as I must have fallen asleep quite quickly.

But how late is it?

I listen to Dominic fumbling about, trying to undress in the dark without waking me. His trainers, thumping quietly one after the other, under the bed. The slither of his scrubs hitting the wash basket.

'What's the time?' I whisper.

'I thought you were asleep.' A slight pause. 'A bit after nine. Your mum said you weren't feeling well or I would have come up earlier.'

'What's everyone doing?'

'They're in the kitchen, playing Scrabble.'

I push up on one elbow, watching his shadowy form in the dark. 'Oh, I love Scrabble. You should have come and told me.'

'What?' He switches on the bedside lamp, looking down at me with an ironic smile. He's wearing nothing but his underpants, and I study his body thoughtfully. 'Are you being funny? You hate Scrabble.'

'Do I?'

He sits on the edge of the bed, and touches the back of his hand to my forehead. 'No fever. So I'm guessing this is just your sense of humour resurfacing.' His mouth twists wryly. 'You haven't missed much, anyway. Robert's dominating the field as usual.'

'I can beat him any day.'

'Now I know you're kidding.'

I reach for him hungrily. 'Come to bed,' I whisper, stroking his bare chest, then I throw back the duvet to show that I'm naked, too. 'Join me.'

He looks startled. 'Right now?'

'Why not?'

'Well . . .' He hesitates, glancing back at the fresh clothes he's gathered together. 'I was going to shower and then head back downstairs. To fix myself a light supper.'

'You can do that later,' I say softly. 'Afterwards.'

He raises his eyebrows, studying my face. He's still smiling, but it's a different kind of smile now. 'Afterwards?'

'Why not?' I take his hand and place it on my breast. I must have failed to turn the radiator up earlier, because my nipples are erect from the cold. Either that or from my growing excitement. 'Unless you're too tired after work?'

For an answer, he leans forward slowly and sucks on my nipple. Hard and deliberate. The physical contact is like an electric shock running through me. Sheer voltage. My back arches and I jerk upwards, groaning. He clamps that breast with his hand, squeezing it, and then bends his head to the other one, teasing me, circling my nipple with his tongue before licking it.

'Suck it,' I order him.

His gaze flicks to my face, a little surprised, but he obeys.

'Yes,' I say hoarsely, and grip the sheet so hard I feel one edge lift free of the mattress. 'Yes, like that.'

He laughs under his breath. 'You're eager.'

'I'm starving.'

'But not for food, apparently.'

I lean back and part my thighs invitingly. 'There are better things than food. Though if you're so hungry, darling, I've got something here you can eat.'

Now his surprise is undisguised. 'Cat?'

'Dom?'

'But you don't like it when I—'

'Hush.' I slip my hands up his spine, and draw him close, moulding him against me. 'A girl can change her mind, can't she? I like it now,' I whisper in his ear, and then lick his throat for good measure. 'Come on, baby. I need your tongue inside me. How much longer are you going to keep me waiting?'

'My God,' he begins, laughing as he pulls away, and I sit up, raking my nails down his bare back. He jerks back at once, angry. 'Shit, that hurt.'

'Then stop talking and fuck me.'

'Hey, watch it!'

'Jesus, you're so boring these days.' I pretend to yawn. 'Come on, be a good boy and share. What does it take to get you excited? Seriously, when are you planning to live up to your name?'

He stares down at me, his eyes glittering with baffled rage. 'My . . . what?'

'*Dom.*'

There's a stillness about him.

Then he snaps me back on the bed, his hands hard. 'Oh, I see what you're driving at. You want to be *dominated*, do you?'

'Well, it would be nice for a change. So far, this is like watching paint dry. Actually, no, I've had more fun watching paint dry.'

'Bitch.'

Hoisting my legs in the air, Dominic hooks them roughly over his shoulders and sinks his mouth between my thighs. I growl in approval. For all of five seconds. Because he's not there to please me, I realise, suddenly aware that I've been outmanoeuvred. I shriek in pain as I feel sharp teeth make contact with my tender flesh there.

'No!'

He only bites me harder though, and I thrash about wildly beneath him, trying in vain to dislodge his weight.

'You . . . total . . . fuck!'

I hit his back and shoulders, pummelling him with my fists. He ignores me, licking and biting in swift succession, pleasuring me and hurting me cruelly.

'Get off me, you bastard!'

He sucks hard, and I scream. They can probably hear me downstairs. But right then I don't care. I don't care if everyone in London can hear me. I just want him off me.

My upper body starts to thump up and down on the bed, my thighs locked like iron manacles about his neck, everything straining impossibly upwards as if I'm trying to reach the ceiling. I can't breathe, my lungs burning from a lack of oxygen. I bite hard on my lower lip, tasting blood in my mouth. My own blood. Then my lips part and I scream again. Not in pain or distress, though it's a close call.

I'm having an orgasm. The best damn orgasm of my life.

I gasp, my arms flailing about.

God, it feels amazing.

With one swift movement, he's up and thrusting between my legs, rigid with excitement himself, harder than I've ever known him.

'You nasty little bitch!' Dominic pants into my face, our sweaty bodies sliding together like pistons. 'This is what you want, isn't it? To be screwed hard. To be taught a lesson.'

I turn my hot face into the pillow and say nothing. He's hurting me, for sure. Hurting me good. But inside, I'm smiling. Because no, actually, getting screwed is not what I want.

But it will do for a start.

Chapter Forty-Three

Later, smiling secretly at each other, we get dressed again and go downstairs to the kitchen, where my parents and Jasmine are still playing Scrabble. Dad's head shines under the ceiling spotlights. He's got a little bald patch developing on top, I realise. Like a monk's tonsure. Why did I never notice that before? They glance up as we come in, and see us hand in hand. Jasmine smiles and looks down at her letter tiles. Trying to pretend she's not thinking what I know she's thinking.

I drop Dominic's hand – we're hardly love-struck teenagers, for God's sake – and stare over Jasmine's shoulder at her letter tiles, too.

'Winning?' I ask.

'Not even close. Your dad's on fire.'

Christ, if only.

I study her letter tiles, then the partially completed Scrabble board, and give a wry smile of my own.

BAGGAGE.

The universe does love to have its little jokes, doesn't it?

'Cup of tea, darling?' my mother asks, jumping up rather too quickly. There's an odd note in her voice. 'And . . . and you too, Dominic? What can I get you?'

Clearly they heard us having sex.

Ah, bless. Mother's embarrassed because we made so much noise upstairs. Screwing each other into the ground. Twice.

How delightfully quaint.

As though I've never heard her and Dad having it off. Poor old bastard, puffing away manfully, and her moaning, trying to sound excited, though really they both know she's thinking about that young man at the gym.

Pyotr. Her personal trainer for the past six months. Polish-born and hung like a horse, by the sound of it.

Not that my mother's ever mentioned his equipment. It's the way she *hasn't* mentioned it that tells its own story. Not a story she'd like to share with my father either, I'm guessing. Despite his own ill-disguised appreciation for all things Polish.

'Such a nice young man, that Pyotr,' she says every time she comes back from her personal training sessions, a slight sheen to her face, her pupils dilated. What is she now? Fifty? Older? Still with plenty of ambition in the bedroom though, oh yes. 'Such a very *nice* young man.'

She's gagging for it, obviously.

And she's not the only one.

Mouth dry, I make straight for the fridge. 'No tea for me, thank you very much. I've had enough tea to last me a lifetime.' I swing open the door and check the wine bottles in the door. Pinot Grigio. That'll do. I extract one of the open bottles and fill a large glass without hesitation, then glance back at my husband. 'Wine, Dom?'

He shakes his head.

My father looks from me to Dominic and frowns. Disapproval. Perhaps even suspicion. What's his problem? He's not usually as prudish about sex as Mum.

But maybe he doesn't like the thigh-length silver dress I'm wearing. I suppose it is a little snug about the chest, and the hips, and . . . well, snug all over. Even Dominic raised his eyebrows when he saw me take it out of the wardrobe. He seemed to approve though, going by the way he smacked my backside several times on our way downstairs.

Clearing his throat, my father reaches for the tile bag to complete his letter allowance, head bent as he fumbles about inside the bag.

I swig back a generous mouthful of Pinot Grigio, studying my father's profile as I ponder the question. It can't be *jealousy*, surely? That would be kind of sweet. Not to mention sick and illegal, of course.

Definitely one for the blackmail list.

'Still here, Jasmine?' I ask lightly, and see my cousin's look of surprise. 'Oh, of course. You're scrounging off us for another few days, aren't you? Just until your parents come home from holiday. Because poor little Jazzy can't be left alone over Christmas. That would be too mean.'

My mother's eyes are wide. 'Catherine, for goodness' sake.'

'What?' I drain the wine glass and pour myself some more. It's not bad, this. A cheeky little number with a bold aftertaste. 'Did I say something untrue?'

My mother blinks.

Jasmine's face is stiff with hurt and offence. My two favourite reactions. 'I offered to pay my way,' she says. 'Your parents didn't want anything.'

'Of course not. Because they're loaded and you're the poor relation.' I smile at her. 'It's like a scene out of Jane Austen. Or is it Charlotte Brontë? I forget which. You get the gist anyway.'

Dominic catches my elbow. 'Hey,' he says, a bite in his voice, 'what do you think you're doing? That was totally uncalled for. Apologise to Jasmine at once.'

'Or what?'

'Excuse me?'

'Or what?' I repeat, arching my eyebrows in polite enquiry. 'How exactly are you planning to enforce that manly command, Master Dom? Put me over your knee? Like you did upstairs?' When he says nothing, staring at me with a face that is beginning to flush with anger, I laugh. 'The second time, that is. The first time, you were a little too preoccupied to bother with good old-fashioned punishment.'

'Fucking hell.'

Behind him, I see Mum suck in her breath in silent protest at his swearing. Which tells me I must have got to him. Dominic's normally so careful to be polite in front of his mother-in-law. How marvellous. The dominant's cage has been well and truly rattled. I want to clap my hands in triumph, but it might spoil the moment.

I haven't finished with them yet.

'That's enough,' Dominic tells me, standing very straight, his shoulders back, as though he still believes he has some kind of power over me. 'What the hell's the matter with you tonight, Cat? It's almost as if you're . . .'

'Yes? What is it like?'

'As if you're a different person.'

I smile.

My father stands up abruptly, his chair scraping loudly in the silence. 'Cat?'

'Yes, Daddy darling?'

Oh shit, that's torn it. Now he's staring at me the same way as Dominic, frowning and suspicious. The two of them are a couple of bookends. With my mother squeezed between them, staring at me too, pale and restless. She's twisting her silver necklace between her fingers, and I can tell what she's thinking.

My mother shakes her head. 'No . . . no.'

I take a long, easy swallow of wine, then murmur, 'Yes, Mummy dear. I'm afraid so, yes', and see her take a few faltering steps backwards.

Jasmine looks up at everyone, still hurt and confused by my comments, to judge by the way her lower lip is quivering. She's put *GAGGED* on the board, her five letters joined to a 'D', and has been writing down her paltry score. My father's going to blow her out of the water with his *KUMQUAT*.

'Did I miss something?' Jasmine says. 'What's going on?'

'Exactly what I want to know.' I pour the last of the wine into my glass. 'And I intend to find out.'

'Find out what?' Dominic's gaze has not moved from my face. He's tenacious, I'll give him that. Poor sap. 'Catherine?'

'Don't call me that.'

'Shit,' says my father.

'Oh, Daddy. That wasn't very polite, was it?' I turn to him with a mock frown, and tut. 'Remember what Mummy always used to say. *Pas devant l'enfant, Papa.*'

My mother collapses back onto her chair, a shaking hand at her mouth.

'But what I really want to know,' I continue blithely, since nobody else seems to be jumping in to break the silence, 'is who the hell was in that urn? Because those weren't Rachel's ashes, were they?'

Chapter Forty-Four

I sip my wine in a contemplative way, pleasantly aware that every eye in the room is on me. I'm enjoying being in the limelight at last. God knows I've had little enough of it this past decade or so. Ever since Daddy decided enough was enough.

I have their full attention now though.

'Shit,' my father says again.

'Exactly, Daddy. "Shit" is the correct word, and you're up to the eyeballs in it. I ought to have smelled the manure a long time ago. But of course I was distracted, because I was playing the game too. A key player, in fact. Not just on the sidelines like you, dear little Jasmine.' My voice sharpens. 'Only I was playing blindfold.'

There's a faint mew from the other side of the room.

I turn, quickly seeking the source of the sound, and I catch my breath. 'Oh my, little Panther. I'd forgotten all about you.'

The sleek black kitten Dominic gave me as a Christmas present steps out from the utility room and into the kitchen. His huge green eyes are on me. As if he too has caught the mood of the room.

I click my fingers. 'Isn't he gorgeous? Here, kitty kitty.'

Mum gasps.

Dominic grabs my wrist. 'No.' His voice is like steel. 'Leave it alone.'

It's as if he thinks I'm going to launch myself on the defenceless little thing and tear it to pieces with my bare teeth.

I glance at Dad, hoping for something equally dramatic. But he's staring at me with that part-shocked, part-bemused look on his face, like someone just slapped him and he still can't quite believe it.

'What the hell do you think I'm going to do?' I ask lightly. 'Strangle the cat? For pity's sake . . .'

Dominic hesitates, then releases my wrist.

'Ouch, so unnecessary.' I give my wrist a shake. It hurts, but no more than what we did earlier. I sneak him a dirty sideways look, and stage-whisper, 'Better save that kind of kinky shit for bedtime, yeah?'

Dominic says nothing but there's a flicker in his face. I'm guessing it's fear. But it could be surprise.

I crouch down, holding out a hand, and Panther comes to me trustingly. As if he knows exactly what to do to horrify everyone else in the room. Gently, I stroke the short black fur behind his ears. At once Panther purrs, half closing his eyes with delight, tipping his throat back for more.

A willing sacrifice.

'Look at that,' I say softly. 'Dear little kitty loves me stroking him. In fact, he's practically *gagging* for it. Wouldn't you say so, Jasmine?'

I smile up at my cousin, who sits frozen in shock, staring at me with her big wide eyes.

'Do you like his name?' I ask nobody in particular. 'Panther.' I smooth a hand along his thin back. 'He's still quite small, of course. A helpless little thing, really. But he looks like he'll be a panther when he grows up, don't you think? It's the black fur. And the eyes, always watching . . .'

I stop stroking Panther, and my mother rushes forward to grab him. She backs away, watching me, clutching the kitten to her chest so hard he begins to struggle.

'Look out, you're the one strangling him now,' I tell her.

'Shut up,' my father says.

I make a tutting sound under my breath. 'Nice.'

Dad glances at Mum. I know that look. It means business. Nasty, unpleasant business. The kind that comes with pills and physical restraints.

'That's it,' he says, 'I'm calling the doctor.'

'Doctor Holbern, by any chance?' I ask sweetly.

'But, darling, it's Boxing Day,' Mum says to Dad in a small, trembling voice. She has put Panther down on the floor at last, much to the kitten's relief. 'He won't come out. He won't be available. No one will be available.'

'He'll come.'

'But darling . . .'

My father is frowning, very much the man in charge. 'Would you get me the phone, please?' he asks, turning to Dominic as his second-in-command, his voice strained but polite. He's preserving the niceties at all costs. Because that's what diplomats do. 'I want to keep an eye on her.'

I watch as Dominic leaves the kitchen.

'Got the good doctor's number on speed dial, have you?' I say. 'In case of emergency. How very convenient.'

Jasmine is hurriedly collecting up the letter tiles and folding the Scrabble board. *So helpful*, I think, smiling at her. She stiffens, no doubt worried that I've turned my attention to her.

'You were going to lose anyway,' I tell her kindly. 'My father had "kumquat". You can't compete with an exotic fruit.'

The door bangs open. Dominic is back with the phone. He passes it to my father, his gaze on my face.

'And the hero returns, his mission accomplished.' I flop with mock relief, one hand pressed to my forehead. 'Thank God for that. We can all relax now.'

'Cat,' Mum says, pleading with me now.

'That's not my name.'

Dad stops pressing buttons on the phone and looks at me. His face is drained of colour.

'Fuck,' he says under his breath.

'My name is not Catherine,' I say loudly, just to be clear, and look around the room at every face. Even the kitten is staring at me from behind Mum's legs. I make a loud 'shoo!' at him and he makes a dash for the utility room. That makes me laugh.

'Yes, it is,' my mother says stubbornly. 'You were christened Catherine.'

'But I renounced that name, didn't I?' I smile at Dominic, who looks back at me in shock. 'That sounds rather impressive, doesn't it?' I say. 'Kind of preachy too. Like renouncing the devil.' I put on a deep pulpit voice that echoes about the kitchen. 'I renounce thee, Catherine, in the name of the Lord!'

'You're still Cat to us.'

'Oh, Mummy.' I put my hands on my hips and tip my head to one side, mocking her. 'Was I a terrible disappointment? Of course I was. Your only child, and a complete nutjob. It must have been hard for you to call in Doctor Holbern. Admitting to the world that you couldn't cope with naughty little Catherine.'

'Don't,' she begs me.

Dad has got through to someone on the phone.

'Yes, hello. It's Robert Bates. I'd like to talk to Dr Holbern. It's urgent.' He glances at me, then pushes past Dominic and goes into the hall to talk. The door bangs behind him but we can still hear him talking. I hear the word 'relapse'.

'What does he mean, *relapse*?' I say. 'This isn't a relapse. It's a return to normal service. A very welcome return, as far as I'm concerned.'

Dominic holds out his hand to me.

After a short hesitation, I take it, and watch our fingers interlace. He's still my husband, after all. And he fucks like a jackhammer.

'What *is* a jackhammer?' I ask. 'I've always wondered.'

He blinks.

'A jackhammer?' he repeats.

I turn to Mum. 'What was in that urn, seriously?' She doesn't answer, but glances at Dominic.

Then I realise and look at him. 'So you were in on it too,' I say softly.

His jaw works, his gaze locked with mine.

'I knew some of it, yes,' he says. 'But only because I needed to know. When we first talked about getting married, Robert gave me a call. We met up and he . . . well, he explained about your past, and what married life might be like for us. What could potentially happen. The signs to look out for.'

'And you accepted the challenge. Wow.' I smile, genuinely moved. For a moment, I drop the ironic tone. 'Well done, you. I was wrong to take the piss before. You *are* a hero, Dominic.'

He says nothing, although his hand tightens around mine.

'But the question stands,' I say, raising my chin as I face my mother. 'What was in that urn? Not the ashes of some unfortunate neighbourhood moggy, I hope. Because it wasn't Rachel, let's face it.'

'I'm so sorry,' Jasmine bursts out, and we all look at her, surprised.

'Jasmine, stay out of this,' Dominic says, a warning note in his voice. Not unfriendly but needing to keep control of the situation. To keep control of me, in other words.

She's still holding the bag containing the Scrabble letters. She dumps it in the box, then shakes her head.

'I can't do that, sorry,' she says, and pushes her hair back with an impatient gesture. 'You don't understand, none of you. Some of this is my fault.' She takes a shaky breath. 'Maybe *all* of it.'

Chapter Forty-Five

I raise my eyebrows. 'How so?'

'I told you about the postcard. I shouldn't have done that. That's what triggered this relapse, isn't it? But I didn't understand.' Her voice rises, agonised. 'I didn't know. I knew you as Rachel. You came to visit us in Birmingham that time, remember? You made our lives miserable. But everyone was calling you Rachel in those days.'

'I preferred Rachel.' I shrug. 'Still do.'

'Then I was told you'd died, but Cat was okay. I thought that must be your younger sister, another cousin I'd never met. I mean, fuck, we live at the other end of the country practically, and I was only a little kid at the time.' She's flushed now, getting hysterical. 'I had no idea what was going on. Someone should have told me. It wasn't fair to keep it a secret.'

'It was none of your business,' my mother says coldly.

'But if I'd known, I would never have mentioned the postcard. Not in a million years. Especially on her wedding day.' Jasmine turns to me. 'I mean, God, that must have been what started all this shit again. Otherwise why would you be tripping out like this so soon afterwards?'

'Tripping out?' I repeat, as icy as my mother but with my own special twist of crazed batshittery for added menace.

'Flipping out, relapsing, whatever you want to call it.'

Jasmine is crying now, tears rolling down her cheeks. Tears of guilt and fear. She's worried my parents will blame her, of course. That's what this is really about. These are tears of self-protection. *Just look at how unhappy I am about this; you can't make matters worse by blaming me, it wouldn't be fair.* She's so transparent, it's embarrassing.

Jasmine sees me looking at her, coolly dissecting her behaviour, and almost shrieks. 'You sent the postcard. You sent it to me. So it wasn't my fault. It was yours.'

'Jasmine,' my mother says, a reprimand in her voice.

I let go of Dominic's hand and keep staring at Jasmine, playing back those words in my head.

You sent the postcard. You sent it to me.

She's right, of course. I must have sent her that postcard signed, so provocatively, *Rachel*. Except I have no memory of doing it. Surely I ought to remember?

Yet it's the only logical explanation. Like the creepy eyeball in the snow globe. Nice touch that. I congratulate myself. I pinched the snow globe from the wooden chest on the landing, procured the eyeball and posted it to myself at work. Later, I cut up my own wedding dress – it made me look fat, anyway, so it was probably a good move – and sprinkled it with animal blood for dramatic effect, then went out to work as usual, being sure to leave the bathroom window open to make it look like an intruder got in. As for the cat noises and the footsteps in the cellar . . .

Well, the mind is a strange and unpredictable thing, never entirely under our control. That's what I love about being me. The not-knowing part.

I didn't know I was Rachel, after all. Not until I read my father's notebook. Or rather, I forgot that I was also Rachel. Or rather, to be completely accurate, I was *induced* to forget. Brainwashing, some might call what they did to me at that specialist clinic in Switzerland. I don't remember much of that either, to be fair. It's all a blur of snow and white rooms and pills. Pills every day. And yoga therapy.

God, I'd forgotten about the yoga. How weird.

So yes, I did it all, I hold my hands up to that naughtiness. I masterminded my own relapse. Because I was sick of being goody-two-shoes Catherine, and wanted badass Rachel back in my life.

'Sorry about that,' I say. I pick up the wine bottle, my mouth suddenly dry. It's empty, of course. 'Shit. Out of wine. Did I do that?'

I place the bottle back on the kitchen worktop but somehow miss the edge. Or maybe I deliberately miss it. I can't be sure which, afterwards. But it drops to the tiled kitchen floor, where of course it shatters.

Glass explodes across the floor.

Jasmine shrieks again. It's almost a default setting with her, I'm beginning to suspect. Mum jumps hurriedly out of the way to avoid the glass shards. Dominic doesn't move from my side.

My rock, I think drily.

Dad comes back into the kitchen and stares at the mess, then looks at me.

Oops.

'Thank God. What did he say?' Mum asks, sounding tearful herself now. 'What did Doctor Holbern say?'

'He's not in England,' my father says flatly. 'He's in the States.'

'What?'

'I know. Talk about bad timing.' He opens the walk-in kitchen cupboard and reaches for a broom. I didn't even realise he knew where the broom is kept. But maybe he and Kasia get kinky in the cupboard occasionally. Dirty bastard. 'Dr Holbern flew out there for a Christmas skiing break, apparently. Some mountain cabin he keeps up in Vermont. He flies home the day after tomorrow. But his PA is going to email him, see what can be arranged for when he's back. We may even be able to get Cat booked back into the specialist clinic in Switzerland. There's been a change of management since she was there before, but they still accept private referrals, thank God.' He starts sweeping up the glass with quick, impatient movements, then stops to look around at me again, breathing hard as though he's been thinking about Kasia. I smile and his face tightens. 'Meanwhile, his PA suggests we do what we did last time, as an interim measure.'

'Which is?' Dominic asks.

'Take away everything she could use to harm herself, and lock her in her room. And try to get a doctor out to her, for an emergency prescription of antipsychotics.'

Dominic nods. 'Leave that last part to me, I can make a call. And I'll stay with her in the room. Keep her safe.'

The largest fragment of the broken bottle, the heavy glass base, is glinting at me, still wet with wine, right at my feet. Like an invitation nobody in my position could be expected to resist. And being me, I don't see the need even to consider resisting.

I stoop to pick it up, and Dominic grabs at my arm.

'Oh no you don't.' He twists my arm behind my back as I struggle. I could be wrong but it sounds almost like he's laughing at me. 'Please don't fight me, darling. This is for your own good.'

'That's what they always say.'

'Well, I'm not them. I'm your husband.' His breath is warm on my neck, oddly reassuring. 'And I can do this all night if necessary.'

'Sounds like fun,' I gasp.

So here we are again. Back to Rachel. Back to ground zero.

I laugh, throwing my head back, and enjoy my wrestling match with Dominic. It's a bit one-sided though. He's strong, and he knows what he's doing; there'll be no getting out of this arm lock. What was it my father wrote in his notebook?

I just wish we could have our lovely Cat back.

Not while I'm alive.

Chapter Forty-Six

I wake up with a start, dragging air into my lungs. It's dark and I'm lying on my side, stiff and cold, completely naked. My back is nestled against something soft. But when I put my hand up, I find something hard in front of me. Just inches from my face. Like I'm in a coffin.

My God, they've actually killed me. I'm dead and this is the afterlife.

I ought to be upset by that idea. Instead, I'm curious, and maybe a little angry. Except it's not wood, I realise. It's too solid for that. And it's been papered. A wall, I think, running my fingertips lightly over the surface. My fingers sting at the pressure, and I pull them back, instinctively sucking them into my mouth like a baby for comfort.

I taste blood. And the nails on my right hand are jagged and broken. What the hell?

Reaching out more slowly, I discover that the papered wall in front of my face is covered in gouge marks. Deep grooves that seem to match the shape of my fingernails, with ragged strips of paper hanging down loose.

Then I remember . . .

It was all very 'Sunday tea with the vicar' at first. Sitting me down after midnight with a very nice woman in a flowery skirt who had come out specially. The duty doctor. She asked a long and irritating series of questions. I answered. I didn't answer. I made shit up. I put my hand on her knee and squeezed. She nodded and wrote things down on a clipboard. Then she gave me two small, white, bitter-tasting pills, with a glass of water. I may have spat them out on her clipboard.

Not very nice of me.

She suggested a second opinion.

'Not yet,' Dominic said at once, quiet and concerned, a voice in the corner. 'Some meds first, and a few nights of peace and quiet here at home. I'll get time off. I'll look after her.'

A second opinion. I knew what that meant. The woman in the flowery skirt wanted me committed.

Definitely not nice.

I was glad then that I'd ruined her notes.

'She ought to be somewhere secure,' the duty doctor said. 'Catherine needs professional care.'

'I'm a trained nurse, and she's my wife. I'll deal with it.'

A hesitation. 'Do you have any experience of psychotic patients?'

'Some, yes. Enough to get us through a day or two until she's seen by a specialist. And if there's any trouble at all, I'll take her to the hospital myself.'

Later, the meds arrived.

I spat those pills out, too. I like spitting, I've decided. It expresses perfectly what I'm feeling, and seems to annoy everyone in the room.

Double whammy.

After the duty doctor had gone – still muttering darkly about a secure unit – they took me upstairs to our self-contained flat on the top floor. They stuck me in the bedroom with Jasmine while they cleared nearly everything out of the living room – previously my bedroom, of course – then trundled me in there, a firm hand on each shoulder, Dominic and Dad.

My guards.

The old lock and bolt on the door had been reinstated.

In we went, then the key was turned.

Bare mattress on the floor. One plastic chair. Nothing else.

I looked at Dominic.

'Well, this is cosy.'

He stroked my hair back from my forehead, then smiled. 'Strip,' he said.

'That's not very romantic.'

'Strip,' he repeated. 'Everything.'

'Everything?' I rolled my eyes at him, gasping in mock horror. 'But what if Dad comes back?'

'Everything.'

I smiled. 'Pervert.'

He hesitated, then reached round for the zip at the back of my little silver dress. 'Okay, if you won't do it yourself . . .'

'Oh, darling. This is so sexy.'

'Don't get any ideas. You're going to sleep.'

'And what are you going to do?'

He dragged my dress over my head and threw it aside. 'I'm going to watch.'

'You're going to watch me sleep in the nude? How unspeakably kinky. Can you film me too? On your phone? So I can watch myself later?'

His eyes met mine at last. He looked exhausted, poor lamb. It must be such a tiring business, looking after mad Mrs Rochester.

'Doctor's orders,' he said wearily. 'Come on, it's really late. And this is for the best. No phones in here. No clothes. No hidden weapons.'

He took off the rest of my clothes. Transparent bra and thong. Not very gently. Then knocked twice on the door. Jasmine opened it, staring in with a worried expression, and he handed her my clothes.

The door was locked again.

'Bed,' he said, pointing at the mattress.

I struck a pose, thrusting out my bare breasts. 'Oh baby, what an invitation. Okay, okay. I'll be a good girl and lie down. But only if you lie down with me.'

Dominic drew breath, then picked me up and threw me backwards onto the mattress. I screamed and tried to scramble back up. He pinned me down, hands to wrists, his full weight on my body.

That was when the fighting began in earnest.

I kicked and screamed and spat at him. He struggled to hold me down. I told him exactly what I thought of him. He said nothing. I gave up trying to escape and attacked the wall instead with my bare hands. Gouged holes in the appalling black-and-white striped wallpaper, tore strips off it, banged my forehead against the wall until I was dizzy. Dominic dragged me away a few times, but I kept charging back, attacking the wall like it was my enemy.

'I hate this wallpaper!' I was shouting at one point. 'This is my bedroom. This isn't how it's supposed to look.'

I'm not sure how long all that drama lasted. But somehow it ended with me rolling onto the floor between the cold wall and the mattress, too drained to do anything beyond moan and swear.

I guess I must have fallen asleep in this position.

'Catherine?'

A voice breaks the silence. A man's voice nearby. Is he watching me? He knows I'm not asleep.

'Catherine?'

My heart rate picks up. I don't respond, though I know that voice. It's not for me.

'Cat?'

'I'm sorry,' I say. 'Cat's not here right now. Please leave a message at the beep.' I raise my voice, strident with defiance. 'BEEP. BEEP—'

'Rachel?'

I smile. I don't mean to, but I can't help myself.

'Yes?'

Dominic laughs. 'Stubborn little bitch, aren't you?'

My rock.

Also the weak link in their chain.

'I'm cold,' I say.

'Tell me about it.'

'You could warm me up. What time is it?'

'Just gone five. And there'll be no warming up. Not until you're better.'

I pretend to sulk for a minute.

'You should try to get some sleep,' he adds.

I say nothing.

It takes him another three or four minutes of waiting, then Dominic breaks. 'Cat?' Quickly, he corrects himself. 'Rachel?'

I roll over and look for him in the darkness. There's a shimmering, man-sized mass over where they placed the plastic chair. So he's not even *trying* to sleep. Just sitting there, wide awake, watching me.

Now I call that cheating.

'Aren't you going to get some sleep yourself?'

'I can sleep later. It's no different from a night shift.' He yawns audibly, then laughs. 'Except for the sitting-still part. I'm used to a rather more eventful night shift than this.'

I slap the wall behind me with the flat of my palm. 'This wasn't eventful enough for you? I must be slipping.'

'Oh, you were right up there with the greats.'

'Name me a great.'

'The morbidly obese woman with the hernia. Who was also incontinent.' He pauses. 'That was an epic night.'

I laugh and sit up. There's an instant stirring from my guard, as though he's steeling himself for some kind of attack.

'Please may I have some water?' I ask plaintively.

Another pause. Then he gets up and turns on the light. I blink, shielding my eyes. Unlike me, Dominic is still fully dressed. Jeans, sweatshirt, trainers, all the same as last night. I bet he's dying for a shower. There's a smear of dried blood on his thigh. I focus on it as he comes nearer, holding out a bottle of water.

'Here.'

He's already removed the cap. Just in case I try to swallow it, perhaps.

I take the bottle and drink greedily while he watches. My body is so dehydrated. I can almost feel my cells plumping up as I pour mouthfuls of cold water down my throat.

I hand it back, empty. 'I needed that.'

'All that wine earlier,' he comments. 'You knocked back most of a bottle in about ten minutes, by my reckoning. Not exactly clever.'

'I was thirsty.' I change the topic, pointing at the stain on his jeans. 'Was that me?'

He glances down, then nods. 'You hurt your hands.'

'You tried to stop me.'

'Unsuccessfully.'

'I'm feeling better now, honestly. No more wall-gouging.'

His gaze moves down my naked body, then shifts quickly away. As if he's unwilling to sexualise me in this state. To take advantage.

I'm not unwilling.

'Seriously though, I'm freezing.' I rub my bare arms and hug myself, pretending to shiver violently. 'Can't I have my clothes back?'

'I was warned not to allow that.'

I make a face, dismissing his concerns. 'Because of the thing with the tights, I suppose.'

'What thing with the tights?'

'Didn't they tell you?' I mime making a noose from tights, and then hanging myself with it. 'After that, they took turns watching me.'

'Jesus Christ.'

'It's okay though. I wouldn't do that now. I was a teenager. Kids always do that wacky, look-at-me crap. It's fine now. You can totally trust me with clothes. Even tights, though personally I hate them. So nasty and unsexy. Catherine used to wear them for work, I know. But God, you wouldn't catch me dead in a pair. Well, maybe if I'd succeeded with the noose thing.' I lean back against the cold wall, making sure he gets a good eyeful of my breasts before I draw my knees up to my chest. 'Look, babe, I'm totally over the suicide vibe. And I'm freezing.'

He checks the radiator behind his plastic chair. 'The heating's on.'

'Still cold.'

'I can't get your clothes back. Jasmine's looking after them.'

'So knock her up.' I give a derisive laugh at my pun, imagining the ineffectual Jasmine pairing off with my husband. 'So to speak.'

He frowns. 'It's five in the morning. She'll be asleep.'

'Where?'

'Next door.'

'You let her sleep in our bedroom? In our *bed*?' My voice is high with outrage. 'What the fuck, Dom?'

A muscle jerks in his cheek. 'Lower your voice, please.'

'Oh, go screw yourself! You've got no power over me.'

'I mean it, Cat. Stop shouting at me.'

'Not Cat!' I scream at him. 'Not Cat! Not Cat!'

'Stop shouting, Cat,' he repeats deliberately.

I want to get up and punch him in the face. To do something violent. Or better still, have it done to me. I glare at him through narrowed, speculative eyes.

'Or *what*, fuckface?'

Dominic takes three swift paces and picks me up without effort, his hands gripping my upper arms painfully. He slams me against the wall so we're at eye level and stares into my face, mere inches away. His chest is heaving, his face flushed, teeth bared. It looks as if he's finally had enough of me and my shit.

'You little . . .'

I flicker my tongue at him suggestively. He watches the movement with sudden intensity. Then I laugh.

'Bitch,' he finishes, and crushes his mouth against mine.

I kiss him back, enjoying the violence, then wriggle a hand down between our bodies, and slowly unzip his jeans.

He doesn't stop me.

Chapter Forty-Seven

Some time later, I hear the door to the other room opening, on the opposite side of the top floor. I hold my breath, waiting.

I'm standing beside the locked door to my prison, my old bedroom, flat against the wall. Dominic is asleep on the mattress, his face grey with exhaustion. I had to wait ages until he fell asleep after we'd finished having sex, and nearly gave up hope of it happening. But eventually his breathing slowed, his body relaxed against mine and he slipped away into dreamland.

I then spent some minutes slowly and gently disentangling myself from his body without waking him, and crawled to the door. It was still locked and bolted from the outside, of course. But I knew either Jasmine or one of my parents would come and check on us early. They would be expecting him to need the toilet, at the very least.

I was hoping it would not be Dad who came first. He's always been the hardest to fool.

My luck is in.

Jasmine creeps across the landing from the other bedroom. There's a tentative knock. 'Dominic?'

I wait a few seconds, then knock back.

Twice.

Exactly the same knock Dominic gave in the night, when he called her to the door. Some kind of signal, I'm guessing. And pathetically easy to crack.

Jasmine unbolts the door, unlocks it and then opens it a few careful inches.

Before she's aware what's happening, I'm out of the door, one hand over her mouth, the other holding her still.

She struggles, her eyes alarmed, making a muffled noise behind my hand.

'You want me to break your neck, Jasmine?' I hiss in her ear.

She stops struggling, meeting my gaze, then shakes her head. There's genuine fear in her face. I wonder what they've told her about me. More than she knew before last night, clearly.

'Good call,' I say, still in a whisper. 'Now shut the door. Quietly.'

Shakily, she obeys me, her eyes fixed on my face.

'Lock it again.'

Jasmine swallows, and then turns the key in the lock. It clicks loudly, and I stiffen, listening. But there's no sound from inside.

Dominic is still out of it. And no surprise, the way he hammered away at me. And standing, too. No wonder they call it a knee-trembler. He must need a full day's sleep after that workout.

'Now,' I say softly, 'back up. Into the bedroom.'

Again, she obeys me, but awkwardly, stumbling into the door frame, watching me the whole time.

Inside the bedroom, I knee the door shut, then look into her eyes.

'I can hurt you if I need to,' I say, and mean it. 'Hurt you badly, and not think twice about it. Nod if you understand me.'

She nods, her eyes wide.

'I'm going to let go of you. But if you make a sound, if you try anything, you're going to need surgery. I hope I'm making myself clear?'

Again, she nods.

Slowly, watching for any sudden movements, I release her. Jasmine backs against the wall, watching me, not even attempting to escape.

Scared shitless, in other words.

I smile.

'Now, turn around. Hands behind your back.' She starts to say something, but I hold my finger up to my lips. 'Hush.'

She turns around, trembling, instantly obedient.

I rummage through my bottom drawer for a long scarf. The thin black one I wear to work is perfect. I tie her wrists together, tight enough to be a little uncomfortable. Then I spin her around so she almost falls, and catch her, grinning at her horrified expression.

'Right,' I say. 'Where are good old Mum and Dad? Still in bed?'

'I don't know.' She hesitates. 'Probably.'

'What time did they go to bed?'

'Three o'clock? Later? I'm sorry, I don't know. They were talking for ages.' She's babbling, getting hysterical. 'What are you going to do?' Her gaze flashes down to my nudity, then back to my face. 'You know you . . . you don't have any clothes on, don't you?'

'What?'

I look down at myself, pretending to be shocked. Then laugh, and remove a thick, fabric scarf from the bottom drawer.

'Open wide,' I tell her.

'Sorry?'

'Time you were gagged.' I laugh again, nudging her. 'Like last night, remember? Your Scrabble word. *GAGGED*.'

But she just stares at me, not laughing, her mouth slightly open. So I wind the thick scarf twice about her head, making sure her mouth is covered, and knot it at the back. I test it for wriggle room, but it's secure. I could silence her more effectively, I suppose. But I don't want to make a mess. Not in my own bedroom.

Besides, by the time she's managed to raise the alarm and free Dominic, I'll be long gone. With any luck.

'Sit,' I tell her, like she's a dog.

She backs slowly onto the desk chair. I use more scarfs and a couple of Dominic's leather belts to make sure she can't escape. Not without taking the whole damn chair with her. I smile, imagining her attempting the stairs, still strapped to a chair.

'Now listen, Jasmine, no doing anything stupid and breaking your neck,' I tell her sternly, checking the bonds. 'Okay? Promise? They'll only blame it on me if you get killed, and then I'll be really cross. I'm sure that's something you want to avoid.'

She says nothing.

I straighten and check myself in the mirror. God, I look wild. Hair in a mess, bruises on my arms and legs, my face flushed with excitement.

And naked.

'You're right,' I say, grinning, and open the wardrobe. 'I need clothes. Can't go around like this all day. I'll get arrested.'

I begin to dress, then stop suddenly, frowning over the mushroom-coloured skirt I've automatically selected from the range hanging in the wardrobe.

'God, what in the name of holy shit is this?' I toss it aside and flick through the rest of the skirts hanging up. 'Dull, dull, dull. Too long, too brown, too . . . grim. And what is this frilly thing? It looks like she wears it to church.' I shake my head, swinging round to glare at Jasmine. 'Doesn't Cat have any clothes that aren't boring as shit?'

Chapter Forty-Eight

Sharon comes out of her office as I saunter into the food bank and drop my shopping bags next to my workstation. Cat's workstation, that is. But mine today. Since she's not here to object.

'Catherine? I didn't think you were coming in today,' Sharon says, staring at me like she's never seen me before. 'Your husband rang to say you were in hospital. That you were really sick.'

'They let me out,' I tell her. 'For good behaviour.'

'Well, that's good news,' she says uncertainly. 'But you're not down to work today, Catherine. Not on the time sheet. You'll have to go home again.'

I look around. The place seems empty. 'Where is everyone?'

'It's still Christmas holidays. We're only open two hours today, for emergency relief.' She's frowning. 'I was just about to close up, actually.'

I study Sharon thoughtfully. What an odd-looking woman she is. Like overcooked mutton. Still, no doubt some men find that look attractive. The scarlet lipstick, tan tights with everything, hair-in-a-beehive look.

'Sorry, but what on earth are you wearing?' Sharon looks me up and down, her mouth slightly open, a little dusting of black mascara splodges under each eye. 'You look like a . . . a . . .'

'Tart?'

Her eyes widen. 'I was going to say "entertainer".'

'My God, what kind of parties do you go to?'

I glance down at the little black PVC skirt I found at the back of a drawer, coupled with a black leotard, plus fuck-me heels and a thigh-length black leather coat. A bit retro, perhaps. A bit Jane Fonda with her knees behind her ears. But definitely a reflection of how I feel today.

'Don't you like it?' I say. 'It needs a belt, of course, you're right. Something thin and silver. But it was the best I could do at short notice. Don't worry though, I've been shopping.' I wink at Petra, who has appeared from a side aisle followed by a grubby-looking couple. Petra also stares at me with a shocked expression. 'No more mushroom-coloured outfits, I promise. And all that beige.' I shudder. 'Why did nobody stop me?'

Sharon appears to be speechless. At least, she doesn't say a word in response, merely gapes at me.

The black leotard is a little tight, I admit. My boobs keep escaping from it. I must have grown since I last wore it. Or rather, Cat did. The cab driver who brought me here from Harvey Nicks could barely contain his lust, staring at me in the mirror the whole way. That was where I bought the leather coat, ditching that horrid woollen thing I found in the hall. I bought a few other bits and pieces, deeply unsuitable designer dresses and skirts and see-through tops, all wildly expensive and guaranteed to annoy my aged parents.

Before hitting the shops, I dropped into The Ritz for a delicious breakfast. Smoked salmon, scrambled eggs, Cumberland sausages and caviar. And a bottle of Dom Pérignon champagne. With Dom in the name, I had to order it, didn't I? It would have been greedy to drink the whole bottle on my own, especially at breakfast, but I did my best. The waiters didn't bat an eye, nor did they complain when I knocked over the ice bucket on my way to the powder room.

Such darlings, and so gorgeously fit, I could have paid them all in blow jobs and not thought twice about it.

But I had the *day* job to think about instead. Couldn't be late for *that*. Moral conscience and all. So I charged it all to dear Dad's debit card instead, since he'd rather foolishly left his wallet on the desk in his study last night. And we all know his PIN, because whenever he runs out of brandy he sends me or Mum to the off-licence with his card. I like to think he did it deliberately. Because he's as sick of Catherine and her beige wardrobe and sensible flatties as I am.

I don't feel even remotely guilty, of course. Guilt is for saps like Catherine. Besides, if Daddy had not told me his PIN, it wouldn't have been so easy for me to clean him out. So it's entirely his own fault, not mine.

'What's the matter with you both?' I look from Petra to Sharon, and laugh. 'Here I am, come to do my very worthy volunteering job, and you don't look at all pleased to see me. Anyone would think I had two heads.' My laugh deepens as I realise what I've said. 'Two heads. Get it?' But they just look at me blankly. 'Oh, forget it.'

I notice the couple behind her. There are probably happier people in the grave, I think, studying them. The woman is skinny and black, maybe about forty, her head a mass of Afro curls, and her partner – presumably, unless he's some random stray she's picked up – is a grey man. Grey skin, grey hair, grey eyebrows. Not a particularly healthy look. And he's coughing, too. Every few seconds, like a nervous tic. Cough, pause, cough, cough.

'Hello? Who have we here?'

Petra shoots me a warning look. 'It's okay,' she says quickly, 'I'm dealing with it. No referral.'

'Not another one.' Sharon shakes her head, lips pursed, then tells the woman, 'Sorry, love. No letter of referral, no food.'

'But he's sick,' the woman says, jerking her thumb at the grey man. 'I'm sorry.'

'He's got lung cancer. He can't work. And I'm his carer, see?'

'I'm sorry,' Sharon says again, in exactly the same tone of voice. Like she hasn't heard a word the woman said.

'But we've no money for food. And his mum's staying with us over Christmas. The social says the money's coming but it could be another week yet.' The woman pauses, looking unhappily from Sharon to Petra to me. 'We don't want much. Just a few things to tide us over.'

'Did they give you a voucher?' Sharon asked her.

'Who?'

'The staff at the job centre.'

'No.'

'Well, you need to go back and get one.'

'But it's not open now,' the woman says. 'It's shut, isn't it? For Christmas, you know. They're all on their holidays. The sign on the door says they're open again tomorrow.'

'Then you'd better pay them a visit first thing tomorrow morning.' Sharon is already shepherding the couple towards the door. 'We can't do anything for you here. Not without the proper paperwork.'

'Oh, that's not strictly true,' I say, following them.

The woman turns to me, her face suddenly lit up. 'You can help us out, then?'

'Yes.'

'No,' Sharon says firmly.

'Yes,' I repeat, not looking at her but at the woman. 'What do you need?'

'Anything you can spare,' the woman tells me hurriedly. 'But tinned food would be great. And pasta and rice. And sauces.'

'And biscuits,' the grey man adds.

'Yeah, and milk and teabags,' the woman says, nodding. 'And coffee, if you have it. And baked beans.'

'We like baked beans,' the grey man agrees.

Sharon is shaking her head, but I've already grabbed a handful of plastic bags. I shake one out, then pass the others to the grey man.

'Open them, would you?' Then I walk briskly down the aisles of food shelves, grabbing packets and tins off the shelves and thrusting them into the bag.

'Tuna?' I ask. 'Or Spam?'

Sharon runs ahead of me and halts in my path, trying to stop me. 'What the hell do you think you're doing, Catherine?'

'Feeding these people,' I say calmly. 'Sorry, was that a yes or a no for canned fish?'

'I hate fish,' the grey man says.

'Tuna,' the woman tells me, raising her voice above Sharon's, who is hysterical now.

'Petra? Don't just stand there! Help me stop her!'

Petra, I notice, is staying well out of it.

I bag a can of tuna, then stride towards the pasta and rice aisle.

'Spaghetti?' I ask.

The woman helps herself this time. Her eyes are bright and she's grinning. The grey man tries to thank me, but goes into a paroxysm of coughing. Poor old sod. Sounds like he's going to cough up a lung right there.

I wonder how long he's got.

We reach the cereal shelves. Sharon is blocking my path.

'You're in my way,' I say.

'Last warning, Catherine.'

'These people are starving. And he's sick. Really sick.' I hand another full plastic bag to the woman. 'What good is a food bank if we're never allowed to make an exception?'

'I know it's not a perfect system,' Sharon says through her teeth. 'But this is a charity, and the rules are there to stop people taking advantage. They can have food. Just not today. Not without a referral.'

I walk on. 'Tea and coffee next.'

Sharon drags me round so hard, she nearly pulls my coat and the black leotard off my shoulder.

'Hey!' I say, tugging them back into position.

'Petra,' Sharon says angrily, 'escort these people to the door. They can keep what they've got. But don't let them take anything else.' I try to move round her, but Sharon shoves me back against the metal shelving. The cereal packets above wobble violently. A few fall, narrowly missing us. 'You stay right where you are, Catherine.'

'Don't shove me,' I warn her. 'Don't ever shove me like that again.'

Her eyes flicker, then she shoves me again, quite deliberately, hard enough to hurt my back this time.

'Okay,' I say. 'But just remember, you asked for this.'

It's a strong punch, straight to the nose. Sharon goes down heavily, legs akimbo, grabbing at the shelves on her way, cereal packets raining on her head. Blood starts to trickle from her nose at once, satisfyingly thick and red.

I look down at her. Sharon is a very irritating woman and this is something I've wanted to do for a very long time. Or Cat has. I'm happy to do it for her.

What are sisters for, after all?

Chapter Forty-Nine

Sharon raises a trembling hand to her face, staring at the blood on her fingertips in disbelief. Then she tilts her head and squints up at me. 'That's it, you snotty bitch,' she growls. 'I've had it with you and your bleeding-heart politics. You are so fucking sacked.'

'Can you sack a volunteer?'

'I'm terminating your volunteering agreement. As of right now.'

I smile. 'Is that it?' I say. 'Is that the best you can do?'

'You hit me. That's assault.'

Time to go, I think.

I'm not afraid of Sharon but I've achieved what I came here to do. The couple have disappeared with their bags of food. I'd better leave too, before things get complicated.

I'm almost at the door when there's a clatter of heels behind me and something strikes me violently in the back, winding me.

'What the fuck?' I say, turning to see Sharon. She jumps on me, half strangling me, her chubby little arms around my neck.

'You're not going anywhere!' she snarls, almost hysterical. 'Not until the police arrive. Petra,' she shrieks, 'call the police!'

I try again to shake her off, but Sharon must weigh about eleven stone, maybe twelve. Heavy, in other words.

'Okay, okay, you win, you win,' I say. 'I give up.'

'You must think I'm an idiot.'

'Of course, but I'd never say so to your face.' I turn and start struggling towards the door, Sharon hanging round my neck.

'You're not getting away,' she says.

I back up against a metal cabinet, and slam her into it. She swears but her grip doesn't loosen. I'm laughing. This is so funny. Her hands tighten around my throat. I shift round and bang her against the cabinet again, hoping to dislodge her, then stagger on a few feet. Petra seems to have disappeared. I'm beginning to worry that she may actually have called the police. If I'm arrested, that would be a bad thing. A very bad thing.

'Bored now,' I say.

I snap my head back and there's a loud crack as it makes contact with her face.

Sharon howls and slides to the floor.

'I told you to let go,' I say.

It feels good to be rid of her weight. I grab hold of my own shopping bags and head for the exit but there's someone in the doorway, blocking my path.

It's Dominic.

Chapter Fifty

'Hey, sweetie,' I say calmly. 'How's Jasmine? I didn't like to disturb her when I left this morning. She looked a bit tied-up.'

He is angry but in control. 'You need to come home, Rachel,' is all he says.

I glance at the car keys in his hand. 'Dad's car. Is he with you?'

'Robert's still at the house. Trying to calm Jasmine down. She's in a terrible state, wants to take the next train back to Birmingham.'

'Best place for her, I'd say.'

He doesn't answer.

'Well,' I continue smoothly, 'I have to congratulate you on working out exactly where I'd be. Or have you been cruising the streets for hours, looking for me?'

'Come on, we can talk in the car.' Dominic looks past me, a sudden flicker of uncertainty in his expression. 'What the hell happened here? Looks like you've been busy.'

I glance round and see Sharon sitting on the floor, her nose and mouth covered in blood, twin black streams of mascara running down her face. One of her high heels has come off and there's something ugly about her tan-stockinged foot.

'She assaulted me,' Sharon tells him. 'I've got witnesses.'

Dominic looks at me. 'Shit, Cat.'

'Wrong name,' I growl.

He makes a face but says nothing.

I walk towards Sharon and she scrabbles backwards, terrified.

'You're a terrible boss, Sharon,' I say. 'And you're such a mess.'

'A . . . a *what*?'

'Why so much mascara? And who wears tan tights these days?'

Sharon stares at me, her mouth open but no sound coming out.

I look back at my husband.

'I thought we were going home,' I say, and then head for the door with him following.

It's cold outside, that grim afternoon-darkening in the sky that means dusk is not far off. Traffic is thickening up, too. But North London is always busy.

'Okay, where's the car?' I ask.

'Round the corner. Assuming it hasn't been towed away by now.'

'Illegal parking.' I give him a flirtatious smile. 'How sexy and rebellious of you.'

'Better move quickly. In case they really did call the police.'

But someone is running after us down the street. I look back, half expecting to see Sharon again.

It's Petra.

'Wait,' she says, gasping. 'Wait.'

I stop, curious.

Her face is flushed when she gets to us. 'I just wanted to say,' she gasps, 'I'm not going to back her up. Sharon, I mean. What she said back there about you attacking her . . . it's not true. I saw her push you first. You were just defending yourself. That's what I'll tell the police.'

I'm moved. 'Thanks, Petra.'

'You're welcome. You deserve it.' She looks from me to Dominic. 'And you have a lovely husband. When he told us about you, I thought it was the most romantic thing ever.'

'Told you what?'

'About your . . . your problems.'

I look at Dominic, my eyebrows raised. 'Oh, you told them all about my *problems*, did you?'

At least Dominic has the grace to look embarrassed. 'It wasn't like that,' he says. 'I just wanted to make sure you were getting on okay at the food bank.'

'Of course you did.'

I jerk away from Dominic's guiding hand.

'Rachel,' he says warningly.

But I don't intend on doing anything awful. Quite the opposite, in fact.

I lean forward and kiss Petra full on the lips, a real smacker, her eyes widening as I hold on to her.

'Thanks, darling,' I whisper when I finally let go. 'I won't forget this.'

She swallows, but seems unable to speak.

'Right, you,' Dominic says flatly. 'Time we were going.'

He steers me swiftly down the street and round the first corner, one hand at my elbow. As if he still thinks I might make a dash for it.

'What exactly did you tell them about me?' I demand as soon as we're out of earshot, trying to contain my temper.

'Me first,' he says succinctly. 'What the hell did you do to Sharon?'

'Look, she had it coming,' I say. 'I have no idea how saintly little Cat stood it for so long. I'd have decked the bitch months ago. And I would *never* have asked her to my wedding.'

I can see Dad's Mercedes ahead of us, parked awkwardly on the kerb.

Double yellows.

'I didn't think she's that bad,' Dominic says.

'Look, you've only met her twice. You can't possibly make an assessment . . .' I wince again, stopping as I make a play of fumbling with my shopping bags. 'Sorry, it's these bloody bags. They weigh a ton.'

He hesitates, then says, 'Here, let me take a couple.'

'Would you, sweetie? Petra's right. You're such a good husband, rescuing me like this. And this one too, it's hurting my hand.' I hand over all the shopping bags, keeping my handbag firmly on my arm, until he's laden down instead of me. 'Thanks, that's much better.'

'What have you been buying? Bricks?'

'Oh, you know. The usual expensive tat from Knightsbridge. Clothes and shoes.' I look over his shoulder and frown as if I've seen something annoying. 'Hey, is that a ticket on your windscreen?'

'Shit,' he says, turning.

And I run.

Chapter Fifty-One

I catch a cab a few streets further on and tell the driver to head for the mainline station at Paddington. Then, if he's questioned later, he won't be able to tell the police exactly where I was going. But anyone looking for me will assume I was planning on catching a train out of London.

I sit back and check the address scrawled on a scrap of paper in my bag. The street I want is Eastbourne Terrace, apparently a short walk from the station entrance. I don't know Paddington well, but I used my smartphone earlier to find the street online, so I have a rough idea where I'm going.

In the taxi bay at Paddington, I hand over some of the big wad of cash I took out on Dad's card and wait until the taxi pulls away before getting my bearings.

I zip up my bag and sling it over my shoulder, then walk briskly away and head through the busy concourse.

Beyond the station buildings, there's a huge Christmas tree swaying in the wind, lit up with hundreds of multicoloured lights. Very festive, I think drily, passing two homeless women huddled together in a doorway, their knees drawn up to their chins, arms round each other's shoulders.

I stop to check the direction on my phone.

A few turns later, I'm wandering along Eastbourne Terrace, gazing through the revolving doors of office entrances and at the brass name plates of buildings. It's getting on for dusk by the time I find it, at the far end of the street.

Jason Wainwright. Private Investigator.

It's a third-floor office in a glass-fronted block. I stare up at the windows, imagining I would find the place in darkness. The poor bastard's just died. It's the Christmas holidays. Nobody's likely to be at work under those circumstances.

But there is a light up there. High up, in one of the front windows.

The glass door at the base of the tower block is locked. I rattle it, but it's shut firm. And there's no sign of life inside. The lobby is dark. I can't see a concierge.

Keeping my head low, I study the metal name plates with their matching buzzers. I need to be quick. The light is failing and I don't know where else to go.

I press the buzzer for Jason Wainwright, third floor.

Nothing.

No surprise there.

I hesitate, looking at the other name plates on the upper floors. Two accountancy firms and a Tempest Textiles, second floor. George's Gardening Supplies is the only occupied office on the fourth floor.

I press the buzzer.

A moment passes, then to my relief there's a crackle. 'Hello?' a male voice asks in a puzzled tone through the intercom. 'Can I help you?'

I adopt a deep voice. And add a Scottish accent for good measure. 'Delivery for George's Gardening Supplies.'

'A delivery? At this time?' Puzzled pause. 'I didn't know there were any deliveries over the holidays.'

I grunt. 'They work us like slaves, these corporate bastards.'

'I'm not expecting anything.'

'It's marked urgent. And I need a signature.'

'Oh, very well . . . hang on.' The crackle stops, and for a few uncomfortable seconds I think I've lost him. Then George presses the intercom again, sounding weary but resigned. 'I'll come down to you. Wait there.'

Chapter Fifty-Two

George is a hulking great bloke in his thirties with an ill-fitting plaid shirt hanging open over jeans, and stubble. As soon as I see him emerge from the lifts a few minutes later, I turn my back and pretend to be rummaging through my bag.

He pushes out through the door. I glance round at him and smile invitingly. He looks me up and down, then stares at the empty street. He has an unkempt brown fringe that lifts in the wind.

'You seen a delivery guy?' he asks, sounding irritated.

'Oh, was he for you?' I point vaguely along the road. 'He rode off on his bike about thirty seconds before you appeared. Some courier service? I think he had a parcel with him. I guess he couldn't wait any longer.'

'For God's sake,' he mutters, and pulls a face, beginning to retreat back into the building.

'Hang on,' I say, and grab the door before it closes. He stares round at me in surprise, and I smile cheerfully, putting on a breathless little-girl-lost voice. 'George, isn't it?'

'Erm, that's right.'

'Linda. Tempest Textiles. I've left my phone up in the office. Can you believe it?'

My heels clacking, I walk breezily past him and across the black-tiled vestibule, heading for the lift with purpose. As if I have every right to be there.

'Had a good Christmas?' I ask.

He follows more slowly, frowning. 'I'm sorry, I don't . . .'

'You don't remember me? Oh George, I'm wounded. We've met *several times*.' I press the button to call the lift, and then burst out laughing at his blank expression. 'I'm obviously not that memorable.'

George looks me up and down again, taking in my fuck-me heels, the PVC skirt, the skin-tight black leotard visible under my open coat. 'I think I would have remembered you.'

I laugh. 'You flirt!'

The lift arrives. We both get on, his gaze on my legs. 'You're fourth floor, yes?' When he nods, I punch the '4' button for him, then hit '2' for myself and check my reflection in the mirrored wall. Ugh, my little tussle with Sharon has taken its toll on my lipstick, which is looking a bit smudged. And there's a long scratch down one cheek.

No wonder he's staring.

'Party,' I say, tweaking my short skirt.

His eyebrows rise. He hasn't missed my scratched face. 'Did it get rough?'

'I haven't gone yet. So who knows?' I give him a dangerous smile. 'Would you like to come?'

George takes an instinctive step backwards in the constrained space, his eyes widening. 'No . . . no thanks. I need to get home to my wife.'

I pretend to study him with interest. 'Pity.' The lift stops at the second floor, and the doors slide open. 'Well, this is me.'

'Good luck with the party,' George says awkwardly as I give him a little wave. 'See you after the holidays.'

I saunter away from the lift, my hips swinging. The doors close.

At once, I return and watch the light display above the door as the lift rises to the fourth floor. Above, I hear the doors open and close again.

Then silence.

I turn to the staircase, and head up one floor. The stairs are chilly and deserted. Reaching the third floor, I swiftly locate the office of Jason Wainwright and check the door. It's locked, unsurprisingly.

I knock, just to be sure. No reply.

The lock is a Yale.

I check the other offices. There are three suites on this floor. Jason Wainwright's, and two that appear to be unoccupied. The office doors are locked, but the toilets and communal kitchen are both open.

I close the kitchen door and put a chair under the handle to prevent it from opening. Just in case. There probably isn't a guard who patrols the office building at night. But better safe than sorry.

To my relief, my phone has several bars when I stand by the kitchen window. I hunt through my bag until I find the business card Bianca gave us at La Giravolta, then ring the number and stare out at the city lights.

It rings three times before someone picks up.

'*Pronto?*'

A husky male voice. Rather gorgeous. Very Italian.

'Hello. Are you Bianca's brother, Giacomo?'

'Yes, who's this?'

'I'm a friend of Bianca's. From La Giravolta bistro.'

'Is Bianca in trouble again?'

I smile.

'No, it's nothing like that. But I'm in a bit of trouble myself, and she gave me your number. She said you might be able to help me.'

'What kind of trouble?'

'I've locked myself out of my office.'

Slight pause. 'Whereabouts?'

I tell him the building address, and he changes his tone, asks me to wait. I hear frantic whispering in the background. Definitely female. I wonder if it's Bianca, or if he has a wife.

'I'm sorry,' Giacomo says, coming back to the phone. 'It's late, you know, and the kids need their bath.'

'I'll pay double.'

Another pause. More urgent whispering.

'Okay.' He takes a moment to write down my name – in a moment of inspiration, I tell him I'm Joyce Wainwright, the investigator's late wife, which will fit the name on the door when he arrives – and the address and my mobile number. 'I'll meet you there?'

'Thanks.' I can't resist adding, 'Bring your tools.'

He laughs and disconnects.

I set my phone alarm to go off in forty-five minutes. That should be enough time for a quick nap.

I should really stay alert, in case someone comes along. But I'm a bit ragged with exhaustion now, and all I can think about is lying down. Sad old lady, or what? I check my reflection again in the darkened glass of the microwave door. Hair all over the place, which isn't necessarily bad. But there are distinct shadows under my eyes too, and a weary look in my eyes.

I used to be able to pull all-nighters, no problem. But I suppose all that frenetic rolling about with Dominic in the early hours used up my reserves of energy.

I grin at myself, and flick back my messy hair. Too much sex is always an acceptable excuse for fatigue.

There are two shapeless fabric chairs in the dining area of the kitchen.

I study them, then pull down the window blind as far as it will go, which is only three-quarters of the way. I push the two fabric chairs together to make a rough sort of bed. Not desperately comfortable, but it will do for a nap.

Forty-five minutes later, my phone buzzes.

As I sit up on my makeshift bed, surfacing from a confused dream, my stomach rebels and I feel suddenly nauseous.

Bloody hell.

I groan, closing my eyes and clutching my belly. Something I ate? Though I haven't eaten since breakfast, I realise. Low blood sugar, perhaps. No wonder I was so tired before.

I shake off the sickness with an effort and reach for my phone. It's a text from Giacomo.

I'm outside your building. Where are you?

I text back, *Down in five*, and splash my face with cold water a couple of times, then pat it dry with kitchen paper. Finally, I reapply my lipstick, and blow my reflection a kiss.

I feel better after that, if a little unsteady on my feet.

Weird though.

It's only as I'm heading down the stairs to let Giacomo in that I think of another, more horrifying possibility for my moment of sickness.

I can't be. Am I . . . pregnant?

I push the thought away, unable to cope with it.

Downstairs, I open the front door to the building and Giacomo looks at me, toolbox in hand.

He's broad-shouldered and broad-chested, but tall with it, like his sister Bianca. He looks strong, too. A guy who can handle himself. With thick black hair and the typical olive complexion of the Mediterranean region.

'You okay?' he says.

'Bad tummy.'

He looks me up and down, incredulous, even a little mocking. I glare back at him without smiling. I'm seriously beginning to regret my outrageous outfit now. Though maybe he's amused because I'm holding my heels in one hand rather than wearing them.

'My feet were hurting,' I say.

He shrugs. 'No problem.'

The third floor is dark and silent. The lights come on automatically the second we leave the elevator.

I come to the door. 'This one's mine,' I say.

Giacomo stops and looks at the door plaque. *Jason Wainwright, Private Investigator.* I half expect him to ask for ID. But without even waiting for an answer, he crouches to open his large blue toolbox and search through it. 'Yale lock. Shouldn't take long. You're paying double, yeah?'

'Absolutely.'

'Cash?'

I nod to the office door, my expression nonchalant. 'You know where to find me. Why not just invoice me?'

'What do you take me for?' he asks drily. 'A fool?'

I don't know what to say.

'Bianca was there when you rang tonight,' he continues, looking at me quizzically over his shoulder. 'My sister? She said she doesn't know any Joyce Wainwright, and she certainly never told any woman to phone me today. Then we checked the name and address on the Internet.'

I hold my breath, thinking fast.

'Okay, *signorina*. Time for the truth.' Giacomo straightens and stares into my face, an aggressive look in his eyes. 'I know you aren't Joyce Wainwright. She died in August. And this guy, he's dead too. So who are you, and why the hell are you trying to break into a dead man's office?'

Chapter Fifty-Three

I consider spinning another elaborate story like the one I used for gullible George. But it doesn't seem like a good time for more lies. Especially given his threatening look.

'My name is Rachel.' I bend to slip my high heels back on, so that my face is slightly flushed when I straighten up again. 'And I'm the one who killed Jason Wainwright. Probably.'

'Probably?' he repeats, frowning. 'I read online that he killed himself. Threw himself under a train on Christmas Eve.'

'I may have thrown him under that train.'

'You don't know for sure?'

'Nothing's ever simple.'

He gives me a direct look. 'Killing a man is pretty simple, Rachel – or whatever your name is. Either you killed this guy Wainwright or you didn't.'

'I was next to him on the platform. There was a big crowd. Everyone was pushing. Including me.' I take a deep breath, then continue. 'He went under the train.'

'Did you push him?'

I shrug.

'Did you tell the police?'

'What do you think?'

'Well,' he says, after a brief pause, 'I wouldn't have told them.' And he spits on the floor. 'I'm no friend of the police.'

'Me neither.' I consider spitting too, but decide against it.

'Okay,' he says, 'but why break into the man's office? What's he got on you?'

I hesitate.

'Please,' he says, 'no more lies.'

'That's another thing I don't know for sure.' I nod towards the door. 'It's why I'm here. To find out why Wainwright was following me.'

'So he was investigating you.'

'Yes, I just can't figure out why.'

'Huh.' He looks me up and down again, more deliberately this time. 'You married, Rachel?'

'Very.'

Giacomo spreads his hands wide in an expressive gesture. '*Allora*, there's your explanation.'

'You've lost me.'

'Your husband is the one who had you followed. This man Wainwright was a private detective, yes? Your husband doesn't trust you, so he put Wainwright on your tail.' His gaze lingers on my legs in the short skirt. 'Such a nice tail too.' He winks at me. 'Can't say I blame him.'

'You think Dominic was behind this?'

'Who's that?'

'My husband.' My head is hurting and I feel vaguely sick again. I push the thought away. 'You're suggesting Dominic had me followed? That doesn't make any sense. He was with me that night. He was right next to me when Wainwright died.'

Except he wasn't, was he?

I remember looking for him, and finding him just out of reach, standing on the edge of the platform beside Sally.

The two of them chatting, their heads bent together, intimate.

'Sally,' I mutter.

That husband-stealing bitch.

Giacomo, rummaging once again through his toolbox, looks round at me in surprise. 'Sally? Who's Sally?'

'My husband's boss.'

'Ah.' He waves a hammer in the air. 'Is he having an affair with her?'

'Maybe.'

'It's always the boss. Late nights. Working all hours. Then one time she doesn't bother coming home, and next thing you know . . .'

'You too?'

'Divorced. She went off with her boss. Guy made tapas for a living, for God's sake. These fucking little dishes . . . It was so humiliating. Spanish, too. Not even Italian.' He shakes his head, throwing the hammer back into the toolbox with a loud crack. 'Now I'm on my own with three kids. Three kids, for God's sake, I ask you. Bianca is looking after them tonight. If it wasn't for her, I wouldn't be able to cope.' He smiles. 'She's a good sister.'

The back of my neck prickles. 'Keep it down, would you?'

'Sorry.' He stands up, grimacing, and weighs a crowbar speculatively in both hands. 'Okay, no need to change the locks. So we make this look like a burglary, yes?'

'Thank you.'

'Once you're in, I go home.' He eyes the door. 'The place may be alarmed. You should get ready to run, just in case.'

I slip off my high heels.

'Payment?' He smiles, his dark gaze meeting mine. 'Or we could come to a more interesting arrangement.' He looks down at my bare feet, then up my legs, raising his eyebrows suggestively. 'I expect this Wainwright has a good strong desk in his office. You like desks?'

I smile too, but this is hardly the time.

'Maybe another night.' I grab a large handful of cash from my handbag – the remnants of my raid on Dad's bank account – and thrust it towards him. 'Will that do?'

He doesn't bother to count the notes, but stuffs them rapidly into his pockets.

'It's . . . acceptable.'

'Right. Clock's ticking. Time to do your thing.'

'Whatever you say.' He grins. 'Boss.'

I stand back, my heart thumping.

Giacomo levers the crowbar into the crack between the lock and door frame, and with a quick jerk of his arm breaks the lock with a loud splintering sound.

We both wait for a moment. No alarm.

Nobody has come running to find out what the hell's going on. The building seems to be empty. It occurs to me that even George may have gone home by now.

Giacomo swiftly packs away his tools and salutes me.

'*Arrivederci.*'

'Goodbye, and thanks.'

I watch him go down the stairs and then the silence is complete.

I push my feet back into my high heels, and crunch over wood splinters into Wainwright's outer office. Some kind of waiting room. Very posh. Leather armchairs. Potted plants. Even a miniature fake Christmas tree on a table, white with red baubles.

I open the door into Wainwright's office. It's a spacious room with broad windows looking out over the street. I flick a switch. Spotlights come on overhead. My heels sink into the soft beige carpeting. Bloody beige. There's some kind of geometric painting on the wall. Beside it is a huge map of Greater London, covered with pins and strings like something the police might put together for a crime scene analysis. And a free-standing whiteboard, wiped clean except for a date in the top right corner.

24 December.

The day Wainwright went under the train.

The large desk near the window has elegantly turned legs and a green marbled leather top. It looks respectably strong.

I consider calling Giacomo back.

There's a large computer on the desk. An Apple Mac.

I sit down and turn it on.

The password box lights up, cursor blinking ready.

'Christ.'

Undeterred, I check in the desk drawers. That's what people do in films, and invariably find the password written down somewhere inside.

But there are no helpful password hints in the drawers. No cryptic clues scribbled on scraps of paper, no primers or lists or anagrams taped secretly to the underside of any of the drawers. Plenty of pens though, whiteboard markers, spare staples, bags of rubber bands, and dozens of torn chocolate-bar wrappers.

Jason had a sweet tooth, I think, chucking them out onto the carpet in my search. Presumably Joyce disapproved. 'No more choccies. You don't want diabetes, do you?' Otherwise the wrappers would be in the wastepaper bin standing behind the desk. She may be gone now, but he'd probably got used to hiding them.

Exasperated, I try various passwords at random.

WAINWRIGHT123

123WAINWRIGHT

HOTSEXWITHJOYCE69

Nothing works.

I didn't really expect them to. I blame Daddy, of course. I never learnt much about computers as a kid, kept out of school for years and home-taught. Phones aren't much hassle, but my hacking skills are non-existent.

I stare at the blank screen of the Mac, wrestling with a burning desire to smash the computer to pieces with the leather swivel chair I'm sitting on.

But I don't want to make that much noise.

Then I notice the filing cabinet, a few feet from the desk.

I get up silently and stand in front of it. It's a large metal cabinet with five drawers. A plant pot on top containing a decorative fern. Attractive and sturdy, rather like the desk and the Jag he drove. Jason Wainwright had expensive tastes. I expect he charged substantial fees for his services. So who hired him to follow me about, if that was what he was doing?

I try the top drawer, holding my breath.

It's not locked.

Chapter Fifty-Four

I have no idea how much time has passed before I hear the lift doors open and close, then footsteps coming along the corridor in my direction.

I don't move at first.

My neck hurts from being hunched over, reading. Papers and documents from several folders I found in the filing cabinet are strewn over Wainwright's desk. And my eyes are sore from crying.

Damn you, Daddy.

Fucking damn you to hell.

Except I don't believe in hell. I do, however, believe in revenge. How dare you hide all this from me? How dare you play God with my life?

Someone enters the outer room of Wainwright's offices, crunching over the wood splinters. Not a security guard. A security guard would have raised an alarm by now, on a radio or phone. A security guard would be unlikely to enter the scene of a break-in late at night without back-up. Nor would he approach Wainwright's office so openly and without hesitation.

I screw up the paper I'm reading and thrust it into my bag. Then I turn, leaning back against the big desk.

'Hello, Daddy,' I say.

Only it's not my father who enters Wainwright's office.

Anger is my first emotion. Then a sense of bitter hurt.

That surprises me. I thought it was Cat who was in love with him, not me. But maybe strong emotions can bleed through from one persona to another.

Dr Holbern would know.

I don't.

'Hello, Rachel,' he says, without a single quiver in his voice. 'I thought I might find you here.'

Dominic looks at me from the doorway, then I see his gaze move steadily past me to the leather-topped desk. The glossy black-and-white photographs everywhere. Papers scattered about. The drawer of the filing cabinet wide open. Folders spilt on the carpet. Everything in disarray, including my heart.

'How did you know?' I ask, my smile false and brittle.

'About Wainwright?' Dominic shrugs. 'I've known for some time. Isn't that obvious?'

'Nothing here is obvious,' I say savagely.

'Right.'

Dominic slides his hands into his jean pockets, and leans against the door frame. He's making no attempt to come any further into the room, I notice. Doesn't want to spook me, I suppose. In case I run again.

Though I have no idea where I would go. Not after what I've just read.

I recognise that look on his face. He's hiding something. Something I haven't found out yet among all this crap in Wainwright's files. But what?

'You're angry,' he says.

'Does that surprise you?'

Without looking at them, I run my hand over the papers and photographs on the desk, then dash them furiously to the carpet.

A photo lands almost equidistant between us, face up. Dominic and me – or rather Cat – walking arm in arm on our way home from a restaurant. I remember that night, the woollen dress, the icy weather. The pavements had been slippery and Dominic had held my arm to make sure I didn't fall. It was about a fortnight before our wedding.

I ask, 'Okay, *how long* have you known?'

'Known what, exactly?'

He is studying my face. Probing to see what I know before he gives anything away.

I need to be cautious, too.

'That Wainwright was following us.'

'*Us?*'

'Fine,' I say coldly, and correct myself. 'How long have you known that Wainwright was following you?'

'It was something Sally said.'

My stomach churns with jealousy at that name, and I struggle to hide it, hating him more than ever.

'Enlighten me.'

'Sally didn't know who Wainwright was, but she spotted him hanging round the casualty department day after day. Once she'd pointed him out to me, I kept seeing the same guy everywhere. In bars, in shops, once even on the Tube. He got off at the same tube station as me, then got out a map and tried to pretend he was lost when he realised I'd seen him. That was when I worked out he was watching me. Before that, I had no idea.' He grimaces. 'I know that sounds naive. But I was so focused on you, I couldn't see what was going on around me.'

'I killed him,' I say, without really meaning to.

He frowns. 'Wainwright?'

'I pushed him under the train.'

'No, you didn't.'

'Look, I know it was me,' I say angrily. 'He was right there one minute, the next he was dead.'

Dominic smiles. 'Is that guilt talking?'

'No. I just thought you should know.'

'Well, you can forget it. You didn't kill him,' he says dismissively. 'It was an accident.'

'You seem very sure.'

'That's because he was standing closer to me and Sally that night than he was to you. If you'd pushed him under the train, I would have seen.'

'Dominic,' I say, trying to keep my fury under control, 'are you having an affair with Sally?'

He hesitates. 'Define "affair".'

'You bastard.'

'Oh, come on.' His mouth twists. 'A stray kiss here or there, what does it matter? Besides, you don't care what I do. We're hardly love's great dream.'

'So why marry me?'

'I didn't marry *you*,' he points out.

Something jolts inside me. It's a blow but he's right. I can't deny it. To deny it would be to deny myself.

He's still watching me. 'Who did I marry, Rachel?'

'Cat,' I whisper.

'Speak up. I can't hear you.'

'Cat,' I repeat, my voice raised in sudden fury. I hate the way he's talking to me. 'You married Catherine.'

'And who are you?'

'Rachel.'

He nods, his whole body taut. 'Cat's not your alter ego though, is she? Not really. Deep down, she's you.'

'She's not me,' I say with cold emphasis.

'For God's sake, stop lying to yourself. This is bullshit. You are Cat, and Cat is you. There is no Rachel. There never was.' His voice has hardened. 'Rachel was the girl you invented to take the blame for all the appalling things you did as Cat.'

'No!'

He points to the files I've been reading, contempt in his voice. 'You still haven't faced the truth yet, have you?' he says. 'You're a fake, Catherine. Everything about your life is false. And we all know it. You're the only person who won't admit it. And you're a born liar.'

I shake my head in instant denial. 'No, you're the liar. You're the one in disguise.' My voice sharpens. 'And Wainwright knew it, didn't he?'

'You're Cat,' he says doggedly.

'No.'

'Yes. Admit it. Say your real name.'

'No.' I'm shouting now. 'I'm Rachel.' I run at him, claws out, determined to hurt him as much as he's hurting me. 'I'm Rachel, you fucking bastard. Cat is dead.'

He catches me by the wrists and bears down violently, leaving my skin burning. Then he spins me round to face the desk, wrenching both arms behind my back. I fight, kicking backwards and catching his leg.

'Stay still,' he hisses in my ear, pushing me face down over Wainwright's desk. 'Or I'll be forced to hurt you.'

'Don't flatter yourself. You can't hurt me.'

'Then why were you crying when I walked in?'

'Fuck you, Dom.'

He laughs, breathless, pressing hard against me. 'Oh, such a tempting invitation. Only wish I had the time, darling. But we need to get out of here.'

'I'm not going anywhere with you.'

'Not willingly, maybe.'

'What do you mean?'

His weight keeping me pinned me to the desk, Dominic fumbles in his jacket pocket as though retrieving something, then clamps a hand awkwardly over my mouth.

I struggle to breathe.

He's stifling me with some kind of sweet-scented cloth, his voice suddenly far away. 'Hush, relax. You've been up for hours, poor darling. You must be exhausted.'

'No,' I try to say, but my tongue is so heavy. He's drugged me, I realise with a shock. Finally, he releases his grip on me, and I stumble away, then fall to my hands and knees. 'No.'

As the room blurs, I stare up at my cheating husband's melting face and think, *Wainwright was on your tail all right, you lying bastard. And you killed him for it. But that's not the whole story, is it?*

'Who . . . ?'

My mind forms questions I can no longer ask, my eyes closing against my will.

'Time to sleep, Rachel,' he says softly. 'Goodnight.'

Chapter Fifty-Five

Icy water is trickling down my lips, my chin, onto my chest.

'What the . . . ?'

I'm slumped in the passenger seat of a car. Dominic is sitting next to me.

We're parked in a suburban street with a plane tree growing beside us, its branches stark and wintry. The side window is misted up with condensation but I catch glimpses of sky out there. A grey pre-dawn.

'Good, you're awake.' Dominic leans on the steering wheel, studying my face. 'But is it Cat or Rachel I'm talking to?'

I don't answer.

He sighs, then reaches for my face. I jerk away, realising in that instant why my arms and shoulders feel so heavy. He's tied my hands behind my back. But he's not going to hit me. He's just wiping my chin with a handkerchief.

'I got bored waiting for you to wake up, so I gave you a little splash of water. Sorry about that.' His smile does not look apologetic. 'How are you feeling? Dry mouth? Headache? Bit nauseous?'

'Fuck you.'

'Excellent.' He puts away the handkerchief and sits back. His fingertips drum on the steering wheel. 'After-effects of chloroform. Not my finest hour. Sorry about tying you up too. But I could tell you weren't planning to cooperate.'

'Did you ever think I would?'

'No,' he concedes. 'Hence the need to drug you.'

I nod. 'You came prepared.'

'It was important to get you out of there before you were seen.' He shakes his head at me. 'Breaking and entering. Not very clever. Especially given your relationship with Wainwright.'

'I didn't have a relationship with Wainwright.'

'The man was a private detective, investigating your husband. Then he died next to you in suspicious circumstances, soon after which you were caught breaking into his offices.' Dominic half smiles. 'Even Robert would have had trouble hushing that up if it had got out.'

He sounds bitter.

'What makes you think it won't get out?' I say. 'When the police walk in there—'

'They won't find anything.'

'But all those photos, the files . . .'

'Gone, destroyed.'

'Wainwright's computer.'

'Also gone.' He's serious. 'It'll look like a break-in. Thieves. Pure and simple.'

'I don't believe a word of this. All on your own, you cleared that office out and carried me down all those stairs?'

'There was a lift,' he says drily.

I look at him, unable to believe what I'm hearing. 'Okay, maybe you can make the computer and all those files vanish. But he must have had back-ups.'

'I've got that covered.'

I stare, incredulous. 'What the fuck, Dominic? What's all this about? Wainwright must have had something really big on you. Otherwise why kill him?'

'I told you. That wasn't me.'

'Yeah, of course.' My laughter is hollow. 'I forgot it was an accident. But then, lots of the bad shit I do is accidental. Like tying up Jasmine yesterday. That was a complete accident. I don't know how it happened.'

His face hardens.

'Poor Dom. You really like her, don't you?' I ignore the stab of jealousy. That's Cat's emotion, not mine. 'Where is Cousin Jasmine, anyway?'

'On her way back to Birmingham by now, I should imagine. Cursing your name to the heavens.'

'She had it coming. She tried to pretend not to know anything. But she couldn't fool me. Jasmine was in on the big lie, same as the rest of you. Thinking you could keep Rachel under wraps forever.' I laugh. 'You should have seen her face when I tied her up. She looked so shocked.' I purse my lips and roll my eyes in mock horror. 'Like that.'

'You selfish bitch. Don't you ever think of anyone but yourself?'

'Of course I don't.' I look at him in surprise. 'I'm a psychopath.'

He becomes serious at that word, his face pale. 'Well, at least you can admit it. That's something I never expected to hear from you.'

We sit in silence for a few minutes.

I watch through the misted-up windscreen as a milk float trundles slowly past. It will be dawn soon, the sky is lightening by the minute. People will start to stir in the houses on either side of the street, most of which are still dark and quiet, their curtains drawn. I wonder if my parents are awake yet. And if they know that Dominic has me. Or even care.

So many burnt bridges behind me, I've lost count. A shiver runs through me. It feels cold enough to snow.

'Why are we here?' I ask.

'To pay someone a visit.' Dominic sounds strained, no longer sure of himself. He studies the houses on the right as though in sudden doubt.

For a moment I watch him hopefully. I think he feels sorry for me. Whatever he's got planned, maybe he's about to change his mind and let me go.

Then he shifts, snatching the key from the ignition. 'Right, it's time. Come on.'

I cough, leaning forward. 'Untie me?'

He hesitates, then uses a pocket knife to cut my hands loose. Some kind of black plastic tie, like the kind of thing my mother uses in the garden to support roses. I wince and stretch out my aching arms, then rub my sore wrists, trying to get the circulation going again. There are red marks on the skin.

Dominic watches me with a wary expression, as if he's not quite sure he has done the right thing by freeing my hands. 'Don't bother trying to run, okay?' he says. 'There's nowhere to go. Besides,' he adds grimly, 'this is something you can't avoid facing.'

'I can do what the hell I like.'

'No one can outrun their past.' Dominic gets out, slamming his door. He comes round to let me out of the passenger side. 'Not even you, Rachel.'

Chapter Fifty-Six

Dominic leads me to the front door of one of the semi-detached houses, holding me tightly by the elbow, his face unreadable. The garden path has crazy paving, a few slabs missing, weeds growing in the sandy gaps, and a sad-looking rosemary shrub in a pot beside the front step. There's a silver Renault hatchback parked on the drive, with a Green Party sticker in the rear window.

Dominic presses the doorbell. A long, hard press, as though designed to wake anyone who might have been considering a lie-in.

'Who lives here?' I demand, but he doesn't answer.

I take a step back, Dominic still gripping my arm, and look up at the window above us. Have we been invited or is this a surprise visit?

The curtains upstairs are still drawn.

'Did they know we were coming?' I ask. 'Maybe we should come back another time. Let's go somewhere for breakfast instead. There must be an early-opening café somewhere round here.' I yawn and stretch again, though secretly I'm worried. What the fuck is all this about? 'I could murder a fry-up.'

He drags me back to his side, his face tight. 'Behave.'

'Yes, master.'

His gaze flicks to me, but he says nothing.

'You're a tough audience,' I say.

'Shut up.'

I set my teeth at his tone, wishing I could make a run for it. But I know he would only catch me and drag me back.

The downstairs window is covered with thick net curtains, a dingy grey colour. Who the hell lives here and why does Dominic want me to meet them? The house looks ordinary enough, even a little run-down, paint peeling from the door frame, a faded sticker on the glass door panel: *NO SALESMEN, COLD CALLERS OR CANVASSERS.*

I feel sick again.

'Bacon and eggs,' I say, struggling to hide my nausea. 'With fried bread and mushrooms and tomatoes and black pudding. And a hot, sweet cup of tea.'

Then the door opens.

A large black woman with dreadlocks looks out at us, a weary look on her face like she's been awake all night. She's wearing a pale-blue uniform with some kind of flower logo on the collar, and a badge that says *Nurse Trudi*.

'Good morning, sir.' She clearly recognises Dominic and is not surprised to see him, despite a hint of irritation in her tone. Her gaze locks on me with interest though. 'You didn't say you'd be bringing someone new with you.'

'Is that a problem?'

'Of course not, sir.' Her lips purse as she continues to study me. 'Though it's a little early for visitors.'

'I'm sorry about that. But like I said on the phone, it can't be helped. When does your shift end?'

'Nine o'clock.'

There's a clock on the wall inside. The time is coming up to half past seven. He glances at it. 'We'll be gone by then.'

She shrugs, and steps aside for us.

'Right, you first.' Dominic pushes me past the nurse into the hall-way. 'And don't try anything stupid,' he tells me.

I halt inside, uncomfortable and a little scared now. What is this place? A flight of stairs reaches into darkness to the right. Ahead of me is what looks like a kitchen, its door partly open, electric light spilling out into the hall. The carpet under my feet is worn almost to nothing, only a few dark blue stripes remaining along each edge from its original colour. The whole place reeks mustily of tomatoes, which I can see growing on a windowsill in the kitchen.

Everything smells damp and neglected.

It's a little early for visitors.

Who are we visiting?

'I don't want to stay,' I say, turning around. 'I don't like it here.'

Dominic says nothing, but spins me back round by the shoulders and gives me another shove, pushing me further inside.

'Bastard,' I mutter.

'Should I put the kettle on, sir?' Nurse Trudi asks, watching us.

'Yes,' Dominic says at once, as if eager to be rid of the woman. 'Tea would be nice, thank you, Trudi. Give us some time first though. Say, half an hour?'

She looks at me curiously, seeming almost as bemused by this visit as I am, then nods and disappears into the kitchen, closing the door behind her.

It's dark in the hallway once the kitchen door shuts.

'Dom,' I whisper, suddenly panicked. 'What are we doing here? Whose house is this?'

He does not answer but feels for the light switch, and I sag against the wall in relief as it comes on, my heart thumping under my ribs. I've always hated the dark. It's like death.

'I want to leave,' I say raggedly. 'I hate this place. It smells like an old people's home.'

He points silently down the hall. When I don't move, he puts a hand on the small of my back and pushes me. I stumble, hands out, nearly falling.

'For God's sake . . .'

'First door on the left,' he says coldly.

I come to a halt outside the door. The once-cream-painted wood is grimy with age.

It's closed.

He stands behind me, his face tense. 'Open the door,' he says.

'I don't want to.'

'Open it, Rachel.'

I pout, turning away towards the kitchen. 'I said, I'm not going in there. I hate you. And I don't want tea anymore. I want a coffee. Strong black coffee.'

'You are going in there, and I don't care if you hate me or not.' Seizing me by the arm, he jerks me back to the door so hard I almost smack my head on the wood. 'It's time to face up to what you did.'

'Fuck you!'

He takes my hand and forces it down on the handle. 'Open the door, Rachel.'

I stare back at him, the two of us struggling in silence, our gazes locked. But he's stronger. The handle gives, and the door opens a little.

At first, all I can see is that the front room of the house is small and dim. There are net curtains at a window, filtering the dawn to a milky light that dapples the plain white wallpaper like a pattern. I can hear the steady pump of a machine somewhere out of sight, and high-pitched electronic beeps at regular intervals. There's a green armchair near the door, and a half-finished jigsaw puzzle on a table beside it. An oval mirror on the wall.

I catch my face in the mirror, my eyes wide with fear, and Dominic's dark head behind me, like an avenging angel.

Then he pushes the door open wider, and I get a proper look inside. I shake my head at what I see and try to back out of the room, but Dominic stands firmly behind me, pushing me forward.

'No,' I say. 'I don't want to look. I don't feel well.' My voice sounds scared, but I'm not, of course. I'm just pissed off at him for putting me through this. 'Take me home, Dom.'

'Get inside,' he says harshly, thrusting me back into the room. There's no love or humour left in his face, not a spark of the Dominic I thought I knew. 'Not nice, is it?' he says. 'Take a good look. A good, hard look. This is your doing, Rachel. This is all your fault.'

Chapter Fifty-Seven

Dominic closes the door and points to a large bed near the window. It is standing on a thick plastic sheet. The bed has raised metal sides, the whole frame on wheels like a hospital bed. Next to it is a tall standard lamp.

A woman in a white gown is lying on the bed, apparently asleep, under a white sheet that covers her body from the chest down. Her bare arms rest by her sides. Two soft white pillows are under her head. Her eyes are closed. She looks peaceful in the half-light, like a fairy-tale princess resting on a bed of feathers or snow.

There's a vase of flowers and a book lying face down on the cabinet beside her bed. I glance at the title on the spine.

Through the Looking-Glass, and What Alice Found There.

Dominic treads softly as he goes to one side of the bed. He looks down at the woman for a moment, his expression unreadable, then switches on the lamp.

The illusion of beauty falls away under that harsh light. She is painfully thin, almost skeletal. Her cheeks are gaunt and her eye sockets hollow and dark. Her head has been shaved. There are plastic tubes taped to her mouth and nostrils. She is completely unmoving. Her face is so pale that she looks dead.

I draw back in horror, wondering why the hell I have been brought here, why I'm being shown this dead woman.

But then I see her chest gently rising and falling. She isn't dead. Merely asleep.

Not a natural sleep, however. I study the machines ranged on either side of the bed, connected to her body via various tubes and wires. A ventilator, I think, and a heart monitor, and other machines I don't recognise.

'They keep her alive,' Dominic says, watching me inscrutably. 'Until I decide this charade has gone on long enough. That it's time to let her go.'

'I don't understand.'

He draws a slow breath, then lets it out. Controlling himself.

'Don't you, *Rachel*?'

I hate the way he says my name with such deliberate emphasis. As if he's contrasting me with Cat. My pale shadow. The person I no longer want to be, according to Dr Holbern's philosophy.

'I don't have a clue,' I say. For once, I don't know how to play this. I want to scream at him to take me home, but I don't quite dare. Not when he's looking at me with such an accusing expression, as if I've done something dreadful. Only I have no idea what. 'Why don't you tell me what this is about, Dom? Who is she?'

He strokes a finger down the woman's cheek, gazing at her with real tenderness. 'This,' he says, 'is Felicity.'

I frown. 'Felicity? Sorry, is that name supposed to mean something to me? Because it's not ringing any bells.' I stare at the woman. 'Who exactly *is* Felicity?'

'My half-sister.'

'Your half-sister.'

'That's right,' he says. 'Same mum, different dads.'

'I don't understand,' I say again, frowning. 'You told me you didn't have any close family still living.'

'I lied.'

I'm nauseous again. My head buzzes oddly, like there's a wasp in there, beating against the inside of my head, desperate to be free.

'Look at her, Rachel,' he says, and studies his half-sister. 'Felicity wasn't just my half-sister. She was my best friend too. We were so close growing up, she always knew what I was thinking. Like she was inside my head. And her laugh . . . God, it was so bubbly, so infectious, you couldn't hear it and not laugh too. We all loved her madly. I can't tell you how much I miss her.' His voice chokes. 'How much I'll always miss her.'

I stare at my feet. My high heels are pinching, so I kick them off. The plastic sheet is cool under my feet.

'Look at her,' he says through gritted teeth.

'I've looked.' I shrug. 'So she's your half-sister. So what?'

'Do you recognise her?'

'No.' I chew at my fingernail, pretending to be bored now, impatient to leave this vile place. 'I'm hungry. Can't we eat yet?' I bite off a jagged sliver of nail and spit it out like a ten-year-old. 'Come on, let's go. I hate the smell of this place.'

'Don't you even want to know what happened to her? Why Felicity is here?' Dominic grabs my wrist and yanks me closer to the bed, his voice angry. 'Why these machines are the only thing keeping her alive?'

The wasp in my head buzzes violently. Suddenly, I feel like retching.

'No,' I say.

'Liar!'

I don't see his hand come up until it's too late. He knocks me backwards with one blow, a slap across my face that leaves me breathless and shocked, staring up at him from the floor.

'You should want to know,' he yells, 'because you did this to her!'

Stunned, I cup my throbbing cheek.

'Years ago, you lied your way out of taking responsibility for what happened to her. But this is where the lies stop.' He stands over me, his face dark with emotion. 'Fuck! I thought that once you were Rachel again, you'd remember for sure.'

'Remember what?'

'A wet night. Your dad's car. He'd left his keys on the kitchen table.' His eyes are like slits. 'You took them. Stole the car. Even though you were only a kid, even though you had no idea how to drive.' His voice thickens, furious. 'The car was a classic Jaguar. Big, sleek, powerful. Automatic transmission. A lethal weapon in the wrong hands.'

He takes a step towards me and I fear he's going to kill me.

I reach out blindly, scrabbling about, and find one of my shoes. I throw it at him, but it just bounces off his thigh.

'Felicity had gone out to train at the leisure centre that evening. She often trained late, then walked home.' He glances back at the woman on the bed, and his eyes well with tears. 'She was a promising swimmer. Regional champion. There was talk of her working towards Olympic selection.' His voice cracks. 'Until you came round the corner too fast, and lost control.'

'Me?'

'It was raining. The Jag skidded, mounted the pavement.' His voice becomes a howl as he stalks towards me, and I can tell he means to do me harm. 'She was crushed against a wall. She didn't stand a chance.'

I start to crawl away on hands and knees, but Dominic follows close behind. Grabs me by my short hair, dragging me back to my feet.

'You ran away, you bitch!' he spits out. 'You left my sister for dead. Felicity can't even breathe on her own. She's brain damaged. She's been in a coma ever since the accident.'

'No!' I can barely hear my own voice through the buzz of angry wasps in my head. 'No!'

'What you did ruined my family. My mum killed herself soon after the accident. She couldn't handle it. My dad eventually drank himself to death two years ago. Felicity's father refused to visit her, but he always was a useless bastard. Then he died too. Now I'm the only one left to

317

care about her . . .' Dominic's voice is like a knife in my ear, his breath hot on the back of my neck. 'All I've been able to think about since it happened is revenge, and how to get it.'

'I don't remember,' I tell him frantically, struggling to be free. 'Please, I don't remember.'

'You should have gone to prison. You should have been punished.'

'But I'm telling you, I don't remember any of this. I don't understand. You . . . you said your parents died in a house fire.'

'I lied.' His voice is merciless. He seizes my wrists as I claw at the air, dragging my hands painfully down behind my back. 'But no more than you, Rachel.'

'Maybe you're lying now. If you're telling the truth, why does nobody know what I did? Why wasn't I sent to . . . to prison, or a remand centre?'

'Because it was all hushed up, of course. Clever old Robert pulled some strings. His diplomatic contacts, I suppose. I was too young at the time to understand why you hadn't been punished for your crime.' Dominic releases my wrists, twisting me round to face him. He looks almost insane, his eyes wild, his face darkly flushed. 'Beyond the law, my dad used to say. Not your fault, just your psychosis. You weren't well, the doctors said.' He laughs viciously. 'Dad didn't believe that any more than I did, but he accepted it in the end. It was the only way he could come to terms with what had happened to our Felicity.'

The sickness builds in me, and looking at Dominic only makes it worse. I try to bury my face in my hands, but he won't let me.

'The judge who oversaw the case insisted you got proper treatment,' he continues in that harsh, unrelenting way. 'So your parents flew you off to that fucking specialist clinic in Switzerland. Meanwhile, the doctors told us Felicity's brain damage meant that keeping her alive was useless. They were poised to pull the plug. My dad said he'd go to the papers with the story, embarrass your family. So your father's money paid for this . . .' He drags me back towards the bed, forcing me to look at his sister. 'This living death.'

'I was a child!'

'You're not a child now.'

'Dominic—'

'Shut up!' He shakes me like I'm a rag doll, my head rattling. 'You don't get to say my name ever again, do you understand? We're strangers, and don't you ever forget it.'

I cover my mouth, holding back the sickness.

'I married Catherine, not you,' he says. 'They fixed you at that clinic, Rachel. They made you whole again. But nobody will ever be able to fix my sister.'

'So why marry me, for God's sake?'

'Because you had to be punished. You couldn't be allowed to walk away from this. My parents were blinded by Robert's money. His promise of round-the-clock private nursing, the newest experimental treatments, all in return for our silence . . . But none of it worked. My sister never woke up, and she never will.' He sounds like he hates me. 'I always knew Rachel was still inside you, just under your skin. All I had to do was strip back those layers, one by one, until you were mad, until you became Rachel again.' From behind, his hands come round my throat, squeezing hard enough to throttle me. 'And then your life would be ruined too.'

His grip tightens about my throat, and I struggle helplessly against his strength. I stare down at the pale young woman in the bed, my vision blurring.

'When my dad died, I decided to get closer to you,' he says next to my ear, his voice hoarse. 'It was so easy to pull the wool over your parents' eyes. Everyone called me Nick as a child, and I have a different surname to Felicity. At first, I only wanted to hurt you, to get some revenge for Felicity. But it was so easy to seduce you. Laughably easy. It was as if you wanted it too. As though you were *desperate* to be punished.'

His hands slacken off, and he turns me to face him. I'm choking, gasping for air. Bending his head towards mine, his face suffused with hatred, Dominic finds my lips, crushing them with his mouth. I feel his control, his fury. When he raises his head, we're both breathless.

'Then I asked you to marry me, and you said yes. Just like that.' His voice sneers at me. 'That was when I knew.'

I stare up at him, my lips barely able to form the words, 'Knew . . . what?'

'That you and I were meant to be.' His gaze locks with mine, our faces close. 'I knew then that the universe was on my side. Because this is karma. Don't you see? Deep down, you needed to become Rachel again, to be shown what you'd done to my sister. And so you let me into your life.'

He releases me and I stagger backwards, trembling and clasping my throat, amazed that I'm alive. That he hasn't strangled me.

That's when I realise the truth. Dominic is not going to kill me. He was never planning to kill me. Instead, he's done something far worse. He's opened a door that can never be shut again. A door into the dark, twisted depths of my own psyche.

'Rachel?' he says, taking a step towards me.

But I moan incoherently and back away, shaking my head.

I'm not Rachel.

There is no Rachel. No evil sister.

I'm not Cat either. Not anymore. How can I ever be Cat again, now that I've met Rachel face-to-face and been told what she did?

He's watching me. He knows what's happening to me. And he doesn't care.

I can feel everything inside me starting to crack, to collapse under the strain of that one horrifying glimpse. But I can't let him see that. I can't let him win.

'D-does Louise know?' I'm stammering again. Somehow I can't bear the thought of her knowing what I've done. Knowing and lying about it to my face. Louise is probably the only person in the world that I might call a friend – and mean it. 'Does she know about Felicity? What I did to her?'

'No,' he says huskily.

I'm relieved, though I hate him seeing it. Hurriedly, I change the subject.

'B-but what about my father? Why didn't he try to stop you marrying me?'

'He would have done, if he'd known. But I was careful never to discuss my family with anyone who might come into contact with you. Not having the same surname helped. And my aunt and uncle were well briefed not to mention Felicity at the wedding. I told them I didn't want you to feel sorry for me.' Dominic grimaces. 'It hurt, having to airbrush her name out of my life for the past couple of years. But it was worth it. Robert didn't get suspicious until after I sent you the snow globe. I think that was when he began to guess the truth, or something close to it.'

I glance at the door, wondering if I can distract him when Trudi arrives with our tea. Long enough to escape the house, at least.

'I don't understand how you even got hold of the snow globe.'

His smile chills me. He moves between me and the door, as if he can read my mind. 'Kasia let me into the house. I told her some lie, said I was there to collect something you'd left behind. Then it was a simple matter of finding an object from your childhood that I could use to' – he pauses as though searching for the right word – 'unbalance you.'

'Well, it worked.'

'Of course. The eyeball was a nasty touch. Just right for a nasty piece of work like you. I wanted you to know you were being *watched*.'

I shiver.

'Destroying your wedding dress wasn't easy. The stench of pig blood. I started to think I wouldn't be able to go through with it. But then I visited Felicity again, and just seeing her in this bed . . . it gave me the strength I needed to see it through. It made me more determined than ever to punish you. To get Rachel back.'

'You sent Jasmine the postcard?'

Dominic nods.

'And wrote my name on the wall beside the hangman game.'

'And in your old paperback romances in the chest,' he says softly, 'where I knew you would be bound to find them. Just a touch here, a change there, and you were halfway back into madness. It was so simple; it was almost laughable.'

I'm frowning now. 'But Rachel's signature on those sheets at the food bank . . .' I begin.

'I went to see Sharon,' he says. 'Pretended I needed her advice about a wedding present for you. She let me wait in her office while she dealt with a query. I saw the sheets on her desk . . .'

I remember what Petra had said to him outside the food bank. That he'd discussed my 'problems' with her and Sharon. 'So that's what Petra meant,' I whisper. 'I thought you must have spoken to her at the wedding. But you'd been there before.' I can hear faint noises from outside the door. Is that Trudi returning with the tea? Discreetly, I edge closer to the door. 'What else did you do? Did you put a cat in the cellar?'

'It wasn't a real cat, just a recording taken from the Internet. I hid down in the cellar and played it back at top volume on my phone.' His smile is grim. 'Kasia nearly caught me sneaking back into the house that morning; I had to hide in the utility room until she'd finished cleaning downstairs. But it was vital to get you into the cellar. I knew you wouldn't be able to resist the idea of rescuing a trapped cat.'

'Why did you need me in the cellar?'

'Apart from wanting to lock you down there forever, you mean?' he asks, his tone vehement. 'While I was helping to clear out "Rachel's" bedroom before we moved in, I took a load of old furniture down to the cellar. That's when I saw the old filing cabinet. Finding your dad's journal in there was a godsend. I thought about planting it somewhere in the house for you to find. But I couldn't risk Robert finding it himself. So I tried to lead you to it without being too obvious.' He pauses, an odd expression on his face. 'Not a brilliant plan, in the end. I didn't mean you to get hurt.'

'Of course you didn't.'

His face hardens. 'But all my little mind games made Robert suspicious. So he hired Wainwright to find out more about me.'

I stare, my full attention back on him. '*Dad* hired him?'

'Of course, who else? I didn't realise I was being followed until after we got back from our honeymoon. I was a bit slow there. Then one night I gave Wainwright the slip, doubled back and followed him to his office. That's when I realised he was a private detective.' He makes a face. 'I had to stop visiting Felicity after that. I knew it was only a matter of time before he worked out my connection to her.'

'So you did kill Wainwright?'

Dominic laughs. 'Nothing so dramatic. It happened exactly like I told the police that night. Wainwright was knocked under the train in the crush, pure and simple.' He shrugs. 'Or maybe he realised I'd sussed him, and panicked, and that's why he lost his footing. I guess we'll never know for sure. For what it's worth though, I'm sorry he died.'

I don't believe him, and my eyes tell him that.

'I'm not like you, Rachel,' he points out, his tone cutting. 'I'm not a stone-cold killer.'

I look away from him, back at Felicity's pale face. Her shrunken figure in the bed. The pumps work steadily, the electronic beeps continue, her chest rises and falls, her face still and composed. She is growing older every day without having lived.

'I'm not a killer,' I whisper. 'I don't even remember hitting her with the Jag. I don't remember any of it.'

But that's not true.

And he knows it. 'Don't lie to me.'

I see bright lights dazzling me. A car coming towards me. I taste fear in my mouth. The sickening sideways wrench of a car too powerful for me to control.

I throw up my arm, hiding my face from those lights. 'Please . . . !'

'Back when you were still Catherine, you told me what Rachel did to some unfortunate cat. Tormented it cruelly, gouged out its eyes.'

'No.'

'Only it wasn't a flesh-and-blood cat, was it?' His voice nags at me, implacable. 'It wasn't even a metaphor for yourself, for Cat.'

'No.'

'It was a car with the figurine of a big cat on the bonnet.'

'No, I told you—'

'It was your father's classic Jag, the one you drove into my sister, leaving her here in this bed, with no idea who she is or what happened to her.' He stares at me furiously. 'Rather like you, shutting off completely from Rachel after the accident. Reinventing her as your big bad sister. The sister nobody talks about. Only I've found a way to bring her back, haven't I?' His smile is worse than his threats. 'And now you'll never be rid of her again. Rachel's here to stay and she's going to pay for what she did.'

He reaches for me again, but I jerk away.

'Wait, wait,' I say urgently. 'Does Dad ever come here?' My voice is high-pitched, unrecognisable. 'You said he pays for all this. Does he visit her too?'

'Robert Bates doesn't give a damn about Felicity,' Dominic tells me. 'He pays for her care because of a deal he made with my dad. A financial arrangement that kept all the embarrassing details out of the papers, and let my dad hope she might recover one day. But she'll never recover, and my dad's dead now.' He swallows, suddenly paling. 'It's time to let her go. Turn off these machines. Then your dad will be free of it. But you never will be, Rachel.' His voice hardens again. 'I'm going to make sure of that.'

'So you're reading to her, are you?'

He looks blank. 'I don't read to Felicity, no. I talk to her, and bring flowers, and play her music. The music she used to love as a teen.'

I point to the book on the bedside cabinet. 'Then what's that?'

'Nurse Trudi, perhaps. Or one of the other nurses who come in to look after her.'

I slip round the bed and pick up the book, *Through the Looking-Glass*.

He's instantly furious again, chasing after me. 'What the hell are you doing?' He grabs my arm. 'Get away from her.'

'It's not one of the nurses who left this,' I say huskily, and show him the flyleaf, where my name is written. My other name. I read aloud, '*To Catherine, on your twelfth birthday, love Daddy*.' I give a harsh laugh and close the book. 'One of his little acts of rebellion when I was going through my Rachel phase. Daddy hated calling me Rachel, even though he knew it made me even crazier when he didn't. I threw the book out of my bedroom window that morning when I saw which name he'd used. He ran outside in the rain to rescue it. In his slippers.'

Dominic stares down at the book, momentarily speechless, then says slowly, 'I don't understand.'

A deep voice asks, 'Don't you?' from the doorway.

We both turn.

I start in surprise and horror, tears springing to my eyes. Dominic does not release me, his hand squeezing my wrist even harder.

Dad watches us, filling the doorway with his tall figure. 'Hello, Rachel,' he says, then looks at the woman in the bed, his voice softening. 'Hello, Felicity.'

'Daddy,' I gasp.

'Get away from my daughter,' he tells Dominic, a steely note in his voice.

Dominic hesitates, his face tense, still grasping my wrist.

'I know who you really are, Nick,' Dad continues icily. 'I've known for some time, thanks to Wainwright.'

Dominic's eyes widen at the use of his childhood name.

'I didn't want to precipitate a crisis with Cat, so I said nothing. But that horse has well and truly bolted. So your little charade here is finished.' Dad pauses, his face a mask of cold authority. 'If you stay away from Cat, I won't pursue this any further. But if you persist, I will intervene, don't think I won't. I doubt the police will believe you weren't involved in Wainwright's death, for instance.'

Dominic says nothing, but I can feel his sudden stillness.

'I'm sorry for what happened to Felicity. It was a terrible tragedy, a talented young life cut short.' Dad glances towards the woman in the bed, a sudden throb of emotion in his voice. 'Yes, I come here some-times to sit and read to her. And ask her to forgive me. Though I've never been able to forgive myself.'

I stare at him. 'For what?'

'For not managing your condition better. And for not being a stricter parent at times. Perhaps if I hadn't let you have your way so often . . .' He shakes his head, then looks at Dominic, a significant edge to his voice. 'I'll do whatever it takes to protect my daughter. Do we understand each other?'

Dominic hesitates, then nods silently.

'Good, I'm glad.' Behind my father, I can see Nurse Trudi hanging about in the hallway, peering over his shoulder with a curious expres-sion. Dad lowers his voice, choosing his words carefully as though aware of this unwanted audience. 'Because none of us will come out of this unscathed if you decide to go public. You've had your revenge. You've turned Cat back into Rachel. Don't make things any worse than they already are.'

I twist away from Dominic and run towards my father.

'I'm sorry,' I tell him wildly. 'I'm so, so sorry.'

Dad opens his arms.

'Hush, darling, it's all forgiven,' he says, and clutches me to his chest, then kisses my forehead. 'Are you hurt?' He puts a finger under my chin and raises my face to examine me, his eyes dark with concern. 'Christ, what's that on your cheek? Did that bastard hit you?'

I bury my face in his chest. 'Take me home, Daddy,' I say huskily, not looking at Dominic again. 'It's over.'

Epilogue

'You can't put the genie back in the bottle,' Dr Aebischer tells my father, his tone apologetic. 'We've come to the end of our usefulness, I'm afraid. To keep Catherine here any longer would be against her best interests. The best thing you can do is take your daughter back to London, and continue with the therapy sessions we've started here.'

I ignore them, staring out of the window at the snow instead. It's been a poor year for the ski resorts again, one of the warmest springs for a decade, but the mountains are still white-capped. Anyway, what does it matter what these doctors say? I've been here for weeks now, locked in this bedroom, only let out for exercise or therapy sessions, and Dr Aebischer is about the fifth specialist to assess me. The others have said the same, but Dad doesn't want to listen. He won't give up but I'm beginning to wish he would.

The bedroom is cold, but through choice. I turned down the thermostat deliberately. I wanted to feel the cold.

My dress is white, knee-length, buttoned up to the neck. It's prim and controlled, the sort of outfit Catherine might wear.

I hate it.

But it's what I need right now. To be controlled.

'Medication can only do so much, you see,' Dr Aebischer continues in that very correct Swiss accent. He's the clinic director, a large man with a bald head and a kind smile. I like him instinctively. He tends to oversee treatments rather than deal with patients individually. 'As my colleagues have informed you, it's a question of therapy now. Therapy and integration.'

'I thought it was a question of money,' Dad says coolly.

The clinic director inclines his head. 'Your donations to our research work have been most generous, and we are very grateful. But whether Catherine stays another month or another year, it will not change our recommendations.'

'Last time we were here—'

'Last time your daughter attended this clinic, other doctors were in charge. Doctors whose views are no longer held to be valid by the current team. Also, Catherine was going through adolescence. Highly suggestible, subject to hormonal surges, her personality not quite formed.' Dr Aebischer shakes his head. 'She's an adult now. The same aggressive approach will not work, whatever your Dr Holbern has told you.'

'I don't see why we can't at least try.'

'I'm going to be frank with you, Mr Bates. I've read Catherine's notes in some detail. All the records we held on file from her last visit, in fact.' The doctor pauses. 'I understand why Dr Holbern has recommended you go down the same route as last time. It did work with Catherine, to a certain extent. But we don't do those particular therapies anymore. They were discredited some years ago. Too many cases of patients regressing after treatment. Even worsening.'

I look round at them, interested at last.

'So reinstate them.' My father sounds impatient. 'Make an exception for my daughter.'

The doctor's smile is thin. 'I'm afraid we can't do that, and I wouldn't make the attempt even if it was permitted. The industry is more tightly regulated now, and quite rightly. What your daughter was forced to undergo as a child was brutal. Little better than brainwashing, in my opinion.'

'But it worked.'

'Forgive me, sir, that's hardly the point.' Dr Aebischer looks past him at me. 'I'm sorry, Miss Bates. I don't see what else we can do for you, other than the therapies already put forward by my colleagues.'

I'm surprised. He's the first of the senior doctors at this clinic to talk to me directly, except when asking questions aimed at elucidating my condition.

'Wait,' I say as he walks to the door.

Dr Aebischer looks round at me, clearly surprised. 'Yes?' He pauses, glancing at my father. 'You have a question, Miss Bates?'

'Who am I?'

He frowns, clearly puzzled. 'I'm sorry?'

'Who am I?' I take a few steps towards him. The doctor backs away slightly, his face wary, and I stop. 'Am I Catherine?' I stare at him, pleading. 'Or am I Rachel? Can you at least tell me what my name is?'

Dr Aebischer clears his throat. 'Yes, I see.' He thinks for a moment, then says carefully, 'You are both and neither.'

'Sorry?'

'You are both Rachel and Catherine now. But that also means you are neither. Not entirely. I wouldn't want you to see that as an admission of defeat, however, but as a beginning of something new. A different phase in your life.'

'I don't understand.'

'Since it's proved impossible to reverse your psychotic relapse into the Rachel persona,' he says, 'you should aim instead to manage your condition through acceptance and integration.'

'Integration,' I repeat slowly.

'That's right. As I've discussed with your father, what you need to do is integrate both personae into one new personality.' Dr Aebischer hesitates, then gestures to the large glossy document folder my father is studying. 'You can do this via the meds we've been able to prescribe you, and the continuing therapy sessions we've set up for you back in London. Someone who is basically Catherine but is nonetheless aware of Rachel, and able to manage that part of herself in a controlled way.' He smiles uneasily. 'For your own safety as well as that of your family.'

'The meds aren't very strong.'

'Yes, I'm sorry about that.' Again the awkward look. 'Maybe later you can increase the dosage. But that's not advisable right now.'

I say nothing but turn away to gaze out of the window. The mountains are so white and cold.

That's how I feel inside.

I hear the door click behind me as the doctor leaves. I keep staring out at the snow-capped heights. I feel a hand on my shoulder.

'Darling?'

Dad has stopped calling me either Cat or Rachel these days. Now it's always 'darling' or 'sweetheart'. He's gentler too, more understanding. When Sharon accused me of assault, he didn't once complain when he had to settle out of court. That darkness I used to sense in him has gone.

It hasn't gone from inside me though.

I want to be like the snow.

Pure. White. Empty.

But I know it's going to take a long time before I can return to zero. Perhaps I'll never be able to get back there.

'Darling?' Dad is hesitant now, which is unlike him. 'I have to go and sort out some paperwork with the doctors. Make sure we have everything in order for your return to London. The address of the clinic, the medications you'll need. I'll call your mother, let her know how things stand . . .'

I shrug.

'Will you be all right on your own for a bit?'

'I'm not a child.'

He kisses me on the cheek. 'If you need me, sweetheart, you only have to call. I'll be in the office at the end of the hall. Stick your head out of the door. I can be back here in seconds, if necessary.'

I look at him. 'Okay.'

'I love you,' he says abruptly. 'You know that, right?'

'I love you too, Daddy,' I say, surprised by his sudden seriousness. His eyes search my own as if he doesn't believe me. Once it might not have been true, perhaps. But he's been my anchor these past few months. Someone familiar to cling on to as I've battled the darkness and chaos inside. 'Honestly.'

He nods, then leaves me. But he's clearly reluctant.

I look at the single bed with its white, turned-down sheets, fit more for a nun than for someone with my history. My suitcase is tucked beneath it, and for a moment I consider pulling it out onto the bed and starting to pack. But I don't have the energy. Not right now. I need all my strength to deal with what's happening. With the idea of going home to the noise and chaos of London.

I turn back to look out at the snowy mountains. Then very deliberately place my hand on the window and spread my fingers wide.

The glass is icy, glinting with white.

Suddenly, I seem to see another hand pressing from the other side. A child's hand, its smaller fingers fitting easily within mine. I stare, holding my breath, but its impression fades as soon as I pull my hand away.

I stare at the emptiness outside.

'Rachel?' I whisper.

I'm filled with the most intolerable sadness. I've wasted so many years of my life. And done the most appalling thing, wantonly destroying the life of another human being. I didn't know what I was doing, and couldn't always control myself. And yet what happened to Felicity is part of me. I can't deny or undo it.

All I can do is live with the aftermath of that horror, and try never to let the madness take hold of me again.

It's not easy though. Rachel was so real to me, a living, breathing sister who existed in my head for all those years. I may have imagined my interactions with her, constructed all those family scenes and conflicts in my head to help my subconscious mind process her 'death', to ensure I never slipped back into being Rachel again. But the pain of her absence is a real thing, too.

Rachel was me, and I was Rachel.

Now I have to accept that my 'sister' is gone forever. And I'm alone with the terrible understanding of what I did in her name.

Behind me, someone knocks on the door.

'Come in.'

The door opens almost silently.

'Hello, Cat.'

I turn from the snow, staring in disbelief at the man in front of me.

Dominic is leaner than ever, his jeans loose on his hips. He has cut his hair, I realise. It's almost painfully short now. But I suppose I've changed more than he has.

His eyes widen as he takes in my figure, then he shakes his head. 'I didn't believe it when I heard,' he says, still staring. 'Not until now.'

I move clumsily and he hurries forward, ready to support me.

'I don't need your help,' I snap at him.

He backs off, hands held high. 'Sorry, of course not. My bad.' He steps away and looks out of the window instead. At the snow I've come to love and hate. Its frozen, ice-locked purity. After another moment, he says, his tone subdued, 'I'm sorry if I startled you. You must be wondering why I'm here.'

'Top marks.'

'Robert rang me a few weeks ago. He thought I should fly out to visit you. I didn't want to at first. It felt like the wrong thing to do.

333

Disastrous, in fact.' He comes close again, and this time I don't push him away. 'But then he rang again, and told me—'

I interrupt him. 'You're too late. We're on our way back to London soon. As early as tomorrow, maybe.'

'I know.' He leans his forehead against the glass, closing his eyes. 'Robert told me just now.'

I'm silent for a moment. 'He should have let me know you were here.'

'I asked him not to.'

'Why?' I'm tense, furious with them both. How dare they interfere?

'You know why.' Dominic looks round at me, studying me with wary incredulity again. 'I wanted to be here last week, but . . . Well, I'm here now.'

'And you can go away again.'

'I deserve that, I suppose.'

'You haven't exactly been in a big hurry to visit.'

'There was something I had to do first. It wasn't easy.' His face is bleak. 'I spent a few days sitting with Felicity, telling her everything I could think of, holding her hand, letting her know how much I loved her. How much we all loved her. Then I turned off the ventilator myself.' He's very pale. 'She only lived for thirty minutes. I buried her last week.'

'I'm sorry.'

'Are you?' He searches my face, frowning. 'Well, I said it was time to let Felicity go. I just didn't realise how hard it would be, in the end. She was such a huge part of my life.' He draws an unsteady breath. 'Like you.'

'I'm sorry about Felicity.' I pull out the chair from under the desk. 'But I'm not part of your life anymore, Dom. And you're not part of mine.'

'Understood.' He closes his eyes as though in pain, then opens them again, meeting my gaze directly. 'One question though, Rachel, Catherine or whoever you are now . . . Is it mine?'

I sit down and pass a hand over my swollen belly. 'It's a she,' I say. 'And what kind of stupid question is that?' I glare at him, angry now. 'Of course she's yours. I never played away. You're the one who couldn't keep his hands to himself.'

'That's not true.'

'Sally?'

'We never . . . It wasn't like that. It was a flirtation, that's all. I only ever had eyes for you.' Dominic comes towards me and I shake my head. 'Please, Rachel, Cat . . . don't do this, don't push me away. I've tried living without you and I can't do it. And now this.' He stares at my pregnant bump. 'Whatever mistakes I made, she's my baby too. You can't shut me out.'

'You only married me to get revenge for your sister.'

He nods, looking almost sick. 'True.'

'So why the fuck are you here?'

'Because I'm in love with you,' he blurts out, then looks away, staring out at the mountains, his face contorted with agony. 'I bloody well fell in love with you.'

I stare at him. How can I believe a word he says?

'I thought I'd get over you eventually,' he mutters, still not looking at me. 'But it didn't happen. After the first month without you, I started walking past your parents' house, even dropping in sometimes, hoping you'd eventually come home. But it was only ever your mum there, alone.' He grimaces. 'I begged Ellen to let me know how you were.'

'But she refused?'

He nods. 'I told myself it was for the best. Until Robert called me out of the blue. Told me about the baby. I couldn't believe it at first. But then I saw it was just another of those cruel tricks life plays on us sometimes. Only this is a trick that doesn't have to be cruel. Not unless we let it.' He pauses. 'Robert also told me some other things about you. That you're depressed. Badly depressed. That he's never seen you like this before.'

I close my eyes.

Dominic drops to his knees beside me. 'Listen, I know you're deeply unhappy. I know you're out there on the edge with no one to hold your hand. I know because I feel like that too. And maybe I don't deserve a second chance, after all the shit I put you through. But you're no saint either. Are you?'

I look at him warily.

'My condition could be hereditary,' I remind him.

'Then let me be there for you both,' he says quickly. 'Whatever the outcome, we can face it together.'

He takes my hand and I don't pull away this time, though I'm tempted to kick him in the balls instead. But that would be a Rachel response, and I've promised myself to be Catherine as much as possible. To keep taking the meds and going to the therapist and put all that horror behind me. For the baby's sake, if not for myself.

'I love you.' He kisses my hand gently. 'Let me be your husband again. Let's put the past behind us and try to make a life together.'

'Because of the baby?'

'Because it's what we want. What we both need.'

I almost hate him for that. 'I don't need you,' I tell him hotly. 'I don't need anyone. Not even Mum and Dad.'

'Really?'

He turns my hand over and presses his lips passionately to my palm.

I shiver, trying to pull away, and he reaches up, grabbing hold of my shoulders. 'No escaping this time, you hear me?' He's breathing hard, his eyes intent on my face. 'You may not need your parents. But you need this. I know I need it. In fact, I think I may be addicted to you.'

I struggle but he's too strong. He holds my face still while he kisses my mouth. It's not a gentle kiss. It's a hard, searching kiss. A let's-go-to-bed kiss.

It reminds me what I've been missing.

Craving, perhaps.

'Oh God.'

I clutch at his hair and drag him closer, our mouths fused together in heat. Someone must have turned the thermostat up again, I think, because I'm so hot all of a sudden. I can hardly breath, my skin is feverish, and I'm shaking with urgency.

There's no point pretending I don't want him.

I may even love him.

He looks round at the narrow bed behind us. 'Now,' he says thickly, and kisses my throat, already unbuttoning the front of my white dress. 'Here.'

'Say my name first.'

'Names are for ordinary people. Not us.'

I hold him off, frowning. 'You don't even know if I'm Rachel or Cat.'

'I don't care who you are. Only what you do to me.'

'You're crazy.'

He lifts me easily out of the chair, despite my swollen belly, and I lock my legs about his waist. 'Then we're made for each other, aren't we?'

'Bastard!' I growl into his neck as he carries me across the room.

'Bitch!'

'Don't waste time undressing,' I tell him urgently.

Dominic throws me down on the bed, landing heavily beside me. 'Who said anything about undressing?'

I keep my eyes wide open as we love each other the way other people hate. Neither of us can help being this rough with each other. It's pure instinct.

But such wild behaviour is normal for people like me and Dominic. *We're made for each other*, he said, and he's right. This thing between us is elemental, unrestrained by ordinary rules and expectations. It's natural, not something we need to pick apart in a clinical setting and psychoanalyse. It stems from our personal baggage and how we've learnt to deal with it. The violence of our lovemaking is what sweeps everything clean every time and brings us back to ourselves, back to some semblance of sanity. Back to life and out of the darkness.

Just before climaxing, he cries out, 'Rachel!'

I don't correct him.

He may be right, after all. Who knows?

Afterwards, cradled in the circle of his strong arms, I gaze out of the window at the white mountains, and my eyelids grow heavy as I listen to the steady drip-drip-drip of thawing snow.

Acknowledgments

I am vastly indebted, as always, to my dynamic and brilliant literary agent, Luigi Bonomi, and also to Alison and Danielle at LBA, for their continuing support (not to mention all those life-saving email chats).

Many thanks to my lovely editors at Thomas & Mercer, Jane Snelgrove and Jack Butler, without whom this book would not exist. I'm also grateful to the whole Amazon Publishing team for their belief in me and their hard work, especially Emilie Marneur, Eoin Purcell, Hatty Stiles, Victoire Chevalier, Shannon McMonagle and Sammia Hamer. Many thanks also to Ian Pindar, David Downing and Gemma Wain for their insightful and entertaining editorial comments.

Plus, a very special thank you to Stuart Gibbon, of gibconsultancy. co.uk, for his expert help and advice with matters of police procedure. Any mistakes are entirely my own.

As ever, I thank my fantastic cohort of readers, many of whom have become friends over the years on social media and in Real Life – thank you, Martha Dunlop! – for having my back, and pushing me on with your enthusiasm. Also to my fellow writers, who understand all too well how much of your soul goes into every published book, and who lighten each day with hilarious memes and cat-pic shares. All of you keep me writing and hoping.

Lastly, my grateful thanks to my loving husband Steve, and my children Kate, Becki, Dylan, Morris and Indigo, for being there when I need you, and for not being there when I need a quiet house instead. And for all the cups of tea . . .

About the Author

Jane Holland is a Gregory Award-winning poet and novelist who also writes commercial fiction under the pseudonyms Victoria Lamb, Elizabeth Moss, Beth Good and Hannah Coates. Her debut thriller, *Girl Number One*, hit #1 in the UK Kindle Store in December 2015. Jane lives with her husband and young family near the North Cornwall/Devon border. A homeschooler, her hobbies include photography and growing her own vegetables.